# TWENTY TWENTY

Compiled & Edited by
Ben Thomas & D Kershaw

# Also available from Black Hare Press

## DARK DRABBLES ANTHOLOGIES

WORLDS
ANGELS
MONSTERS
BEYOND
UNRAVEL
APOCALYPSE
LOVE
HATE
OCEANS
ANCIENTS

## BHP WRITERS' GROUP SPECIAL EDITIONS

STORMING AREA 51
EERIE CHRISTMAS
BAD ROMANCE
TWENTY TWENTY

## OTHER VOLUMES

DEEP SPACE
WHAT IF?
KEY TO THE KINGDOM
BEYOND THE REALM

Twitter: @BlackHarePress
Facebook: BlackHarePress
Website: www.BlackHarePress.com

John Dillinger and Baby-Faced Nelson
in a dream together
--one shooting holes thru
theories of his untimely death,
the other frying in an old-time
(e) Electric Chair
with balloons waving, bonbons
going off, the crowd in a joyous,
boisterous mood.

The marquee reads:
"Public Enemy Number One
laid to rest in a
shallow grave as
gravelly as the heart
that beat in his stoney chest."

An adjacent sign noted,
crime does pay the undertaker
but other, good-hearted folks
need look no further than
the Dempsey-Tunney fight
to see which has the
bigger box office draw.

*1920s Flicker* **by Paul Cameron Brown**

# Table of Contents

# BLOODY PROHIBITION

by Zoey Xolton

The back-alley speakeasy tucked away in the very heart of New Orleans was a cacophony of sound. Trumpets filled the air as a jazz band played and a dark-haired, red-lipped siren in a short, tasselled dress teased the bar's patrons with her natural allure and husky voice. Laughter, the scent of spilled liquor, and cigar smoke permeated the hazed atmosphere as a woman carrying a pair of martinis brushed past Alexander with an impish smile.

Approaching the crowded bar, the suited gentleman tipped his hat and made eye contact with the barman who nodded knowingly. He jerked his head to the back booths. "Table fourteen," he mouthed, before returning to his cloying customers.

Alexander wove his way through the throng of jostling bodies to the rear of the speakeasy. Slipping past a crimson curtain into the reserved booth, a golden-haired beauty awaited him. Her milky skin was perfumed with jasmine, and her pouty lips were painted with a shimmering shade of tangerine. Her lacquered eyelashes framed intelligent, bright blue eyes; they regarded him with amusement and thinly veiled attraction.

"Back so soon, Alex?" she purred, petting the beige vinyl seat beside her.

Alexander placed his hat on the table and shrugged off his coat before sliding onto the bench seat beside her.

"Drink?" she queried, raising her empty glass.

"Allow me," he said, pouring the illegal whisky over the remaining ice.

"Thank you, kindly."

"My pleasure."

Taking a slow sip of her whisky, the woman smiled, her cheeks flushing a becoming shade of pink. "You know, Alex, if I didn't know better, I'd think you'd actually developed feelings for me."

Alexander poured himself a drink and slugged it back with a smirk. "I like you, Pamela," he said. "But it's what you provide that I love."

Pamela pouted for a moment but laughed quickly after. "I guess you could have your choice of women," she pondered aloud. "And yet, you choose me."

Alexander's eyes darkened as he focused on the purple vein pulsing visibly beneath the soft flesh of her throat. "You taste like the ambrosia of Greek legends," he said, his cultured accent thick with lust. "Like fine honey, and fiery aged whisky all at once."

Pamela revelled in the compliment, biting her lip. Alexander inhaled deeply and sighed. His heightened senses picked up on the fragrant scent of her womanhood as it moistened her lace panties. He leaned in, his lips whispering against her neck. He kissed it reverently, each touch of his lips against her flesh, a prayer.

Pamela wiggled beside him, teasing. "You know, Erik paid me a visit, earlier."

Alexander stiffened beside her, drawing back to meet her eye. "Erik?"

"Yes, he stopped in for a quick bite," she giggled. "He asked me to pass on a message to you."

The handsome but ancient vampire set his jaw, and the cool, but stoic human façade he normally maintained effortlessly, began to slip. "And what precisely did he have to say, my dear?"

The golden-haired beauty adjusted her pearl-adorned headband, before finishing her glass. When she met his eye, hers were glazed and vacant.

Alexander peered at her. *She's been compelled*, he realised.

"He said that he's coming for you, so you might as well enjoy your last drink while you still can." She then tilted her head, offering her throat to him, forced into obedience by the equally ancient vampire.

Alexander snarled, his fangs descending over his lip. So, the Heretic, the vampire that hunted vampires, thought he could outplay him, did he? If the night's promise was combat, so be it; he'd take the gift offered. The more he fed, the stronger he would be. Drawing back his lips, he swooped like a beast, sinking his fangs into Pamela's tender throat. He supped viciously from her carotid artery until he felt her go limp in his embrace.

Letting her fall unceremoniously to the table, he wiped his mouth with a silk kerchief and grinned. "Alcohol might be in short supply, but blood never is." He moved to stand, straightening his shirt, when a sudden wave of nausea washed over him, followed by a lung-arresting coughing fit. His vision swimming, he stared in horror; his crisp white sleeve was stained crimson. Wrestling into his jacket, he slipped from the booth, whooshing through the drunk and disorderly patrons, and out the back door, faster than the human eye could see.

He gasped, choking for air as he fell to his knees in the filth of the alleyway.

"You've slipped, old friend," said a familiar voice as a pair of high-shine black boots encroached on his field of vision.

Alexander spat out a dark mouthful of blood, and with a great effort, lifted his gaze. Erik shook his head, stake in hand.

"What did you do to me?" Alexander rasped as he felt himself weakening further.

"I had Pamela drink Holy water," Erik answered simply. "You've gotten cocky and careless these last few hundred years, Alexander. It's a shame, really. I have enjoyed our game of cat and mouse, but all good things must come to an end."

"Why?"

"This world belongs to the humans, Alexander. The time of Darkness is over. Do you not remember what it was like—to be human? I will rid the world of our kind until I am the last, and then, I will end it once and for all; humanity will finally be free of our shadow."

Black veins etched their way across Alexander's

flesh in intricate patterns, like dark spider webs, as they burned within him. He collapsed, rolling onto his back, his breathing ragged. "Be done with it then, *Heretic*."

Erik grimaced, taking a knee beside his once brother-in-arms. Drawing the stake back, he smiled apologetically. "I'm sorry old friend, but the bar's closed."

Alexander gurgled, laughing despite himself, as he drowned in his own blood. A moment later the stake came down, piercing his centuries old heart. Erik withdrew the stake and stood back as his frenemy's corpse ignited, bursting into sudden, glorious flame. He stood in the darkness, watching for a time—in respect, in regret? He wasn't sure anymore. Killing never felt right, but he would do what must be done.

From within the bar, a piercing scream broke the night.

"Damn," said Erik. They'd found Pamela. *Poor dame*. The scream was muffled, and the patrons sworn to silence as they scurried out of the illicit establishment like rats off a sinking ship. The mob wouldn't be far. The speakeasy was theirs, and they'd clean up the mess before the pigs ever caught a whiff of the trouble.

Slipping the bloodied stake into an interior coat pocket, the ancient vampire tipped his hat to the now

# TWENTY TWENTY

smouldering pile of ash and left the scene, whistling the *Charleston Dance* on the way to his next mark.

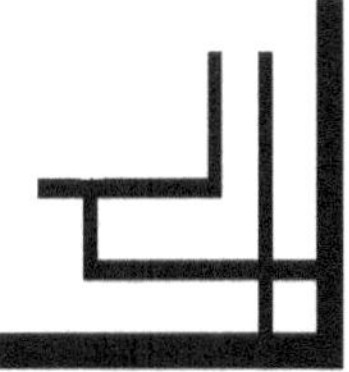

BLACK HARE PRESS

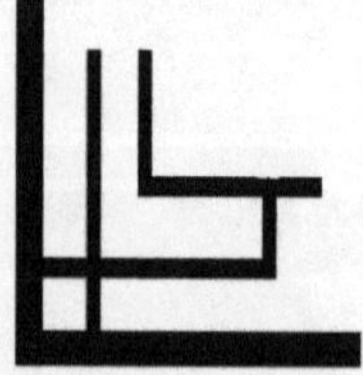

# THE SPEAKEASY

by Sam M. Phillips

**June 29, 1922**

Dreams of tentacle monsters haunt John in his sleep. He runs, crashing through branches in a dark forest, but they follow him. Emerging on the shore of a lake he dives from a high rock into deep waters. Sinking, with bubbles rising around him, the black depths suffocate him. As his lungs are crushed, all the air within them spent, he is sure he is going to die. At the last possible moment, an arm reaches down to clutch him, pull him from his watery prison.

John coughs up water as he squirms on the shore's lake, the arm still holding him, almost gently. He looks at it, his wet face shaking with shock as he sees the suckers of the octopus man's tentacle unravel…

And reach for his throat.

John wakes up with a start, covered in perspiration.

The blankets are tangled around his limbs, and he struggles to free himself from their grasp. Cursing, he tumbles to the floor, banging his knee hard. A shout of pain and shock is accompanied by knocking through the floorboards; the old bat in the apartment below protesting at the noise with her broom handle. John stomps his fury.

"Damn you, you cow, what time is it? Who cares about the noise?"

He looks at the pulled curtains. Light streams through the gaps. It must be late afternoon, which is a normal rising time for him. He gets up, struggling with the last curls of blanket, and as he throws them on the floor, he scrabbles around for a cigarette, or the chamber pot, or some bloody water. Finding a tumbler containing a few dregs of whiskey and half a cigarette, he figures it's close enough to suit his many morning needs. Downing the booze, ignoring the cigarette stub, he pisses in the glass and throws the contents out the window.

Looking in the mirror he realises he looks like crap. The whole apartment looks like crap, so John figures he fits right in. But it just won't do; he's out of hooch and there's fun to be had when the nighttime comes, drinks to down, revelry to enjoy, and women to tumble. Still,

there're hours until then, and so John throws himself back on the bed, and gives in to the tentacle monsters once more, knowing they can do nothing worse to him than he does to himself.

* * *

In the recesses of darkness lurk the deep desires of the human soul. Sex, strong drink, and wild abandon to the accompanying tune of a big band call to every man and John is no different. He cuts a fine figure now, all his scruffiness polished up, shaven face, brushed suit, polished shoes. All the money John has goes towards the pursuit of his desires, and his desires require him to look good.

He steps out of the cab on the corner of May and Newton, failing to tip the driver. John needs all the money he has if he's going to get his fix tonight. Prohibition bites hard and hooch only flows where money does.

His pockets full of ill-gotten gains, he sidesteps traffic as his cabbie curses him, speeding off. John shrugs and twirls a finger, his mind already dancing a jitterbug. Tapping his feet playfully as he walks, John ducks off down an alley, escaping the lights and attention of the busy thoroughfare.

For a moment, he is alone and able to fully grasp the pleasure of anticipation. Something stirs at the base of his spine and tingles all the way up into his brain, wrapping his mind in a soft blanket of expectancy. If it weren't for this feeling, he'd be suffering right now; alcohol withdrawals, very likely, depression, most certainly. But with the coming surety of excess, he is not worried.

He raps a jolly number on a nondescript door. A slit opens, and two baleful eyes stare out.

"What's the password?"

"Highball."

The slit slams shut and there is a moment of panic which flood's John's brain. Then the door creaks open and he smiles, stepping into the shadowy void of the underground speakeasy.

* * *

"The place is jumping tonight," says John's friend, Ted, and he's right. Flappers and willing chaps fill the dance floor. It is a riot of colourful dresses, bouncing feathers, fake pearls, and highly polished shoes, the men's suits a sombre background to break up the

shimmering sea of gyrating and twirling bodies.

"The band is phenomenal!" It's a swinging big band, with the bandmaster bouncing his hands energetically as the horns blow a jazz fanfare and the drummer pushing an insistent beat. A clarinettist throws himself into a lively solo. John can't help but tap his feet and clap his hands.

"You want another drink?" asks Ted.

"Gin fizz," says John, not taking his eyes off the band. The bartender in his white suit pushes the drinks to Ted, who hands one to John. He takes a big sip.

"Ah, that's bully, thanks. Few more of these and I'll be ready to trot."

"Got your eye on any particular ladies?" asks Ted.

"None yet, just the usual fare, go off with a bang and then the regret the morning after," says John, casting his connoisseur's eye about the room.

"Bit like a gin fizz or two, then," says Ted, laughing.

John downs his drink and wades into the throngs of dancers. He gives a few willing flappers a twirl, but he was right in his initial assessment: nothing to get too excited about.

The band hits a high note, the trumpets shrilling, cymbals crashing, the clarinet shrieking up and down the scales. Everyone stops and claps as the number comes to an end. The lights in the club change, throwing shadows on the dance floor and illuminating centre stage.

John's jaw drops as a svelte lioness of a woman strides into the spotlight. Her dress is a shimmering mass of crystal faux diamonds, sparkling bracelets and earrings to match. Long black hair cascades down over a long, lily white neck, framing a perfect face, punctuated with ruby red lips and ocean's deep eyes of sapphire blue. She bats her long eyelashes as she steps up to the microphone.

Then she sings and John falls in love.

* * *

The number is a slow, intimate number, and several women approach John and try to engage him to dance. He simply ignores them, his eyes locked onto the object of an all-consuming desire. The world flows around him and he falls out of time as the song passes, and then another. After a third, the woman speaks to the crowd and says her goodnights. Her voice is husky and impossibly sexy. John is in raptures as she invades his ears and creeps down his spine and into his soul.

She leaves the stage and John is thrown out in the cold. He stands there, stunned, wondering what has happened to him. Ted is at his elbow, nudging him with his arm. John turns, the spell momentarily broken.

"Gin fizz?" offers Ted, holding out one of the drinks in his hands.

"Ah, yes, thanks." John throws the drink back in one pull. It temporarily numbs him from the shock, sending a warm slither through his limbs which now seems like a meagre shadow of the real pleasures possible in life.

"Looks like you could use another one, let's go to the bar," says Ted, already leading the way as the band strike up a lively number and the dance floor packs out.

Another gin fizz or two and John hasn't said more than two words. Ted smiles wryly.

"So, she's caught your eye, then?"

"Who?"

"The belladonna, of course," says Ted with a flourish towards the stage. John looks, suddenly feeling very empty. Ted nods eagerly. "The beautiful lady."

"Oh, yeah, she's a knockout."

Ted laughs. "She's one of a kind, that's for sure. The magnificent Joanne Fitzgerald, the most sought after bootleg speakeasy singer this side of Chicago."

John gulps, recalling the effect she had on him, a feeling he has only just got under control with the help of libations from the bar.

"She's certainly very talented," he finally manages.

"She's the best. Everyone is in love with her."

"Everyone?"

Ted nods seriously. "Oh, yes. Did you think you were the only one? She takes them ten at a time, chum. She's a *man-eater*."

"What did you say about her?" John clenches his jaw, the hooch boiling in his blood, making his face go red.

"I said, men love her, and she eats them alive!" says Ted, ignoring John's venomous gaze.

"It's not true," he says, suddenly deflating.

"Oh, yes it is. She'll take any man who brings her a bottle of *that*." Ted points to the most expensive bottle of brandy perched behind the bar. "And that's not all." Ted leans in and raises a conspiratorial eyebrow. "I've heard tell she applies red lipstick to her lips."

John leans back. "So? She was wearing lipstick on stage. Lots of women do nowadays. It *is* the '20s."

"No, no, not on *those* lips." Ted glances down and back up with a wry smile.

"Oh…" says John. Ted nods.

"And she…*applies* it for the pleasure of her…male guests?" ask John.

"For her own pleasure, man," says Ted, ribbing him with an elbow.

"And all I…all one has to do is buy her a bottle of expensive hooch?"

"That's what I heard," says Ted with a shrug. "Hey!"

Ted is distracted by a female friend who blusters up to them, all smiles and bobbing feathers. They chat for a moment, ignoring John, and then she pulls him onto the dance floor, Ted feigning reluctance.

Left alone, John's head is spinning, and it's not just the gin. He takes a moment to contemplate the level of his audacity. Deciding he needs one more drink to muster the necessary pluck, he quickly downs it and orders a bottle of the speakeasy's most expensive bottle of brandy.

* * *

A close hallway with flickering gaslights, John stalks it like a cat closing in on his prey. Turning left, he is confronted with a doorway with a star on it. 'Fitzgerald' is printed on it in flowing script. The letters themselves are seductive, like the inviting waves of a beckoning lover. He raises a hand to knock, realises it's shaking. With an effort he stills himself, taking several deep breaths, his head swimming with the heat of the gin.

John goes to knock again, but the door opens under his fist. He almost accidentally strikes the man who quickly shuffles out the door, pulls it hurriedly shut behind him. The man is quivering, sweat pouring down his face. He looks straight through John like he isn't there, and, with a quick pause to tug at his tie and loosen his collar, the man disappears down the hallway.

John watches him go, his face a numb mask, but his mind doing backflips. Jealousy and hate war with blind lust. He can't make up his mind if he's inflamed with anger to witness the man emerging from the lady's dressing room, or simply overwhelmed with desire for a loose woman.

He shakes himself, disgusted by his own thoughts. Hefting the bottle of brandy like a talisman of innocent love, of pure intentions he can't even convince himself of, he knocks on the door.

A sing-song voice from within beckons him. Tentatively he tries the doorknob. It's locked. He shakes his head, checks himself, wondering why he had the

audacity to come here. What business did he have imposing on this woman?

He turns to walk away, thinking for once with his brain. The door behind him creaks open. A drop of sweat snakes its way down his brow to his collar, cool and sobering on his neck. Little hairs stand up on the back of his hands and he almost drops the bottle of brandy.

"Well?" says the voice. "Are you going to come in?"

John tries to resist, but it is a siren's call, and he feels emboldened by the invitation. His loins tug at him, and he is pulled along by a puppet string, into the dark room, closing the door behind him.

* * *

Soft temptation tickles his nostrils; a scent he recognises from his most torturous dreams. The light is languid and lazy, just a few flickering candles hidden behind frosted glass. Hanging silks and a faded rug, a chest of draws and a table covered in open pots of makeup. There is a changing barrier strung with clothes and an overstuffed leather couch with a beautiful body stretched upon it.

She looks like a living corpse in the low light, her

skin so translucent as to glow white. Her eyes have the predatory reflective nature of a cat, and suddenly John feels the situation sliding out of his control, all his desire draining away at the thought that he himself might not be hunter but prey.

"Hello," says Joanne, stretching herself out. She's wearing just a silk shift which hugs her slim yet curvaceous body. She looks like a sea creature, something you pull out of a shell, a fleshy, succulent thing to slide down the throat as an aphrodisiac.

She raises her eyebrows expectantly and John realises he's standing too stiff, shocked by the power of her presence.

"Oh, hello," he says. "I'm…a big fan."

"Are you?" she asks, looking him up and down, her eyes lingering on his crotch for a moment before snapping up to meet his nerve ridden gaze.

"I…I brought you this." He lifts the bottle. She rolls her eyes.

"Put it with the others." She flicks a bored wrist at the top of the dresser in the corner. On it stand a dozen bottles of the same. John tries to ignore them as he places his with the rest. He doesn't want to be just another one of many, and wonders what he can do to impress her, to stand out. Spinning around suddenly, he decides to be

bold.

"Someone told me about your little friend," he says, and her eyebrows shoot up in question, her eyes still lazy and hooded.

"My friend?"

He walks over to the couch, sits next to her. Placing a hand on her thigh, he can feel her writhe beneath the thin, smooth cloth of the shift.

"Your lips," he says, looking down between her thighs for just the most fleeting of moments.

She smiles, her eyes momentarily lighting up. "Oh, you mean, my second mouth?"

John squirms under the strange verbiage, yet gulps, and nods, excitement rising in him.

She suddenly sits up shock straight, pushes him. "Over there, sit there, on that chair." She points insistently and repeatedly. He gets up and reluctantly obeys her orders to move away from her.

With John sitting in the seat, she slides like a ghost across the room, picks up an object from amongst the makeup on the dressing table. She sits back down on the couch and smiles as she spreads her legs.

John's pulse hammers in his temples as he catches the first glimpse of thick dark curls. He's leans forward in his chair and she looks down and back up, drinking in his reaction as she pulls the cap from the lipstick and slowly, seductively turns the base. The red stick emerges like an obscene phallic symbol. Down it dives in her hand as her legs grow further and further apart. The thick curls become thicker, thicker, growing into a mass of dense strands which…

John's eyes go wide.

The lips pout and blush as the lipstick is applied and John nearly falls off his seat.

And then the lips speak, a deep, wet sound, and he really does fall off his seat. The mouth shouts and gibbers and John scrabbles back across the floor. Struggling to regain his feet he thinks of the man he saw emerging from the dressing room, and now realises the cause of his strange fear.

Tentacles grow from the thick mass of hair around Joanne's second mouth as it spews green bile and bloody chunks upon the floor. John sees an eyeball amongst the filthy mass and screams.

He rushes for the door, but the tentacles have him around the ankles. They tug him from his feet, and he scratches helplessly at the rug as he's pulled back.

Joanne laughs maniacally, throwing her head back in ecstasy as her second mouth distends like the jaw of a python and swallows its struggling prey whole.

# TWENTY TWENTY

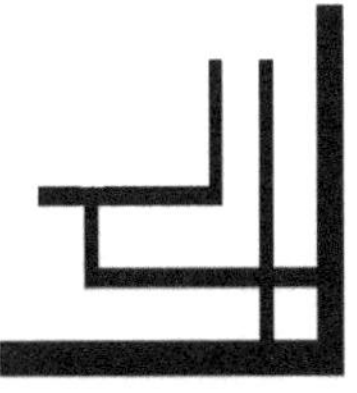

BLACK HARE PRESS

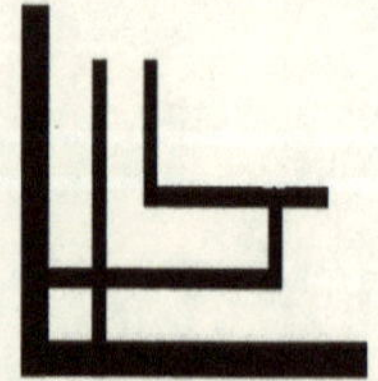

# The Death Of A Nation

by Derek Dunn

A sea of spotted amber and vermilion foliage swept over the hills surrounding Maple Grove. Death had entered the valley as beautiful as ever. The leaves were changing. Many things were changing. Half the population had left, gone up north to work for Chrysler, General Motors, or Ford. Those who remained had banded together, pledging an oath of loyalty and communion to their ancestral roots. They were the true labourers of the land, tobacco farmers and mill workers who'd sustained it for generations.

But their small community verged on extinction. No one travelled the old trail through the valley anymore. Anyone looking to cross the mountains now used the highway through Knoxville. Maple Grove was all but forgotten.

Robert wanted to go north too, but his father wouldn't have it. Edwin Tuft's great-grandfather had settled these parts over a century ago. His grandfather had fought alongside General John Bell Hood in the civil war. Edwin himself had poured his blood, sweat, and tears into this land. He wasn't about to let his son become a Yankee.

Robert knew not to bring the matter up again. He kept his mouth shut and went to work, day after day, slaving in the heat of the grist mill, listening to the creak and grind of the water wheel and millstone. The only thing that kept his spirits up was the chance of seeing Virginia Ross on his walk home. He'd circle around her family's store until he finally caught a glimpse of the blonde beauty.

The girl was a few years younger than him. She was still in school but worked at the store in the evenings. Her daddy had bought the place from Walt Milton before he packed up his family and headed north. In fact, her daddy had bought a lot of land as folk uprooted themselves from the valley. He offered lower than fair prices, and the deserters accepted, seeing as no other

offers were on the table.

Word around town was that Clarence Ross was looking to buy them all out. No one knew why he came to Maple Grove or what his true intentions were, but there was plenty of gossip on the matter. Some said he'd discovered gold in the mountains and wanted it all for himself. Others claimed he was hiding from the government. Some believed him to be a German spy. All anyone knew for sure was that he wasn't taking any more land. This was their home, and they weren't going to give it up to some outsider no matter what he offered. Besides, the Rosses didn't go to church with everyone else. They were Catholic or Jewish or heavens knew what blasphemous denomination. Whatever God they worshipped was apparently too good for the rest of them. While everyone else went to hear Reverend Moats preach on Sunday mornings, the Rosses stayed home. In fact, they even opened their store for business. The nerve of such people, Robert's father had said, trading money on the Sabbath. It was sacrilege.

It did trouble Robert somewhat that Virginia didn't go to church, but he figured she had her reasons. And who was he to judge? A true Christian wouldn't cast stones at his neighbour when his own faults lay before him. No matter what Reverend Moats said about her family, Virginia Ross was the most angelic thing he'd ever seen.

He'd yet to make conversation with her, only smiling as they passed. Sometimes a wave was thrown in for good measure; and even a hello was uttered when their eyes met once.

The store was just around the corner. Robert hoped she was there, sitting on the porch, reading one of her favorite books as she so often did. His legs stiffened at the thought of her being so close. Nerves shot through his veins. The girl had an effect on him like none other. Robert spat in his hand and swept the unruly curls from his face. He rounded the corner—but she wasn't there.

A wave of disappointment washed over him. Maybe tomorrow, he thought. Robert picked his head up and turned to cross the street, but something made him pause. His heartbeat quickened as the nerves returned. He couldn't keep waiting for chance encounters. Today was the day. He turned back to the store, a surge of confidence flowing through him.

Two steps led to the covered porch. He skipped them both and drifted across the creaky wooden boards toward the open door. Virginia stood behind the counter, a book in hand. She lit up the darkened room brighter than any lamp or flame.

She was alone. The stars were aligning for Robert. He reached into his pants' pocket. Two nickels clinked against each other. He figured he should at least buy something. Though he was committed to talk to the girl, he still needed an excuse.

A gust of cool air accompanied him over the threshold. Virginia looked up and smiled, then returned to her book. Robert sauntered across the room. He could afford two bottles of cola, one for him and one for her. It was the perfect plan. He examined the shelf full of sugary treats and drinks. The Rosses carried a lot more goods than Walt Milton ever did. Old Walt kept the store filled with bread, cornmeal, vegetables, and milk; but he never had the delicacies the Rosses were bringing in. Robert didn't know where it all came from, but he was glad for it.

He clasped a hand around two glass bottles and carried them to the counter. Virginia looked up and met his eyes. Robert lost himself in those sparkling emerald pools and almost forgot he had to pay for the drinks. He fumbled through his pocket to find the coins, dropping one to the floor as he pulled them out. The nickel rolled across the splintery wooden surface, forcing Robert to crouch and grab it before the runaway coin could make its escape. He stood, avoiding Virginia's gaze, and simply placed the five-cent pieces on the counter.

"Will that be all?" she said. Her voice, sweet as honey, sent a tingle down his spine. He pushed one of the bottles across to her.

"This one's for you."

She reached for it just as Robert released his fingers. The soft touch of her skin brushed against his for a fraction of a second. Her warmth filled his soul, eliminating all doubts and concerns. For the first time in his young adulthood, Robert felt alive. All dreams of going north vanished in that moment. This was where he belonged.

Robert wouldn't remember what else was said that night, but he enjoyed every minute of it. He went home a changed man, barely able to sleep with the slew of exciting possibilities racing through his mind. In the following weeks, a budding romance emerged between the young lovers. Others took notice, too. As Robert left Sunday worship one morning, Reverend Moats shook his hand a bit harder than usual and asked that he join him in his office.

"I see you've been spending a lot of time with the Ross girl," the reverend said, closing the door behind him.

"Yes, sir." Robert stood in front of the desk as there

were no chairs for him to sit. Though it was clean, the room was far from inviting. The white walls were mostly bare except for one lopsided cross. In one corner stood a shelf with several knick knacks piled among tattered books. Robert noticed a neatly folded white cloth lying on top of another garment with a pointed end. It was a hood. A pointed hood.

Robert had heard of men in white robes and hoods forming groups across the country—Klans they called them. The Ku Klux Klan. Was Reverend Moats a member of the Klan?

The old man rushed across the room to shield the clothes from Robert's view.

"We cannot be having that," the reverend said, his chin held high. His long nose arched toward the ceiling.

"What?"

"You must not visit the Ross girl anymore." The man, who was a half foot shorter than Robert, took a step closer. Somehow, he'd managed to get on the boy's level, staring deep into his eyes, penetrating his very soul.

"I don't understand."

"The Ross family is not benevolent. I fear evil intentions in their hearts." The man backed away and clasped his hands behind his back. "For your own sake, please do not see or speak to the girl again."

He smiled, like a loving father satisfied with his son's good deeds.

Robert swallowed a gulp of air. Though his desires were contrary to the reverend's, he didn't dare defy him. "Okay," he said, choking on the word as it came out.

The man motioned to the door. "You may go now."

Robert went straight home. Virginia would be waiting for him by the creek with a basket of fresh biscuits and jams, but Robert couldn't ignore what he'd been told, much less what he'd seen. Images of Reverend Moats in a white robe and hood flooded his mind. The revelation of such deception and hatred from a man of the cloth instilled a fear in him far greater than any godly rebuke. He couldn't see Virginia that day.

For several days, in fact, Robert avoided his new-found love. The emotions and desires he felt so strongly had to be buried in the deepest recesses of his heart. He took the long way home from work each day to bypass the store. It wasn't until Virginia showed up at the mill one day that he finally spoke to her and disclosed the reasons for his absence.

"He's just a backwoods hick who's scared of anyone who threatens his lifestyle," she told him.

"But he's a good man. He baptised me, for

goodness' sake."

"He's misguided."

Robert couldn't disagree with her. Reverend Moats had lost his way. Confused by the devil's cunning, he'd taken a wrong turn.

"I don't think you should go to his sermons anymore," she said. "Who knows what other tomfoolery he's putting in your head?"

"Do you really think he's with the KKK?"

"I don't know. Anyone could be in the Klan, far as I know."

Robert had heard about the march in D.C. Thousands had gathered to rally their cause, all in white robes and hoods. They were everywhere. But here, in Maple Grove? He couldn't believe it.

They continued to meet in secrecy. If Reverend Moats was in the Klan, then who else was? Robert trusted no one. There could be spies all over town watching him, doing the reverend's bidding. He took added precaution in every move. He'd decided, however, to take the path by the Ross's store once again. Even if he couldn't see Virginia, knowing that she was close eased his soul.

One night, after leaving work later than usual, Robert found Mr Ross lying face down on the front porch. He rushed to the man. He'd been badly beaten and could barely move. Strange inscriptions had been carved into his forehead.

Robert's hair stood on the back of his neck. This was far more sinister than he could have imagined. What kind of man could do such a thing?

Mr Ross looked up at him through swollen eyes. "They took her."

"Who?"

"They took Virginia."

Robert's heart sank deep in his bowels. "Where?"

The man pointed behind him. "Into the woods."

Robert looked up. It was getting dark, but he had no choice. "Will you be okay here?"

"Yes, please go."

Robert ran inside and grabbed a rag and some water. He wiped the blood from Mr Ross's face.

"Please, hurry," said the injured man.

Robert stopped and looked into his desperate eyes. He grasped his hands, careful not to squeeze too hard, and placed the rag in his broken fingers.

"I'll bring her back," he said, then raced for the woods.

There was no path to follow. The weeds and shrubs had consumed the ground and twisted around the trees.

# TWENTY TWENTY

The setting sun barely shown through the overhead canopy of dying leaves. But Robert didn't surrender. A strange sound, like a familiar hymn he'd heard in church years ago, echoed through the forest. Only it was different. The ethereal chants of unfamiliar words grew louder as he followed the droning hum. Robert had no idea what these people were capable of. He'd heard stories of what they did to black folk after the war, but surely that barbarity had ended.

The final rays of sunlight disappeared overhead. Robert hadn't thought to bring a light. He'd been in such a hurry to rescue his love from whatever unspeakable horrors awaited. Nevertheless, a burning flame appeared ahead. At first just one, but as he neared, the fiery orb diffused into a number of waving flames. The chants grew louder. Branches thrashed at his legs. The black shrubbery consumed him. All he could see were the slits between the giant oaks and maples, guided by the lights of Virginia's tormenters. He weaved through the tangled mess, emerging victorious over the forest's wrath when he finally reached the clearing.

But the battle was far from over. Dozens of eyes fell on him, peering through holes in white pointed hoods. Robert felt naked among the deathly congregation, his identity exposed but theirs still hidden.

Who did all those eyes belong to?

The chanting had stopped. Only the crackle of flames broke the night's silence. Robert crept forward. The figures parted, clearing a path to the centrepiece ahead.

A large cross had been erected; and there, tied to its wooden arms, hung Virginia. Matted hair fell on her face. Flames reflected off the tears in her eyes. Robert felt as though the world had stopped turning. Everyone stood there, frozen in place like an army of marble effigies. They all waited on his next move.

Robert stepped forward. He stretched a hand toward Virginia.

"Stop!" Reverend Moat's voice was unmistakable, though it held an urgency Robert had never heard. "You shall not touch her."

Robert continued and brought his hand to Virginia's face. Tears soaked his fingertips.

"Please son, come here."

Robert turned. His own father stood just feet behind him, masked in a silly costume like all the other lunatics.

"Listen to your father, Robert," said Uncle Clyde, standing beside him.

Was the whole town here? Robert glanced at the masked faces. He couldn't see them, but he knew who they were. People he'd trusted and respected. What evil had befallen them to put an innocent girl on this cross? What kind of spell had Reverend Moats put on them?

He turned back to Virginia and retrieved a small knife from his belt. The blade was dull but would have to do. He held it tight, slicing as fast as he could through the ropes that bound her limbs.

"No!" cried the men behind him. "Don't do it!"

They scrambled to stop him, but Robert wrestled them back. With only one purpose left in his being, adrenaline rushed to his aid. He pushed and shoved, focusing all his energy to the liberation of his dear, Virginia, until finally the bands were cut.

The girl dropped to the ground, landing on her feet.

A chorus of lamentations swelled through the forest. White-robed figures sprinted for the trees in all directions. Some fell, too terrified to move. What madness had overcome them?

Robert reached again for Virginia—but her hand shot up and seized his arm. A tight grip clenched his wrist. Her skin glowed a fiery red, igniting flames to life. Smoke rose from Robert's burning skin.

Tighter and tighter Virginia's fingers clutched until a crack split the air. Pain shot through Robert's arm and sent an agonizing scream from his lungs. His hand fell limp to the side. The lifeless appendage hung loosely from his wrist, blackened and shrivelled from the girl's bone-crushing grasp.

Virginia raised her head. Eyelids rolled back, revealing black spheres, darker than the darkest night. Robert wanted to run, but he couldn't. It was too late. The beast was free.

# JUST ONE BOTTLE

by Amber M. Simpson

"Kiss your willy for a bottle," Sally called to a group of young men passing by. The men snickered and elbowed each other, but none took her up on her offer. In the darkening alleyway off the main drag, Sally stood close enough to the entrance to solicit any promising buyers, yet deep enough to hide in the shadows should a copper pass by. Her hands shook as she brought a Lucky Strike to her red-painted lips and twisted the fake pearls at her throat.

"You there!" she called to an attractive elderly man in a dark suit and fedora. He looked the type to have a small bottle to spare. "Kiss your willy for a bottle? Just one bottle! Cheapest you'll find on any street!" The man shot her a disgusted look before hurrying on his way.

Sally sighed and slumped her back against the wall beside the dumpster, squeezing her eyes shut against the pounding in her brain. God, she needed her medicine; just one little drink. It'd been over twenty-four hours since her last one, and her body was starting to rebel.

"Goddamn you, Charlie," she murmured, dropping her cigarette and crushing out the ember with the heel of her Mary Jane. Charlie had been her main supplier ever since Prohibition began, cooking up big batches of gin in his kitchen. But someone had squealed and got Charlie locked up, leaving Sally nowhere to go but the streets for her fix.

And the fish just weren't biting tonight.

Knees trembling, Sally slid down the wall and plopped on the ground, hanging her head in defeat. She didn't notice the man who ducked into the alley until his shiny black wingtips strode into view.

"Hey, doll," he said, smoothing back his greased hair. "I hear you're looking for some hooch." He opened his jacket to reveal a small bottle, and Sally's heart leaped as she began climbing to her feet.

"Yes, I—"

"Get back down," he spat, pushing down on her head. His small beady eyes were hard and cold. "No need for you to stand."

He was a bit ruder than Sally would have liked and looked like a thug with his too-greased hair and his dress

shirt unbuttoned on top. But the hooch was right *there;* she could smell it on his breath. Without another word, she got to work, pulling down his trousers and taking him in her mouth.

After a few moments, the man grunted in displeasure, pulling himself away.

"Your mouth is as dry as my dead grandmother's cunt," he snapped.

"I—I'm sorry," Sally cried, clutching his jacket to keep him near. "I haven't had a drink all day, is all. If you could just give me a little to wet my tongue—"

"I don't pay up front," he scoffed.

"Please," she pleaded, pulling him closer. Working up as much saliva as she could, she spit on his semi-erection and tried to put it back in her mouth.

"Aw, Christ," the man snarled, jerking away. "I think I'll go 'round the block and find some other broad to do the job right." He headed for the street, pulling up his pants.

Sally lurched to her feet, desperate. "Mister, please wait! What about her? I promise you, she's as wet and warm as they come." When he turned back to face her, she lifted her dress, exposing her curly blonde pubic hair. "Same price," she added when he hesitated.

She held her breath as the man once again

smoothed his greased hair, licking his lips in deliberation. He pulled the bottle from his pocket and took a deep swill, Sally's insides squeezing in agony.

"All right," he relented. "But if it's as dry as your mouth, you'll get nothing from me."

Sally could have cried with relief. "Right over here."

She led him behind the dumpster and bent over at the waist, raising her dress to expose her bare bottom. The man got into position behind her, pulling down his pants, but she whirled around before he could take himself out.

"Hey, what—" he began, but his words were cut off— by the six-inch blade Sally shoved in his windpipe. Hot blood spurted as she yanked the blade back out, spattering her face and dress. Gurgling, the man wrapped his hands around his throat, the blood gushing between his fingers. Sally calmly gazed into his shocked, wide eyes—no longer scary, but scared.

"Sorry, poor sap," she apologised, snatching the bottle from his pocket as he fell to the ground and raising it to her lips. "But a gal's gotta drink."

As the man writhed at her feet, choking on blood, Sally tossed back her head and downed the full bottle.

With a loud burp, she giggled, the juice humming through her veins. She rifled through his pockets—swiping some change and half a pack of Chesterfields—then wiped the blood off her face and blade with the hem of his jacket.

Whistling a tune, she emerged from the alley and crossed the main drag, tottering in her worn heels over cracks in the pavement. She wandered the streets, her vigour renewed, until she found another dark alley. Sally stood close enough to the entrance to solicit any promising buyers, yet deep enough to hide in the shadows should a copper pass by.

"Kiss your willy for a bottle!"

Just one more.

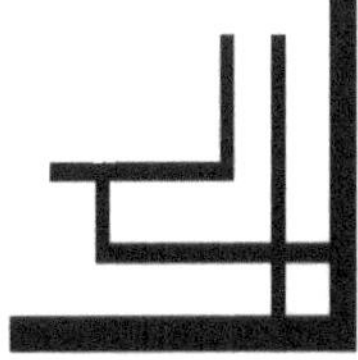

BLACK HARE PRESS

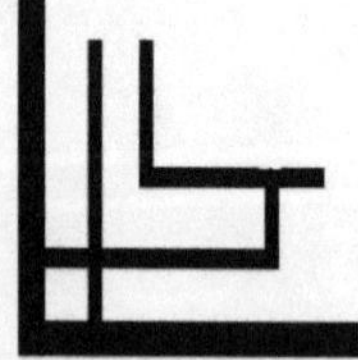

# LITTLE BRASS TIN

## by David Bowmore

Welcome, welcome to The Little Brass Tin. I'm always glad to see new patrons in my humble establishment. What would you like to drink?

Oh, I see…

Well, we sell nearly everything here; from booze to milk and even dancing girls, if you take my meaning. But not many know that I might occasionally sell the white powder to a select circle of friends.

They say it keeps one going for longer, and you know how those bright young things like their parties. They're the ones who mainly seek me out. And apparently, one of them has being telling tales out of school. Oh well, never mind. Felix, the tricky minx, it seems, has been let out of the bag.

Did you know that Sherlock Holmes believed it

made his mind sharper and wittier? I won't talk about what it does for the reproductive organs, not while there's a lady present. And it's available in so many forms. One can chew on the fresh leaves and get a very pleasant, if a little numbing, sensation. We sell, quite legally, two brands of coca wine. Especially liked by some of our more famous ladies—Sarah Bernhardt was a big fan of Vin Mariani. Are you sure you wouldn't like some of that instead? No. Can't say I blame you. In truth, it's not what it used to be.

So, what do you want to drink? This is after all a bar. You should at least be seen to be enjoying yourself in the expected manner. Splendid. Two White Lady's while we chat and I decide if I like you enough to sell you my prize commodity. Forgive me if I dominate the conversation. As you have no doubt noticed, I like the sound of my own voice a little too much.

You know, I first got a taste for the stuff on the front line in 1916. Much nicer here in a warm, dark bar than a cold and muddy trench, wouldn't you agree? I was a seventeen-year-old second lieutenant with no life experience other than six weeks basic and four weeks officer training. I'd been a schoolboy up to a few months previously, and schoolboys were sent clothes at Christmas, bought their books in the holidays and waited

for acceptance to one of the universities. I skipped on Cambridge. As far as I could see, I was ready to be a man, and being a man at that time meant preparing for war.

The NCO who drilled us told me, in one of his more civil moments, "Eat everything, Dervish. Don't waste anything. If it moves, kill it and then eat it. If it's already dead, just eat it. If it's free, eat it. If you can cook it, cook it, but the important thing is to eat it." And then he forced me and two others to eat the remains of a blackbird pie; bones, beaks, feathers—the lot.

His point being, food was scarce on the front line, and what food there was, was of poor quality. You were never sure of what you were eating, or when you would eat it. And one had to get one's energy from somewhere, didn't one?

Cigarette? Here, please take one of mine.

Where was I? Oh yes, the little brass tin with the word 'Harrods' embossed on the cover was always a very welcome gift; one which I soon looked forward to with great expectation. It came with a loving note from Mother, and it lifted the spirits. Looking under the lid and seeing the vial of morphine with an accompanying needle and a separate cachet of white powder, always brought a sense of relief. There is nothing better for giving one enough energy to face the enemy than one of those cachets—it beat seven bells out of boiled vermin, I can tell you—and when most of the guns were silenced (although, there is never any complete peace in Hell) an injection of morphine helped send one on the sweetest sleep.

I was eventually pulled out of a hole, bumped up to major and shipped back to blighty, minus an eye.

After that, it was a desk job for me, but I still missed the euphoria such a little brass tin would bring. To be honest, I still need it to silence the shells and the screams that continue to berate the old thinking machine.

When the war ended—gosh, has it really been five years?—one had to pay chemists and stores large amounts for a rapidly shrinking commodity. So I turned to the streets of Soho, where one could find it by the barrel load, after said barrel had fallen off the back of a horse and cart.

And then I struck a deal with a nasty piece of work.

I've been running this bar for the last year now. I don't have any trouble from the law or racketeers peddling protection, but if I do, the aforementioned nasty piece of work is never far away to deal with them.

Are you okay? You look sleepy. So does your lady friend for that matter. The chaps in the band call them

'Jazz Cigarettes' and they can have a rather soporific effect to the uninitiated. What you need is a little pick me up. Come with me to my office. It's in the cellar, I'm afraid.

Yes, there are a lot of stairs. I think that's because of the underground. You can hear it all around sometimes; above, below, far away and close by. I agree, it is hot down here. It might have something to do with the torches on the walls.

There you are. Sit yourselves down and rest easy. Who? Oh, him in the alcove, in the corner. Don't mind him. He's the nasty piece of work I struck up a deal with. Yes, you're right. He does look like the Devil, although I am assured he is just one of His minions. A demon whose name I fail to pronounce every single time, so I won't embarrass myself by trying again. But there is no doubt about it, he is a demon. You can tell by the glowing red eyes and cloven feet. The horns tend to draw a bit too much attention in public. That's why he lives in the basement of my little bar. Or is the Little Brass Tin a doorway to Hades? I'm not really sure.

No, no, no, don't try to run. Your legs won't be able to carry you up the steps much less get you to the front door. You see, I'm afraid you've had a rather large dose of opiate. Wrong of me, I know. But I won't tell anyone

if you don't, eh? Mum's the word, right.

That's it. Lie back, close your eyes, and let oblivion take you. Soon, I'll lay you on the sacrificial slab, one at a time, and then Hell, oh I am sorry, I mean *he'll* feast on your souls and I'll be able to feed myself for a couple of weeks too.

Old habits die hard and all that… But this is the price I pay to silence the shells of Passchendaele.

# WHAT THE BUTLER SAW

by Tim Mendees

Jenkins heaved with all his might and finally helped the near-comatose Colonel Peterson back onto the edge of the bed. Peterson was as drunk as a skunk. All the guests at his master's party were drunk as skunks. Party season was one that everyone in his line of work dreaded and this Christmas was living up to all of his worst anxieties.

"There you go, Colonel. Is there anything else I can help you with?" He purred as deferentially as humanly possible under the circumstances. After half-carrying the eighteen stone walrus of a man up two flights of stairs then nearly blowing his back out helping him off with his trousers, all he wanted was to slip quietly back down to the servants' quarters. There he would have a crafty smoke, straighten the kink out of his spine and calmly await the next disaster.

"Jenkins, my good chap." Peterson's moustache fluttered. "Go and get me a drop of brandy, there's a good fellow."

Jenkins rolled his eyes. "Very good sir." He crossed the lavish guest suite to the small bar in the corner and poured a generous measure of the finest cognac from a crystal decanter. He replaced the stopper, swirled the liquid in the glass and returned to his guest.

In the brief moment he was occupied, Peterson had slumped back on the bed and passed out. Jenkins sighed and placed the brandy on the bedside table. The bluff old military man couldn't half snore. It sounded like a man sawing logs. Jenkins swung the man's legs onto the bed and left him to his stupor.

Jenkins switched off the light and shut the door on his way out. "Oaf," he muttered to himself as he straightened his attire. This year had been a trying one, and this party was the icing on the faecal cake. As the distant hideous sounds of a raucous singsong around the baby grand drifted up to him, he seriously considered making nineteen-twenty-eight the year he sought out

other employment.

He knew without looking whose clumsy fingers were tickling the ivories; it was his bone-headed master. The tortures of the Spanish inquisition paled in comparison to the sheer agony of one of his piano recitals. The deluded man was entirely bereft of talent but convinced that he was up there with George Gershwin.

Jenkins sighed again and started his long walk back down to the main hall. Not wishing to jump back into the fray just quite yet, he slowed his footfalls on the plush carpet to a crawl.

*Slap!*

"Ahhh."

Jenkins stopped in his tracks. The unmistakable noise of rumpy-pumpy firmly grabbing his attention. He looked at the number on the door from where the sound emanated and quickly rattled off the guest list in his head.

"Miss Worthington," he muttered under his breath. Cor, she was a corker and no mistake. Jenkins didn't recall seeing her retire with any gentleman friend, but a beauty like that could have any man she wanted.

An internal struggle started to Build in the thirty-something gentleman's gentleman. He had managed just under a year without so much as a peek. He knew it was wrong. He knew it was voyeuristic and perverted, but damn he enjoyed it.

The struggle was ultimately lost as he reflected that there weren't many perks to this job and seeing Miss Worthington *en flagrante delicto* would definitely qualify as a perk.

Jenkins rubbed his white-gloved hands together and hitched up his trouser legs to avoid splitting his backside when he squatted down. Once in position, he pressed his ear to the door. *Splendid!* It sounded like Miss Worthington, and whomever her lucky beau was, were going at it hammer and tongs.

The young socialite's cries bordered on the painful and the bed creaked under the motion of the activity. Sweat started to bead on Jenkins' forehead and his breathing quickened, becoming short and ragged.

*Slap!*

"Ahhhh."

That was it. He could stand it no more. He closed his right eye, his hands pressed against the polished oak, and let his left descend to the keyhole.

"Nuts!" he mouthed, silently.

All he could see was the silk lining of Miss Worthington's elegant jacket hanging on the door

handle.

Jenkins recoiled from the door, his body trembling with unfulfilled lust. Directing some blood back up to his brain from his nether regions, he tried to think.

The sounds from the room continued to build in ferocity. The sounds of flesh slapping and thrashing about on an antique four-poster were almost hypnotic.

Jenkins patted his jacket and located the fresh taper that he carried in his pocket. His eyebrows knitted together as he tried to gauge the length of the stiff, wax-coated wick. It was around twelve inches. That ought to do the job.

Carefully, he placed the taper in the keyhole and pushed it against the jacket. With every extremity crossed that the noise of the falling apparel wouldn't alert the participants in the wild horizontal dance.

With a shove and a sharp intake of breath, he knocked the jacket off the handle and quickly withdrew the taper. The next few seconds were agonizing as he held his breath and prayed that he hadn't been detected. There was no slowing down of the coital harmony if anything it seemed to continue building towards an ecstatic crescendo. His eye descended once more.

It took a few seconds for his eye to adapt to the gloom. The room was lit only by candlelight. It wasn't the best angle to see the bed from, but it would suffice. He breathed harder as his eye focussed on the shape hanging over the edge of the bed.

"Cripes!" he mouthed in titillation.

Miss Worthington was bent backwards, her back arched and her nipples pointing up at the chandelier. The feather on her sequin headdress brushed the floor as her body moved back and forth rhythmically.

Jenkins bit his lip as his eyes wandered over her body. He couldn't see who she was with. There was just a shadow-clad shape on the opposite side of the bed. A big shadow-clad shape.

He looked at Miss Worthington's face. Despite the yelps and moans, her face was completely passive, and her eyes were rolled back in their sockets revealing only the whites.

"Blimey," Jenkins mouthed whilst reaching for his belt buckle. "That guy must be hung like a don..." He looked at the figure again. It seemed to ripple. He squinted harder. "Wait. What is that? Is that a tenta..."

Hundreds of blazing orange eyes on the bulk of the figure snapped open in an instant. The shape started to bubble and ripple. It was changing. Metamorphosing.

Jenkins froze with horror. His breathing got louder and louder. His trembling vision settled once again on

Miss Worthington's face. Her eyes snapped back to pupils and glared directly at the keyhole, her lips twisting into a cruel smirk. The worst thing about the shock Jenkins received... Her eyes too were burning orange.

"Aargh!" Jenkins let out a panicked scream and fell away from the door. He landed on his posterior and scrambled backwards like an upside-down spider. He slammed his back into the wall opposite and tucked his knees under his chin.

*Slam!*

The sound of a slamming door snapped his head away from Miss Worthington's door.

"What the blue blazes is going on out here?!" It was the Colonel. Roused from his slumber by the commotion. Jenkins stared in horror at the sight. Standing before him in sock-suspenders, stained underwear and no trousers was a rotund drunk man with a glass of brandy in one hand and a revolver in the other.

"Jenkins?" Peterson slurred. "What the devil is going on, man?"

Jenkins couldn't speak. He raised a finger to his lips in a plea for silence and pointed a shaky finger at the door.

"What? What is it, man? Spit it out, damn your

eyes!"

Jenkins shushed him again. This made Peterson's blood boil. His face turned the colour of a boiled lobster and his cheeks puffed out. He stood to attention and tipped his head back. He was about to give the impertinent butler a good roasting when...

*Slap!*

"Ahhhh."

The noise halted Peterson in his tracks. Jenkins watched as all the colour on the Colonel's face settled in his cheeks and a wolfish grin spread across his lips.

"You sly old dog." He winked. "Come on, let's have a look."

Jenkins shook his head and mouthed, "No."

"What? Shocking is it?"

Jenkins pleaded with his eyes and continued to shake his head.

"Ahh, too much for you is it?" Peterson's bloodshot eyes danced with perverse glee. "Well, I'm not so easily shocked. I could tell you tales that would turn your hair white." He approached the door and got down on his knees. "When I was in India, they have this book called the Karma Sutra and I tell you what—"

Peterson was cut off by another shush from Jenkins.

"Oh," Peterson lowered his voice to a barely

audible whisper. "Quite right." He put his finger on his lips and grinned.

As Peterson lowered his head to the keyhole, Jenkins grabbed him on the shoulder and tried to pull him back. Peterson slapped it away sharply.

"What the devil is the matter with you, boy?" he bellowed in a whisper. "It's just a bit of nookie for heaven's sake!"

Peterson's eye met the keyhole and in a split second, his body went rigid.

Jenkins scrambled to his feet by sliding his back up the wall, dislodging a priceless Turner seascape as he ascended.

"Well, I'll be blown," Peterson hissed. "That chap is really going for it, what?"

Jenkin's started to back down the hallway in the direction of the stairs.

"Wait." Peterson panted. "Is that a tenta—"

*Splat!*

The back of Peterson's head exploded as a rush of steaming gelatinous matter burst into his eye socket. Jenkins nearly fainted. His knees buckled, and he had to steady himself on a tea-trolley. The wheels squeaked and the china rattled furiously.

The shapeless blob surged over the Colonel's body,

engulfing him. His bones cracked as the creature devoured him.

Jenkins turned to run. The eyes appeared on the creature's body and appendages grew from it organically, seemingly at will. Jenkins ran as fast as he could to the staircase. Leaving the creature to finish absorbing the Colonel.

* * *

The party fell silent as the deafening screams of Jenkins preceded him down the stairs. He crashed into the room, knocking two debutants and a bottle of bubbly crashing to the floor.

Ladies gasped in shock. Men grumbled in disapproval.

Jenkins screamed.

His wiry legs sent him sprinting through the assembled guests, his belt buckle jangling loose and his arms flailing in the air.

His master detached himself from the clutches of a drunken dowager just in time to see his butler slam through the front doors and disappear into the night. He shrugged and resumed his canoodling.

Jenkins didn't look back once during his flight. He

just ran until his legs gave out.

The following morning, the assembled guests were shocked by the sudden announcement of the impending nuptials of Miss Worthington and Colonel Peterson. Heads were scratched and tongues started to wag almost instantly. The couple looked happy. Like they were already joined at the hip. Everyone was so caught up in the gossip that they failed to notice the foul smell of the pair and a distinct sheen to their skin.

Jenkins never returned. He was never heard of again. Some people say he went mad and threw himself off the Blasted Crag. Some people say he ran off and joined the circus.

However, one thing that *was* certain... His master could butter his own crumpets from now on.

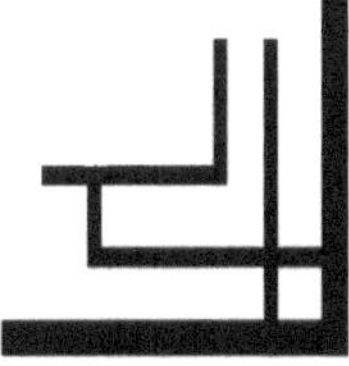

BLACK HARE PRESS

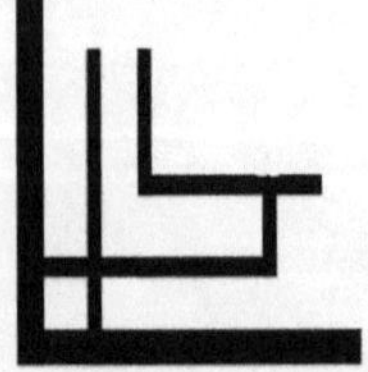

# 1921

by Paul Benkendorfer

It is a time when the living envied the dead. The dead found peace and an end to their suffering. The living had to carry on, with the cold and hunger. Once it was only the cold that bothered us, and we were hungry, yes we were hungry, but we could endure it as we always had. But this was a different kind of hunger.

We were promised things would become better. We were promised the people would be free, and we were promised we would know the luxuries of prosperity. We were promised. But when the Soviets had won the war, everything changed. The army ransacked all our food, saying they needed it for the war effort, leaving us with nothing to feed ourselves. Out of desperation, we ate our reserves and the seeds we needed for the next harvest. When the summer came, we had nothing left to grow

food with.

Then came the winter and her unforgiving cold. And with it everything started to die.

We pleaded to Moscow for relief, but the war had destroyed most of the rail lines. Both messages and supplies were difficult to get through. Now we were left with nothing. We were abandoned by those who promised us something better. If this is what freedom and prosperity looked like, then I gladly welcome back the chains of the Czar.

There was another funeral today, the third one this week. There were dozens of funerals every month. Seeing wagons filled with bodies carted through the streets became a common sight. Now we were burying the five-year-old son of my neighbour, Lev. He and his wife walked behind the cart carrying the boy, his body covered with a brown, stained blanket. Their faces stared blankly off into the distance.

My daughter, Yelena, gripped my hand as she walked beside me. My little devushka. The thought of the Hunger taking her next filled me with fear, as it should any father. I pitied her. She was old enough to understand the concept of death, yet too young to experience it.

Her bony fingers pricked me from beneath her wool

mittens. Another cramp from the pains of hunger must have surged through her bloated belly. Little plumes belched forth from her tiny mouth, like little vapours. She began to tremble. I picked her up and carried her. She buried her face into my chest, hoping to soak in what little warmth my body offered.

The people of the village watched on with vacant eyes. A year ago, everyone in the village would have gathered to mourn the loss of a child. Now the sight of bodies was a regular part of daily life. They had no more tears to shed. They had become wraiths roaming the streets. I could feel some of the villagers' eyes watching me and my daughter, like vultures, wondering when she would be next. Lev and his wife knew what was to become of their son, though they would not say. We all knew. We did not discuss it, but we all knew what happened to the bodies after they were buried.

We all knew.

The procession carried on to the graveyard. I knew the vultures followed us from the shadows. Hunger does terrible things to men.

* * *

That night my wife enveloped herself in a blanket

along with Yelena. Hunger did not stave off the cold of winter, brutal as it is.

I poured boiling water into a pot with some mushrooms and herbs from the reserves I stored away before winter. I stirred the soup and poured it into two wooden bowls. I gave one to my wife while I held the other bowl for my little devushka. Her little arms were too weak to hold the bowl on her own. I held out a spoonful of soup to her which she eagerly sucked it down.

My wife stroked Yelena's delicate sandy blonde hair. Once my wife and daughter's faces were bright and full of colour. Now they were as pale as ghosts.

"Papa," she whimpered. "Aren't you going to eat?"

"Papa had some food earlier, Printsessa," I lied. "I am not hungry now. You and mommy eat up."

I looked at my wife, her once pristine green eyes now grey, stared at me in sullen silence. I loved those eyes. They reminded me of the spring. When Yelena was born it brought me great joy to see she had inherited my wife's beautiful eyes instead of my dull grey ones.

"You should eat something, Pyotr," said my wife.

"I am fine, Fyokla," I said, placatingly. "I will eat another time."

"And when will that be?" she asked, scowling. "I

have not seen you eat in three days."

"You exaggerate," I said.

"I do not! You think I don't see you wasting away? You think I don't see how you suffer from hunger pains?"

"We all feel the pain of hunger, Fyokla," I said, waving her off. "I am no different."

"You suffer more than most," she said.

She brushed my curly brown hair with the palm of her hand. The touch of her soft, gentle hands always soothed me.

"Pyotr, you cannot carry on like this. You must eat."

"I will find something to eat in the morning when I go to town. I am sure the train with the rations will be arriving soon. I just know it. You and Yelena eat for now."

I could tell she was not satisfied with my answer. I knew she was worried about me. But I wasn't going to bury her or Yelena. I will not allow the vultures to take either of them. Not them. The thought of such a thing sent a chill through my soul. They could have me and most likely they probably will. I have come to accept that, but they will not have my family.

"There is no food in town, Pyotr. It's been months

since the last shipment of rations came."

"Fyokla, I appreciate your concern, but your concerns are misplaced. I promise you, I will be fine."

Before she could protest, I retired to bed. I did not feel like arguing with her, and I knew she did not have the energy to argue with me as well. She sat huddled by the fire with Yelena, both would soon fall asleep after dinner. I got no rest that night.

* * *

The next morning, I headed into town praying the supplies from Moscow had arrived, though I didn't have much hope. Fyokla was right, they hadn't been here in months. They may never come. They didn't care about us. We were just poor peasants and farmers. I huddled under my coat for warmth. They became more frigid as winter carried on. My legs weak, ready to give in with each step. But I had to press on.

As I trudged through the mud, not much further from the village now. Something caught my eye, a dark red puddle near the side of the road. The snow beside it sprayed crimson. I knew I should leave it alone, but my curiosity was getting the better of me. Scattered snow and a large divot indicated a struggle must have taken

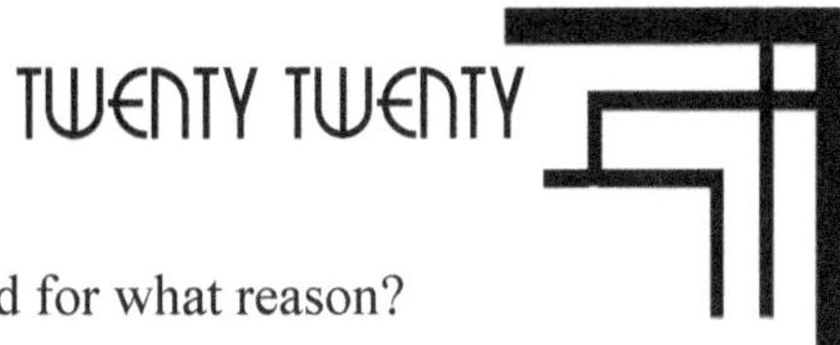

place here. But who, and for what reason?

I came to the realisation that it was blood. I felt queasy. A trail of red snow meandered from out the divot passed the road. I followed it. I told myself it was a bad idea, but somebody could be hurt and in dire need for attention. My gut told me to turn back but hunger pervaded my mind.

I followed the trail around the bend until I came upon a familiar cottage. The home of my friend Deklatov and his wife, Taisia. The front door was ajar.

Worried, I approached the door, seeing frozen blood plastered on the wooden steps. I knocked but received no answer.

"Hello?" I said, opening the door.

It creaked loudly on its hinges.

"Hello?" I said again.

I entered the darkened room overwhelmed by a rancid charcoal smell. An eerie chill filled the cottage. A strange cold, unlike the cold from the winter outside. I couldn't shake this unsettling feeling in my gut. Little light crept in through the curtained windows. Somewhere in the darkness I heard the sounds of grunting and tearing. I felt my heart freeze in my chest.

I made out two figures, one lying in the centre and another sitting over it.

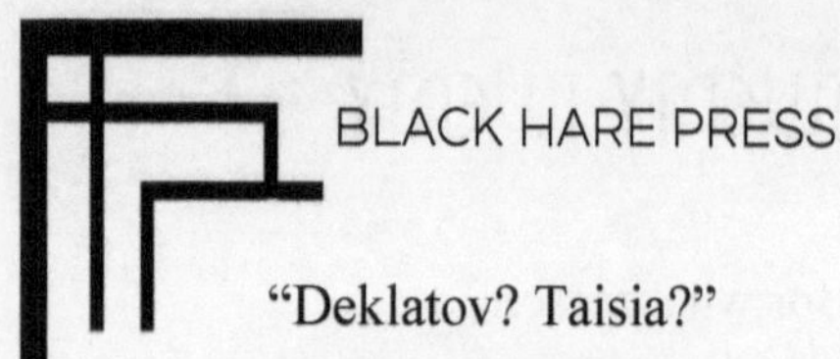



"Deklatov? Taisia?"

I knew I should have turned back right there and then, but worry for my friend drove me forward. As I neared the charcoal smell grew stronger, almost nauseating. The sitting figured grunted. It was then that I realised that the figure lying on the ground was a body, though to whom it belonged I could not tell. The sitting figure buried his hands into an open crevice carved out of the body's chest.

"Deklatov?"

The sitting figured turned to face me. I was barely able to make out my friend's face in the darkness, but I knew it was him. His face smeared red and black, blood dripping from the whiskers of his beard.

"Stay away, Pyotr," he sneered.

He grabbed a knife and pointed it at me. It was still coated with a fresh layer of blood.

"This is mine! You hear! Mine. I found it, it's mine."

"Deklatov, what are you doing?"

I held my hands, a gesture that I intended no harm, and took a step closer. My friend's eyes blazed with insanity I had never seen in a man before.

"You think I'm the only one?" he laughed.

"Deklatov, this isn't you. Where is Taisia?"

"You best return home, Pyotr. Go, now. Stay away or it will be you who I kill next."

"Kill? Deklatov, you don't mean--"

"Go, Pyotr!" he roared.

I turned and ran from that forsaken place. I ran out into the snow, my legs giving way. I crashed hard into the snow, feeling the bitter cold pierce through my clothing. I rose to my knees, dry heaving and coughing. The vultures I understood. People had become desperate in times of the Hunger. But at least they waited for their victims to die first.

* * *

That night I watched the fire silently while Fyokla and Yelena ate their soup. The two huddled under the blanket. Fyokla soothingly stroked Yelena's sandy blonde hair.

"Pyotr, please you must eat something, tonight," Fyokla said.

"Not tonight, Fyokla," I said. "I have no appetite."

"What's wrong?"

I looked at her, then to Yelena, my little devushka, sleeping peacefully in her arms.

"I saw Deklatov today," I said, turning back to the

crackling fire.

"What happened?"

I shook my head.

"The Hunger has made monsters of many a man."

Deklatov's repeated in my mind.

*"You think I'm the only one?"*

Fyokla gently rubbed my arm.

"Please, Pyotr, you must eat," she said. "You have to keep your strength up."

I took the bowl; nothing more than a few bites of food left. I had no appetite, the images of Deklatov feeding on the corpse fresh in my mind. I looked back at Fyokla, seeing the worry in her eyes compelled me to take the bowl. I smiled at her and ate what little remained. If there were others like Deklatov, I would need to keep my strength up. Just in case.

* * *

The next morning I returned to the village, carrying my woodcutting axe. If the Hunger had managed to cause Deklatov to turn into a beast, I could only imagine what it has done to others. Before I left, I told Fyokla to lock the doors and not to open for anyone except for me. I knew that my words terrified her, but it was for her and

Yelena's safety. She pleaded with me not to go, but I had to. I had to see if any supplies had come into the village. But I promised to return. I will return to them.

When I reached the village, I noticed a large crowd gathered around the train platform. The sound of roaring engines and the sight of a large plume of black smoke rose into the air and the smell of sulphur filled the streets filled me with hope. The trains had arrived!

"Get in line!" A man in an officer's uniform barked. He stood erect on the train platform surrounded by soldiers. "The rations will be distributed fairly. Get into line."

Chaos erupted. Villagers stormed the platform, clawing and seizing at whatever they could reach. Soldiers used their rifles in a futile attempt to keep the villagers at bay but were overwhelmed by sheer numbers.

Villagers fought over the sacks of grain. The fabric tore causing the contents to pour out onto the snow and mud. The surrounding villagers scrambled for it. Some shovelled what grain they could into their mouths while others stuffed handfuls into coat pockets.

"Get back into line!" the officer roared, unholstering a pistol. "I said get back into line!"

He fired into the crowd. Mists of blood sprayed

through the air. Villagers crumbled to the ground. A woman shrieked as some of the villagers turned to flee. Others became enraged and lashed out against the soldiers.

The officer continued to fire. Bodies falling before him. The soldiers joined in turning their rifles onto the crowd. Cries of panic erupted. Streams of blood mixed in with the snow and mud.

More soldiers rushed onto the scene.

The officer barked orders. While he was distracted, a member of the mob grabbed hold of his arm. The two wrestled for a bit before both were dragged into the swarm of bodies below.

I spotted one man break through the mob carrying a sack of grain in his arms. Others followed behind them, but they were either shot dead or tackled to the ground. The man barged his way through before a bullet ripped through his chest causing him to collapse to the ground. The sack fell out of his hands only feet away. I dropped my axe lunged for it.

No sooner had I held the sack in my hands I felt someone grab me from behind. Their hands slithered around my neck. I rolled forward, throwing them off. I turned to run, but I was quickly assaulted by another attacker. He grabbed hold of the sack and attempted to

pry it away from me.

He was strong. With great heaves, he tossed me about, yet I held firm. I tried to balance myself but my feet slipped and slid in the mud and ice. I dug my fingers into the rough fabric. In desperation, I tried to kick my attacker, only for my feet stumbled in the slush.

I felt my grip on the sack begin to slip. My attacker was just about to rip the sack away from me when suddenly I felt a shower of warm blood wash over me. My attacker groaned; a single stream of blood trickled from the corner of his lips before he toppled dead into the mud.

I ran as fast as my feet would carry me. A sharp burning pain pierced through my left shoulder. I toppled hard into the mud. A wave of warmth washed over as blood poured from my wound. The sack lay beneath me.

Barring my teeth, I forced myself back up. A sharp, burning pain erupted in my shoulder coursing through the rest of my body. I let out a cry of pain. My vision blurry from pain and wet snow and mud. Grunting, I forced myself back to my knees.

All around me I heard the cries and wails of the villagers; the shots of rifles; the thuds of bodies hitting the frozen ground; the smell of gunpowder and blood intoxicating. This isn't how it was supposed to be. This isn't how it was supposed to be.

I got up and ran. I ran and I ran and I ran. I held onto the sack for dear life and I ran. I ran until my lungs were about to burst. I ran until the bones in my legs snapped. And I ran some more.

* * *

I arrived at home, pounding on the door. My lungs burned. My shoulder burned. My body soaked with blood; the warm liquid now turned ice in the cold. Every gasp of air caused a searing pain to radiate through me.

"Fyokla!" I cried. "Fyokla, open the door!"

The door swung open. My wife standing there looking at me mortified.

"Pyotr, what's wrong? What happened to you?"

I entered the house and slammed the door shut behind me and locked it. Tossing the sack, now drenched in mud and blood, onto the floor I fell to my knees exhausted. Tears flooded from my eyes.

"Pyotr?" Fyokla said, wrapping her arms around me. "Pyotr, what's happened?"

I didn't know what to say. I hugged her back.

"The Hunger," I said. "The Hunger has made monsters of us all."

# THE EMPEROR'S CURSE: THE GREAT KANTO EARTHQUAKE OF 1923

by Lyndsey Ellis-Holloway

The smell of the broth simmering on the pot had him salivating. It had been a long morning; training with his men, and going over numerous, tedious files. Hirohito was ready for this meal.

He watched in eager anticipation as Kazue ladled the soup into a bowl. Takahiro reached out to claim the bowl and Hirohito laughed, slapping the man's hand away, waggling his finger and tutting. His men laughed, poking Takahiro in the chest, mocking him as they mimicked Hirohito's tuts.

Hirohito eagerly reached out for the bowl, but then the earth beneath him began to shake so violently that the entire building shuddered around him and his men. Kazue yelped, the soup sloshed out of the bowl, onto his exposed hand. Their cooking pot turned over with the force of the earthquake, and Kazue's pained cry escalated swiftly as the overturned pot set fire to the tatami mat and Kazue, who was nearest to it.

Hirohito's eyes widened in fear, and it took him a moment to realise that the flailing mass before him, screaming, had once been his friend and ally.

"Hirohito-sama! We *must* go!" Takahiro's voice cut through his shock, dragging him back to the reality of the room being devoured by flames around him, the heat of it prickling the back of his throat with every breath.

Scrambling from the burning building, Hirohito and others stumbled into the street, joining the chaos washing over the city like a tsunami.

The streets were flooded with people. Fire spread, flickering and biting at the sky as it fed on the buildings around them. Tendrils of flame lashed at the poor souls who managed to escape their homes, only to find

themselves trapped on the streets.

Cries filled the air, frenzied wails singing in eerie harmony with the agonised screams of the dying. Despite the acrid taste of smoke and ash, there was something else, something unknown that sent a shiver down Hirohito's spine.

The heat at his back should have been enough to drive Hirohito forward, to force him to flee this place, but he had seen something dancing amongst the flames. There were creatures fuelled by fire whose own flames fed the already devastating inferno. Something he'd only heard about in stories.

As a child, he'd read countless texts on the Oni and Yokai of his country, but never imagined he would face them. They were folklore. They were myth. They were silly stories told to children to keep them in line!

If it were not for the black eyes that stared at him from the orange glow of the flames, he would not have believed it himself. There was no mistaking the fiend that stood before him; the ridiculously elongated nose, mouth filled with fangs like tusks, and a wiry black beard upon a prominent chin—a Tengu.

The Tengu's eyes met his, and the fiend smiled, lips curling as best they could with teeth that overlapped them.

Hirohito's hand trembled as it reached for the hilt of his sword. These creatures attacked his people, people who would one day call *him* Emperor upon the advent of his father's demise. These people were *his* responsibility. He was Major of Japan's army and Lieutenant Commander of the Navy. He would die before he allowed these demons to devastate all his father had built.

Beside the Tengu, other faces floated amongst the flames. Bodiless horrors with dead eyes and terrible smiles that shuddered and sent out sparks, grinning wickedly when another building, or person, caught fire. These creatures, called the Kechibi, would destroy the city if he didn't do something.

"Help our people. Get them out of the city. Get them to safety," Hirohito commanded his men, snapping him from his thoughts to focus on the task at hand. The wave of fear facing these legendary beasts caused his senses to abandon him, and he'd almost forgotten his men were with him.

"Hai!" they replied, bowing sharply. They scattered down the streets which hadn't caught fire yet so they could direct anyone they encountered to head out of the city where they might be safe…or at least safer than they were.

"Brave little boy." The Tengu laughed, one clawed hand resting on the hilts of the pair of swords at his hip. "Do you believe you can defeat us? We, who are ancient and forgotten by you, except for the Shrines you visit without any real conviction? We, who have spent centuries planning your demise?"

"I will do whatever it takes to keep my city and my people safe," Hirohito replied, fingers curling around his hilt and scabbard. He lowered his shoulder slightly, but never took his eyes off the Tengu.

"You are *failing*. Can you not see? Your city belongs to us now. Emperor Sutoku will reclaim his seat, and a new era will spread across all of Nippon. The fire shall spread, our army shall advance, and your people will bow before our Emperor. You and your father will *beg* for your lives."

Emperor Sutoku had cursed the Imperial line upon his death, swearing that he would have his revenge for all the wrongs he had suffered, damning Japan and all future Emperors…or so the legend went.

"Never!" Hirohito roared. His sword sang, the flames glinting off the blade until the steel ran red with them. "My life for Nippon!"

The Tengu howled with laughter, drawing his own swords and leaping from the rooftop. A crash echoed as the building collapsed in his wake.

As Hirohito entered battle with his enemy, eyes narrowed, the tremble in his hand vanished, replaced by his resolve. He would forfeit his life if it meant even one more person got out of Tokyo alive. His people would survive this, and they would be stronger because of it.

Gritting his teeth, Hirohito thrust his sword forward, pushing his enemy away from his body, though he narrowly missed being cut in half by the Tengu's second blade. He was outmatched, and outnumbered. Even if he beat this fiend, how many other Oni or Yokai would he be forced to fight before he could deal with the fires threatening to overwhelm the city? No, he could not think like that. One step at a time, concentrate on staying alive, and then he could think about the next course of action.

Their swords clashed. Hirohito was always on the back foot, only just holding his own.

Fire began to encircle the square, threatening to cut off every exit. Parrying another blow, he swallowed the horror he felt at facing the Tengu. The terror of that niggling feeling he had died in the fire alongside Kazue. He teetered dangerously close to the peril of despair, but he found strength in the steel in his hands and the knowledge that his city needed him.

He had to get out of this square; had to find somewhere to fight this demon where he didn't have to keep an eye on his escape routes. Again, the Tengu swung his blades, but rather than parry with his own sword, Hirohito ducked beneath them, taking a chance that the demon would not expect such a move from him. Steel clanged against stone as the Tengu's blades narrowly missed Hirohito's exposed back. The Emperor's son rolled out of the way—but not before he sliced across the Tengu's waist.

Blood, hot and sticky, poured over his blade as steel connected with flesh and the subsequent roar from his opponent told him damage had been done. Not enough to kill, Hirohito was not arrogant enough to believe that, but enough to wound and give him a chance to escape, and to renew his resolve.

Without hesitation, he scrambled to his feet, ducking down one of the last remaining streets that had not been blocked by the fire. The road beneath his feet was hot, despite the fact that the flames had not yet overwhelmed this part of the city. He looked over his shoulder, relieved to see the Tengu had not yet followed him, though he knew this reprieve would be short-lived.

With his plan formulated, Hirohito made his way through the streets, his path obstructed several times by whirling flames and lesser Yokai that sought to stop him. With every diversion, he glanced over his shoulder wondering how long he could evade the Tengu. It had his scent now, and he had drawn its blood with his blade, that could not go without punishment.

"Please! Anybody! Help us!"

The pain-filled cry tore at Hirohito's heart. He turned a corner and was horrified by the scene before him. Flames flickered overhead and smoke filled the street. His eyes stung but he could still see the ghastly scene quite clearly.

The tarmac had begun to melt. The poor souls who had ducked down this street in the hopes of escape had become stuck, their feet sinking into the molten path, unable to pull free. On those closest to him, Hirohito could see the blisters forming on their exposed skin from the heat beneath their feet. Several had fallen during their struggles to escape their fate and had already died from the shock and pain.

"Please! Help me, get me free!" A woman wailed, arms outstretched to him, her face covered in soot and sweat, eyes wide with fear and pain.

Hirohito reached out a hand to her, desperately wishing he could reach her, but knowing that to step forward would mean his own demise. Closing his eyes,

Hirohito hurried away, fearful of falling to the same fate they had, grateful when the smoke swirled about in the breeze, blocking his view of the woman as he continued on his path. Closing his eyes as her agonised wails followed him.

Tokyo was almost unrecognisable. The whole city seemed to glow orange. Hirohito felt he had become deaf to the screams of the people around him, and the joyous cries of their enemies. The beating of his heart was so loud that it had drowned them out. He could only hope that his men had done as he asked and saved as many of their people as they could while taking out some of their enemies in the process.

His senses were dulled by fire and smoke, his nose filled with the smell of charred flesh and burning wood, his skin sensitive thanks to the heat, his eyes dry and stinging to the point of madness, but all of this fuelled the anger welling in his heart. These fiends had come and hurt his people over a centuries-old curse, Sutoku's anger was over a grudge that had nothing to do with the citizens of this city, they did not deserve this.

Jogging around the corner, Rikugun Honjo came into view, along with the tens of thousands of citizens who had gathered there for shelter against the flames and the aftermath of the earthquake. Hirohito's gaze was drawn to the roof of the army depot where three Tengu stood. To the left, his skin as red as the flames at Hirohito's back, was the one he had tussled with before, blood staining his clothes from the wound Hirohito had inflicted. To the right stood a Crow Tengu. With skin as grey as the smoke-filled sky, feathered wings furled at its back. Sharp black eyes fixed on Hirohito as he moved into the open street, a strange smile spreading across the fiend's beaked face. The people below looked to their Emperor's son for guidance against this living nightmare.

It was the figure in the middle who truly caught Hirohito's eye, for he had seen hundreds of pictures depicting *this* man's image. "Sutoku," he uttered, eyes transfixed upon the man's blue and bloated face. His black hair and beard grew long and wild, sharp yellow eyes set deep against a fierce and unforgiving face. Blood poured from his mouth in a constant flow. "Stop this madness, these people do not deserve your wrath, your argument is with me and my family, with all those in line for Emperor, leave our people alone."

"Emperor Sutoku has come to claim what is rightfully his, but first he must show his strength so that you pathetic creatures learn your place," the Crow spoke. "So *bow*, you woeful creature, before your true

Emperor."

"He is no Emperor of mine, an Emperor protects his people, he does *not* use them as an example!" Hirohito snarled. "As long as I live, you shall not take this city."

Sutoku smiled, a wave of blood from his tongueless mouth, pouring over his chin. He looked to the Crow, who nodded and took off into the sky, as the other Tengu escorted Sutoku down to the street below.

Hirohito's eyes followed the Tengu's path, hand tightening upon his sword hilt, readying himself for an attack. The Crow moved over the city, behind Hirohito, and with a snap of his beak he began to beat his wings furiously, whipping up the wind, catching the flames and creating a whirling tornado that raced over the buildings towards the depot, and the people huddled together in fear.

What little colour was left, drained from Hirohito's face as he realised what the Tengu had intended. "No!" he roared, instinct forcing him to throw himself backward, away from the flames and what was to come, his compassion desperately trying to drag him towards it, to save those who had taken shelter within…but he could do nothing for them.

The tornado inhaled the building. Thousands of men, women, and children. Their images burned into his mind, flesh blistering and charring in an instant. The smell of their burning bodies was nauseating and filled his nostrils.

The screams of those caught in the inferno clamoured to a terrible cacophony, and Hirohito clasped his hands over his ears, begging them to stop. That sound would haunt him until his death, and as he felt the heat of the fire, he hoped that it was sooner rather than later. Tears burned against his dry eyes, his heart ached as the sound of the blaze blissfully drowned out the cries of those souls now lost forever.

Hirohito could not move, his body had given up on him, the anguish of what he had just witnessed paralysing every muscle.

He'd lost.

They'd all lost.

A cry of pain and a dull thud broke through his mourning, and Hirohito looked up, his eyes fixed on the fallen body of the Crow—blood gushing from its limp frame.

He scrambled to his feet as three of his men, covered in soot and blood and burns, tattered and exhausted, hurried into the street beside him.

He was their leader.

He was their future Emperor.

It was time to act like it.

His eyes met Takahiro's, and the two men exchanged a nod.

The Tengu he had fought before came at them quickly, it was Takahiro who immediately charged forwards to engage this opponent, the rest of Hirohito's men racing after him. They knew where their fight lay, and where Hirohito's lay. He was grateful to them, to their loyalty and their strength, and he drew his own from that.

Sword in hand, Hirohito sprinted toward his own opponent. Sutoku was his, the Emperor was no fighter, those days were gone. His curse was all he had and all he needed. Sutoku smiled wickedly.

Hirohito's chest tightened, his vision blurred. His entire body shivered in a wave of panic and all-consuming despair that stopped him in his tracks. His body froze in place, barely a step away from where Sutoku stood. The world seemed to be devoid of light and warmth, as though the life had been sucked out of the air, leaving it hard to breathe. His heart raced exponentially.

Hirohito gasped, blinking furiously, desperate to rid his mind of the fog threatening to drain him of his strength. The battle raging behind him, between his men and the Tengu, was coming to its violent, bloody end, the Tengu's death cry pierced the vale in his mind, breaking through the barrier, shattering Sutoku's hold on his heart. His men's strength, their loyalty to him, to their city, it gave him hope and brought him back to himself, to the promise he had made to the Tengu in the beginning. His life for Nippon.

Blade held by his side, Hirohito swung with all of his might, lopping off the head of his enemy in one clean blow. Sutoku's head rolled away from his body in a spray of blood that splattered Hirohito's face.

With the fall of their Emperor, the remaining Yokai and Oni wailed, turning to flee the city, falling to the soldiers and citizens who remained.

Hirohito bent over, fingers entangling in Sutoku's hair as he lifted the decapitated head from the floor. He fixed his gaze on Sutoku's lifeless eyes. Sutoku had seen this city as his, had seen the people of Tokyo as lesser than himself.

His sword slipped from his hand, fingers limp at his side. His knees gave way and his body pitched forward. The last thing he remembered was looking out at the flame ridden, ruined streets of their city. So many people lost, they would survive, but at what cost?

Eyes closing, exhaling deeply, he fell unconscious.

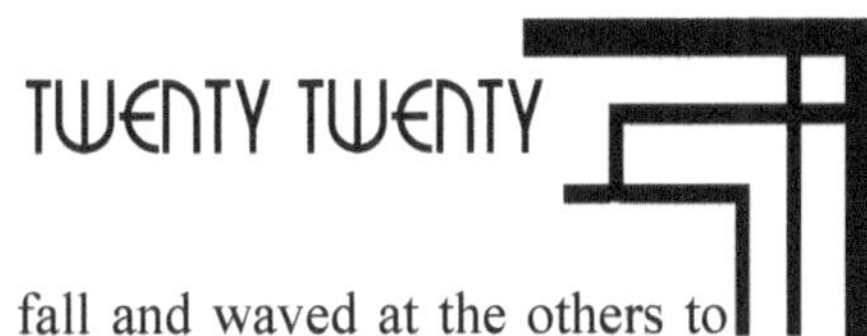

Takahiro saw him fall and waved at the others to help him retrieve their leader and friend.

"How do we come back from this?" Daiki whispered, looking from Hirohito to Takahiro for guidance as they gathered the unconscious man from the floor.

Hirohito stirred in their arms, slowly opening his eyes, the lids impossibly heavy as he fixed his gaze upon his companions before he spoke to them in a whispered tone, "Our greatest glory is not in never falling, but in rising every time we fall."

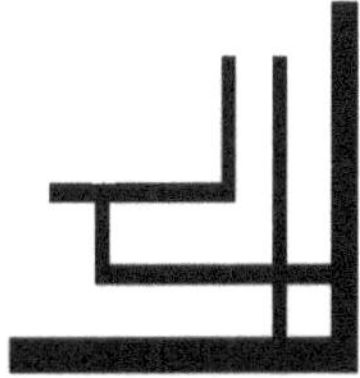

BLACK HARE PRESS

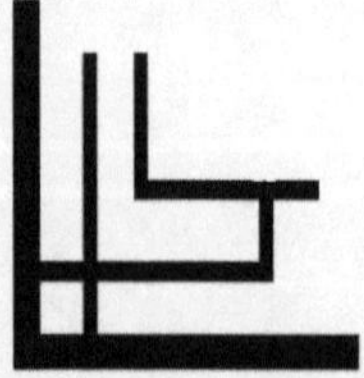

# Taxi Dancer

by Jacqueline Moran Meyer

People would be shocked if they knew what some men expect in return for a measly dime!

My dancing 'student' of the moment is holding me so tight I can't breathe, let alone squirm free. His movie-star looks don't fool me. I used to think men who look like Rudolph Valentino would be the cat's pyjamas. But I soon learned men were men, gorgeous or not and stopped swooning over the handsome ones three months into my current misadventures. No white knights on horses will gallop in to save these dancing damsels in distress. I'm past wanting to be saved anyway.

"Aww...come on, Doll, give a guy a kiss. You ain't gettin' younger by the minute."

*Shop's closed, weasel!*

I fake a wet sneeze in the chump's face, which

throws him off a bit and gives me a perverse sense of pleasure. While he stumbles all over my toes, I wince but manage to break free. We continue dancing. I try to recover from being mauled; while he's trying to find a way to smash the more...personal...parts of his body against mine. *Hallelujah!* I let out a quiet breath as the orchestra starts playing the foxtrot and I can relax. Not because it's a slow dance—the dance is fast—but the trot is the least handsy dance I know.

For five years now, being a taxi dancer, a dime a dance girl, has been my profession; ever since I lost my sweetheart in the Great War. Part of my soul died along with young Edward, and I will not say more on the heart-breaking event. Prohibition soon fell upon us, and my Pop's bar went bust. So, I left my small town for the big city and managed to steal a waitressing job. The hours were long, and I still barely made enough lettuce to survive and hated my octopus of a married boss.

One day, Rocco, a man who could sell ice to a polar bear, came in and changed my life. He was no looker, my Rocco, a fat, sweating man, twice my age with an ever-present cigar hanging out of his mouth, or dangling between two tar-stained fingers. Rocco is the owner of the Stardust Dancing School and offered me a job.

"Baby-doll, you listen to Rocco," he said as he eyed

me from head to toe. 'How would you like to make a lot of clams dancing the night away teaching dashing young men how to waltz or do the Charleston?'

"I can dance, sir," I said eagerly. Dancing sounded like a lot more fun than pouring coffee. Wouldn't I have been a fool to turn down more dough and maybe stop struggling to pay the electric? Why would I ever say no?

"Call me Rocco, Doll."

The same night Rocco offered me the job, I got all dolled up. I ignored the catcalls and hoots, coming from the trail of men waiting in the unending line to buy tickets, and walked into the dance hall. The place—lit by multi-coloured string lights hanging from the ceiling—did little to brighten the room, but the orchestra played loud and lively. I stood at the edge of the dance floor with the other gals waiting to be selected by a customer. I wore my prettiest dress, which ended up not being appropriate with its drab floral print and granny lace collar. The dancers were chic in long gowns, stylish hairdos and painted faces. The younger girls like me smiled, chatted, and one greeted me.

"Be careful baby-vamp, don't take any wooden dimes?" Her friends behind her looked me over and laughed.

The older gals, in their late twenties, stood apart

from the others, with their arms crossed, their expressions exhibiting utter boredom and maybe disdain. When a man asked an older gal to dance, she lit up like a bonfire while sliding her arm into his.

The first night, I made three times more in a single evening than I made in a week slinging hash at the dump of a restaurant. I decided to keep dancing. Rocco took an immediate shine to me. I did not return his interest. Now I realise the advantages of having a sugar daddy, or two, or three, could be a swell thing.

Customers—all sorts of men, any man imaginable—pay ten cents to dance with one of us for thirty seconds. We are taxis—picking them up, moving them around, bringing them where they want to go, and we drop them off and kick them to the curb unless they pay for another ride. I keep half of the ten cents they pay. With an average of forty dances per hour, the nickels can't help but add up, and the better I look, the more money I make. My gowns are beautiful and long. The necklines are cut as low as I can go without getting fired or arrested.

When I started dancing, I wasn't as sophisticated as I am now. Rocco says I'm not classy, I'm tired and grumpy. The first time a middle-aged man asked me to hold him tighter, I complied. But I'm smarter now. I went from not allowing any hanky-panky to getting paid for a squeeze or a grope.

I learned how to succeed in this business: manipulation. The customers want something from me, and I want something from them. A simple arrangement. We each play our roles, like actors and actresses, to make sure we both get what we want. But I am tired of the games.

Some men are sweet, though. I like the country boys best; some travel from their farms to learn how to dance.

"You are a swell dancer. Thank you, miss."

Us gals aren't the friendly sort with each other; we are competitors. No one calls me Clara, not for years. When I introduce myself to the men, they never repeat my name. Never a 'Thank you, Clara' or 'may have this dance, Clara?' Sometimes I use a fake name, knowing it doesn't matter. I am Doll, a toy; not human.

I used to feel sorry for the lonely men, but now I can't help but view them as pitiful creatures who should find an ounce of gratitude for the simple fact of being alive. My young Edward, my lost soldier, would love to be here, be one of them dancing with me.

"How 'bout we go in the corner, tomato," an old man may say while grinding into me.

If one of them gives me a severe case of the creeps, I wave over the chaperone, a walking wall of a man we call Fire Extinguisher. The offender will either find some gal willing to fill his desires, behave or F.E. will kick him out the door.

The most fun and lucrative—but also the easiest to handle—are the married men. These husbands have a lot to lose if I go extra-curricular with them, which I don't do as much now because I'm with Rocco. But if Rocco's on business for a few days, I do what I want because I don't wear a handcuff on *my* ring finger. I wear some long-sleeved gowns now and again when he's suspects me of cheating, because I usually receive a beating, but he never kicks me out. When I sense the gifts and friendship ending—dinners, jewellery, furs, gowns—from a married male suitor, a mild hint of a scandal gives me a nice financial send-off. I'm lucky to have dipped into the deep well of hitched men without getting myself killed; dancers do go missing once in a while. Rocco always claims the girl eloped or went home, although all her belongings are still in her flat.

Rocco schools all the girls on what to never do and what to always do: "No dates with customers. No accepting gifts. No inappropriate behaviour. But always make the customers believe they are special." He might as well say: Do whatever it takes to drum up business but don't tell me about it. Does Rocco think I bought furs and jewellery for myself before I became his number one dame?

The dancing joint's a front for his real money maker, bootlegging, and he doesn't want any trouble from the cops. He's worried about his own ass, not ours, for sure.

Since we've been an item, I go on a lot of hooch runs with Rocco. The police don't pull a man over if a woman is in the car with him, since we women are so naïve and innocent; we wouldn't be doing anything as complicated as breaking the law. Police officers can't search women either, so I hold the wads of cash, any flasks of moonshine and stash a gun in my garter belts.

I'm working a run with him tonight. Rocco isn't always respectful toward me, but he pays me generously, so I'm willing to risk jail time. Small mercies.

After the dance hall closes, Rocco's voice booms through the hall.

"Hey, Doll, ready to scram?"

I'm starting to think Doll is my real name. I wonder if Rocco remembers my name.

My name is Clara Bradford.

"Pos-i-lute-ly, Big Daddy," I say in the cutesy voice he favours.

He gives me a wet kiss on my mouth; his breath smells of whiskey, cigars and other women.

"You slay me. I'll meet you outside."

"That's a girl. I can't wait to slip you out of this beautiful dress."

He winks at me.

After I settle myself in the passenger seat, Rocco hands me the items to place under my dress. He watches me closely, relishing the view, while I complete this task. He starts the car and drives out of the city.

"Where we off to, honey?"

"Business at Ransom's shack. He'll also set us up with some shine, so we can get sozzled."

"Whoopee! Butt me please," I say while I wrap my arms around his neck and give him a peck on the cheek. He nods, and I place my hand in his coat pocket and pull out his silver cigarette case and light a smoke, cracking the window a bit.

"So, Doll, been thinkin'... Not many dancin' years left for you, are there?" His tone was solemn.

"What are you getting at?"

"You're what, twenty-seven...twenty-eight? Men don't like dancin' with spinsters."

"Are you planning on giving me another job, Rocco? Partners?" We both laugh at this because I'll never be his partner.

"Well, they're always looking for girls down at Miss Amy's. She's a new customer of mine."

Miss Amy's is a brothel.

*Never.*

I can't reject him outright, not if I want to leave this car without any bruises.

"I'll think about your offer. Mighty kind of you to be always thinking of me."

"Well, I experienced first-hand how...talented you are," he sneers.

*The bastard.*

"You're too generous to me," I say with a giggle. The role I'm forced to play—and my talent at playing it—disgusts me.

"Of course, Doll. I'll always stand by you."

*What a prince.*

"Ooh, Rocco. Can you pull over? I need to do number one. One hopper was plying me with soda all night."

"OK, Baby-doll."

I open the car door.

"Don't you get the money wet," he warns me, with

a laugh.

"Don't worry. I'm a pro at this." I *am* a pro at this. It has taken me years to earn this man's trust. I've purposely asked to pee during every ride. Between the cash I've saved and stuffed under my dress tonight and Rocco's wad of dough, I'm as wealthy as I'll ever be. I can stop this tiresome life, this charade.

I ease out of the car into the still black night, feeling the tall grass against my fingertips. We're in the back country; not a house for miles around.

I squat, pretending to pee and remove the gun.

"Oh, no! Please don't be mad, Rocco," I yell, adding a note of panic to my voice. I stand and face the car. He unwittingly plays his role perfectly.

"What'd you do? Did you ruin the money?"

"It was an accident. I'm sorry," I say in a shaky voice.

"Damn it!" Rocco roars, heaving his sweaty, overweight body out of his car as fast as he can. He waddles toward me. This arrogant fat penguin will soon never be able to control me again.

Rocco stops when he sees the glint of metal in my hands. He puts his hands above his head.

"What's eating you, Doll?"

His eyes are wide. Rocco's mouth hangs open, his

cigar falls in the grass.

"Kneel."

Moving is not an easy task for him. He bends his knees, doubles over, and ungracefully lowers himself to the ground. I glare at him, ready to do as planned.

"Doll. Think. Where will you be without me?"

I laugh. Rocco somehow still thinks he has some power here.

"I was joking about Miss Amy's. Calm down and give me the gun."

I laugh louder.

"Sure thing, Rocco. I'll give you the gun. We'll pretend none of this ever happened."

I can tell he's shocked, and not solely by my actions. The coquettish voice he's gotten used to hearing simper out of me is now rough, harsh. I'm not playing his games anymore and I am not giving him this gun.

"I won't hurt you. Look—"

"You finally got something right, Doll," I reply. I revel in the feelings of freedom and power coursing through me.

He reaches into his pocket, curious, I wait because I have touched him enough tonight to know he is not, and would not be, packing another pistol.

He pulls out a small black velvet ring box and opens

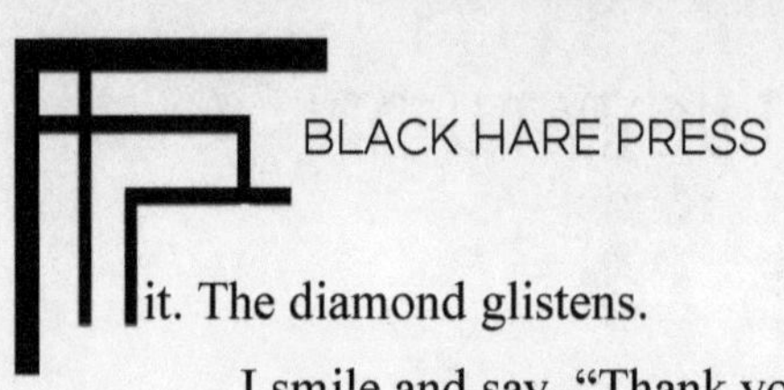


it. The diamond glistens.

I smile and say, "Thank you."

Rocco smiles too.

The click as I release the safety is the loudest sound echoing in the stillness of the night until I pull the trigger.

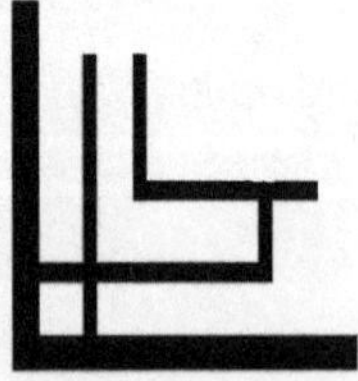

# ANOTHER DAY

by J.W. Garrett

Tom blinked, letting his eyes open painfully to another day. At least it wasn't sunny. Rain streaked down the window in long sheets—matching his mood. What was this hell on Earth that had ruined him and robbed him of his future? Just on the cusp of a new decade and 1929 had turned to shit with no end in sight.

He scrubbed his hand down his face and eyed the woman beside him only partially covered in blankets. Nodding in appreciation, he let his gaze linger over the length of her exposed leg, her slender waist. He kissed her shoulder. *What was her name again?*

"Oh, tell me it's not morning yet." She ran a hand lazily down the stubble dusting his jaw.

*Angel. That's it. The dancer from last night.* "No, it's early yet. Go back to sleep, darlin'." Tom threw his legs over the side of the bed and gripped the bottle of Jack with his right hand while steadying the glass on the nightstand with the other, then poured, downed the contents, and helped himself to another.

A trail of stockings, various undergarments, and a sequined sparkly flapper dress littered the floor. Tom's lips lifted in a half smile despite himself. He tugged on his pants and glanced over his shoulder. *Damn…she's something*. And for a little while, she'd eased the mind-numbing ache.

Abandoning his glass, he grabbed the neck of the bottle, took a long pull, and then strode toward the window. People rushed by, only to wait in long lines for money that would never come. The dead look he'd seen in their eyes mirrored his own. The hurry…the rush? None of it mattered. He was no different from the farmers. Except maybe even they had more hope of a future. They could always have another crop to sell—eventually. Now Tom was less than worthless.

Desperation had seeped into his soul. Had moved in and taken up residence. And worse, it tightened his chest, fighting him for the breaths he took with each successive day. His banking career was over. When his loans had been called in, he'd had nothing more to give. Thirty years of working, achieving a level of success, all reduced to this…Hell. At least his son was with his aunt, so he didn't have to witness what his father had become over the past several weeks.

Picking his way through clothing and other discarded items, Tom headed to his office, bottle still in hand. The hours he'd spent in here… Tom crossed the floor, leaned against his mahogany desk, the solid feel of the wood lending him strength. The picture of his wife, Susan, graced the table behind his desk, and next to hers was their son's photo, Tommy Jr.—almost sixteen now.

When his wife had died five years ago, it had been him and Tommy against the world, and what a team they had made. He'd be a man soon. *Tommy would be fine*, Tom argued with himself. He and Susan had made a great kid, but Tom was an empty shell with nothing more left to give his son—besides maybe this damn worthless desk that no one could afford to buy.

Tossing his head back, he gulped another large swallow of Jack. His office looked and smelled like success. He used to fit in here—the faint odour of ink, the slight mustiness of the neatly stacked papers, the crisp scent of the leather that bound the books along the wall, the rich smell of the tobacco lining his pipe—but no longer.

A calmness washed over Tom, and with it, his wife's voice whispered through his thoughts, beckoning him. He wasn't alone anymore. Susan appeared, reaching out a hand to him. *Susie, I didn't think it would come to this. Soon, at least, we'll be together.* As he sat down, Tom heaved a settling breath, set his jaw, and grabbed his .38 Special from the top drawer of his desk. He'd always kept the gun loaded, but Tom checked the chamber methodically just the same and pushed it closed with a soft *click.*

The cool metal added to his resolve, a secure weight in his hand. Unlike his shredded existence, a ghost of who he used to be, here, now, he had control. Sliding the barrel in his mouth, his last thoughts were of his son, hoping that someday he might understand Tom's words he'd written to him. Words that he'd carefully chosen while stone-cold sober.

A shot echoed, followed by a distant scream. The S&W revolver clattered loudly to the floor. Drops of blood splattered then drifted down Susan's picture, bathing the black-and-white photo a deep crimson.

# BROADCAST

## by Raven Corinn Carluk

John pinned the second bicycle lense into place, ignoring the lingering scent of tea. He'd washed the used tea chest several times to no avail. Nothing else was a good fit, so he had to put up with the tantalising aroma.

He leaned back and pushed his glasses back up his nose. The televisor was coming together well enough. The glue held the hat box in place, the sealing wax filled all the gaps, and he had just one more lense left to pin in place before he could fit the Nipkow disk. Thankfully, he had enough spare darning needles, in case one broke.

Someone knocked on the door. John coughed, forced himself to his feet, and crossed the small workshop to answer the door. "Mister…er, Dantalion. Miss. Won't you come in?" He shuffled aside for the demon, bowing his head.

The Great Duke sauntered into the workshop, dressed in the latest fashion from America, a cigarette trailing smoke in his wake. *Her* wake. John couldn't keep up with the demon's appearance; Dantalion wore whatever face he chose, every man and woman available to him. Or her.

Dantalion struck a pose in the middle of the space, the fringe on her dress shaking and shimmering. Amber eyes locked with him, and the demon took a long pull on the cigarette before speaking. "How progresses your toy, Mister Baird?"

John set his chin, returned to his work. "It's almost finished. Are you here for…the spell?" He fiddled with the bicycle lense, wanting to place it, but uncomfortable beneath the Great Duke's amber eyes. The loveliness of his female form only added to John's nervousness.

Heels clunked on the dusty wooden floor as Dantalion approached. Chills worked their way up John's spine. The same as whenever the demon stood in close proximity. Evil and warm and cold and heavy, penetrating straight to the man's soul. John feared yet needed the strength and power offered.

"It's not very much to look at," Dantalion murmured, leaning over the set of boxes, cherry red lips a moue of curiosity.

John wanted to snatch it closer, but he knew the demon wouldn't hurt his televisor. It was Dantalion who had helped him, had allowed John to read the Great Duke's Book of All Knowing, had promised to bring the invention to life. "My calculations say yes. With the disk and your spell, it will become exactly what I said."

Dantalion pulled hard on her cigarette, then let the rich smoke out with a long purr. John coughed, weakness stealing over him. The coast air of Hastings had only done so much for his health. He would need a long rest after the Great Duke left.

"I suppose you're ready for this," the demon said, softly, fumbling at her tiny purse, cigarette holder clenched between sharp teeth. Coins clunked as long fingers rustled through the contents, seeking for far longer than possible.

Then she pulled a Nipkow disk free, easily twenty centimetres across. It gleamed in the gaslight, coppery, though richer than any copper John had ever seen. Dantalion faced him and offered the disk, a bloody sigil painted on the surface. "Exactly as specified."

A thrill ran through John, overriding the weight of the Great Duke's presence. He accepted the Nipkow disk with gentle hands, measuring the spaces with his eyes. The perfect spiral; just as needed to capture

moving images.

"I'll let you mount your disk and finish your toy. Have to go get the sacrifice anyway, so that should give you plenty of time." Dantilion left the workshop, but John was too focused on completing the televisor to notice.

Time flew as he finished, pinning the last lense, mounting the disk, and lighting the lamp. John cleaned his glasses, admiring his work, then noticed that Dantilion had returned. He turned, startled, and stared at the demon and the bound girl at her side. "It's ready," John whispered.

Dantilion smiled, amber eyes flashing with red fires. "Then we shall finish." John swallowed a sudden lump in his throat and nodded.

The demon's smile grew larger and larger, revealing far too many teeth. She drew a Kris knife from her tiny purse and began her incantation. The words seemed to burn the air, stealing all the warmth at the same time. The girl beside Dantilion screamed through her gag, struggling to rise.

Her words ceased, and she plunged her knife into the girl's heart. The scream came to a sharp end, blood spraying across the room.

John flinched back, closing his eyes, avoiding the

splatter. Power crackled across his skin, reeking of ozone, biting his nerves. He ached as something built inside him, outside him, all around. Crushing, pressing, boiling, freezing, until it finally burst and released, leaving him drained and weak.

He opened his eyes and stared in awe. The vellum lining on the hat box glowed, silhouettes replaying the sacrifice. "It works," he whispered.

Dantilion giggled, clapping her hands excitedly. "Mortal hands have crafted that which shall control the mortal world."

"With knowledge. Bringing peace."

The demon batted amber eyes. "Of course, Mister Baird. After you refine your design, I will make sure every household has one of your televisors. Everyone shall know your name. They will watch, and they will learn, and they will know, because your device will show them the way. In time, their whole world shall be viewed through this device." She laughed again.

John nodded, suppressing a cough, suffused with pride. His invention would equalise the population, would raise the masses up. No one would be better than anyone else, and wars would become a thing of the past.

He could not *wait* to see what the future held.

# A Lad Named Jack

by Kevin J. Kennedy

Prohibition is only for those without money. I know of clubs all over the city where one can partake in an alcoholic beverage if so inclined.

Being a gentleman of no fixed abode is problematic of course. The lack of substantial housing isn't the problem. The absence of money is the issue that takes precedence when one is feeling rather parched and in need of a fine hooch.

I was a young lad in London, thirty odd years ago, the last time I needed to kill for money. Jack, the newspapers had named me. Never mind. Another whore must die.

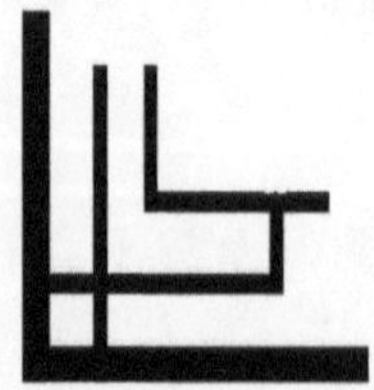

# Clean Sneak

by Matthew A. Clarke

Big Ricky and Frankie Frisco have been casing the clip joint for the past week. Rumour has it there's fifty large in a safe below the speakeasy out back. The real target, however, is Masetti. The fat fucker and his goons sprang up outta nowhere like weeds in shit a few months back and have been clipping our boys for weeks. Respect used to mean something in this city; you don't fuck with other people's business, they don't fuck with yours. Apparently, these guys need reminding that they ain't above the rules.

Getting inside won't be a problem. The two suits that will be working the doors usually head inside at eleven on the nose, once the last of the drunkards have cleared out. However, there will be an explosion in the financial quarter across town at eleven, which should keep the coppers busy long enough to keep us out of the cooler. Once Paddy has dealt with the doormen, the chopper squad will lead the attack to clear a path through to Masetti, with Big Ricky, Frankie, and Knuckles waiting out front to cut down any runners.

From there it should be a pretty clear run through to the speakeasy out back and across to the hatch that leads to the basement. If the boys have been doing their job properly, that's where Masetti will be, holed up like a mouse, counting the takings. At least, that's what he'd usually be doing. Things could go pear-shaped sharpish once the blasting starts.

Bump Masetti, send Jimmy the can-opener in for the safe. Or, keep Masetti alive long enough to open the safe, then bump him off. It should be a pretty easy job. A clean sneak.

* * *

The explosion is surprisingly loud even from this distance, but I figure that could work in our favour. Add to the confusion.

I watch as Paddy puts a slug into each of the doormen before dragging them down the side of the building, toward the dumpsters. I remove a smoke from my deck of Luckies and light it up. The smoke twists and flits to and fro in the cool evening air while I wait for him to reappear. Eventually, he surfaces. Paddy raises a bloodied hand and points further up the street where five men dressed in black suits separate from the shadows, their faces obscured by low-tilted fedoras. As they make their way toward the nondescript entrance of the clip joint, they release the catches on the violin cases they carry, letting them clatter to the floor as they withdraw their gats.

As soon as they cross the threshold and disappear, the shooting starts. My cigarette almost burns my finger—I'd forgotten all about it—and I drop it to the ground and crush it under a polished brogue. Big Ricky, Frankie, and Knuckles now move up to join Paddy by the door and cut down two broads and a goon as they run from the building. I can't tell if they were packing or if it's just a case of wrong place wrong time. I won't lose any sleep over it though, and I know they won't either.

A few moments later the popping sounds have died down. Knuckles looks at me and gives an almost imperceptible nod as the other three take the fresh stiffs the way of the previous two. I check both ways before crossing—you never know when one of those fancy motorcars might be coming—and make my way across to them.

"Five minutes, then we're gone," I say. "Jimmy's waiting out back should we need him. Ricky, you lead. Frankie, cover him. Knuckles, you're with me."

I don't need to give Paddy any further instruction, he's already halfway down the dark alleyway to rendezvous with Jimmy and get the motor ready.

"Boss," Big Ricky replies.

I follow my men toward the entrance, stepping over a pool of tacky blood, peppered with chunks of gore. Looking at the pulp, I'd say one of those runners got nailed pretty good through the eye socket.

The inside of the clip joint is a total shit-show. Three of my choppers lay dead around the room and the smell of iron and smoke hangs in the air and burns my nostrils. I pause as I notice that each of them are missing limbs (*what the fuck?*). I count six other bodies lying still amongst overturned tables and smashed glass, dressed in once expensive suits, now twisted and torn with leaking bullet holes. I catch sight of Big Ricky and the expression on his face says that he's thinking the same thing I am—something ain't right. I kick aside a broken chair and we make our way to the red velvet curtain at the back of the stage.

Two more corpses lay in the corridor, surrounded by bullet casings, both staring at the ceiling. I thought I saw one of them blink, but I know that's ridiculous and put it down to dying nerves. However, I still can't shake the feeling of being watched and I'm not the only one. A wooden door at the far end of the corridor is slightly ajar and I hear movement from within. Then: silence. I look to Big Ricky. He moves ahead slowly, cannon trained on the opening.

A sudden flash of light and a deafening roar catch me by surprise—even though I've experienced it a hundred times before—the tight corridor seems to amplify the noise. Big Ricky drops to the floor like a bag of wet sand. The top of his head has been blown away by the goon with the sawn off and the rest of us are sprayed with warm brain matter. Knuckles pulls me behind him while the other two return fire, pumping the man on the other side of the door full of lead.

Eventually, the firing stops, at least, it sounds like it has—my hearing has been muted by the racket and everything has a high-pitch whine over it. I wave away the smell of gunpowder and death as we pass Ricky without stopping to check the damage. They did us a favour really as no head makes him harder to identify and I don't have to worry about getting the body out of here.

After Frankie has given us the all-clear, we push ahead and enter the speakeasy proper. I'd thought my boys had done a pretty decent number on the club out front, but this is a whole other level. Scanning the room, I count nineteen bodies in total. About a half of those were dancers, now nothing more than shredded meat in bloodied dresses and broken pearls. A canary has been slain where she stood on the stage, the microphone rests atop her cooling body. The rest of the stiffs littering the dance floor are Masetti's goons, and sure enough, the last of my choppers. Again, missing limbs. I shudder as I wonder what kind of weapon could do that.

"The big cheese ain't here," I say. "Keep sharp."

Knuckles nods to the other two and we move up through the room, or what's left of it. Glass shards from dozens of smashed bottles of hooch glint on every surface and the wooden panelling of the back bar has been turned to honeycomb by hundreds of metal bees. I walk around the back of the bar, cursing at the sticky liquids that are clinging to my polished shoes, and come across a man in a grey pinstripe suit crawling toward me. He manages to raise his head and mouth a word that may have been *"mercy"*, but his lower jaw is hanging on by just a few tendons and his speech is sloppy. One end of it scrapes and catches the floor. I crouch and put him out of his misery with a single cap through the temple.

The hatch at the far end is open, propped up against the panelling behind it. A dim light floats up from below and illuminates a set of wooden stairs leading down to the lower level.

Frankie takes the lead without prompting, moving quick and quiet; we're all aware that we're running short on time. I linger for just a moment until I spot what I'm looking for; a bottle filled with a sour smelling liquid. Knuckles takes it and we continue after Frankie.

There's only one way ahead as we reach the bottom—the same way the trail of blood seems to lead to, a single, low doorway recessed in a damp concrete wall. We know what waits for us on the other side of that door; the dough. And a dead man walking. Although, from the amount of blood down here, he may not be walking at all.

We follow the river of red that runs parallel to the labyrinth of pipework either side of the uneven concrete, stepping over two more corpses halfway down. Eventually, we reach the door. Frankie takes a step back before booting it open with an explosive force. Surprisingly, it opens with little resistance. A hollow crack rings out as it collides with the wall beyond before

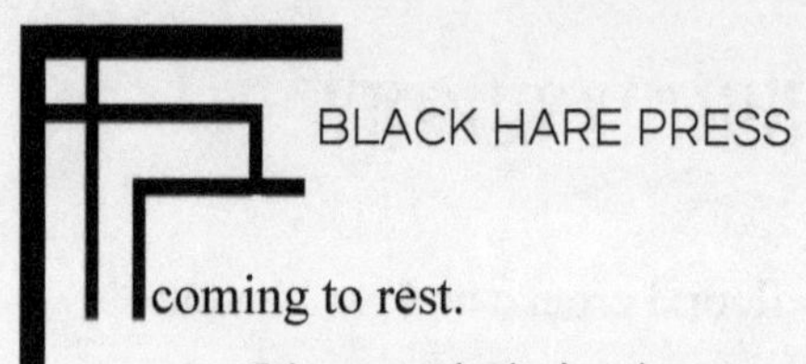


coming to rest.

It's too dark in the room to make anything out inside—other than the skeletal thing with the sharp teeth that probably isn't even there. I've heard that in the absence of light the brain will try to fill in the gaps.

Frankie reaches in, one hand patting along the cold wall for a light, the other grasping his shooter so hard his knuckles are turning white.

I blink, and Frankie has disappeared. Sucked into the void by some unseen force. Knuckles makes a noise that I've never heard Knuckles make before. I can only assume he's seen something that I haven't.

A wet crunching noise taunts us from the darkness and the two of us that remain fire wildly without hesitation. Once again, my hearing becomes dampened, as if the basement has suddenly flooded with a thick gel.

After I finally manage to get a hold of myself long enough to stop frantically squeezing the trigger of my M911, I notice that Knuckles is gawking at something dangling from the bottom of the doorway. An arm. It falls from the gloom and lands on the concrete with a wet slap. A gold Cartier Tank watch adorns the wrist. Frankie's wrist.

"Knuckles. Molotov," I hiss.

The bottle is already lit before I finish talking and I

shield my eyes as he tosses it into the darkness, impacting the floor with a satisfying *whoom.*

A flaming man (*oh shit the skeletal figure*) erupts from the room and dashes towards me, arms outstretched, shrieking. I step aside as much as I can in this narrow passage and shoot some lead at his kneecap. Luckily, the shot connects, and it drops the bastard instantly.

I leave the human torch writhing in liquid death, pausing to watch the fascinating way that the skin peels back from his features and exposes sharp canines, before joining Knuckles at the doorway. His face is void of colour. He takes a step inside and curses as he steps on something that sounds wet and airy. Fortunately, it's not long before he's able to locate a cord hanging from the ceiling. He tugs it and a single, dusty bulb reluctantly flares to life and bathes us in a dull embrace. The room is larger than it appears from the outside. Tall racks of metal shelving line the grey walls with enough weaponry and cases of ammunition to take down a small army. I stamp out the hungry tongues of the fire before they can get any closer – perhaps we can take some of this out with us too.

"Boss," Knuckles says.

I follow his gaze and see the fat man in the far

corner of the room, sitting with his back to the wall and clutching both hands to his stomach.

The safe sits beside him, bolted to the wall.

He laughs at the sight of us. Blood trickles from the corner of his mouth. "Neither of you are getting out of here alive," he says.

I walk toward Masetti, Knuckles by my side. "Oh yea? Because from where I'm standing, I'd say the only one who isn't getting out of here is you."

Masetti winces in agony, the trauma to his stomach getting the better of him. "Once you two are snuffed out, you know what's going to happen next? My boys will be all over your turf in minutes, and by the time the sun rises…" he coughs up a lump of bloody phlegm, "everyone you've ever known and loved will be dead. Your empire will be ashes, burned to the ground. I will personally, ki—"

"Tell it to Sweeney. We're a little short on time. So if you could be good enough to open that box for us, we'll be on our way. Leave you to die with some dignity."

"Fuck you."

I gesture to Knuckles to do his thing and he moves forward with a smile. He grabs the fat man by the collar of his suit and smashes his oversized fist into Masetti's

nose with explosive force. I can't help but smile as his head bounces off the wall behind him, then hangs slack on his shoulders.

"Again," I say.

Knuckles delivers another devastating blow, this time, to Masetti's right eye. It instantly flares red and puckers up like fish lips.

I move up, knocking Masetti's hat to the floor and lifting his face to mine by his wiry hair. A sharp backhand across his right cheek brings him back to the room with us. The trickle of blood from his mouth is now a torrent, as is joined by two more from his nostrils. My hand throbs from the impact of the blow, so I'm satisfied he must be getting the message.

"Open it," I say, yanking his head to the side so he's now facing the safe.

"Fuck...you."

I can't believe my ears; it sounds like the fat bastard is still trying to laugh.

"You see something funny here, Knuckles?" I ask.

"No boss. All I see is a dead man," he replies.

Masetti chuckles and shakes his head. As his bloated stomach jostles, I can see the thick pink ribbons of his intestines poking out from between his fingers and find myself wondering how he's even still alive.

Knuckles yelps, I look to him just in time to see his eyes bulging as he is yanked backward with incredible speed for a man of his size.

The burnt man is standing behind me. I can smell him, hear the harsh rasping of breath in a choked throat. I turn and my fears are confirmed. Knuckles lays in a folded heap to the side of the doorway. Somehow his head has been torn clean from his shoulders and comes to a rest on the patch of scorched ground. His eyes are still wide with fear as he looks toward his killer. I wonder if it's true what they say, if his brain hasn't got the message that he's dead yet.

The burnt man appears to be staring at me—sizing me up—although his sockets are empty and crusted over with blackened flesh.

I stare back. I watch, numb, as my pistol is aimed at the abomination and discharges the last of my rounds. The thing still stands. It appears to be sneering.

Behind me, Masetti's is quiet.

I want to turn, but I'm too afraid to take my eyes off the thing stood before me.

Masetti steps into my line of sight. He wipes the blood from his face with the back of his sleeve and stands tall. Although his suit is still torn up, the pink flesh beneath it has completely healed over, and his face

looks unharmed.

"I expected a little more from 'The Butcher' and his mob, I must admit," he says. "You've done me a solid, really. We was gunna hit you pretty soon, but you've just made it much easier for me, coming right to us like this. I'd like to thank you, sincerely," he extends a hand toward me, which I ignore.

"What the fuck is even going on here?" My eyes dart between the two dead men stood before me.

"I wouldn't worry yourself with specifics, you're going to be snuffed in a minute, anyway. After all, we're a little short on time." Both men cackled.

I hear footsteps approaching from the hallway outside. A lot of them. I look beyond the twisted remains of Frankie and Knuckles and watch as the first figure bends down to enter the room.

"Paddy! Snuff these two!" I shout.

He doesn't. Instead, he folds his arms across his chest and steps aside to allow the rest of the crowd in.

Just when I thought this night couldn't get any more insane, it does.

One by one, the dead enter the room, forming a semi-circle behind Masetti and the burnt man; several men wearing suits covered in bullet holes—I recognise one of them from the corridor—that blinked as I passed.

The broads from upstairs are here too, smiling, wearing their elegant headgear and ripped, stained dresses. My eyes stop on another familiar face, the canary with the broken necklace from the stage. Her pale skin is without blemish, she doesn't have a single mark on her. She catches my eye and winks.

"What…what is this?" I stammer. My legs fail me as I try to take a step back and crash to the floor, landing hard on my coccyx with an audible crack. I feel the fight go from the rest of my body as the mob closes in around me.

I think of Frankie, Knuckles.
At least it's going to be quick.

# A DRY RUN

by John H. Dromey

The private investigator was clearly out of his element—far from the paved streets and city sidewalks which were his regular beat.

Although Murphy fought valiantly against a compulsive, irresistible urge to look back over his shoulder, it was a losing battle. He was so preoccupied with eluding his pursuers he forgot to watch where he was going. He tripped over an elongated object half-buried in the sand. The weary traveller took a couple more stumbling steps forward before falling face down on the ground.

For a few heartbeats—with a mouthful of grit and a headful of regrets—the PI lay motionless. Then, sputtering like a pernickety toddler, whenever an unfamiliar food failed to please the tiny tyke's taste buds, Murphy raised his head and looked around. There was not much to see.

Ahead of him was a dune that effectively blocked his view in that direction. Behind him a single set of footprints and the unexpected obstacle he encountered earlier. The contour suggested a human being was concealed beneath an uneven coating of sand. Was it a recent corpse or a relic from antiquity? Murphy shuddered at the prospect of the latter possibility, but he needed to know for sure. Springy, rather than rock hard, he remembered the stumbling block yielded slightly when he stubbed his toe. At the point of contact, the dislodged sand revealed a bit of fabric. Murphy squinted at the spot and determined the cloth was modern. That was a relief. There was no immediate threat of his being attacked by a reanimated mummy.

How did one of his pursuers manage to get out in front of him? Perhaps—after the sandstorm wiped out their tracks—they were going around in circles, just as lost and disoriented as he was. If so, their primary concern, like his, should be finding a way out of the trackless waste.

For the first time in what seemed like many hours, Murphy enjoyed a brief respite from a waking nightmare. It was a time for reflection.

* * *

The day before his desert misadventure, Murphy was walking down a darkened corridor leading to his office when he was accosted by a shadowy figure. A seemingly disembodied hand reached out and tugged at the investigator's sleeve.

"Why don't you come into my office where there's some light?" Murphy asked.

"It ain't safe for us to be seen together," a gruff voice said.

"Is that you, Barney?"

"Shhhh! No names. There's no telling *who* or *what* might be listening."

Murphy was intrigued, but wary. *Who* might be listening, he could understand. He sometimes dealt with highly sensitive situations which would spark the interest of newspaper gossip columnists and extortionists alike. *What,* was a different matter entirely.

Murphy considered the source. The Barney he knew was somewhat of a dinosaur. A man who lived in the past, or tried to, anyway. Someone whose fondest wish was to return to a simpler time, to those good old days before the Great War. Before his day-to-day subsistence in the trenches. Before his exposure to mustard gas. Before he emerged from the chrysalis of his uniform as a shell-shocked remnant of his former self. Especially, before he took to drink in an attempt to recapture his lost youth. Nearly a decade later, Barney still struggled. A hulking creature with a bulbous nose and rosacea, in a certain light his face had a purplish hue.

For Barney, Prohibition was little more than a bump in the rocky road of his existence. The quality of alcohol he consumed may have changed, but not the quantity.

The downside of Barney's excessive drinking was a looming threat of delirium tremens should he be deprived of spirituous libations for an extended period of time.

The private eye could detect no sign of the DTs. The hand grabbing his sleeve was steady. There must be some other explanation for Barney's strange behaviour.

"Are you in some kind of trouble?" Murphy asked.

"Not just me," Barney said. "All of us are in great peril. An army of mummies is on the move."

"Were they riding pink elephants?"

"No," Barney said. "This is not a good time for facetiousness, either." He enunciated every word clearly without slurring a single syllable.

Murphy was suitably impressed and agreed to

investigate.

Barney gave him an address. "I'll meet you there," he said, before slipping silently back into even deeper shadows than before.

* * *

It was nearly sundown as Murphy took a taxi to the warehouse district of the city. The driver stopped next to an empty lot.

Murphy was startled by the *ah-oogah* of a car horn. He looked back over his shoulder and saw Barney getting out of a cab.

"You didn't tell me the mummies were invisible," the PI chided his client.

"They're not." Barney led the sceptical detective to the rear of a dilapidated building a block away from their rendezvous point.

They climbed a rusty fire escape and entered the structure through a glassless window casement.

Once inside, taking their cue from Gilbert and Sullivan's Pirates of Penzance, they proceeded with cat-like tread across the dusty floor. The warehouse was as silent as a tomb and not much better lit.

After pressing his extended forefinger to his lips,

Barney led the way to a hole in the floor.

Murphy crouched next to the opening and gazed intently into the crepuscular depths. He could just barely make out the shadowy outline of a vaguely humanoid shape.

From somewhere in the bowels of the warehouse an engine announced its presence with a mechanical roar.

Near the periphery of Murphy's restricted view, a single lightbulb flickered a time or two and then gave off an eerie glow. The incandescent illumination revealed an elongated gauze-wrapped figure stretched out full length below the peephole. Without any apparent articulation of its tightly wrapped limbs, the figure gave a spasmodic lurch and then appeared to float away on a horizontal plane. A second figure came into view shortly thereafter, and then it too slowly drifted out of sight.

Murphy was not fooled for long. The mummies were moving, all right, but not under their own volition. A stationary gas engine was powering a conveyor belt.

"Where do you suppose those critters are headed?" Murphy asked.

"Follow me," Barney whispered.

There was a narrow stairway at the far end of the

building.

"What's down there?"

Barney shrugged his shoulders. "Beats me. I'm afraid to look. I don't want to risk falling victim to the curse of an angry mummy whose burial place has been disturbed."

"Isn't that just a myth?"

"Not according to newspaper accounts. Nearly a dozen victims in the last several years, counting Lord Carnarvon in 1923. For all we know, one of these mummies is a distant cousin of King Tut."

"That's a sobering thought," Murphy blurted out.

"I could use a stiff drink or two about now," Barney said. He pointed down the dusky stairwell. "Especially, if you intend to go chasing after those stiffs."

Murphy descended the stairs with great caution. Aware that his outline might be observable in the dim reflected light of the warehouse, he stood perfectly still.

He watched as two men took the mummies from the moving conveyor belt and loaded them into the back of a truck.

The PI nearly jumped out of his skin in reaction to a barking sound near his right ear. It was an inopportune time for Barney to have a coughing fit.

Barney coughed again. This time Murphy heard a

follow-up sound coming from a different direction. Was there an echo in the warehouse?

Murphy turned his head in the direction of the answering sound just in time to see a muzzle flash. Immediately afterwards, a lead slug gouged a charred furrow in the doorframe.

Barney stopped coughing long enough to gasp, "Now, do you believe the mummies are dangerous? They're *shooting* at us!"

"No, they're not," Murphy replied. "The mummies' arms are wrapped tight to their bodies. They couldn't even work their fingers into a trigger guard, let alone point and fire a gun. It's a mortal man out there doing the shooting."

"Why aren't you shooting back?" Barney wondered.

"Technically, I'm an intruder, and it's possible the shooter has just as much or even more right to be here than I do."

Barney leaned forward and stuck his head through the door.

A couple of heartbeats later, a bullet whizzed past his left ear. He ducked back inside the stairwell and commented, "That guy's aim isn't very good."

"Either that, or he's deliberately firing warning

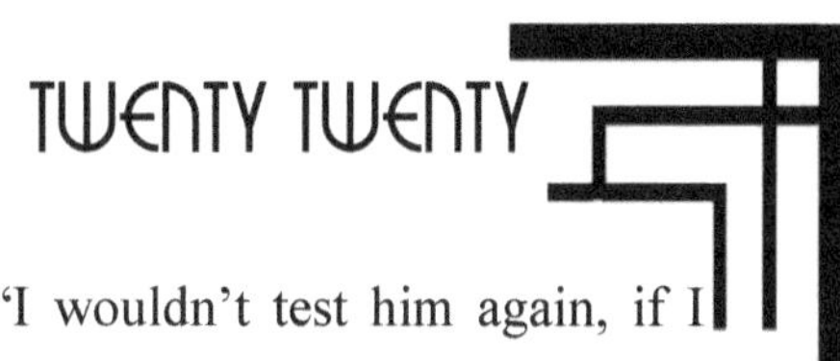

shots," Murphy said. "I wouldn't test him again, if I were you."

"What should we do?"

"We wait. In my profession patience is a virtue."

A short while later, the stationary engine fell silent, the light went out, and the conveyor belt coasted to a shuddery stop.

The truck engine started.

Murphy waited until there was a discernible change in the pitch of the truck's engine. He drew his firearm and stepped to the interior door in time to see the departing vehicle. The canvas cover on the back of the truck was lowered and tied into place with a rope. There was no sign of the two men.

Barney peeked around Murphy's shoulder. "They made a right turn at the intersection. They're headed for the desert road. You need to follow them."

"How? It's dark outside and I'm on foot."

"There's a car here," Barney replied. He took a flashlight out of his pocket.

"Why didn't you use that light before now? I could have broken my neck stumbling around in the dark."

"Are you daft? I didn't want to let the mummies know where we were."

On the other side of the conveyor belt, Barney

pulled the dust cover off of a two-door car. He climbed into the driver's seat and said, "I'll set the spark. You can do the cranking. Give the handle only half a turn at a time. I don't want you to break your arm."

It took several tries, but eventually the engine coughed a few times and then started running smoothly.

Barney climbed out and said, "It's all yours. The gas tank is topped off and there's an auxiliary tank that's also full. You can drive all night if you need to. The lights don't work, but that's a good thing. This way, you can sneak up on the bad guys under cover of darkness."

Murphy got behind the wheel.

"One more thing," Barney said. He went to a dark corner of the warehouse and retrieved a duffel bag which he tossed into the passenger seat.

* * *

Once he got clear of the distraction of the city lights and his eyes adjusted to the semidarkness, Murphy was able to see the road clearly in the moonlight. There were only a few scattered clouds in the sky.

At first, the PI tried to get as much speed out of the unfamiliar car as he could. Eventually, he saw taillights up ahead of him going in the same direction he was. He

slowed down and followed from a discreet distance.

The sun rose in an overcast sky.

After a long night, the investigator was bone-weary and desperately needed rest. If he was going to catch the crooks, however, there was no way he could stop to catch forty winks. Two or three winks maybe—while still on the move. The second or third time Murphy's sagging head jerked upward, as he resisted a powerful urge to fall under the Sandman's spell, the PI realised the truck was no longer in sight.

He speeded up.

A few miles farther on, as he crested a hill, Murphy saw the truck an uncomfortably short distance in front of him. He braked immediately and hoped the occupants would not spot him either in a mirror or by direct line of sight.

Another few miles down the road, at the top of another hill, Murphy's worst fears were realised. The truck was parked off to one side of the motorway.

A heartbeat later, one of his borrowed vehicle's front tires exploded. In an instance, the wheel was wrenched from his hands. The car swerved off the road and became mired in the sand.

Murphy was shaken up, but there was no time to check himself for injuries. After piercing the passenger door, a bullet struck the duffel bag and ricocheted with a high-pitched whine into the roof of the car. The shooter meant business. That was not a warning shot. Its lethal intent was foiled when something inside the bag saved the PI's life.

Murphy grabbed the strap of the cloth satchel and took it with him as he ran a zigzag pattern toward the shelter of an outcropping of rocks. He was encouraged to move faster by the crack of a rifle and the subsequent spurt of sand kicked up by a bullet striking too close for comfort.

When he reached the safety of the rocks, Murphy inventoried the contents of the duffel bag. He found a canteen of water, a silver flask—presumably filled with something more potent than $H_2O$—a gasmask, and a crowbar with a shiny scratch on it where it deflected the would-be assassin's bullet.

What should he do next? If he made a run for it, the rifleman could pick him off. If he stayed put, pinned down by one man, the other man could use a flanking manoeuvre to approach him from an angle for which the rocks provided no protection.

Murphy was a sitting duck. Despite being deathly tired, he needed to remain vigilant. He took a sip of water and waited. His head drooped, and he closed his

eyes.

After resting his eyes for an indeterminate time, the PI woke up with a start. The sky was getting darker by the minute. That didn't seem right somehow. He checked his watch. It was still early morning. He scanned the horizon for any sign of movement. In the distance, an impossibly high wall of sand, threatening to blot out the sun, was rushing toward him across the desert.

Murphy quickly put on the gas mask, and with his right arm entwined in the strap, did his darnedest to hide behind the duffel bag.

* * *

After the sandstorm died down—as soon as the dust settled—Murphy started walking. Initially, he headed away from the road, intending to put some distance between him and the shooters before doubling back.

When he tripped over a dead body in the sand, the PI revised his plan. He decided to crawl to the top of the nearest dune and look around. If no one shot at him, he could look for a recognisable landmark to help him get his bearings.

The first thing he saw when he peeked over the

ridge stopped him cold. A mummy was advancing slowly but surely up the other side of the dune. It was not a mirage. Instead of shimmering and hovering in place, the mummy was moving its lower limbs in a series of jerky, scissor steps without bending its knees.

Murphy could not help but wonder if Barney was right. Was there a curse of some kind in play?

Fearing for his life, the PI drew his pistol and aimed at the mummy's upper torso. He squeezed the trigger. There was an explosive puff of dust at the point of impact and then a white grainy substance gushed out, leaving a large gaping hole in the mummy's chest. The mummy continued to advance. How was that possible? Apparently, the creature was heartless—with all its organs removed during the mummification process.

Murphy fired again, aiming for the same spot as before. His hand trembled slightly, but his aim was true. This time some red liquid spurted out of the wound. The mummy—as rigid as a marble statue—toppled forward and lay motionless on the hot sand. Only then was its secret revealed. The mummy was propelled along by a man who balanced the mummy's feet on the toes of his boots.

Murphy did not recognise the dead man. The corpse was not one of the two shooters. Perhaps he was a driver

who sat out the storm inside the vehicle. If so, the PI could follow the man's tracks back to the truck and thus to the road, where he could wait to be rescued.

That's what he did.

* * *

In the police investigation that followed, the alleged driver's motive for removing one of the so-called mummies from the truck was revealed. The gauze-wrapped mannequin that Murphy shot was partially filled with white sand which kept its cache of stolen jewellery from rattling. It's likely the thief's intention was to bury the dummy mummy in the sand and then return for it later.

The remaining cargo in the truck included one genuine mummy which was probably intended to serve as a decoy if discovered during a border crossing. In that theory of the case, if customs officials could be deceived into thinking the driver was working for smugglers of antiquities, the faux mummies would likely receive only a cursory inspection instead of being impounded as evidence.

Murphy was greatly relieved no one asked him about the origin of his pursuit vehicle—now a sandblasted derelict abandoned in the desert—and he didn't volunteer any information on the subject.

* * *

Murphy and Barney split the reward paid by the insurance company for the recovery of the stolen jewellery.

Afterwards, the two men shared a meal to celebrate their good fortune.

"Although you were right about an actual mummy being involved, Barney, your fears of the supernatural were unfounded. There was a logical explanation for everything."

"What about the timing of the haboob?"

"The what?"

"The sandstorm," Barney translated.

Murphy didn't have an answer for that. He concentrated on eating his filet mignon.

# Speakeasy Jane

## by Erica Schaef

The Blind Pig was crowded, its air so thick with tobacco smoke that it made even *my* eyes water. Beneath the layers of salty BO and drenched-on perfume, the faint scent of mildew lingered undisguised, wafting up from the damp cement floor to mix in with the heavy haze of the place. Hardly surprising, we were in a basement after all, and not an overly clean one.

Jazz music drifted down from the nightclub above us, becoming louder whenever someone opened the door at the top of the wooden staircase.

I sat at the back of the room, wedged on a barstool between two oafs who reeked of stale beer, a glass of amber whiskey clutched in my hand. I'd never been much of a drinker, but something about Uncle Sam's recent forbiddance of alcohol teased at my rebellious nature, making me insolent. I was stubborn like that, or maybe it was just plain immaturity. Anyway, the stuff was making my time in the dirty room at least a little more tolerable as I waited.

She was taking her time, this girl, the one who had called me up, crying. It had been *her* idea to meet here. Strange choice, I thought, but after so many years in the business of private detection, hardly anything actually surprised me.

The jazz music got loud again, and I watched the staircase. A young woman was coming down. She wore a very short, flapper-style dress, and some kind of black, feathery concoction at the crown of her stationary, dark hair. I kept my eyes on her as she walked lithely over to the bar, her well-muscled legs drawing almost every male gaze in the room. This wasn't my girl, her angel face didn't seem as though it had a care in the world, and consequently, no use for my services; but still, she was worth looking at.

My girl came later, in an olive-green walking suit and a matching, lace-trimmed hat over hair that actually swayed a little when she walked. Even without the tear-sodden eyes, she'd have been conspicuous in a place like this.

Her movements were small; tentative. She was a

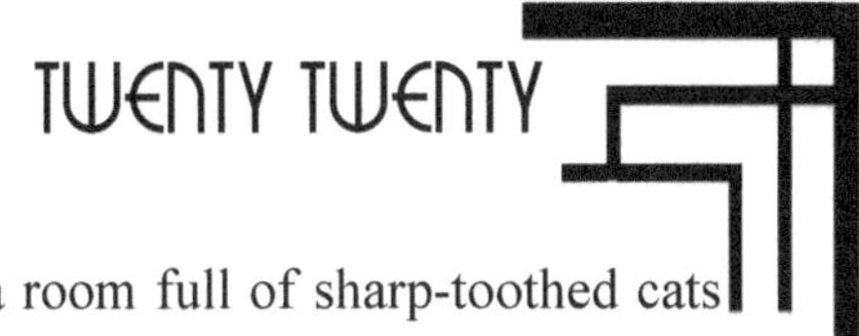

pretty little mouse in a room full of sharp-toothed cats and she knew it.

I stood up, questioning again what it was that had made her want to meet up here, and at this time of night. Her eyes didn't meet mine as I approached her. She was scanning the crowd, looking, at once, both let down and hopeful.

I stopped just in front her, so that I was looking down at the top of her hat.

"Hello…"

She cut me off. "Sorry I'm meeting someone, and I'm afraid I'm terribly late." She brought up a hand deliberately to adjust the strap of the bag she carried, fingers titled upward so that I couldn't miss the sparkling silver of a wedding band. "Excuse me."

"You aren't Molly Baker?" I asked, but didn't attempt to block her way.

She stopped beside me, looking up with two round eyes the colour of delphinium flowers.

"Mr Wexler?" She put a hand to her temple. "So sorry. I thought you'd be…"

She paused, as though second-guessing what she'd been about to say.

"Yes?" I prompted after a moment.

"Well, never mind. Should we sit down?"

I led her over to one corner of the bar where two seats had been recently vacated.

The barman noticed my strawberry-blonde companion almost immediately and came over to ask what she would have.

"Just a water, thank you." Her voice was polite, but I could sense a kind of urgency in her manner.

"What is it that I can help you with, Mrs Baker?" I asked, once the barman had gone away for the drink.

"Call me Molly, please." She twisted her fingers around the napkin that had been placed in front of her, giving me a long, assessing look.

"You seem awfully young to be in this line of work, Mr Wexler, if I may say it."

"Luke, please. And that's just the magic of dim bar lighting, Mrs Ba… Molly."

"I hardly think so." Her eyes searched my face in a way that made my heart quicken its beats.

"If you doubt my experience, you are free to engage another Private Detective. The city is practically swarming with them." I shrugged.

She pursed her lips together tightly before answering.

"No, no. You were recommended to me, I'm sorry if I've offended you. It's just that, well, this matter is one

very near to my heart, you see."

I nodded. "Why don't you tell me about it? You didn't say much over the phone."

"It's my brother, David. He owns a little bookshop on 3rd Street, Class B Books, which he is *very* committed to." She drew a long breath. "About a month ago, he started seeing a woman, his neighbour, Jane. I'm afraid I don't know her last name, but ever since he's met her, he's been showing up at the store less and less. Two weeks ago, he stopped coming in altogether, and hasn't been seen at all since. I have been to his house every day, and almost every night, and have seen no sign of his coming or going. I've checked with his neighbours, but they haven't seen either him or the woman, Jane, in all that time. I went to the police, of course, but they have entirely dismissed my concerns, saying that two adults have the right to spontaneously elope if they choose to, and that I will doubtlessly hear from him soon."

"But you don't believe that?"

She shook her head. "I know my brother better than anyone in this world, Luke. He would never leave the city without telling me. But there's something else, too."

"Oh?" I watched her intently.

"Gina, one of the girls who works in the bookstore, and has met Jane once or twice, said she saw her *here* last night. She said she disappeared before she, Gina, could reach her, but she was sure that it was Jane. There was no trace of David, though."

"And you want me to…?"

"Find this woman. Jane. Question her, follow her if you have to. Find out what's happened to my brother. I'll pay you well. I've brought three hundred dollars with me here, as a retainer, in fact." She reached into her bag, but I put a hand on her arm.

"And what if the police are right about him?"

"They aren't." She said rigidly. "But if they *were*, then no harm done. You'd still be paid for your time, of course."

"Okay. Save your money for now, though. What does this Jane look like?"

Molly's expression brightened. "You'll do it, then?"

"I'll see what I can find out. But I really do need to know what I'm looking for."

"Descriptions, right." She pulled a small notepad from her purse. "Okay, I've never seen Jane for myself, but according to Gina, she's a tall, attractive woman with black hair cut into an orchid bob. That's like this." She drew a hairline with her index finger across the side of her head, coming down to a point in front of her ear.

"She always wears bright red lipstick, and a beaded black hairband with feathers coming out to one side. Gina said she likes to wear glittery flapper dresses when she goes out, ones that are a little too short for her legs. That's what she was wearing last night, with no jacket or anything."

As she was speaking, I let my eyes drift slowly over to the raven-haired beauty who had come in just before Molly: black headband, short skirt, and lips so brilliantly scarlet they might have been painted with blood. I didn't want Molly to see her, though; didn't want a scene just now.

"I think I have the general picture. What about your brother?"

"David is tall as well, and rather lanky. He has short hair that's just a shade or two darker than my own, and light blue eyes. He wears glasses with round rims and very thick lenses, and has a large white scar in the centre of his chin, from when he was thrown from a horse many years ago."

"Fine," I said, "that's plenty. Let's get you home now. I'll stay and keep an eye out here."

"Are you sure…"

"Yes. I think it's best, for now at least, if you aren't seen."

"Alright," she conceded. "If you say so."

I paid the barman and led Molly up the stairs, through the noisy nightclub, and out through the front door. As we strode along the sidewalk, I became aware of someone standing in a darkened corner across the street from us. All I could make out clearly was the shadowy silhouette of a man in a cock-eyed top hat. I couldn't even tell whether it was us or the nightclub he was looking at.

"Why didn't you bring your husband with you? Or, better yet, send him to meet me instead, Molly? This isn't exactly one of the better parts of our fair city."

She glanced down at the pavement, fiddling with the ring on her finger.

"I'm not married. I just thought it might dissuade men from approaching me tonight, if they thought I was."

"Not the kind of men who come to places like this," I told her bluntly.

She smiled, her periwinkle gaze coming up to meet mine from under long, pale lashes.

"It's a good thing that you were here then, Mr Wexler."

"Because you arranged for me to be. Why don't we go somewhere less rough next time? My offices maybe."

I held up my arm for a cab.

"Sure." She pulled a card from her bag and put in the pocket of my jacket. "Call me, okay? Any time. Especially if that woman shows up tonight, I want to know about it."

"Will do." I assured her, as a bright yellow taxi pulled up to the curb beside us.

I helped her inside, and, wishing her goodnight, closed the door and waved the driver on.

As I straightened, I saw that the man in the top hat had not stirred from his position in the corner. I kept him within the confines of my peripheral vision as I walked back toward the nightclub. By the time I reached the door though, he'd moved only once, to pull a cigarette from his pocket and light it. I went on in, pushing the thought of him aside as I descended once again to the overcrowded speakeasy. Once there, I kept close, but not too close, to the red-lipped girl in the beaded headband. I waited there, watching the throng of admirers that surrounded her practically fall over themselves to gain her attention. Finally, after about twenty minutes, my break came.

"Another martini, Jane?" The barman addressed my query.

That name was all the confirmation I was going to

get. Grinning to myself, I backed off. I kept her in my view, but just barely, I didn't want her to notice me in any way. She took the drink, then another, not having to pay for a drop of the hooch herself, what with all the admirers.

It was another half an hour before she rose to leave, amidst the adamant protests of her adoring companions. I followed her, discreetly of course, as she walked up and out through the nightclub's main entrance. She didn't hale for a cab once she'd reached the pavement, though, just kept walking. Her high heels clicked so loudly on the cement, that I didn't worry too much about keeping quiet myself. The man in the corner perked up, I noticed, then hurried across the street toward Jane. They talked for a moment, then, arm-in-arm with each other, led me through a labyrinth of narrow, nondescript streets.

Eventually, they stopped in front of a massive, gothic-style house, with a sign at its front that read, *Lady M.'s Cabaret Theatre and Social Club.*

I hung back as they crossed into the lighted entryway. The man, though tall, I thought gloomily, did not otherwise fit the description of David that Molly had given to me. Again, I waited, letting another ten minutes go by before approaching the door myself. Once I'd reached the porch, I tapped on the obnoxious showpiece of a knocker that jutted out from the dark siding. The girl answered, the one I'd been following. She was even prettier up close.

"Hello," I smiled. "I'm looking for a young woman called Jane, I thought I might find her here. Name's Wexford." I showed her my ID.

She regarded it with sparkling, sherry-coloured eyes. "I'm Jane. How can I help you?"

"Well, Miss…"

"Doe."

"That's cute," I quipped.

She wrinkled her nose at me. "You can't be too careful these days, Mr Wexler."

"True," I nodded. "But somehow you strike me as the type of woman who is able to fend for herself, Miss *Jane Doe*."

She shrugged noncommittally. "A bunch of us girls live here at the theatre together. We kind of look out for each other. But I think we're getting off track, Mr Wexler, won't you come in?"

The Sheba opened the door wide, letting me move in past her. "Thanks."

"Have a seat in there, please, Detective." She motioned toward a butter-yellow parlour room off to one side of the foyer. "I'll get us some coffee."

I thanked her again and sat down on a dainty-looking couch with pink, frilly cushions. On the wall across from me, women in various states of undress were depicted in large oil paintings. *Interesting place*, I thought.

Jane returned to me after a moment, balancing a tray of mugs, cream, and sugar in her arms. I stood up to help her deposit it on the table in front of me.

"Thanks," she said, throwing herself down on the cushions beside me. Her skirt came up to reveal a dangerous amount of smooth thigh as she did it, and I forced my attention to the coffee.

"Now, what can I do for you, Mr Wexler?" her eyes were dangerous too, bright and knowing. I shifted in my seat.

"A Miss Molly Baker has recently engaged my services, in her search for her brother, David Baker. He owns a bookstore…"

"I know David," she said excitedly.

I arched my brows at her. "Yea? Do you happen to know where he is now?"

"Of course." She leaned her head back against a cushion. "He's been staying here. Come on, I'll take you to him."

I rose beside her, thinking that this had all been just a little too easy. I wasn't going to complain about that, though.

She led me down a dark corridor. The paintings here were more haunting than erotic, the women in them posed with long, sallow faces.

We reached a large, fire-lit study, where someone rested in a chair, turned away from us, with a deep purple wrap covering his or her hair. As we stopped, I became aware of a very faint hissing sound emanating from the direction of the stone fire-place, and told myself that I would mention it to Jane, after I spoke to David.

"Yes, what is it, Jane?"

I was surprised, and slightly disheartened, to hear the distinctly feminine voice coming from the person in the chair.

"A young man to see Mr David Baker, Lady M," Jane answered smoothly.

"Very good, Jane. Very good, indeed."

The woman, Lady M., rose slowly, and as the wrap slipped back from her skull, I noticed that the hissing sound became much louder. I gasped when the bit of fabric fell away completely. Instead of hair, I was looking at a dozen wriggling *snakes*. They squirmed and weighed and hissed their tongues in every direction.

I opened my mouth to speak, or yell, or anything, but the woman turned around, piercing me with cold, grey eyes, and I couldn't move. It felt as though the very soul was being pulled from me as she stared with that dead, slate gaze. Across her neck, running the entire length of it, a jagged scar burned white against her skin.

"*Oh, Jane.* He's so deliciously full of life. Have some for yourself, girl."

For a second, the draining sensation stopped. Then, Jane moved to stand in front of me, her mouth opening into a vast, gaping hole, like some sort of mythical succubus. Again, I felt the energy seeping out from my pores.

They took turns like that, until I was nothing but dried up grey-stone. I couldn't even blink; could do nothing but watch in horror as they stared back at me with sated expressions. Jane was even more radiant than before, her flawless skin practically glowing.

"Cleo, Sarah, Maddie!" Lady M. called out, and three more young women in flapper dresses hurried into the room.

"Yes, Lady Medusa?" the first one asked, eyeing me with undisguised interest.

"Help Jane to take our new fixture to the basement

please, girls. Then we must all get ready for the show tonight."

The women scurried over to me, whispering and giggling to each other. It took all four of them to lift my sclerosed body.

I was carried to a large basement and set down gently upon my feet. Across from me, the stone statue of a man in round-rim glasses and a small scar on his chin stood beside a similar one in a cock-eyed top hat.

"He's sorta cute." One of the women said, wiping her forehead as she looked up at me. "Know who he reminds me of?"

"Perseus," Jane nodded, "I thought the same thing. That jawline."

They laughed and turned away then. I could do nothing as I heard their departing footsteps; could only watch the room's single light go out, leaving me in complete and utter darkness.

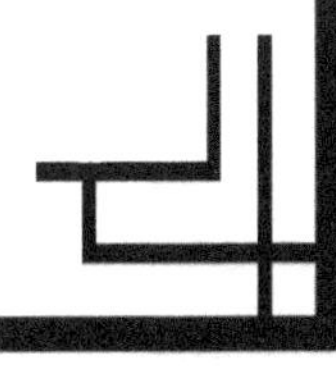

# The Lovers

by Destiny Eve Pifer

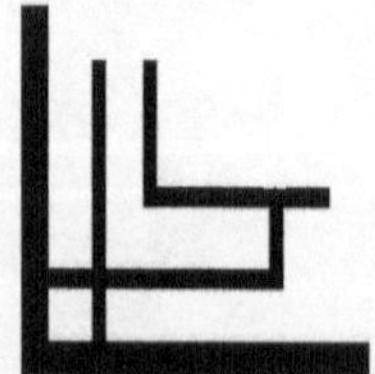

Down the crowded streets she walked, all dressed in black, past the jazz clubs and laughter. She walked down the dark alley and waited patiently for him to come; her unseen lover, always hidden in the dark shadows. Motioning for her to come, he took her in his arms. Then he moved his mouth to her neck and sank his sharp teeth into her soft flesh as she held tight. She could feel the blood running down her back as her lover took his final bite. Together they would remain in the shadows of darkness as a new world unfolded.

# THE WEEK OF BLACK THURSDAY

by N.M. Brown

Mama's been an absolute killjoy this whole week since Daddy's been gone. I'm not sure when he's coming back. When I asked Mama about it, she had kittens; saying something about putting his love of panther sweat above the law and his family, and that he promised he'd never leave us. She calls him a heartless wise guy before the tears come. That makes me a jumbled mess of both mad and sad; my Daddy ain't one of those drugstore cowboy types.

The start of next year marks the beginning of a new decade. I pray it's better than this one.

She keeps telling me that we should stay inside

because it looks like it'll rain. She must take me for a sap, there isn't a single cloud in the sky. Other mamas must've told their kids the same thing. No one else is playing outside today. The weather is perfectly warm for an October afternoon.

The town feels off, like it's been frozen in time or forgotten about. New York is usually bustling with activity. Just hours earlier, the street in front of the exchange building was flooded with people. It should be noisy outside from the breezers, but it's as quiet as death.

Dad's not the only one who went away. Mr. Fredricks left in such a hurry that he left his stove running. Mama says Mr. Schwigel will never grace the clubs of Kansas City again. Even the Carlsons left. No one seems to want to stay anymore. I hear people say that they lost everything, but all I see is the world losing its people.

Mama says it looks like rain. Maybe it's because she's sad. The cupboards are empty. I stole some root vegetables from a farm last time Mama took us to the country, but they're almost gone. She was happy for the food, but I doubt she'd let me do it again.

Maybe Daddy didn't like moving to the city. We moved hours away to a small apartment when he got his new job. I loved it right away. The ritzy Savoy Hotel is across the street from us. It's usually a bustle of face stretchers and floor flushers. But is now empty; I can see it from our balcony window. The people flitting in and out remind me of ants.

Mama got a phone call from someone about Daddy failing to settle a beef at some juice joint. I'm guessing she headed out to get him and bring him home. I might as well get a wiggle on and go outside until it rains, seeing as she's not here to stop me. It doesn't look like it's going to rain.

Wind whips through my hair as I run through the empty street. No one's here to see my ragamuffin clothes. No reason to doll up for an empty street.

The silence is no longer unsettling as I begin to conquer it with silly noises and whistled tunes. Sunshine blinds my eyes as I silently scorn Mama for lying about the weather. It hurts to look towards the skyline.

I stop just outside the ritzy hotel, hoping to get relief from the light. I'm rewarded with temporary relief as a giant shadow falls over my area of the sidewalk.

As the shadow becomes smaller, I begin to hear a noise. Waves of white consume my senses as a baby grand of a man shoves me from where I stand, knocking me across the sidewalk.

Splashes of liquid bounce off my cheeks as torrents of rain start to fall. It's only after a moment that I see puddles begin to form on the pebbles of broken pavement by my feet and the body that caused it to shatter.

A note floats down, grazing my ankles before landing in the puddle nearest to where I sit still in a crumpled heap from being pushed. I barely have time to read it before it's absorbed into a ball of crimson.

*My body should go to science, my soul to the sympathy to my creditors.*

Someone had jumped from the 15th story window of the hotel, his body dashed to pieces the second he hit the ground. The remains of what was once a man was distributed all across the street. Sirens of the fire brigade cut through the masses of screams, including my own.

Mama was right, it had indeed looked like rain. The rain of another casualty of the week of Black Thursday.

# WHEN THE LEONIDS COME

## by David M. Hoenig

*November 3, 1929*

It was a beautiful autumn night in New York, cool and crisp, and I walked the downtown streets in my Burberry trench coat. The smells of roasting chestnuts on street corners reminded me of the old country, though the absence of snow on the ground and ice in the air made me miss the simple days of sauna, cross-country skiing in the woods, and shared aquavit while looking at the cold stars of the night sky over Sweden.

And then I remembered other things—*things!*—from my long ago Sweden and shuddered. I knew better than to dwell on such, but memory is a strange and sorcerous beast, summoned by association and likely to rampage out of all control if not ruthlessly suppressed. Even so, the chill air and the stars high above in their recognisable constellations forced my thoughts to a particular autumn night with fresh snow on the ground and the celestial heavens reflected in the yet-unfrozen Vätttern lake, and what followed when I'd stared at the sight for too long.

And then of the bargain a much younger self had agreed to for fear of death.

A sudden, familiar nausea churned my bowels as sharp-edged memories a thousand years old threatened, and sour, acidic saliva flooded my mouth. I spat it out to the cobbled streets of this foreign city.

Commotion several streets away distracted me from the past. I consulted my pocket watch. *Soon*, I thought, with a quick glance at the stars overhead. I walked unhurriedly forward, and came to the edge of a frantic crowd, all looking up.

I heard a female voice. "Good God! Not even a week since Black Tuesday and it's another one!"

"He might as well do it, he's one of those responsible, am I right?" responded a man beside her. Other fragments of conversation and exclamations slid past.

High above, perhaps twenty or more stories, was a figure on a ledge at a building corner. He leaned forward, his arms behind him clutching at the stone bulwark there. I moved to a policeman who was just finishing ushering some people out of the street to a nearby sidewalk.

"Excuse me." When he turned, I proffered my business card to him. It read, simply: *Gustav Ahlberg, Eldritch Investigations*.

He took it and read. "We've got a situation here, Mr Ahlberg. What can I do for you?" He did a double-take at the card. "What's this 'Eldritch' baloney mean? You a private eye or something?"

"Something." I smiled reassuringly at him. "But in all seriousness, I'd be happy to go speak with that unfortunate man, see if I can help in some way."

"Why bother? Not like we can stop him if he wants to do it, and he ain't the first stockbroker—hell, not even the tenth—to want to splat himself these days. I'm just here to keep people back so they don't get hurt when he dives."

"Perhaps the stars will turn out to be just right for the poor gentleman, if that's even what he is—a bit hard to tell from down here, isn't it?"

"Are you nuts, buster?" He waved a hand

scornfully. "It's definitely another jumper. Well, knock yourself out, just don't expect anything." He then scrawled something on a pad of paper in a small leather folio he carried, tore off the sheet, and handed it to me. "Show them this and they'll let you through."

It was a short walk to the building, and the policeman there read my note. "So you know, the elevator's out, mister."

"I don't mind the constitutional. May I go up?"

The officer went back to looking up as he waved me in, so I went.

The lobby was dark, and the door to the stairs was behind the bank of lifts. The climb up the stairs was indeed long, but as I went, I felt energised by it rather than fatigued. I consulted my pocket watch several times along the way but didn't have to adjust my pace at all. I marvelled at the gifts afforded me be those choices I'd made so long ago, even as I skirted the memories themselves most carefully. The opportunity to think led me to a statement attributed to a politician of the state of Massachusetts nearly eighty years prior, and which resonated for me as few others had in my unnaturally long life: 'Men, in a word, must necessarily be controlled, either by a power within them, or by a power without them; either by the Word of God, or by the strong arm of man; either by the Bible, or by the bayonet.' *Robert Charles Winthrop saw the truth so clearly,* I thought. *He would have made a good servant of the god had the right introductions been made. Who might have guessed that after less than a century of nationhood these Americans would have such clarity about the reality of existence?*

When I reached the uppermost floor, I found myself in a dark hallway. Ahead and to my left was a door which showed light through the gap between it and the floor. I went to it, through it, and was soon at the window closest to the distraught man. I went to it, and leaned out, to see him holding onto the parapet above his head with both hands, several feet away. "Please sir, might I have a word with you?" I said as calmly as I could manage.

He started violently at my words. The wind whipped around us like something alive and violent, and he looked at me with wide, frantic eyes. "You try to stop me, I'm letting go!"

"I don't want to stop you, sir. In fact, if you intend to jump I would be happy to sanctify your death in the name of the god."

He blinked at me in disbelief. "Wha…?"

I kept my tone conversational as I interrupted him. "On the other hand, there are alternatives to death, if you are willing to explore them."

"What are you talking about?" He shifted his feet, trying to maintain purchase on the tiny ledge. "You're crazy!"

"That is the second time tonight I've been accused of insanity—you Americans seem to toss that phrase around far more casually than it deserves." I made eye contact with him and spoke to him in a low voice which held complete assurance. "Sir: I can assure you that the god *is*, in fact, listening tonight. What if I told you that this black time for you and your country will be but a distant memory in the very near future?"

"I've lost everything in the 'Crash', don't you get it? I'm ruined, there's nothing for me or my family but an insurance payout!" He looked desperately below him as he shifted his feet, and I saw that he meant to jump.

I kept my voice even, my tone sure, even as the wind whipped fiercely around us. "Oh, there is more, much more for you and your loved ones, my dear sir, and your life is worth many times more than a negligible insurance payout. You see, I can offer you peaceful rest throughout this challenging and perilous time and ensure that your family would receive the money your death would earn them. In addition, I can offer you a future you will awaken to in which the money lost in the past

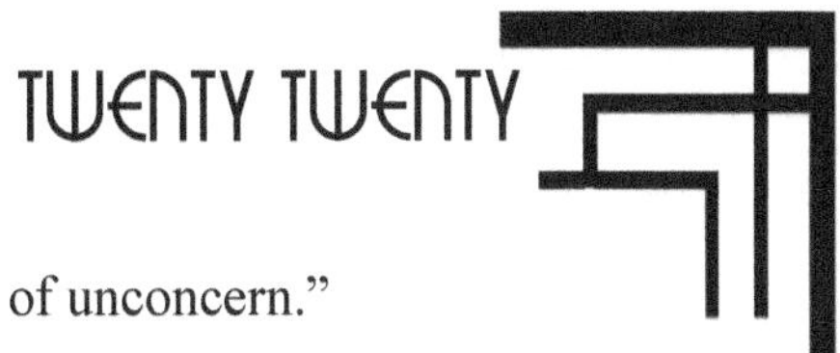

week will be but a drop of unconcern."

He looked at me incredulously. "You can seriously make all that happen?"

I felt the beginning of a smile pull at the corner of my mouth. "And more."

He looked down, and I saw him weighing things before he looked back at me. I brought my right hand from my pocket. "Look into this mirror, friend, and all I've offered will be yours." I tilted it upwards for him, so that when he'd look, he would see the reflected heavens above.

I kept my gaze on him to avoid looking in the glass myself, and our eyes met, held, and then he looked into the mirror. "Oh. Oh my," he said.

I could see the reflection of shooting stars at which he stared echoed in his eyes, and then he shrieked as the god I served entered him. He writhed, face twisted in a rictus of horror as he screamed, and I saw the exact moment when he turned to granite and there was only the sound of the wind. I waited, my hand outstretched as the heavens returned to their cold quiescence.

A different voice then issued from the man's mouth, as though from a throat made of crushed stone. "You've done well, minion."

A dangerous feeling of pride rose in me, but I

squashed it down in order to answer humbly. "The Leonids' conjunction is upon us again, Master."

"I am close, but not yet close enough to manifest fully. My time is still not at hand."

"How long must I wait, Master?"

"As long as it takes! I will arrive in My full power only when the celestial alignment favours My ascendance."

I shivered, but not from the cutting wind.

"Plant more such seeds, minion."

I bowed my head in acquiescence before speaking. "Give me the power, Master, and I will prepare them—as this one—for your coming, that they may be awakened to serve You."

"Yes. And take care you do not fail Me—your centuries of service are not yet done." There was a final grating sound and the gravelly throat fell silent.

I raised my head then to see a statue at the ledge of the building: the man's face distorted in a grimace, clutching the cornerstone of the building just below the roof. I spat sour saliva to the gusty winds around us, leaned back into the room and closed the window behind me. I returned to the streets with a spring in my step, passing through the crowd still staring upwards, pointing and speaking together.

As I was walked away from the building, I felt a tap on my shoulder and turned to see the same policeman who'd given me the pass in the first place. "Well? Is the palooka going to jump or what? We ain't got all day, after all."

*It was so easy to mislead the unwary when they wanted to be misled.* "I'm afraid it was all a case of mistaken identity, Officer. It turned out to be nothing more than a gargoyle at the roofline."

"But we all saw it moving!"

I chuckled. "An amazing optical illusion! A scarf was caught about its neck giving it the appearance of a living man. You can certainly check it yourself, assuming the wind has not driven it from that perch—I had a rather good laugh when I'd finally huffed and puffed my way all the way up to it."

He turned to look, and I simply walked away. *Manhattan could use a few more gargoyles*, I thought as I looked at the tall buildings around me. I couldn't keep the smile off my face as I turned north onto Broadway as more meteors flashed overhead.

"Men, in a word, must necessarily be controlled, either by a power within them, or by a power without them," I murmured aloud. *I made my choice long ago to be controlled by the power within. I think I've gotten the*

*best of that bargain so far.*

I wondered just how many gargoyles this city might hold in a hundred years or so, when the god's time of ascendance finally arrived. It made me both shudder and chuckle as I went uptown in this strange, new city under the same old—*very old!*—stars.

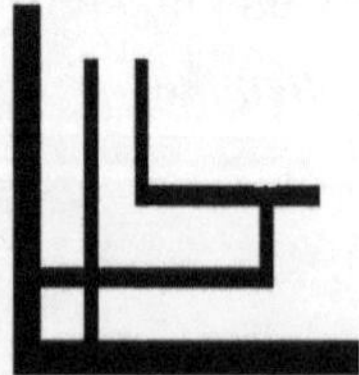

# Someone to Watch Over Me

by Henry Snider

*Moonlight and Roses* echoed throughout the makeshift speakeasy, drowning out most of the conversations. Several couples clung to each other and swayed to the slow song. Hanging lanterns cast a sleepy amber glow on the patronage. Elsie Blankard stared into the shadows wreathing the far end of the great room. There, in the darkness, a solitary man drank from a tin cup. Behind him, shadows had their own momentum, shifting with the subtle movements of couples taking advantage of dim illumination.

"Is that him?"

"Easy, Els." Mary shook a bit of spilled bathtub gin

from her hand. "This stuff's expensive."

Elsie leaned in close. "I said, 'Is that him?'" She pointed at the dark-haired stranger.

Mary nodded a confirmation. "Yeah, that's Charles Machon. Just got in a couple a' days ago. Old money. Had some problem during the war." Another song started up, this one enticing the masses into drunken renditions of the Charleston and forced Mary to speak up. "Nearly got blipped off during some battle and lost his noodle for a bit."

Elsie tapped her heel to the music but never took her eyes off Charles. Her flapper dress sparkled hypnotically. "He's a real sheik, you know?"

"Oh, deary." Mary draped an arm across Elsie's shoulders, "Sheik's so yesterday. We're in the land of talkies now. Haven't you heard?"

She pulled away, skirting the crowd.

"Els! Where ya goin'?"

The blonde threw a wicked glance over one shoulder. "You can't expect me to bump gums with you here all night, now can you?" She slid between the masses, snaking her way into one corner of the designated dance area and narrowly dodged one couple kicking their heels up. A handful of steps later Elsie bumped into the intended quarry.

"I — oh...sorry." She giggled.

He looked down, eyes black in the limited light. "I assume you were looking for me?" His thick, British accent cut against her Mckee's Rocks, Pennsylvania twang and left them both straining to understand each other.

Elsie feigned innocence. "No...I don't—"

"Well," he cut in with a somehow sad smile, "I don't think you were planning on going back there alone?" He nodded to the half a dozen or so couples clutching at one another, actions hidden by well-placed coats.

"Oh." She stood a little straighter. "And you think you're the man for the job, do you?"

Charles looked left, then right before settling his gaze upon her once more. "I think I'm the only man in the vicinity at the moment."

"Brazen." She smiled.

"Just observant." He took a long, slow swallow from the cup.

Elsie moved a little closer. "You're the talk-o-the-Rocks here, Chuck."

"Charles," he corrected.

"Charles. Sorry." She shifted from one heel to the other and looked down at his cup. "Offer a girl a drink?"

"Certainly. I believe—"

Elsie snatched the cup from his hand and took a swallow, making sure to lick her lips slowly afterward, stealing a glance to see if he paid attention.

He was.

"That's not gin," she said. A new song started up and dancers cluttered the floor.

"No. I believe it's made from corn."

"Mash," she said over the increasing din.

"Of course."

"Do you wanna..." Elsie motioned to the dance floor.

"I'm afraid that seems a bit active at the moment. Perhaps you would be content with a walk, miss?"

"You mean leave all this?" She waved an arm at the convention of law-breakers before answering the second question. "Elsie. Elsie Blankard. Now, lead on." Her hand grasped the crook of Charles' elbow. The flapper gave a devilish look, winking across the barn to Mary. This was met with riotous laughter.

The two walked past the dozen or so wagons and spattering of Fords that filled the otherwise empty field. A full moon lit up the night, making the hill country stand out like a minimalist painting.

"Look at that." Elsie pulled free and walked to the

side of a newer convertible.

Charles sounded bored. "What about it?"

"It's yellow," she stammered.

"I like yellow."

She stared back at him, slack-jawed. "You mean this is yours? Is it new?"

He popped the door open for Elsie. "This one is a twenty-three. Only a couple of years old, but I still like it."

"But it's yellow," she repeated.

"I know."

"But they're *never* yellow."

"This one is. My father knows Henry and managed to talk the moose into making this one a colour other than his obsessive black." Charles offered the last swallow from the cup to Elsie, which she took and downed in an unladylike gulp. "Now, about that walk."

"What about a ride instead?"

"You want to go for a ride? With me?" he asked. "A perfect stranger?"

"You don't seem that strange to me. Maybe a little stiff, but not all that strange."

"Won't your friends be worried about you?"

"Them? Nah. They're already trolling for beaus."

Charles opened the door for her before rounding the

Ford, stepping up onto the sideboard and sliding behind the Model T's wheel. "Then a ride you shall have." He retarded the spark and throttled down before turning the ignition switch. A hard stomp on the starter and the car rumbled to life. The sudden noise disturbed the horses. "Direction?"

Elsie thought a moment. "Pull out onto the main road and go left."

"Toward the river?"

"Yeah. There's a place my granddaddy worked one summer called 'The Mound.'" She flicked a lock of bobbed hair behind one ear. "It's an Indian burial mound."

The car turned in a tight circle and started down the muddy field's access. He cut a sideways glance at Elsie. "You want to take me to a cemetery?"

"Not a cemetery. A burial mound. It hasn't been used in ages. Some professor hired Papaw away from the mine to help on a dig." The flapper slid a little closer. "You know, like that tomb they found in Egypt."

"King Tutankhamen?"

She clapped Charles on the arm and he visibly winced. "That's the chap."

"Chap?"

"Sure." A devious grin crossed her face, makeup

exaggerating it in the moonlight. "Isn't that what the British say? 'Pip, pip' and 'cheerio' and 'chap?'" Elsie adjusted her coat as a cut of cool air sliced the side of the car. "Besides, there's a beautiful view of the Ohio River there. We might be able to even see Brunot."

Charles slowed the Ford and navigated a handful of axle-busting rocks at the road's edge before the car turned onto the hard-packed earth. "Who's Brunot?"

Elsie laughed, then choked on a mouthful of dust. "No, no. Brunot's a little island to the south."

"And what's so interesting about this island?"

She shifted, uncomfortable with the jostling vehicle. "I dunno. I just like it. That's all."

Bugs peppered the windshield as they flew down the country road. Sounds changed when the car left the field behind them and entered a wooden grove. Trees whipped by with a repetitive thump-thump sound while scattered beams of moonlight broke the canopy and danced along the forest floor.

"You're going to want to slow down here," Elsie shouted, now unable to suppress an excited grin. A low branch whooshed by and almost snatched her hat.

Charles acquiesced and slowed the convertible to a more reasonable speed. A rough patch in the road jostled the car so severely Elsie almost lost the grip on the dash.

The high bounces rode her dress up. Seconds later she realised this and caught him staring at her legs.

"Eyes on the road, buster," she said with a laugh. "It'd be a heck of a note to be killed because of my gams."

"Killer gams," Charles said with a smirk.

Elsie pointed to the right. "We're nearly there. It's just a cut in the woods. I'm not even sure we can get up there with this bucket."

A darker patch of woods appeared in the general direction she pointed. Charles stepped on the gas, shot off the road and down a slight embankment before spewing rocks as they skidded around a bend.

"Slow!" She grabbed a handful of his upper arm and he screamed, stomping on the brakes until the car skidded to a halt. Charles cradled his bicep, just over her grip. Elsie let go and leaned back. "I didn't mean—"

"It's not you," he managed through gritted teeth. "It's just an old injury acting up."

"Was it—"

"The war? Yes." Charles rubbed his arm through the jacket. "Isn't it always the war for anyone my age?"

Elsie slid closer. "You're not all that old. You're what...thirty?"

He managed a grim smile. "Twenty-three...nearly

to the day."

"So, you went in when you were...?" Elsie let the question drift off.

Charles sighed and looked up at the hint of moon visible through the lush greenery. "Fourteen. I stole my brother's papers and enlisted. By the time my parents sorted out what happened I was already neck deep at the Battle of the Somme under Sir Douglas Haig."

She returned a hand to his arm and mimicked the soft massage. He winced again, and she eased the pressure. "What was it like?"

In lieu of a response, Charles turned and caressed the side of Elsie's face, trailing one finger under her jaw and tipping her head up in preparation for a kiss. Lips met, parted and released tongues to explore new territory.

They shifted, Elsie's hand slid across his body and around his neck, while his own slid from face to arm, to hip and rested on her coat-covered thigh. The time-immortal dominance dance played out in the front seat, Charles urging her to lie back. She pressed her own advantage by shifting and made access to anything other than her lips more difficult.

The kiss broke and left each flushed.

"Would it be more comfortable...?" He nodded to

the back seat, but Elsie had already slid the car's width and gotten out on the far side. She turned and rested her forearms on the door.

"So, are you coming or not?"

"I thought we were enjoying the evening here."

"We are, silly." Elsie backed away, illuminated by the car's headlights. "Up on the mound. I'm serious about wanting to show it to you."

Charles let loose a laugh. "You actually think you're going to entice me into following you into the night?"

Elsie grinned and lifted the hem of her coat and dress, flashing a glimpse of knee.

"You're incorrigible." The driver's side door swung open and he climbed out, alcohol making legs wobblier than when they'd left the speakeasy. "Lead on, milady." He clicked off the lights and followed her through the foliage.

The couple ascended the low hill at a snail's pace. Undergrowth gave way to trees and dried remains of leaves. They peaked the crest and Elsie sat on a rotted pile of lumber and looked down into a cone-shaped depression. The remnants of the dig spanned a good thirty feet and better than a third of that in depth. Just beyond the far side's lip lay a ledge. The Ohio river

flowed past better than a tree's height below.

"My Papaw worked this with the archaeologist from some college. I grew up with him telling me and my brothers' stories about what they found here."

Charles leaned against a tree and hunted for a match. "What, pray tell, did they find here? Gold? Jewels?"

She scrunched her face up as only a young woman still on the shy side of twenty could. "No. They were Indians."

A match bit back the darkness as it jumped to life. "Then what?" He drew deep against the flame, and the cigarette's tip pulsed yellow-red.

Elsie leaned back. "Over thirty Indians. Tools. Seashells. Pottery. They said this mound is probably full of bodies going back hundreds of years."

"Really?" Disbelief hung heavy in Charles' sarcastic tone.

"Yes, really." She stood, walked over and took his cigarette as her own. The ember glowed hot as she drew deep on the oily smoke. "They think there may be hundreds more deeper than what they dug out."

He reached out, put a hand on Elsie's hip and pulled to close the distance between them. "Fascinating."

"It is," she insisted. "The Hopewell Indians took

this area over from the Adena." A schoolmarm quality overtook the flapper, her enthusiasm coming across like a lesson. "They don't know what happened to the tribe. From the artifacts they found, the Adena, at least this particular tribe," she corrected herself, "just died out and then the Hopewell were here."

"Hmm." Charles leaned down and nuzzled her neck. "Sounds like the Hopewell killed them off."

"No." Elsie stepped back, wrapped up in sharing this all-too-well-known local story with someone new. "The Hopewell were peaceful for the most part. The last Adena found were buried like the Hopewell did for their own dead."

"Fascinating," he repeated. Charles closed the distance between them, mind still on the fumblings exchanged in the car. One hand met another, and the cigarette changed partners again.

"Isn't it? Hey, there's Brunot." She pointed through a copse of trees to a split in the river a few hundred yards distant. The land mass lay as a dark patch of blue-green encompassed by a silver chain of water.

He dropped the butt and pulled her tight, lips searching. Elsie resisted for a second then leaned in, pressing herself against him. The couple found their way to the ground but never broke contact. Elsie wrapped her arms around to the small of Charles' back. His palm, hot in contrast to the night air on her leg, rested just below where acceptable modesty placed this season's hemline. She shifted and felt a hand move up a foot before realising it. Fingertips, softer than those of local beaus, danced at her stocking top, though stayed well below the garter belt's fasteners. Knees relaxed, then parted to allow better access. His nails drug upward and slid from silk to naked thigh. Hesitant caresses teased scant inches away from her mons. With no rejection, the journey continued under the short-bloomers and made quick work of her folds. As digits met target Elsie let loose a gasp and drew her own attention to just below Charles' belt buckle. Another hesitation for propriety's sake, then nature took over and she rubbed the front of his trousers, increasing pressure along his rigid length.

Minutes passed as they groped in the moonlight and Charles grew more aggressive with his ministrations. Elsie's pulse pounded in her ears. The flapper's stomach tightened and the forthcoming wash of pleasure made itself known. Then, just short of a quivering release, fingers slid lower, searching for her centre. She stopped him short of actual penetration.

"Whoa," she said through the kiss, "I only pet."

A familiar sigh of frustration escaped Elsie's new

suitor. She shifted her hand, allowing two fingers to slide past trouser buttons, through underlying fabric and actually touched his length in an effort to regain the enthusiasm he'd shown a moment before. He flexed, then pulled away and sat up.

"I...I need a moment."

"I'm sorry."

Charles patted her knee. "It's fine."

Elsie watched him rub at his shoulder. "How bad was it?" The question blurted out and she found herself adding, "When you got hurt?"

He rested elbows on knees and looked into the night. "You know, I knew I would end up out here in the woods tonight."

"With me?" She smiled and propped her head up on one hand.

"With someone."

The smile faded.

"It was a full moon in nineteen-sixteen. Jerry was coming into the trenches faster than the rain. A bomb went off nearby, but it wasn't the same as the others. Smoke and rain kept us from seeing it at first. Melburn saw the cloud at first—this dingy brown mess that covered everything."

She realised he wasn't really with her anymore. The

question put Charles back at that night almost a decade earlier. "I didn't think anyone called the Germans 'Jerry' anymo—"

"We heard the screams from the trenches as soon as it hit them. We thought Jerry was using the cloud for cover, but no one was shooting." His hands shook. Elsie reached out to comfort him, but he pulled away, still favouring the old injury.

"Chuck—Charles," she self-corrected.

"Then it got to us. This oily... It burned and we couldn't get it off. It itched at first, like when you don't get all the soap off from a bath."

Fear crept along Elsie's spine, raising hairs. "We don't have to talk about this."

He turned to her then, mask of kindness gone, now replaced with an anger she'd only seen in men her mother dated over the years. "Oh, but we do, Elsie. We do."

She straightened her dress and coat. "I think it's time you took me back."

"I remember running, jumping over my friends, getting away from the gas."

"Mustard gas." She pulled back into the story at the mention of the horrific weapon.

His look became a sneer. "Of course it was mustard

gas! Another bomb went off nearby. Everything went black. The next thing I remember I'm wrapped up in bandages and lying in bed looking up at a doctor."

"I want to go back," Elsie said simply.

"I saw Jerries along with a few of my friends standing over by the window. They didn't fight each other. They just stood there looking at me." Charles held a hand out as if showing her where to look. He shook his head. "There weren't any Jerries in the hospital and the friends I saw couldn't be there. They were already under mud and forgotten at the Somme."

Elsie rolled onto her side and got up, trying to understand what Charles said. A glance around reminded her just how truly alone they were at the moment. The occasional whisper of music echoed down from where everyone else drank, laughed and danced a mile or so away. She held a hand out and forced a smile. "Come on. Let's get us both a drink and get back to the party. You can drive me home later," she lied.

He looked at her outstretched arm then disregarded it. "They said it was because I died that night. My mind must be hurt from the blast. I wasn't breathing when Walden found me. He pounded on my chest and I came to. I was dead. The men, even the doctors, said it was a miracle."

"Well, that's a good thing." She let the hand drop and decided to push the point. "Look, I'm heading back. Are you going to drive me or not?"

"The moon looked like it does here...just not as sharp." Charles stood, moving between Elsie and the makeshift path back to the car. "I found another two that could see. Both died like me." Moonlight caught his eyes and reflected a soft blue. "Died and came back on the full moon."

Panic nibbled at her. "You're just trying to scare me because I said no." She tapped a nervous foot and tried to stare the Brit down. "The sheriff's my cousin. Do you know what he'll do to you if you try anything?"

The threat fell on deaf ears. "They didn't see the same people I do. We talked about it for days, but never around the doctors. We knew they'd take us for loonies and place us in a sanatorium." She stepped to the left and Charles mirrored the action. "It's only the dead that are around when you come back. None of us saw each other's audience, you see." He stepped forward.

"N-no. I don't see."

Spittle fell from his lips. "The people that came back with us. Our audience."

Elsie looked around for a means of escape and backed to the excavation's edge, glancing warily at the thirty-foot drop to the water below. Charles closed the distance in two steps.

"Riley killed the doctor before he hung himself."

"Ch-Charles—"

He took another step. "Pulled the man's insides out like he was looking for something. I knew he was going to do it. He said that's what they wanted—for him to close the door that being brought back opened. I think...I think the doctor was just because he harassed the private so incessantly." His hands clenched and opened, clenched and opened. "Johnson..." Charles choked on his words for a second. "Johnson clawed his own eyes out so he wouldn't have to look at them anymore. But you know what?" Arms stretched out for her then jerked back. Elsie retreated, working her way around the narrow lip by the excavation's ledge.

"Do...you...know...what?"

Her heel caught on a root and Elsie pinwheeled both arms, righting herself just short of disaster.

"It didn't help. He could still see them...still *hear* them." He stopped the advance. "I shipped home a couple of days later to recover from the burns the gas left on me."

His demeanour changed with a simple exhale of breath. He took off his jacket and held it out to her.

"Here. You look cold," he offered with a grim smile.

One shaky hand reached out and Charles snatched her by the wrist, jerking the flapper off balance. Elsie fell to her knees and he shoved her onto her back.

"And do you know what *my* audience says, bitch? *My* audience says little girls shouldn't tease." He climbed on top of her. Hands went to Elsie's throat and thumbs dug deep, cutting off her air. She kicked out, legs splayed on either side of the Brit in a perversion of the very act he'd striven for earlier. "You bitch," he screamed. "*Du dumme Schlampe!*"

Her eyes teared and she beat at his arms. Strikes against his right side brought a roar of rage and pain from Charles. He squeezed harder.

"*Schlampe*," he repeated. He kept the grip around her throat, lifted Elsie a foot off the ground and slammed her head down against the rocks.

Lights danced.

"Bitch!"

More pinpricks of white pain winked before her eyes. Movement came from all around them. Her body scraped against the rocks as Charles dragged her to the ledge.

Figures in the shadows shifted.

Then the lights were gone.

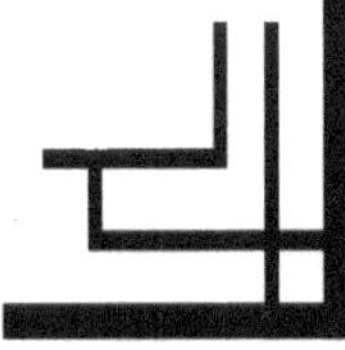

So was the pain.

She was flying.

Her entire body struck something, and Elsie went rigid with a sudden bone-numbing cold. Her gasp came as little more than a wheeze and water flooded an open mouth. Feet found shaky purchase in mud and the flapper pulled herself first to the water's surface then to the river's edge. Elsie looked up at the ledge Charles had flung her from.

"*Schlampe*," echoed a scream from upstream. Branches broke nearby.

Words, guttural and hollow, echoed all around her. Words that made no sense, in some language she didn't understand, but their meaning was clear. "*Get up*."

Elsie shook her head in an effort to clear foggy thoughts. What wasn't frigid from the river hurt. Her face felt like she ran into a door. So did her chest, but it ached deeper, all the way through to her back—the way her grandfather's had when his heart had nearly given out while working a plough. Though a struggle, she inhaled deep past blue lips. Words came faster, overlapping each other until a cacophony of verbiage rattled her eardrums. She pressed palms against her head trying to block out the voices. Foggy shadows moved all around her, shapes appearing more recognisable with

each breath she took.

* * *

"Bitch," Charles screamed again, but barely heard over the other voices as his spirits raged at their prey's escape. "Where are you?" The Brit kicked through a cluster of weeds. A speeding blur of grey caught his attention.

The fist-sized river rock struck home, impacting wetly against the Charles' temple.

Elsie's hands grabbed a broken branch, its raw end jagged and menacing. She staggered over to the moaning form at her feet and stood over him. Moonlight caught her eyes, reflecting a powder blue iris.

"Th-The Hopewell killed off the last of the...." She swallowed hard and forced another breath, "...the Adena tribe. They'd gone inbred and the few remaining weren't right in the head...started doing things that weren't...weren't natural." Elsie rolled Charles onto his stomach and squatted over him with one knee planted in the small of the man's back. A single jerk to the collar of his shirt ripped the fabric free and exposed a large patch of mottled, leathery scars blanketing the entire right side of his back, shoulder and arm. "You...you were right when you said the Hopewell killed them."

Charles didn't move.

"Are you listening?" Elsie smacked her palm against his ruined shoulder blade.

He spasmed in pain. "*Schlampe*," he managed. "Bitch."

"They want...." Another breath. This one came with less effort. "They want...to know something."

"Who?"

"The Adena...*my audience*." She grabbed a handful of hair and turned his head so she could see his profile. Eye shine met eye shine as one predator recognised another. "They want to know what you taste like."

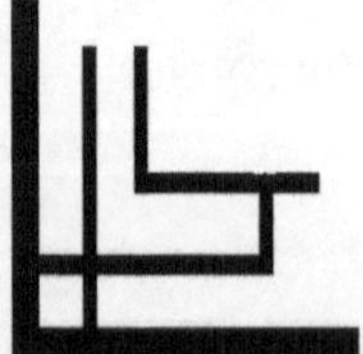

# THE SACRIFICE

by D.J. Elton

Ooooooh, la la! The show begins and the New Year swings into place. This is the era of the vamp, and Celia knows her cue. It's her grand moment; time to burst upwards and out of the huge celebratory cake. She can hear champagne corks popping and the muffled hum of satisfaction. She rises ecstatically through the interior of six tiers of pale pink and white whipped cream, knowing she has found her place. As she throws her arms into the air, smiling widely, a drama queen at her best, she inhales the cool air. There is silence now, and a mild chill. It had been a long twenty minutes inside the shell of the cake, and she had begun to gasp for more air.

A glove-clad hand passes her a thinly rolled one hundred dollar note. White powder escapes onto her fingertips. She licks them clean, then climbs elegantly out of the creaming froth, taking care to adjust her costume, slight as it is. She can feel many eyes upon her as she pats her hair, the jewelled clips in place above her ears giving an elfin look. She is the first of the season. Being chosen is such an honour, so she needs to be perfectly matched. A sacrifice cannot be flawed.

There is a white-clad horned figure. Celia lowers her eyes to avoid his covered face. He is slim and tall, his mask black, contrasting the remaining white of his robed attire, and he stares at her, avidly seeking out any error or misrepresentation. Finding none, he is satisfied.

It is midnight. The clock chimes, a salute to this act of Celia's surrender. She can withdraw if she wishes. It is still possible in these few remaining moments. However, she is certain, has no doubts, no hesitation. She knows this willing act will bring an appeasing to the earth gods, and in time, she will be rewarded in whatever form that may be. To make the gods happy is the greatest gift a human can do, and Celia has it nailed. So she believes.

Celia is led to a stage. Large vases of white goddess lilies stand in each corner, depicting a florist's dream of the moment of life and death. The inhaled drug has brought new insights and clarity, it seems. She is glamourous and adored.

The most important moment of her entire life is just about to happen. She has succeeded. She is glorious, powerful. The gods seek her help, her bonding, her human form. She is loved, by man and the gods. It is a moment of definition, of a perfect sacrifice.

She lies gently on a low table, wide and long, covered in golden cloth with red silk tassels. A pillow, soft beneath her neck, supports her head. Her eyes stare upward where there is a chandelier of many silver bowls holding candles. Not a word is spoken, however she can hear a low ancient chant merging with jazz sounds; a saxophone, a tribute to this time. There are two figures close by, male and female. Both are beautifully naked except for their red and silver masks. Red for the blood of the sacrifice. Silver for the power that restores equilibrium to the feminine.

Celia is ready. The last thing she sees before her cocaine-fuelled ascent are two golden daggers. Long, thin and sharp, gripped by perfect white hands, simultaneously sliding in perfect motion down her sternum. She is totally willing to please the horned god.



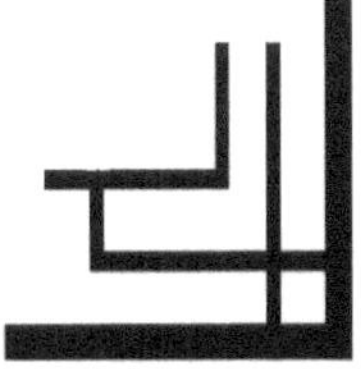

# Transatlantic Plight

## by Evan Baughfman

Lindbergh feared he'd never reach Paris, even with modifications made to his plane.

Storm clouds overworked the *Spirit*, sapping it of much of its fuel supply.

In the cockpit, the Devil appeared. "I'll guarantee you success, Charles," he hissed. "Fame. Fortune. A place in history."

"Is that so?" Controls trembled in Lindbergh's grasp.

"In exchange, however, I ask for…*the life of your firstborn son.*"

Lindbergh hesitated. How easy would it be to replace a child?

Finally, he answered. "Yes. Okay."

The Devil grinned. "Marvelous. Seems our

friendship has taken flight."

Six hours later, Charles Lindbergh landed safely in France.

BLACK HARE PRESS

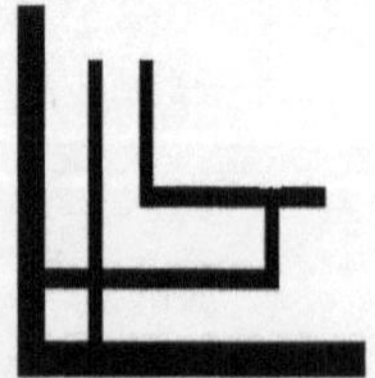

# BATH TUB GIN

## by Jim Bates

Big Ben Barker ran the bootleg arm of Mickey Finn's operation on the south side. He ran it like clockwork and with precision. Mickey called him Ben. Ben Barker's boys called him Boss. And the ladies all called him Mr Big because he was, well, he was rumoured to be well endowed, if you know what I mean.

Yeah, it was a fact that the ladies liked Mr Big and he liked them. Especially Laura Lane. Man, she was something else. A dancer at Club Go Go, she could shake it like no one he'd ever seen. She wore a black cloche hat decorated with gold sequins, and silver silk flapper dresses that shimmered under the spotlights, showing off every curve of her body. Wow! The first time he'd seen her, he wanted her like nobody's business. And the first time she'd slid out of that dress in his bedroom... Well, when they said that the sky was the limit, they didn't even come close. There was no limit as far as Laura was concerned. She'd do anything he asked her to do and leave him begging for more. His desire for her knew no bounds.

No bounds that was until Doris Dalrymple came along. Jeez. She was really the cat's meow. Better built than Laura, Doris knew her way to a man's heart, that was for sure—and it wasn't through his stomach. Whew! If Laura wore him out, Doris did it in spades.

But Big Ben wasn't getting any younger. After a few weeks of trying to manage it with both ladies, he decided one of them had to go. He flipped a coin and was only sad for a moment. Sorry, Laura. It'd been nice to know ya'.

He knew Laura wouldn't go quietly. Plus, she knew too much about his organisation and his business. Enough, anyway, to get nasty if she wanted to, which he figured she would after he gave the news that he was dumping her. So, he came up with a foolproof plan.

He booked the presidential suite on the top floor of the Ritz for that Saturday night. He had his boys fill the gold-plated bathtub with gin, knowing that gin loving Laura would appreciate the gesture. Then, after he'd gotten her good and drunk, he'd drown her in the tub and

claim it was an accident. Easy.

That night he took her to dinner and dancing at the 21 Club. Around midnight, they left and went to Ben's favourite speakeasy for drinks. After they'd had a few, he leaned in close enough to get a good whiff of her Channel, not to mention an eye full of her cleavage, and said, "Hey there, gorgeous. How about you and I blow this place and head for the Ritz? I've got a room for us."

"Oh, honey," Laura said, slurring ever so slightly. "You've got a treat for little old me?" She rubbed her hand against his crotch. "Well, I've got one for you, too." She giggled as she stood up and sauntered off, swinging her hips, driving him and his own personal Mr Big crazy.

He hurried to catch up and took her by the arm, drooling in anticipation. "I'll have one of the boys drive us," he panted.

Half an hour later, they were in the huge bathroom.

Laura purred like a kitten, "Oh, honey, look at all the gin for little old me." She dipped a finger in and licked it.

"All for you, sweetheart." Ben watched her slide her finger around in her mouth and could barely contain himself. *Maybe just once more, for old time's sake*, is what he was thinking as Laura sashayed up to him.

"Aw, honey, give me a little kiss," she said, wrapping her arms around his neck. "Umm. You feel good."

Ben couldn't help himself. In a moment captured by his uncontrollable lust, he grabbed her in a tight embrace and ran his hand up and down her firm behind.

Laura ignored his hand as she felt him grow hard against her thigh. That's all she needed. She slowly turned him until the backs of his knees were propped against the rim of the tub. Then she nibbled on his earlobe whispering, "Oh, my, baby. You feel so good." She rubbed against him sensuously. "Who do you love, honey?" She rubbed some more and took hold of his belt buckle. "Hmm? Do you love little old me?"

She felt Ben's hot breath in her ear. He murmured, "Oh baby, you know how much—" He never finished his thought.

Laura put her hands on his chest and pushed. Backwards he tumbled, splashing into the gin. "What the.." he was starting to say when Laura reached over to the vanity, turned on the electric radio, and dropped it into the tub. Still plugged in. He shook and jiggled and jumped, splashing gin over the sides of the tub and onto the floor.

Laura laughed at Ben's shocked expression. "Do

away with me, baby? Not on your life. Oh, wait. I guess I was wrong. On your life, sucker!"

It took less than a minute, and then he was dead.

Half an hour later, she emerged from the elevator of the ritzy hotel looking every bit the beautiful woman she was. She stopped by the front desk and said, "I think there's a problem up in the Presidential Suite. Something's clogging the drain on the tub."

Then she sauntered across the lobby and out the front door, never to be seen or heard from again. In her purse was twenty thousand dollars, taken from Ben's wallet. Or Little Ben as she now thought of him, because in truth that's what he really was. Tiny, even.

She smiled as she waved for a cab and one pulled up right away. "Airport, ma'am?" the cabby asked.

"Yes, thank you. And please make it a fast. I'm in a hurry."

He saluted and grinned. "You bet, beautiful."

She sat down in back and breathed a sigh of relief as the cab peeled away from the curb. Life was good. She was a beautiful woman, and she had money, more than enough for airfare to the Bahamas. More than enough to start a new life. No one would ever find her. She stared out the window and watched the lights of the city stream past. She'd never see those lights again, and

she smiled. That was just fine with her.

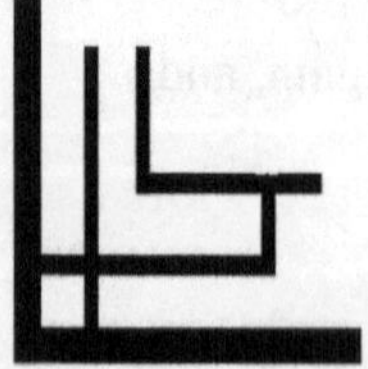

# THE DEVIL'S DEN SPEAKEASY

by J.B. Wocoski

The gangster payoffs corrupted all of us, and it quickly became our way of life. Anyone trying to stop the greed, found themselves riddled with machine-gun fire.

I learned the hard way that the rule of survival is to live off the crumbs the gangsters leave behind. As a detective, it means I take bribes and shut up about what I see going on around me. I only survived by looking the other way as soon as their money greased my palms.

* * *

Our prescient police station had received several

tips and complaints from both the Irish and Italian gang leaders about missing goons and mugs. They complained something wasn't kosher with The Devil's Den Speakeasy, and this is what had led me and Mumbles, my partner, to be staking out the lively bar.

So far, the speakeasy seemed normal enough; men and Women walked into the Devil's Den Speakeasy without incident. It was getting late when Mumbles said to me, "Jake, I think this stakeout is a waste of time."

I slowly nodded in agreement. "Yeah, Mumbles, I reckon these tips we got were just a diversion. I wonder what the gangs don't want us to catch them doing tonight." The stakeout didn't make much sense to me since, earlier that day, gangsters from both gangs had slipped me a couple of fifties to sit in our sedan and watch the place. I'd split the dollars with Mumbles, but it was still too much cash to give to any copper for a diversion.

"You never did say what we are looking for tonight. You mind letting me in on the big secret?"

"It's no secret," I said. "Some gang members disappeared while trying to make their collections from this speakeasy. It sits on the border between the Irish and Italian gangs. Wild gang leader accusations are flying back and forth about conspiring with the speakeasy

owner to knock off the other gang."

Mumbles groaned. "I should have known the gangs wanted us to clean up their mess. What happened, did they run out of hitmen or enforcers?"

I sat there thinking, then commented, "Two Toe Louie and Marco the Machine are two of the missing."

Mumbles looked at me in disbelief. "Those guys are hardcore killers. How are we supposed to stop killers from killing killers?"

I opened the sedan door. "Come on, we're going in."

We checked out our police-special handguns, then grabbed the pump shotguns from the back seat of the unmarked car.

"Jake, do we go through the front doors upstairs, or hit the cellar speakeasy? "

Without hesitating, I said, "The speakeasy! You notice that no one going into the speakeasy is leaving? They have to go somewhere. Keep your shotgun under your trench coat."

"You know their password, Jake?"

"I know the universal password, right here under my arm." I grinned, patting my police special under my coat. "Let's make it official." I took out my badge to flash in the face of anyone challenging us at the Devil's

Den Speakeasy door.

We quickly crossed the street just as some guy started down the cellar stairs to the speakeasy, so we tagged along. He knocked, and when the door to the Devil's Den opened, we overheard the password: "Hellfire."

When we started to follow him in, the big bouncer stuck his giant hand on my chest. "Didn't you forget something?" he demanded of me.

I had planned to kick him in the balls, but instead, smiling wryly, I replied, "Hellfire." Pointing with my thumb behind me, I added, "He's with me, I'll vouch for him."

When the bouncer removed his hand from the front of my trench coat, he didn't even look at Mumbles. We silently moved down a short hallway and into the main speakeasy barroom. The old flickering gas lamps illuminated the packed room in a dim, hellish orange glow, exposing members of different gangs at the tables and along the bars. I whispered in Mumbles ear, "Something weird is going on here. Too many different enemy gangs down here."

I paused when a devilishly good-looking redhead in a tight-fitting fire-red dress came up to us. "Welcome boys. I expected you yesterday, what took you so long

to get here? Jake? Mumbles?"

"I don't think we've been introduced?" I replied, surprised.

"Oh, Jake. You hurt my feelings. Do I have to spell it out for you? Why don't you two get a drink and take a good look around at my clientele? I think you know most of them."

As if on cue, the room fell silent as everyone in it turned and looked at us, their dead eyes fixated on us. I felt a sickening feeling in the pit of my stomach as I started to recognise the faces of the missing gangsters surrounding us.

I looked at the redhead. "I don't understand, I see only dead people here."

Her eyes widened as she grinned. "And?"

I was still standing there, trying to take it all in, when Mumbles muttered, "Jake, you've got bloody bullet holes in your back. I think we're all dead down here and going to Hell."

Laughing hysterically, the devilishly good-looking redhead yelled, "Tonight! We have a winner! Strike up the band!"

She signalled the jazz band to play. The sound of the Charleston rocked the room as one, and everyone started dancing wildly everywhere. The gaslight flames

grew ever brighter, giving the dancers a hellish glow as the floor opened and, one by one, the dancing lost souls dropped into Hell, followed by me and Mumbles.

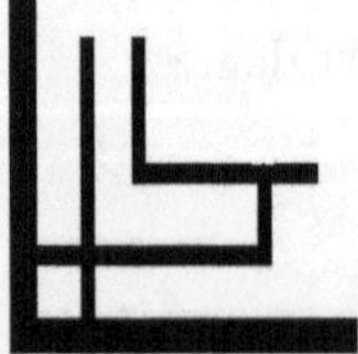

# A FLOOD BIGGER THAN THE RITZ

by Jack Lothian

I suppose it all began on that summer evening in 1922 when I drove to have dinner with my two closest friends—Daniel and Lily Blaine. Lily was a distant cousin, and I'd known Daniel from my college days. In retrospect, we were nothing more than strangers, and this wasn't a beginning; it was the end of everything.

The previous year I'd moved to a modest house in Port Washington, overlooking Manhasset Bay. My new home was nothing compared to the mansion next door, which seemed to have sprung from a storybook. Ivy towers overlooked a grand marble swimming pool, set amongst forty acres of lush green lawn. This was the home of Monroe Harper—or at least that's what I'd been told, as I'd still not crossed paths with my neighbour. That evening though, he was hosting a party. A gold embossed invite had appeared on my doorstep, along with a personalised message.

*I look forward to finally meeting my neighbour...!*

As I left for dinner, I could see the caterers getting to work, setting up canvas awnings and buffet tables, stringing up coloured lights. An orchestra tuned up, their backs to the blue waters of the bay. I suspected Mr Harper was not a man to do things by half. The invite had said I could bring two guests, and Daniel and Lily seemed the ideal candidates. In truth, I didn't have any other friends, finding myself somewhat of a solitary creature, mostly through choice.

"I hear he made his money in black goods," said Daniel as we sat on the veranda of his house, right across the bay from where I lived.

"You shouldn't believe half of what you see and very little of what you hear," said Lily, giving his arm a playful slap.

Her engagement and marriage to Daniel had been something of a surprise. Lily had fallen in with an odd crowd for a number of years, causing concern amongst her family, but Daniel was well-regarded by all; athletic, handsome, born into money. I'd been unable to attend the wedding due to a spell in hospital with what the doctors referred to as 'nervous exhaustion.'

Lily was the only person I'd ever really spoken to about my war-time experiences, an involvement that ended when my ship—the USS *Bedford*—was struck by a German U-boat torpedo. And when the doctors finally discharged me, it was Lily who was waiting, and who found me a job and a place to stay, insisting that Port Washington would be the perfect place to start my life over.

"He's been your neighbour for, what, a year now? And not even a glimpse of the man?" Daniel shook his head as if this was some grave slight on us all.

"I've seen him," I said. "Just from a distance." A few nights, I'd spotted what I assumed was Harper, a subdued shadow on the jetty, staring out over the water, with only the glow of a cigarette for company. It was an image I found somewhat melancholy, although maybe that said more about myself than him.

"Did he serve?" asked Lily.

"I believe so," I said. "If neighbourhood gossip is correct, he was with the Expeditionary Forces at the Western Front," I said.

"I wonder if he killed anyone."

"I'd hope so," said Daniel. "What sort of man goes to war and doesn't take a life? That'd be like going to the beach and not getting wet." Daniel had been ineligible for the draft due to a previously undiagnosed (and unspecific) medical condition.

I looked out across the bay and thought of the Bedford, fire and oil, screams in the night. I didn't say anything.

* * *

By the time we arrived, the party was in full swing. The orchestra had struck up a lively version of 'Rose of Washington Square.' Waiters crisscrossed with trays of cocktails. Girls with bobbed hair and sparkling dresses shimmied across the canvas dancefloor. Everywhere you looked, there was gaiety and laughter. As we walked towards the mansion, it felt as if summer would last forever.

Daniel whisked Lily towards the dancefloor, expertly dipping and swaying her. I submerged my disappointment at being abandoned and busied myself asking partygoers if they knew where Harper was. Our host appeared somewhat elusive; some said they'd seen him at the bar, others spoke of him lounging on the

veranda. One wild-eyed girl said he'd jitterbugged her across the floor only moments before, but her voice was slurred, and I doubted the veracity of her claim.

My enthusiasm for the night started to wear. Too many people, too much noise. Everything seemed to be speeding up, and I could feel the ground tipping and listing like I was back on the deck of the Bedford, cold dark water rushing up to meet me. Then small hands pressed on my arm as Lily gently guided me to the house.

"Maybe we should see what's happening inside," she said, her voice soft and reassuring.

Daniel followed in our trail, breathless from his dance floor exertions. Overhead fireworks split the night sky, coloured shards of thunder.

"I tell you one thing about this Harper chap," said Daniel, as he grabbed a cocktail from a passing tray. "The man knows how to throw a party."

* * *

The mansion interior was a welcome oasis. Yet, as we walked the marble corridors and hallways, past guests and staff, nobody knew where Harper was. I began to wonder if he existed at all.

A turn of the corner brought us into an impressive library, mahogany shelves upon a chequered tile floor. A large man in an ill-fitting suit was perusing the spines with interest.

"Incredible," he said to no-one in particular. "First editions of Barrett and Reuchlin...*Las Reglas de Ruina*...the man's even got a translated copy of the *Cryptomenysis Patefacta*."

Daniel squinted at the shelves. "So, it's worth a tidy sum then?"

"Probably not," replied a newcomer, approaching from behind. "I hear he bought them as a job-lot at some auction."

"You clearly know nothing about books," said the large man.

"You may be right. My accountant did say I paid far too much for them." Then, off the man's confusion, the newcomer extended a hand. "Monroe Harper, at your service."

The large man looked horrified and managed a 'pleased to meet you'—complete with an awkward bow—while Harper turned his attention to the rest of us. He gripped my hand, shook it.

"Tom," he said. "How good to finally meet you. And this must be Mr and Mrs Blaine."

"Mr Harper, pleased to meet you," said Daniel, managing to slur only a few words. Lily offered a more reserved greeting. I thought I saw a flicker of recognition between her and Harper, but that could've been an unspoken apology for her husband's intoxication.

I'd expected Harper to be some boorish socialite, but he had a quiet intelligence and good humour that was most agreeable. He insisted we join him upstairs in his private quarters, leading a brisk route through corridors and winding stairs.

"Aren't you keen to get back to your party?" asked Daniel.

"I'm sure it's managing fine without me," said Harper. He led us into a drawing-room on the third floor, decked out in dark oak, with large bay windows over a writing desk, and a sizable bar running down the far side. A bottle of gin sat next to an ice bucket, and a tray of freshly cut limes, like company had been expected.

Harper gathered four glasses, clinking ice into them. "So, you were in the war, Tom?"

I nodded. "Navy."

"Fair warning—our Tom doesn't like to talk about the war," said Daniel.

"If you were so keen to hear about it, you should've gone yourself," replied Lily.

"Unfortunately, the doctors wouldn't let me," said Daniel. Harper poured a generous measure of gin and soda into each glass, topping it off with a lime. Daniel watched approvingly. "How about you, Mr Harper?"

"Monroe, please. And yes, I served with the A.E.F."

"I'd have thought a man of your means could've found a way to avoid the conflict."

"I believed it was my duty," said Harper.

He made duty sound like the most hollow thing in the world, and I was going to ask him to elucidate but found myself distracted by an object on the desk.

It was a wooden statuette, eight inches high. It appeared to be a carving of an animal, although which kind I could not say. It reminded me of some marine invertebrate—perhaps a cuttlefish—with oval eyes and fleshy cranial appendages. Yet the way it was hunched on what looked like limbs, placed it in an unknown space between man and beast.

Without intending to, I'd crossed the room and picked it up, my fingers brushing over a rough series of hieroglyphics etched on the bas-relief below

"Ugly little thing, isn't it?" Harper was at my shoulder, drink in hand, which he exchanged for the statuette.

"Where is it from?"

"I've no idea, old chap. Found it half-buried in a German trench. Command said we weren't to bring home any souvenirs, but…" He shrugged, placed it back down. "It seems they weren't bothered by what the troops brought back. Or what they lost out there."

The object seemed familiar, but I wasn't sure why. It unnerved me, but so much unnerved me back then that it was hard to bring it into focus. It was soon forgotten, lost amongst a parade of highballs and stories, as Harper proved himself a most congenial host. At one point, I found myself—aided by the gin—telling Lily how much she meant to me. She gave me a sad smile and squeezed my arm.

At the time, I thought she felt sorry for me because of all I'd been through, but I realise now it was for all that was to come.

* * *

A week later, Harper sent a note, asking me to dinner. The invitation extended to Lily, but there was no mention of Daniel. I assumed this was an oversight and would've included him, had it not been for a fortuitous meeting with Harper that very afternoon.

He was on the jetty, hunched over sun-bleached boards, staring into the water. "Tom," he said as I approached. "I was just thinking about you."

"I received your invitation," I replied. "I presume it includes Daniel as well?"

Harper stretched, smiled. "Come on, old man. If I'd wanted to include Daniel, I'd have done so. Dinner is for three. Unless you particularly want Daniel to be there...?"

"I'm not the host," I said diplomatically.

That made Harper laugh. "Bring a swim-suit if you wish. The bay will still be warm."

"I'm not...I'm not one for water," I replied.

"Ah, yes. Lily mentioned you were on the Bedford." He paused, weighing his words. "How many were lost that day?"

I thought of fire on the water, bodies sinking below, the darkness waiting to welcome us.

"Thirty-six."

"You deserved better, Tom. We all did."

I ended up staying the rest of the afternoon, passing the time in Harper's private bar, drink after drink, yet always vaguely aware of that tenebrous statuette in the corner, blankly staring out at us. We talked of many things, from the ongoing tentacles of prohibition through to my work in the city. We didn't speak of the war, but it was an ever-present undertow; those horrific events that'd shaped us, for better or worse.

It was not until dinner that the topic fully emerged, as we sat by the dock, under the glow of daisy-strung lamps. Lily had arrived before sunset, fresh and bright in a simple white dress, which only served to reflect the gleam of her beauty.

"It'll happen again," said Harper. "People call this the war to end all wars, but it's merely an overture."

"I don't know," I said. "I doubt any nation is in a rush to return to conflict."

"Oh, Tom," said Lily. "Can't you see what we've become? This isn't civilization. It's a bloodied beast that demands to be fed. And it's so very hungry… Don't you wish you could just… just wipe it all away and start again?"

I must've been looking at her askew, because she stopped, embarrassed.

"I'm sorry," she said. "Maybe I need to freshen up. And perhaps calm down." She rose, despite my protestations, that all was fine. I watched her walk to the house, confused by her demeanour.

"How long have you been in love with her?" asked Harper.

I shook my head, aware my face was burning. "It's not like that."

"But you're close to her. You confide in her. Tell her things." I caught his eye as he spoke, aware of the shifting tone. "Like what happened after the Bedford sank."

"I don't know what you mean."

"I know what you saw down there, Tom."

And for a moment, I was back there, sinking into pitch-black water, the corpse of the Bedford an iron mountain above. Bodies around me, eyes open, mouths agape, an underwater grave being filled. As death came for me, I stared into the endless dark of the ocean, and the dark opened its giant eye and stared back.

"No," I said. "Whatever Lily told you—she's mistaken…"

"It *spoke* to you, Tom. That's what you told her."

I got up from my seat, unsteady. "No—it was—the doctors said I was sick—imaging things…"

"You're not sick, Tom. You're chosen," said Harper, rising with me. "*It spoke to you.* Do you know how long our people have waited for such a thing?"

"Your people?"

I turned, seeing Lily returning across the lawn. She bore the statuette in her arms, like a fragile child. "Think

of it as a very old church, Tom," she said. "Man has turned paradise into a bloodied, churning field of war. It's time to start over."

"I don't understand."

"It's happened before," said Harper. "A long time ago. You know the story of Noah and the flood—it's a bastardisation of the truth, but the concept is the same. He heard the voice, and he summoned it from the depths."

Lily leaned in close, pressing the statuette into my hands. "You can read it, can't you?"

I stared down at hieroglyphs on the bas-relief, those primordial words etched upon it, feeling them uncurl and unwind in my head.

"Read it for me, Tom," she continued. "Read it and wipe all this away."

Harper gave me a sympathetic look." I know, old chap. We're asking you to snuff out the light of humanity, all before dessert. It's a lot to take in. But we're cattle, and they've turned our world into a slaughterhouse."

A cool breeze blew across the lawn. I thought of how Lily had insisted I move to Port Washington, to the house next to Harper. How she'd always kept me close, on a string, as if waiting for something.

"So, I read this and… and what?"

"It wakes up."

"It being...?"

Harper gestured to the bay. "Something ancient and antediluvian."

"I'm afraid I left my dictionary at home."

"It means before the fall of humans," said Lily. "Before the flood."

I looked at the words and imagined that chthonic being beneath the water, its eye opening, its whispers in my head. They were the sound of a tomb opening, a moon breaking, black stars blinking into existence above.

I drew back my arm and threw the statuette towards the water. It made a small splashing sound and sunk down below.

"I'll pass," I said. I turned, unsteady, and started to walk away. The look of hatred Lily gave me almost froze me in place. Harper took a step forward, and I thought he meant to stop me, but he started to clap his hands, and his smile seemed genuine.

"Bravo, old chap," he said. "I may not agree with your choice but bravo, Tom. Bravo."

I limped home, the sound of his applause fading into the night.

# TWENTY TWENTY

* * *

That was fifteen years ago. I haven't seen either of them since. I moved out of the house the next day and wrangled a transfer to the Pittsburgh office, where I've slowly risen through the ranks to senior partner. I still live a simple and quiet life, mostly by choice.

I received letters from Daniel for a while, full of bitter recrimination. Apparently, Harper and Lily had eloped, leaving him clutching the tattered remains of his marriage. I didn't reply, and after a while, the letters stopped.

There was a postcard from Harper, which arrived almost ten years since that night by the docks. I'm not sure how he knew my address, but it didn't surprise me.

*Tom. I never got to apologise for being such a terrible host. So please, consider this my sincere expression of regret. I still believe one day you'll do the right thing. But belief and reality are rarely the same.*

*Yours,*

*Harper Monroe.*

I think about him sometimes, and Lily, and all they said that night. And some days, after work, I sit in my car and think of words scrawled upon a bas-relief. I think of reports filtering in from Germany, murmurs of a war yet to come. I remember bodies lying in water and dirt, and how far we've drifted from paradise.

But most of all, I think how it's only five hours' drive to the ocean. And how I can remember every one of those ancient words, and how easy it would be to speak them aloud, to see what comes next.

Key in the ignition. Foot on the gas pedal.

Most days, I think I'm driving home, but I won't know for sure, not until I arrive.

# LOVE ALWAYS, VERA

by A.R. Dean

The shattering glass mingled with the heated words. Mildred Thomas was on a rampage. She had destroyed every object she could reach. Snatching up her copy of "Picture Perfect Fan" Magazine, she began pacing across the room. Her slippers crunching on the broken glass. There on the cover was her husband, Lon with Vera Trent.

Mildred screamed as she tore the pages to shreds. The words, "Silent Horror Icons Turned Lovers" floated to her feet. How dare he stray from her?

Mildred spun in a rage to the soft knock at her door. "What?" she screeched. The top of the maid's head poked through.

"Madam, you told me to fetch you when Mr Thomas arrived home." The young woman's eyes rounded at the sight of the room.

"About time," Mildred snarled, "Clean up this mess while I deal with him." She stomped her feet pushing the maid out of her way. The poor girl grabbed the door to keep from falling. Mildred continued her tirade as she stormed into her husband's study without knocking. "You scoundrel!"

Lon glanced up at his wife and slowly continued sipping from his crystal glass. "Good evening, darling."

Mildred continued stomping over, snatching the glass from his lips. With a shout of frustration, she hurled the glass into the empty fireplace. "How dare you cheat on me again?"

"I see you've been reading the fan pages?" he asked raising a dark brow.

"The Romanian tramp of all women." She clutched the front of his shirt, pulling him closer to her.

Shaking his head, he chuckled and removed his wife's clenched fingers. "I can't accept you read those ridiculous scandal rags. The studio is spreading rumours to promote the Vampire's Groom."

"Studio rumours?"

"Of course. With all the studios in an uproar about this talking picture nonsense they are demanding that the silent stars double the profits."

Her fist came down on to his shoulder. "I don't believe you. That woman devours men."

He twisted away shaking with laughter he approached his desk. He poured himself another drink. "You can't deny a modern woman her appetites."

"Vera Trent is a witch," Mildred hissed, "I will not allow you to be one of the many men she devours."

"You're paranoid, my dear. At this very moment, she is seducing Valentino. I promise that it is passing gossip." He sipped his illegal whiskey.

"That woman has had five lovers just this year and you expect me to accept you are being wrongly accused? I will not have my husband follow the course of her other two lovers that disappeared."

Annoyed he slammed his glass onto the desk sloshing liquid everywhere. "You dumb-Dora, haven't you heard a word I said. I am only her co-star and friend. There is nothing more between us."

Mildred gasped, stumbling back from her enraged husband. "You've never spoke to me like that."

Lon raised his left hand showing off his wedding band. "After four years of wearing this manacle I'm about sick of you Mildred. All these years of your unearned jealousy. I'm tempted to walk."

"You can't leave me. My father owns your contract.

You walk and he will make sure you never work again." She hissed.

He threw his head back in a bark of laughter, "The studio makes too much money off of Lon Thomas, the hero of horror films, to even think of getting rid of me." Lon waltzed up to her his breath stale with imported liquor, "Your threats don't hold water anymore. Now go chase yourself!"

Mildred gaped, her blonde bob shaking with fury, "How dare you!"

"Go away," Lon turned his back strutting to the seat in front of the empty fireplace. With a sigh he flopped down in the chair. "The premier is this weekend, and since you can't behave, you are no longer invited to attend."

As she reached for the door Mildred bristled, "You can't do that. I have to be on your arm, or it will fuel more gossip."

"Now you're on the trolley. Stop being a wurp, Mildred. Go clean whatever tantrum-fuelled mess you made of our bedroom. I don't want to lose another maid."

Mildred grabbed the nearest vase, hurling it at the wall beside him, "Drink your panther-piss. You and your harlot can have fun at your petting pantry, Lon.

You haven't heard the last of this." He lit his cigarette as she stomped her feet in retreat.

Four days later Mildred followed her husband to the premier of his film. She watched from the crowd as he approached the director for a firm handshake. His dark locks slicked back shining in the lights. His pencil-thin moustache twitching with every word he muttered. Mildred longed to run her fingers along his well-tailored tux.

Lon's face was a grim line until the photographers started snapping their cameras and shouting. Much to Mildred's displeasure Vera had arrived. The look of pure joy on her husband's face when he saw Vera caused her heart to sink.

Vera's beauty was considered legendary and Mildred could see why. Her unfashionably long ebony locks curled to the middle of her back. The silken emerald evening gown dragged behind her as she strolled the red carpet. A fur wrap covered her shoulders. A small crimson smile adorned her pale face.

Mildred's blood boiled at the sight of the sparkling diamonds that Vera was swathed with. Her locks were arranged around a glistening bandeau, also of diamonds. The howls and whistling of the men began then. Mildred was disgusted by the display. Vera however seemed delighted as she blew kisses back at the fans. Her frame was curvy with full breasts unlike Mildred's boxy one.

Mildred felt her lip snarl when the woman looked towards her way in the crowd. She pulled her cloche down over her eyes. She could see Vera's gloved hand as it waved to the audience. Vera then continued to slither her way up the walk where Lon waited his hand outstretched. He pulled Vera into an embrace where she kissed him gently on the cheek. The crowd roared as the camera bulbs hissed.

They laughed together as Lon tucked Vera's arm into his elbow before guiding her into the theatre. Vera's head turned up as Lon's bent down in a scheming manner.

Everyone dispersed as the movie started. Mildred waited, tucking in her wool coat against the winter chill. She paced back and forth behind the theatre, waiting for the film to let out. Lon had sworn that he was attending the after party at his director's home.

Mildred was not surprised when Lon and Vera climbed alone into a limo headed in the opposite direction. She hailed a cab to follow behind. They travelled up into the new Hollywood Hills property where Vera had her mansion built.

The mansion made the Thomas home look like a

Rueben shanty. The rolling gardens and tall gates surrounded the pristine two-story Tudor revival. Mildred paid the driver and walked the cobblestone driveway among the trees. She glanced around removing her t-straps before racing across the lawn; the shoes clutched tightly in her fist. Light poured from the tall wooden windows. Crouching she pushed the bushes aside so she could settle beneath an open window. She glanced around the rest of the terrace where she saw shadows dancing across the French doors.

The soothing jazz flowed out to her hiding spot. Mildred glanced inside to the study where Lon paced, alone. The built-in mahogany bookcases glowed against the mustard-coloured walls. Vera's fur and diamonds discarded carelessly on the settee along with Lon's coat. Vera glided into the room, a silken ruby robe tied snuggly around her waist. She pushed her raven tresses out of her eyes as she rubbed her face between Lon's shoulders.

"I did not see your wife tonight, my darling. Is she ill?" Vera murmured in her thick Romanian accent.

"No. I made the bluenose stay home. I was sick of her trying to interfere with us." Lon turned, embracing Vera in a sultry kiss.

Mildred growled from her hiding spot. Her grip

tightened on her shoe, ready to bludgeon both with it.

"Does she know?" Vera purred, breaking the kiss.

Lon chuckled as he rained kisses on Vera's neck. "Mildred has her suspicions, but it's nothing I can't dissuade her of."

Vera giggled swatting Lon away, "No, Iubi, not the affair. That you will be leaving her for me."

Lon laughed as he turned away from her, "Listen Vera you're a real Sheba. I mean your bubs are the best in town." Vera's eyes narrowed as he droned on. "You know that its career suicide to divorce in this town."

"So, your words of love mean nothing? I am a fling?" Vera's accent grew thicker as she trembled in rage. Mildred chuckled from beneath the window. "Are you leaving me?" Mildred glanced inside to see Vera clutching tightly to Lon's arm.

"Now Vera, my dear, you know this wasn't forever. I'm a married man."

Mildred's heart leapt in triumph. Lon may stray, but he always came back to her.

"Do you love her?"

"Marriage has nothing to do with love." Lon chuckled nervously as he rubbed Vera's back. He began kissing her neck again. "Now stop acting like a jealous wife I can get that home."

Vera clung to Lon like a wet rag. "I apologise my darling one. Can I get you a noodle juice or giggle water?"

"Yeah I'll take a jorum of skee," Lon ordered as he settled in a chair.

Mildred knew when she heard the swishing of Vera's retreat that her moment had arrived. She would burst in through the terrace doors, confronting her husband. The embarrassment would send him running back home to her arms sooner. She scuttled over, reaching for the door, just as Vera appeared, a goblet in hand.

"Thank you." Lon downed the glass.

Vera grinned as she caressed his cheek. "You're mine forever, Lon."

"What are you yammering…" Lon trailed off clutching his stomach he roared in pain. Falling forward he slammed into the Persian rug he writhed in agony.

"No one leaves me, Lon. To love me is to never leave." Vera smiled down as he eventually stopped moving. Mildred watched as Vera kicked Lon snorting when he didn't move. As Vera waltzed towards the French doors Mildred dived back to her hiding place under the window.

Vera pushed open the double doors, inhaling

deeply of the California air. "Oh, Lon, it's a beautiful night." She turned, heading to her desk. She wrote a quick note before carefully folding it and placing it in her bosom. "Doru, come help Mommy."

A tall, muscular man in his teens came to her call. He carefully picked up Lon and followed his mother to the terrace. Mildred held her breath as they brushed past her. Down the stone steps they lumbered towards the garage.

Carefully, Mildred followed. She watched as Vera opened a door in the grounds and disappeared below. Doru followed, carrying her husband's dead body. Mildred watched for several minutes until the teenager finally emerged, heading back to the house alone. The faint sounds of a phonograph being played could be heard, a sweet song of love coming from the pit where they had taken Lon.

Mildred stepped softly to the hole. The wooden steps creaked beneath her weight as she followed them down. She couldn't believe her eyes. It was an old mine shaft lined with torches. Pushing her body against the dirt wall, Mildred inched her way down the shaft to a cave. Inside, the cave was lined with stone chests. The phonograph was on a round wooden table, a soft chair beside it. There was no sign of Vera.

Mildred rushed over to the open stone chest where her husband lay. She gasped, realising that they were stone coffins. Glancing around, she could make out twenty in the dim firelight. She brushed a shaking hand against her husband's cold face. On his chest was the note Vera had written.

*My Darling Lon,*

*I am sorry that it has come to this. No man is allowed to leave me. So now you will be forever mine. Don't worry about Mildred, she'll be with you soon.*

*Love Always*

*Vera*

Dropping the note back upon her husband's chest, Mildred turned ready to flee. Her path blocked by an enraged Vera.

"You dumb-Dora! You couldn't just leave things alone. He would have stayed had your jealousy not gotten in the way," Vera screeched, her accent thicker than ever.

"I'm sorry, Vera. You can have my husband," Mildred stammered.

"No, he wanted to go back to his wife. He needed you, Mildred. Now he can have you forever." Vera swung the cane that was hidden at her side, connecting with the other woman's skull. Mildred collapsed to the dirt. With a sigh, Vera gathered up the smaller woman, placing her in the sarcophagus with Lon. Humming along with the song from her phonograph, Vera lifted the stone slab, sealing the couple inside.

# MIDNIGHT SHOESHINE

by Pedro Iniguez

Archie LaRue's shoes tapped against the floorboards, shattering the silence of an empty boardwalk on Christmas night. The vendors had long shuttered their doors, most of them, permanently. It was just as well. People could seldom afford to partake in leisurely strolls along the beach these days. Times would be different now. He didn't blame them. Not one bit.

He exhaled a deep sigh while he strolled past an empty carousel and the nearby sounds of a Wurlitzer chiming its cheerful tunes. It had been far too long since last he'd brought Camille and Bobby, the result of a demanding acting career which, recently, had gone bust. Now, he'd never get the chance to bring them again. Not after Camille ran off the way she did.

He turned toward the Santa Monica pier and dipped

his head as a frigid breeze swept against his body, nipping at his hands like small razors. The wind blew a newspaper across the floor until it wrapped its pages around his leg. He plucked it and held it against the light from a lamppost. It was an October issue of the Los Angeles Times. The day the markets crashed. He scoffed and released the paper, offering it back to the wind.

Ahead, a string of lampposts flickered and buzzed erratically, casting eerie, dancing shadows upon the planks of the old pier. If he hadn't been drunk, he would've sworn on his mother that he saw the shadows of three shapes scuttling underneath the floorboards. He mumbled a prayer under his breath and made his way to the tip of the dock where the waves crashed against the pillars below.

Archie leaned forward and scanned the ocean. Nothing but darkness waiting to swallow him whole. It was just as well. He'd exit the stage on his terms, for once. He planted a foot over the bottom rail and hoisted himself onto the ledge. His insides twisted themselves into knots, his body offering protest to his final intended act.

"Hey, Mister," he heard a soft voice cry out.

Archie turned to find a young, dishevelled boy, no

older than ten years of age, stepping forth from the shadows. His face had been smudged with grease and his clothes looked like they hadn't been washed in weeks, perhaps months. The boy nestled a shoeshine box under one arm and wrapped the other around his chest. His purple lips quivered before opening them to speak. "Care for a shoeshine?"

"Christ Almighty, boy," Archie said, startled, "you're gonna die out in this cold." He scanned the pier for a sign of the boy's parents. Nothing, not even a single drunkard stumbling across the boardwalk. "What are you doing in the middle of the night offering shoeshines?"

"Things have been rough," he said scratching his cheek, smearing the grease on his face. "My Pop just up and left after he lost his job. I'm just trying to feed my family."

Archie nodded. "Admirable. What's your name?"

"Eloy, sir. Nice to meet you. So whaddaya say?"

"Kid," Archie said, pursing his lips. He considered telling Eloy what he was about to do. Thought about telling him to turn and walk away as he took the plunge into the void. He thought better of it and shrugged. "Eloy. What makes you think I need a shoeshine?"

"You've got a beautiful pair on your feet," he said

nodding at Archie's shoes. "But in their current state, how's anyone supposed to appreciate them?"

His two-toned wingtips had dulled and caked with booze and mud, vestiges of countless nights ambling drunk about town. "What's it matter to anyone what my shoes look like?"

Eloy smiled. "A man's gotta look good no matter where he's going. Besides, I promise you'll feel better the minute I'm done."

Archie regarded Eloy for a moment. A clean haircut and a good shower and the kid wouldn't look too different from Bobby. He bit his lip and fought the urge to cry. "Alright, kid, you got yourself a customer." He hopped off the rail and patted Eloy's shoulder.

"Thanks, Mister. My family will be eternally grateful." Eloy knelt and unpacked his rags, his eyes gleaming with joy. Archie placed a foot on his rickety box and crossed both arms over his chest, the night progressively getting colder as his body burned through the liquor.

"You smell like my Pop," Eloy said as he got to work.

"How's that?"

"Gin and Tonic. It was his favourite. He said whenever he was having a bad day, a little went a long

way."

"What's your point?"

"You must be having a bad day. You can tell me about it. Everyone should let off a little steam."

"Kid," he said, shaking his head, "not that it matters to you, but I've lost everything."

"Lot of people losing their jobs, lately."

Eloy ran a cloth across his shoe, scrubbing off the filth the last two months had brought him. His tiny fingers were white from the cold, but his face showed no signs of discomfort. Archie supposed he was just happy to land a client at this time of all places.

"No, I don't just mean my job. I lost my savings, my investments. My wife left and took my son Bobby with her. Said I'm no good to them without money. How's that for family support?"

"I'm sorry, Mister. What did you used to do?"

"You ever been to a moving picture show?"

Eloy shook his head, ashamed. "I don't get out much during the day." He retrieved a vial of shoe polish and applied it generously across the crusted leather.

"It's alright. It's a dead art, anyway. They're making those new sound pictures. Lots of old actors losing their jobs on account they can't remember so many lines of dialogue."

Eloy smiled and nodded, keeping his eyes focused on his task. He dismissed Archie's first shoe and brought up his other, settling it gently on the box. He rummaged through his tools, sifting aside a hammer, assorted nails, and a filthy sponge, until he found a fresh rag. He then set to scrubbing the shoe.

The wind blew fiercely as it tugged on Archie's sweater vest. A shiver ran along his limbs, turning his hairs all prickly. Now, more than anything, he wanted to disregard the whole idea. He wanted to nestle his tired body in his warm bed and forget the whole thing. He sniffled and regarded Eloy, unflinching as he toiled away. He wondered if he'd doomed Bobby to a similar fate. No. He shook the thought. There was still time to make things right. There had to be.

"All done," Eloy said, tossing his rags back into the box.

Archie's shoes glistened in the flickering light of the pier. They looked the way they used to when he was on top, when he used to be someone. He gazed on the poor boy. The wind blew tufts of his hair over his pale face. He was malnourished and scraping by in dangerous places no child ever should.

"Hey, Eloy," Archie said digging for change in his pockets. "Where's your family live?"

His cheeks flushed. "We don't have a home."

"Listen, I've got a nice, big house not too far from here." Archie bent over and placed a half-dollar coin in Eloy's box. "How would you and your family like to—"

Eloy snatched the hammer and brought it down against the back of Archie's head. All Archie heard was the wet crunch before the sound of the waves became muted. His skull throbbed and his legs buckled, sending his body collapsing onto the cold, wet planks. Eloy lunged at him and sank his teeth into his throat. Archie opened his mouth to scream but could only produce a wisp of vapor. The warmth of blood cascading down his neck brought small relief against the night's chill.

The flickering lights illuminated the twisted forms of a woman and a young girl crawling forth from the underbelly of the pier. They approached, snarling like rabid dogs, sets of fangs protruding from their mouths. Their faces were as gaunt and pale and hungry as the boy's. Archie stretched out a hand and tried to pull himself forward, but all strength had left his body. He thought once more of Camille and Bobby. He allowed himself only to dwell on the happy moments. Then, Eloy and the terrors knelt beside him, each plunging their teeth into his flesh, until the darkness greeted him forever.

# UNTOUCHABLE

by Tracy Davidson

Prohibition brought mixed blessings.

The creature preferred feasting on blood and organs untainted by alcohol—pure, piquant, natural...as human flesh should be—but...sober people didn't stagger down dark alleys late at night. It limited his options. His prey, alas, were mostly drug addicts. They tasted worse than drunks.

The creature had to emerge from the shadows if he wanted prime cuts.

Now he sensed something...the scent of purity, strength, sobriety. He ventured into the road.

"What was that?!"

"Sorry, Mr Ness. I think we hit an animal. Should I stop?"

"No, drive on. We've work to do."

# SQUEEZE ME DEADLY

## by Peter J. Foote

"Bennie, where have you been? Mario's been staring daggers at us for twenty minutes now, these folks won't buy his bathtub gin without the tunes!" Clyde hisses under his breath as his deft fingers pluck the strings of his bass guitar and a phony smile takes in the milling patrons of the speakeasy.

"Someone broke into my flop and stole my horn, man! I don't know what to do. I can't go back to my Pa's farm; that's a dead-end life," Bennie cries as he stomps up the rough plank stairs to the makeshift stage in the bowels of the warehouse cellar.

"What are you on about, man? Your horn's right

there. Some dude dropped it off a while ago, said you dropped it or something. You drinking your rent money again?" Clyde says under his breath before waving to the red-faced Mario at the bar, his fake smile dialled up a notch.

Ducking under lightbulbs strung throughout the cellar, Bennie hurries over to the leather case beside his stool, ignoring glares of bandmates, Gerry and Francis, as they smoke and wait for their trumpet player.

"This isn't my case," Bennie mumbles as he tunes out Mario and Clyde arguing at the edge of the stage. The black leather case with silver trim is superior to his battered brown leather, though the feel of the leather makes the hairs on the back of his neck stand on end.

Tugging his handkerchief from the chest pocket of his tuxedo jacket, Bennie wipes his fingers, but the sensation persists. As the voices at the edge of the stage become louder and angrier, Bennie unfastens the silver clasps and opens the horn case.

Instead of his surplus army trumpet, the one inside the case, cradled by red velvet, is an example of master craftsmanship.

The reflection on its silver surface from the low light of the cellar causes the trumpet to shine, emphasising the remarkable sweep and curve of its lines as if it were an organic artefact rather than something created by mortal hands. His fingers moving of their own accord, Bennie lifts the horn from the case. The metal is warm and pulsing like a gentle heartbeat.

"Snap out of it, man. Mario will do more than just fire our asses if we don't start soon. We'll be lucky to get out of a beating. You might not give a damn, but some of us have wives and families relying upon us," Clyde hisses into Bennie's ear and grips the trumpet player by the back of the collar.

"This isn't my horn..." Bennie starts, his voice faded and wistful as if coming from a dream.

"I don't give a damn. We will perform and give the people what they want and hope Mario forgets about the late start. Try to keep up!" Clyde snaps and nods to Gerry and Francis as they take their places at the piano and drums.

The first couple of tunes flow through Bennie as if in a dream; he sways back and forth, which garners odd looks from his bandmates.

*I've never played a horn like this before. Notes so crisp and sharp, it's as if it has a voice aching to get out.*

The song finishes and Clyde leans over his bass, cutting off Bennie's musing.

"You ok? You're acting a little odd, even for you."

"I'm good, just feeling the music. You having a hard time keeping up?" Bennie replies without looking up.

"We're doing fine, Bennie," Clyde says, his tone losing the kindness he had been rebuilding for the trumpet player. "This crowd is bracing to dance, and we need you to bring your best."

Bennie shifts to face his bandmates, the trumpet cradled in his arms like a baby, his constant swaying now imitated by the crowd of the speakeasy behind him. With eyes gleaming silver, and lips full and red, Bennie speaks, his voice distant, "I always bring my best, but tonight will be something extraordinary."

"Man, are you *on* something?" Clyde asks, but Bennie just laughs, lifts the trumpet to his lips, and turning to his audience, begins a simple melody.

Dismissing the other members of the band from his mind, Bennie closes his eyes and plays his last song. It opens like the steady rhythm of a heart out for a pleasant stroll, then the pace speeds up, and the trumpet takes over, sealing the fate of them all.

Fingers meld into valve buttons, lips fuse into the mouthpiece. Flesh and metal become one as the trumpet takes control and a tiny part of Bennie's brain recoils in

horror, unable to stop himself.

As the music quickens, so does Bennie's pulse, and he can see it mirrored in the audience as faces flush and sweat glistens on every brow. Try as he might, he can't halt the trumpet; it has seized his body along with those in the speakeasy. Everyone within the club is on their feet, dancing uncontrollably, even owner Mario with his two thugs in their expensive suits bulging with revolvers. From the corner of his eye, Bennie sees that his bandmates are likewise on their feet, dancing like puppets on a string while continuing to play their instruments.

On and on the deafening music plays. Waves of it reverberating off the bricks of the warehouse cellar and drilling into the minds and souls of the people captured by it. Faster and faster the revellers dance, sweat pouring down faces, eyes wide in fear, and still the trumpet demands more.

First, it's Mario who clutches his chest and collapses unto the sawdust-covered floor, legs still striving to respond to the orders of the trumpet until they, too, stop the dance. Mario's death is the herald of the rest; in minutes, waves of bodies join his on the teeming floor. Some have a clean death—their hearts simply giving out—others aren't so fortuitous as the boots and shoes of dancers stomp them to death.

All reason flees from Bennie's mind, and he views the floor of the speakeasy as it becomes awash in blood and sweat. The song of the trumpet dislodges his last morsel of sanity and he becomes a husk, a tool of the trumpet.

Only when, at last, the final reveller has collapsed and become still, does the body that was once Bennie the trumpet player stop his murderous song. Flesh separates from metal, fingers and lips reform, all evidence of their fusion with the murderous trumpet gone. Bloodshot eyes scour the cellar of the warehouse that is now as silent as a grave before fingers place the trumpet on the nearby stool. Its vessel spent, the trumpet releases the body, allowing it to fall off the stage to lie with the other victims.

* * *

"No one move, this is a raid!" a sharp voice yells as the door of the speakeasy splinters apart and a torrent of cops wielding flashlights and revolvers storm into the warehouse cellar to find a scene of horror.

Careful to keep his shoes out of the congealing pools of blood and sweat, Lieutenant Arnold examines

the masses of crushed and twisted bodies that litter the floor. Tiny footprints in blood prove that the rats were the first on the scene.

Wrinkling his nose at the stink, Lieutenant Arnold joins his Sergeant up on the rough plank stage, out of the chaos and the teams using stretchers to cart the bodies away.

"What do we have, Sergeant?" Lieutenant Arnold asks as he turns his back on the carnage, trying his best to ignore the sound of bodies being scraped from the floor.

"Don't rightly know, Sir. Drugs, maybe. Doc says it looks like their hearts burst. And as coarse as the bathtub gin is that Mario and his crew made, I can't believe it would be lethal enough to do this."

Nodding, Lieutenant Arnold finds his gaze drawn to the silver trumpet, clean and unmarred from the bloodbath around it, and can't help but pick it up. The metal is warm to the touch, and a slight vibration flows through the police lieutenant's fingers as if a bell had just been rung.

Crouching down, Lieutenant Arnold opens the black leather case and places the trumpet inside. As he snaps the clasps closed, the Sergeant says, "Sir?"

Standing up with the trumpet case tucked under his

arm, Lieutenant Arnold says, "My boy's birthday is next month, and his mother wishes him to learn an instrument, it's not like anybody here will have any use for it."

"As you say, Sir," the Sergeant replies, his tone neutral. "And the report, Sir?"

"Drugs sounds most likely to me Sergeant, someone spiked the gin, maybe a rival gang. Looks like someone did our work for us. You finish up here, I have paperwork back at the station," Lieutenant Arnold says as he steps off the stage, stepping through the sticky combination of blood, booze, and sweat, the trumpet case secure in his arms.

# THE BIG PRETEND

by Tristan Drue Rogers

She was black as the day she was born. It hadn't been many years since that birth and, although many had taken to calling her grown, she was in fact still a child. Her death wasn't a surprise to anyone, either. With exceptions to how it may have gone down, most would have only pinned a few more years to her marketed life expectancy.

The girl only knew two things: that her body was lying right there in front of her, completely lifeless from a blunt smack to the head, and that her momma wouldn't ever be told that she died with a baby in her belly. Also, that she never even learned what year it was because she didn't care. She did know what her price was, however. And one day, she was meant to be a dancer.

Okay, so she knew many different things according

to the laws of the world.

She didn't know what else she was supposed to do, so after a few dozen minutes of crying, she wiped her nonexistent tears and sat down, waiting for someone to come and get her. Her body wasn't doing anyone any good just sprawled out like that in front of that big white house, but she remained there for quite some time. It was daylight when she saw that static little girl surrounded by blood, and now the sun was about to tuck itself into the land for a good night's rest. This gave her no small end of worrying.

Normally, she'd do everything in her power to look her Sunday best every day of the week. That was what Mister Rusk told her to do. He was the owner of this farm and he helped to shelter her and her family along with a bunch of other black folks in exchange for work. He didn't pay too well, but, "It's easy to save money if none of us pay rent," her momma said. The girl would brush out her hair and sew any holes in her dresses, trying her best to look beautiful like white girls who have tea parties in the middle afternoon. The type of girls that Claire, Mister Rusk's daughter, fraternised with. The type that talk about all kinds of interesting topics under the same sun the girl had been raped under over and over again ever since she caught Mister Rusk's eye. That same sun that she was losing—that friend who was always with her, never telling a soul, even though it tried since it was so bright and all. At least those women would later have the fortune to dress themselves in shiny clothes for the night, heading out to the big city of Harlem to see jazz players and men who smoke cigarettes.

Mister Rusk would call what he did to her "The Big Pretend" since it was all about keeping quiet, no matter how good it felt. The girl never understood that, though. It never felt good. It hurt every time. And it hurt in different ways every time, too.

He wasn't due back from fishing for a few more days, so she wouldn't have to look ragged in front of him if they cleaned her up nicely for the funeral.

They were supposed to keep quiet so that Missus Rusk didn't catch them. She was a kind woman, but with a strong hand if you stepped out of line. Lately, she didn't do much except have Tall Joe do walkabouts, hollerin' and slappin' his folk that offended her. Whether it had to do with her sickness or old age, her realisation that there were no consequences to any of her actions, so long as they were against any of those whose skin colour didn't match hers, caused her to be mighty fowl when she had the inclination.

The girl finally mustered up the strength to stand up when the moon rose into the sky. It was awake and it was almost full, so a little empty. She took one last look at herself, noticing that her eyes, still open wide, were a little empty as well—the flies hadn't gotten to her yet, but the sun had burned them out; they looked like little black shadowy spirits that moved to the rhythm of the wind.

She looked up at an empty barn not too far across the dirt path before her. She had never been to that barn before, but it did seem to call out to her. It was brown and looked so small. Small enough to fit her spirit inside.

She couldn't smell anything along the way. She even tried as she passed by daisies, which were her favourite flowers due to them being yellow—which just so happened to be her favourite colour. Claire once gave her a yellow ribbon for her birthday. It was the most beautiful thing she had ever owned. It lasted a few days before Mister Rusk used it clean himself after he was done. She left it where it was, which at the time was right beside her, covered in dirt under that old sun. It stayed there for days before it just disappeared, probably swept away by Missy Meredith. She was a sweetheart and a dang good cook, too. Perhaps Meredith would miss her, she thought.

# TWENTY TWENTY

A group of black boys were inside the barn. It was bigger than it originally appeared. At first, she was startled by the look on their faces, right at her like a fox with a chicken in its jaws. Soon, she discovered that they were actually peering through her and at the barn door that finally swung closed after she opened it. They were all dressed in colourful suits that were a little worn down, but lookers the each of them.

"Did you hear that?"

"I didn't hear a thing."

"I saw that, right there, look!"

One of the boys that weren't spooked by the movement of barn door told them to hush up and offered them some more of Mister Rusk's homemade moonshine. That there moonshine was famous around these parts, but the girl was hard pressed if she knew how these black boys gotten their hands on it.

"It's nineteen twenty, boys," said the moonshine aficionado. "A new decade and a wild world we live in. Even the little women can vote on laws and presidents and such."

"Not our sisters," said one of the spooked boys after chugging down a half jar of moonshine. "They made sure of that this last August, so they say."

"So who says, Zeb?"

"Well, now, George," said Zeb. "I heard it on the radio. It says Southern states don't want no coloured girls voting."

"Probably for the best," said George. "Ladies are a delicate thing—too much thinkin' could cause them a big heapin' o' headaches. Hell—I'd say the same even for them white ladies, too, I says."

"Shoot, even Mister Rusk says so. I saw him smack Claire around when she was bein' mouthy." Zeb proceeded to replace his empty and foggy glass of moonshine with a slightly rusty trumpet. His hand and the instrument fit one another like a wet man wearing a glove.

The girl, realizing that she had been gazing too long, opened the barn door and walked back out onto the farmland. A few of the boys bolted outside, wide-eyed and lost at what they were privy to once again.

George wasn't too far behind, voicing his concerns along the way. "It ain't that dark to see, fellas, and the wind is too much perfect, so either we got us a spirit or someone is playin' an awful joke on us."

"Maybe we should go now. The walk to Harlem is mighty long anyhow and I'm already seein' double!"

"You right, we may just be staying out our welcome. Don't want no Mister Rusk to catch us

drinkin' his finest."

The boys packed their instruments and started walking toward the dirt road. One of the boys smoking a cigarette tossed the cherry off to the side, almost hitting the girl, and pulled out a clarinet. His arm was incomplete until he held it. He started playing, and the boys who could, did so, too. George even started singing. It was nice for the girl to hear. All in all, there were nine boys and four who could play. The girl figured only three of them could talk, but only two had the gumption.

She listened until they faded away like most excitement does. It was still dark, but not cold. The girl wasn't sure she could feel anything anymore anyway, so she walked back to her body through the grass and onto the bare dirt, finding nothing to notice no how. The body was gone and there was no blood to be found.

She thought a queer thought, but went ahead and did it anyway. The girl mimicked the resting placement of her dead body before it was moved. She looked up into the clear night covered in nothing but blackness and starlight. She wondered why she wasn't up there with the rest of the dead and she also wondered if this is what John Henry last saw when he beat that steam-powered rock drilling machine and died for the effort. The girl knew nothing about steam-power, but she did know that a black man bested a white man's machine and if that wasn't one hell of a story, nothing was. Again, she kept wondering. The girl held her hands up into the sky, controlling the cosmos with her fingertips, tracing the stars and planets, and creating new constellations. At first, she traced a cute little bow. Then, she traced herself. She traced and traced and traced the stars until the last figure she wrote was that of a baby, just between the Milky Way.

Momma told her that the Milky Way Galaxy is home to all kinds of planets and peoples and more marvelous things than anyone has ever attempted to describe and that even the Good Book hadn't come close to scratching the surface entailing all of its wonderful mysteries. The girl stopped what she was doing, lowering her hands, digging them into the earth. Once again, she wondered. She wondered why she wasn't born some other place. This place that she hated so damn much. This place that let a child go up into the heavens before it was born and that forced another to haunt the grounds where she was repeatedly abused.

The girl turned away from the night, instead looking into the many individual grains of dirt beside her. There was a calm that eclipsed her anger, covered by the muck that she knew so well, and so she gazed into it for a prolonged period of time, watching little bugs move around it. She noticed a deep imprint of that dirt, the size of her body, looking as though it was dragged from her death and into some other predicament.

Standing up, she followed the trail. Circling back around toward the front of the big white house, she saw Tall Joe in the dark beside her body sprawled out onto the dirt. Both Missus Rusk's husband's and daughter's motorcars were missing from the open shed beside the house. Mister Rusk took a big loan out from the bank so that he could obtain Claire a shiny new cab and she didn't let it gather any dust save from the big city. Missus Rusk was sitting in her old rocking chair and pointing her finger every which way, shooting words directly at his skull, to which he simply nodded, walking down the steps of the house and grabbing the legs of the girl's body. The radio came in and out, playing music against static.

For a time, Tall Joe and the girl walked with one another, sharing company with a lifeless corpse. The girl inspected Tall Joe like she never had before. The man's history shown on him like a beacon of light used to uncover criminals in the darkness of the city. He was tired of this life, yet he knew no other. Like many others that happened to have the misfortune of being born black and under servitude, Tall Joe closed the door on turning his life around. He preferred having a meal every night and a place to sleep. If he had to kill a few uppity black folk from time to time, so be it.

The tall grass shrouded them in a darker shade than before.

He took no leisurely time in digging a hole for the girl. That's just what it was. A hole. It weren't a grave and it weren't made to be comfortable for the passing of the corpse into the other side, either.

The thing is, the girl didn't know what to expect anymore as Tall Joe slid her body into that hole. The sound it made was something like *KERPLUNT-TCHUNK* as he kicked her down.

What transpired afterward was a thing of symphony. One by one, black folk from all around, different ages and different clothes, started to surround them. Tall Joe paid them no mind as he threw the dirt on top of her.

Attempting to speak, the girl was quickly hushed by an older black lady wearing a pretty golden hat. The golden lady said, "Be quiet now, girl. We tryin' to help you pass onto the other side."

They held each other's hands tightly, gripping and

steadily preparing for a strong force to brush against them from the stars. Those stars started burning with a deep and raging fire before the girl closed her eyes one final time. She heard the breeze and she heard the songs of the dead as she listened to her own soul for the first time.

The girl only knew two things: that her body was buried under a pile of dirt and that her momma would never know any of it. None of it. She'd probably still remain on the land, working for the Rusk family until her dying day. Also, she finally knew what year it was. It was 1920 and the year was almost up. Of course, she still knew her price.

Tall Joe set the shovel down against the tall grass.

She'd never be a dancer, but perhaps she could use her status in the afterlife as something more.

Okay, so she knew plenty.

Her little fingers began to wrap around the wood of the shovel. The girl lifted the shovel into the air. Tall Joe didn't notice anything, sitting down beside the grave, wiping sweat from his brow and breathing heavy.

"What a beauty is the night," he said.

*KERPLUNT-TCHUNK.*

She hit him upside the head over and over again. Her face was still, not a presence of life resting atop it.

*KERPLUNT-TCHUNK.          KERPLUNT-TCHUNK.*
*KERPLUNT-TCHUNK.          KERPLUNT-TCHUNK.*
*KERPLUNT-TCHUNK.          KERPLUNT-TCHUNK.*
*KERPLUNT-TCHUNK*

She found that breathing was unnecessary. As was sweating.

The girl dragged the shovel, blood leaking from it as if it were once alive, all the way to the big white house.

The spirits of old released each hand they held, watching her disappear into the tall grass. The girl heard one of them say that they should warn the others before they all get blamed for what transpired.

Before she made it to the big white house, sounds of doors slamming and sights of lights going on and off were overwhelmed by folks screaming and sights of blacks running toward the dirt road leading into town. They couldn't see her, but those that looked her way saw a floating shovel drenched in blood. She hoped her people were clever, too, and in the proceeding moments, they quickly proved that they were.

Missus Rusk was still atop her rocking chair. She was rocking back and forth with no rhythm and no soul with every care in the world that she had held onto her face. The girl dropped her shovel to find the radio on the porch. She placed her fingers over the knob and turned it to the only station she knew. It started playing that music that moved you, that sound that made you a dancing fiend, that play so good you could smell it, that good ragtime jazz band magic.

With her eyes popping out and her lips spread out real wide, Missus Rusk turned her head to the radio and uttered two words. She said, "Bayou voodoo."

The girl went back for her shovel.

Missus Rusk saw the shovel, floating in the night's air. She saw the droplets of blood scattering onto the dirt from whence it fell.

"Go back to the jungle you jezebel! You indelicate flower! You hussy dog!"

The girl smacked her over the head with the smooth end. The girl didn't know it, but this meant she wasn't going to die quickly.

Missus Rusk started twitching and the girl liked the vibe she was putting out, so she raised her hands in the air and started flapping all about. The music was blaring and the heat was just starting to rise when the police finally arrived.

All they saw was an old lady cradling a shovel. Soon they found Tall Joe and figured Mister Rusk had something to do with it. Funny thing was, his daughter

Claire didn't show up for a week. They asked where her daddy was, but she didn't have a clue.

When Claire finally arrived at the farm, she parked her machine in the shed and walked into that big white house.

Claire jumped onto her bed, made nicely and smelling of lilac. She put her face into the pillow and let out a big sigh before hearing "Crazy Blue" by Mamie Smith begun on the radio. Turning around, she saw one of her most elegant flapper dresses from the Boutique floating under the golden day light.

Together, they danced their lives away.

No pretending anymore.

# THE DEVIL'S OWN

## by Emma K. Leadley

Rose sat on Maggie's bed, turning her hand in the light to admire her nails as they dried. "It's such a good colour," she said, lips twitching up at the corners as she anticipated her friend's reaction.

"It's very…red," Maggie replied. "A girl can get a reputation far too easily, you know."

"It's just a bit of fun. Besides, it'll suit tomorrow night. You are coming, aren't you?"

Maggie looked down and bit her lip. "I can't, Rose. Only last Sunday, the pastor told us we'd go to Hell if we visited the new dance hall. He said jazz is the work of the devil."

"Since when have you been so religious anyway?" Rose watched Maggie's cheeks colour. "Oh. It's Eddie, isn't it?"

"Well, yes," said Maggie, flushing pink. She picked at her fingernails and still didn't look up. "And the name of the place isn't exactly subtle, is it?"

"Tell you what, I've already said I'll lend you a dress. Come with me to *The Devil's Own*, just for an hour, and if you truly think it's corrupting your soul, we'll leave." A wheedling tone entered Rose's voice, one she knew her oldest friend wouldn't refuse. Maggie inclined her head in a quick nod.

The following night, the two women walked towards the new dance hall. Gaudy lights strung across the signage, and when the doors opened, jazz tones spilled out into the street. Maggie grimaced, repeatedly smoothing the front of the borrowed mid-calf-length dress. Rose had given them both an up-do, with smoothed curls and sparkling headbands complete with feathers. "It's all the fashion," she'd told Maggie, before applying rouge and kohl to both their faces. "You'll get used to how it feels."

Feeling her friend hesitate, Rose linked their arms together and pulled Maggie along, slowing a little as she felt Maggie wobble in her unfamiliar shoes.

"Good evening, ladies. Entry for two is it?"

"Yes please," said Rose, turning to Maggie and grinning. "Just an hour, okay? Let's go have some fun."

The doorman pulled back the handle to the dance hall from the foyer with a sweep and they entered. A stage at one end was the focus of the room with bright spotlights marking where the musicians would stand. Booths lined the room and Rose enthusiastically pulled Maggie to one that was empty.

"Look, we can sit here and watch what people are doing. And I can go dance if you don't fancy it." She sat down and looked around, grinning broadly in anticipation of what was to come.

Maggie nodded, a slow up and down movement, as she started to look round. "I suppose you're right."

Just then, all the lights dimmed, and a man in a dinner jacket and bowtie strode on to the stage, spotlight on him as he twirled drumsticks in both hands. He took up a spot behind the drum kit and grinned before letting rip an impressive array of kicks and drum beats. Cheers and clapping filled the room.

He took the sound down to a low rolling drumbeat, and in the darkness of the stage, the outlines of other musicians could be seen moving into position. A double bass joined the drumbeat, the spotlights glinting off trumpet, sax and trombone. Rose gripped Maggie's hand in excitement.

A man in a velvet jacked strode to the microphone,

pulled it off the stand, and made his way down the side of the stage as far as the wire would allow. He stopped at each table to greet its occupants, smiling and shaking hands. The drumbeats stopped, and the man's voice boomed out in silky tones. "Welcome, ladddiiiiiiieeeeeeessss and gentlemen. What a treat we have in store for you tonight. Looking round, I can see we've got some fresh blood."

Maggie shivered. The compere stood at their table, staring at both her and Rose. After a brief pause, he ran back to the stage, fixing the microphone on its stand just in time for the band to burst into song. A blaring cacophony of trumpets and drums started, supported by the piano. At the strumming of the double bass, and the man in the velvet jacket starting to sing, the room was on its feet, moving and clapping, finding a common beat with each other and the stage. The music sped up and so did the dancers, whooping and hollering, ducking and swinging, the whole place coming alive like nothing the two women had ever seen.

Maggie clapped her hands over her ears and leant over to Rose, "I don't like this," she shouted. "It's not music, it's just noise."

"You said—" started Rose, as the music stopped for a pause. "You said," she said again, more quietly, "that you'd give me an hour." She frowned at Maggie and opened her mouth as if to say more but turned as she felt the seat of the booth move beside her. It was the singer from the stage, a mild sheen of sweat across his face, giving him a slightly other-worldly look.

"I couldn't help but overhear," he said, in a voice as smooth as molten chocolate. "You lovely ladies can't be leaving already. Just stay for one dance, and if you still don't like it, you can leave." He grinned, a broad smile showing off the whiteness of his teeth, before winking at Rose and sliding out the booth.

Rose gave him a coy wave, but he was already gone. "Oh, he's a handsome devil."

Maggie rolled her eyes. "You say that every time a man gives you any attention. It'll be the death of you, you know."

"C'mon." Rose pulled her friend to her feet and they made their way to the centre of the room, the band starting up again.

"I don't know the dances," Maggie started saying, but it was too late. She looked round to see what other people were doing, but everyone was moving differently. Some smooth and fluid, others jerking as though they weren't comfortable in their skin. Everyone somehow blending with the beat. She looked back to

Rose, who seemed to be in a world of her own. With hesitation, she started to move to a random beat and soon forgot her awkwardness as her body took over, shoulders dipping, arms waving, feet stamping, sliding into a euphoric haze.

The music stopped again, the musicians pausing between songs. "They must be as exhausted as we are," said Rose, breathing heavily, sweat gathering on her forehead. "I'm just going to sit out for a number and then I'll be back. Are you coming?"

Walking towards the booth, nothing happened. Her feet seemed glued to the spot and when she looked at Maggie, she saw her friend doing the same walk on the spot. It was as though they were both magnetised in position.

"I'm frightened, I want to go home." Tears formed in Maggie's eyes and she wiped them away with the hem of her sleeve.

Rose grabbed her hand, not knowing whether it was her or Maggie shaking. "Me too."

"Keep dancing, ladies and gentlemen. It's nearing the witching hour." The singer's voice boomed out, dropping to a conspiratorial tone for the last couple of words. The crowd "oohed" at his words. He looked directly at the two women. "Keep dancing."

The music started up again, and still holding hands, Rose and Maggie moved, finding themselves caught up in the spell woven by the band. It became more and more frenetic until the band cut out, playing a loud note in synchrony, the singer counting down over the top. "Three...two...one...midnight."

The dancefloor was pitched into darkness. Rose heard Maggie whimper and winced as she felt her friend's fingers grip her arm. The two women huddled closer together, and as quickly as the room had gone dark, they were illuminated under a spotlight.

"You're still here, ladies."

"You said we could leave," shouted Rose into the darkness. Her throat was tight and a tremble in her voice betrayed her nerves.

A laugh filled the room. "Yes, I did. But I didn't say how."

Grunts and shuffling noises approached them in the darkness, a scratching noise like nails on a blackboard, a clacking of far too many heels hitting the floor. A laugh came from directly behind them and the two women spun round trying to see the source, gripping onto each other tightly.

"Their eyes," whispered Maggie. "Have you seen their eyes?"

Rose heard her breathe faster and faster. "We'll be okay," she lied.

"I'm dizzy, Rose, I—"

Maggie's grip on Rose loosened and a second later a sickening crack rang out.

"Maggie?" Rose asked, voice rising in panic. "Maggie?" There was no reply. The spotlight swung to show Maggie collapsed on the hard dance floor, a halo of blood surrounding her head. Rose crouched down to her friend, feeling for a pulse and reaching for her hand. "Maggie?" she whispered.

The musician walked into the light. "My, my, looks like she really has left. Oh, and I did say fresh blood." He squatted down next to the two women, swiping two fingers through the sticky liquid halo before pushing them into his mouth. "Delicious."

He grinned, white incisors reflecting in the light, and winked, eyes glowing in bright red pinpricks.

Rose screamed.

"Oh, I thought you were made of stronger stuff than that." The musician shook his head. "I'm disappointed in you."

Rose scrambled away, slipping and sliding in the pool of blood until she froze in panic, exhausted and panting. A slurping noise came from the darkness behind and she shuddered. The noise approached until it—something—landed on Maggie's chest. A hairy insect-like creature with spikes on its torso and legs stood there. It flicked a proboscis onto Maggie's face and rasped upwards, rows of spikes splitting open the tender skin to channel blood up through transparent, straw-like growths on the surface of its tongue. It probed again, shredding Maggie's face until it pulled over her eye, stretching her eyelid up to expose her eyeball.

Rose couldn't even scream as it exploded.

More hideous creatures slid forwards, as though they'd been signalled. They slithered and clambered over the body to slurp at every drop of blood. Sharp teeth and claws ripped into muscle and sinew, the tearing noise deafening as they ripped it from the bone and feasted.

Rose vomited. More monstrous creatures crept forward, probing the emesis, and reaching towards Rose. She battled off the unknown attackers, hands and arms bleeding as they caught on unseen spikes and claws. Something coated her in fetid, stinking mucus and she vomited again.

"Having fun?" asked the singer next to her ear, his silky soothing tones in direct contrast with the horror.

"You…you…monster!" stuttered Rose, her hoarse

voice barely a whisper. "What have you done to Maggie?"

"You are in The Devil's Own, sweet Rose, and even Maggie tried to warn you. What did you expect?"

Multiple appendages wrapped themselves round Rose from behind, pulling her to her feet and higher. Arms trapped by her sides, she wriggled and squirmed but had no strength left to fight. Hot breath burned her neck and she was squeezed tighter every time she moved.

"Let. Me. Go." she panted, breath catching high in her throat as her lungs were emptied out

"Oh no," said the singer, scraping his slimy forked tongue up her neck and over her cheek. "I'm going to savour every single last little bit of you. You are now, after all, the devil's own."

# THE HEALER

by Drew Starling

The twenties were a time of change in the west, a little after 'the frontier' and a little before 'cowboy country.' Sometime inbetween. People've always called it 'wild.' I s'pose you could call it that. The moniker fits. I've been here all my life and it ain't never really been tame.

I was born on the very same day as our state. The fourteenth of February nineteen hundred and twelve. So, I guess that makes me about ten or eleven when it happened. When he came. I don't remember exactly. It's been so long now. Either way, I's just a tyke, and the important parts I do remember.

Over the years, I've noticed odd things tend to happen during times of change like the nineteen twenties in Arizona. It's almost like people aren't really lookin'. Too busy keepin' their eyes on the road, lookin' out for what's in front of 'em and not payin' no mind to what's up, down, or sideways.

It might be a bit fanciful of me to say that when the doors of time slide open, sometimes things slip through that aren't s'posed to. Our fella here sorta fits into that category. I never did deduce whether he was s'posed to be here or not. But he was here alright, so I guess there ain't much point in wonderin'.

Anyone who was alive back then is old now. Most will say they don't remember him. Always thought that was funny. I don't see how a fella could forget. No one's fault, of course. A lot's happened to our part of the world in the time that's passed. People came. Cities grew. Fields of catclaw and blue palo verde were paved into strip malls. Soon enough, the desert didn't look like itself no more. Lookin' back on it, them times felt like another world completely. If it helps people to forget the things they can't explain, well, I don't hardly blame 'em.

Always thought myself an observant boy, so maybe that's why I remember. I'd set outside for hours and just look. Watch. Listen. Dig my hands into that volcanic gravel and feel the dust slip through my fingers. Fill a saucer with sugar water, stick it the crook of a prickly pear, and wait for the hummers to come. Set out and watch the great big ball of fire in the sky rise above the floodplain and fall behind the canyon.

And so there it was one day. I set there lookin' at the sunset. An orange semicircle, its one round edge all a-flutter in the desert haze. Then a small, black dot appeared in the middle of it. I thought I was seein' things, because the dot was smack dab in the center of that sun. I thought, surely, ain't no way somebody could line it up that perfect. But I kept watchin' and the dot kept gettin' bigger until it wasn't a dot no more but the silhouette of a man on a horse, all black against the shadow of the night, ridin' through the bullseye of that sunset.

He came up through the quarter without commotion. Slow. A dark man ridin' on a dark horse, not so different than any other. 'Cept for one thing: on his whole person, only a sliver of his skin was showin'. It was that space between the brim of his hat and the bandana over his nose. I might be old now, but I still got my wits about me. I'm tellin' ya' here and now, the skin between the hat and that bandana was a deep blue, almost indigo, like a patch of desert bluebells. And his eyes was yellow, like a cat in the night. Oh, a chill run through me when I seen them eyes. I remember that 'cause the night was sweltering.

He didn't make no eye contact as he rode on down the quarter. Didn't even turn his head. But I hid there behind the porch and I watched him. I think I might'a been the only one who seen him come up, but I ain't the only one to see him that night.

I crept around the inn and peered through the glass. He entered, his back to me, and I seen the colour fly right off the proprietor's face. Guess he gave some more to this blue lookin' fella. Anyway, this old proprietor, Hoskins they called him, he looked at this blue skinned stranger with a fear I ain't never seen in a grown man. His lips quivered with whatever words he mumbled, none of which I could hear at my distance. I seen the man give Hoskins the tender and then watched Hoskins show him to the room. Simple as that.

The man stayed there that night and for two more nights after. He never come outta that room. Not one time. Hoskins stabled his horse, kept him fed, and took care of whatever needed taken care of. I heard someone ask Hoskins who it was. He couldn't even start to say. Word started gettin' around. Word of a 'blue man.' Even heard the term 'devil' thrown around, as one's liable to do 'round these parts. By that third day, a fever pitch had built itself beyond moral reason. Sheriff Jackson rallied his deputies to storm the blue man with yellow eyes, but

Hoskins held 'em off. And it's a good thing he succeeded.

It was the day after that when a posse rolled through from Phoenix. We hadn't seen one like it in some time. Must'a been fifteen or sixteen of 'em. Shootin' at this, yellin' at that. They rummaged through little towns like ours, lookin' for whatever gold and women they can gather. Sometimes, they'll kill everybody first and then go get what they came for.

These bandits entered from the floodplain and stormed the buildings one by one. Arlen Mannix was shot on sight simply for standin' up at the wrong time. They threw him plumb out the window and he died right there on the porch. I heard a woman scream. Then another shot, another scream. Then more. Sounds of carnage from all directions instead of just from the east where they come in. They engulfed the town. They ravaged us and they moved fast.

Me? I scampered on out the house. Ain't no use settin' in the bedroom, waitin' for slaughter. I took my sister by the wrist and we ran 'round back. We shimmied through the ocotillo bush and under the house to a crawl space just big enough for us kids. She closed her eyes, but I watched it all unfold. Somethin' I can't explain compelled me to do that.

In the midst of it, I became drawn to a point on the horizon toward the western line. It was the blue skinned man. He was just standin' there, watchin' same as I was, 'cept he was out in the open, almost like an invitation. One of the bandits drew his thumb-buster on him and missed. He fired again and missed again. The bandit looked at his gun, walked up to the man, fired again, missed again. I realised those bullets wasn't missin' before that bandit did. They were bouncin' right off, and he had the holes in his topcoat to prove it.

The bandit yelled somethin' sinister into the sky when he saw his opponent's blue skin and yellow eyes. The blue man stretched a hand forward and placed it gently on the bandit's cheek, and within seconds, the ol' boy just collapsed in a heap. I could hear the smack of his head as it hit the caliche. Blood come out his ear and that was 'bout it for him.

The posse seen what happened and they came down to him. The man with the blue skin stood still. Twangs and ricochets rang through the quarter. Two more came over to fight him, but he did the same as he done to that last fella. Just touched 'em is all. The life sucked right outta both of 'em, headin' off to Lord knows where.

You can imagine this was some sight. Pretty soon, the hollerin' stopped, and everybody just set there gawkin' at this man standin' out in the open with three bodies beside him. Then the leader of the posse come out. He drew, fired, and that bullet bounced right off, too. Sounded like it hit a piece of steel, but we's all lookin' at a man, a man with just a sliver of blue skin showin' and them yellow eyes.

The posse leader stepped closer, and quicker than a rattler nabbin' his breakfast, the blue skinned man thrust his hand clear through that posse leader's skull. I ain't never seen such a thing. That hand just went right through the face and clear out the back of his head. Sounded the same as steppin' on a pile of dry twigs. Just a bunch a little snaps all in a row like that.

Well, that there about turned the whole affair on its head. Whatever's left of the posse run off with whatever they had in their hands. Some of 'em escaped with their lives and that was enough.

The townsfolk looked at this blue skinned man standin' there. They didn't know what to make of him, and when he took a step forward, they gasped. When he kept movin', they ran inside, away from this otherworldly thing that just saved their town. He walked fine enough. Normal gait, a calm pace. He walked right up to the porch Arlen Mannix clattered onto when he got shot down.

The blue man, if you'd even call him a man, looked down at the heap of Arlen and knelt beside him. With the same hand he drove through that bandit's skull, he touched the wound in Arlen's gut and held it there for a minute. I swear on my mother's grave, Arlen Mannix just got up from where he lay no worse for the wear.

A woman come out from a shack with her young daughter in her arms. Dead. Shot by the posse. She ran like hell through the quarter and placed the girl at his feet. He stepped back and put his hand on the wound. 'Bout a minute passed when that girl opened her eyes and slowly got herself up. She looked up at the man, into those yellow eyes, and then she ran off screamin'. The girl's momma leapt up to hug the man, but he jumped back. He didn't want her to touch him. Seein' as how some people came back to life when he touched 'em and others dropped dead, I always thought it was his way of tellin' her not to take no chances.

The man stayed there on the porch as four more townsfolk brought him dead bodies. One by one he raised 'em. This boy a little older'n I was even brought his dog. Took care of him, too.

Sheriff Jackson, who was fixin' to kill this fella just a few hours ago, sat in the sun just bawlin' like a child. He come over to the man and asked him who he was,

how we could pay him, askin' what we could do to thank him. He made no reply. He just retired on back to the inn.

Even though we's all quite curious about the nature of this fella, people let him be that night. I guess that was his reward.

Well, everyone, that is, 'cept one person.

I don't know what got into me. Maybe it's 'cause I's the one who first seen him come into town, ridin' through that orange sunset. Sorta felt like I knew him. Aw, hell, I don't know. I was just a curious kid who couldn't mind his business.

So, I headed into the inn. I tiptoed up to the man's room and I set down there. Didn't hear no sound at all comin' from behind the door. I lowered myself to the keyhole and I seen somethin' through the hole in that door that eats me up to this day. Somethin' I…I still can't…

Well, I seen the man with no clothes on whatsoever. His back was to me, and I seen him just standin' there, not doin' nothin' 'cept starin' at the wall like he's in some kinda trance. The man was blue from head to toe and wasn't built like no regular man. His arms and legs were all skinny, his back looked completely flat and he had no buttocks really to speak of. Whatever clothes he'd had on musta' been piled up high on the inside to mask the real thing underneath.

Then he whipped his head around and glared at me. It was almost like a record skippin'; one second he's lookin' away, and the next, he's lookin' at me with them yellow eyes. His face was featureless. No mouth or nose or ears or nothin'. Didn't really even have a neck. Just them eyes. Them yellow eyes that looked like an animal's eyes. As if the rest of it wasn't enough, them eyes told me for sure, whatever I's gazin' up at was not natural. It was not from this world.

So, I scampered right on outta there and back on home. Reckon I've never run so hard in my life. The next day he was just gone. Didn't check out, didn't come down, didn't even open the door. Hell, he didn't even pick up his horse. His clothes were still in the room, but he wasn't. Just gone. In our lives one moment and gone the next.

For a while there, we called him 'the healer.' I guess that's what he did, but if you wanna put a body count to it, I think he did more killin' than healin'. 'Course we didn't complain. Then he sorta became like an urban legend. Some folk didn't wanna talk about it. Didn't wanna think about what they couldn't explain. I can appreciate that, I s'pose. What's there to say 'bout

somethin' that don't hardly make no sense to nobody?

I remember him all these years later. I remember our moment in the inn and the wild yellow eyes that cut right through me. Believe it or not, I still ain't quite made up my mind on the whole affair. Maybe I's young enough that I didn't need to ask too many questions. Maybe if I'd been older, it would'a been different.

I'm eighty-two now. The man with blue skin, 'the healer' as they say, came into my life seventy some odd years ago. I'd not seen him since, but I did ponder the whole ordeal quite often. And I ain't got no more answers than I did back then.

'Bout three or four days ago, I's settin' in the diner I've come to every mornin' for twenty-five years. My order's always been the same: eggs over easy, plain toast, and black coffee. Anyway, I's settin' there readin' the paper. Readin' about this mess they got over in Waco. Can you believe some fella started tellin' people he was Jesus and then went and shot 'em all up? I can't hardly wrap my mind around it.

Well, soon as I lifted my head up from the newspaper, I look down the row of booths and I see him: the man with the blue skin and them yellow eyes. Settin' there in the last booth all by himself. And what was he lookin' at? Me. Lookin' at me with them otherworldly yellow eyes. Hadn't felt them eyes on me since the inn. All them years ago. Well, I 'bout spit out my coffee when I seen that. Didn't think we'd ever cross paths again, that's for sure.

He just set there not movin'. I s'pose that's his way. Face covered up again, this time under a baseball cap and coat wrapped 'round his muzzle area. Lord A'mighty, I cannot tell you how scared I was. When the waitress come over, I asked her how long the man's been settin' there. She looked down, looked back at me, and said she kindly didn't get my meanin'. She ain't seen no one settin' in that booth.

Well, I come back the next day, there he was again. I come back this mornin', I see him again.

But then I started ponderin' somethin'.

I'm an old man. Wife passed back in eighty-five, Lord rest her. I started thinkin' maybe this fella come back for me and he's offerin' me, I dunno…a way out. I seen what he done to that posse back when I's a kid, and I s'pose it never occurred to me how quick it was for 'em. Here one minute, gone the next. Now, ain't that the way to do it? Ain't that better than lettin' the life get sucked outta ya little by little? That's how my wife went. Cancer. Tore her up and me up, too. I ain't been myself since. Watchin' someone die like that, well, it just makes

a fella wonder.

I s'pose tomorrow, or maybe the next day, or maybe next week, I might just set down in the booth with the blue skinned man. I reckon he'll be there. And I reckon that's why he's come, too. For me. This old man's body's got so much pain runnin' through it now. It's all busted from years of livin' a good life. A life he saved many years ago.

Maybe when I'm ready, I'll join him over there. Buy him a cup. Put my hands out on the table and look into his yellow eyes once again. See if he can't heal me.

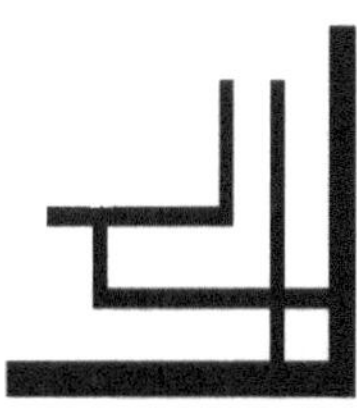

# WHITE WEDNESDAY

by Hannah Retallick

I saw you at the glittery parties, drowning in champagne, tassels spinning around your youthful thighs. I saw you with your fine suits and alluring smiles, excess seeping from every pore.

You dance back along the city streets in flapper frocks and sparkling costume jewellery. I watch from a hidden doorway, gun prepped and ready. It's been a long time coming, hasn't it, my darlings?

You say goodnight, enter your houses, and extinguish the lights. Sleep finds you in beautiful obliviousness, while I hide in shadows.

My name is The Great Depression.

I will destroy you all.

It starts tomorrow.

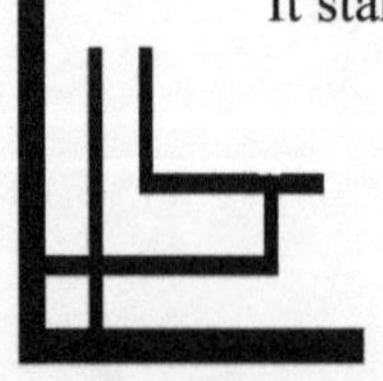

# A BLOODY PROPOSITION

by Stephen Herczeg

The hatch slid open and a pair of blood shot red rimmed eyes stared through.

"What you want?" said the gruff voice of the eyes' owner.

"I wish entry into this establishment," Lucien answered, a wry grin on his handsome face.

"Password?"

"I haven't received one as yet."

"Piss off then," the hatch shut with a dull clang.

Lucien was not to be perturbed. He waited a moment then knocked again.

The hatch slid open revealing the same set of eyes.

"What you again? I told you to piss off."

Before the hatch could shut, Lucien waved his hand before the gruff man's sight. His eyes suddenly cleared and took on a glazed quality.

"My dear Sir, I think you are mistaken. Regardless of my lack of password, you should give me entry to your establishment."

The gruff voice became more relaxed. "Yes. Yes, I should," it said. The hatch slid shut more gently this time, a moment later several locks were unfastened, and bolts withdrawn. The door creaked open letting out a waft of thick cigar smoke.

Lucien's expression changed to surprise as he regarded the extremely short and ugly man, who stepped down from a footstool and held out his arm in greeting.

"Please welcome to the Palais de McGee," the ugly dwarf said, "Make yourself at home."

*Oh, I thoroughly intend to.*

Lucien smiled and placed a coin in the short man's open hand. The dwarf looked at his palm, smiled and quickly pocketed the coin.

"Thank you, Sir." He closed and quickly locked the door before sitting back on the small step stool built into the back to await the next customer.

Lucien ignored him and strode into the thick cloud of smoke. A low stage in the centre dominated the room.

On the stage, two voluptuous young ladies danced with each other to the upbeat music from a swing band at the back of the room. Articles of clothing they had removed from each other, as their act progressed, littered the stage.

A full room of patrons sat drinking the booze on offer and eyeing off the girls on stage. Several topless waitresses walked amongst them, carrying fresh trays of drinks.

A bar ran along the wall farthest from the stage. Several bartenders poured drinks and placed them on the waitresses' trays ready for the customers.

*Wonderful, this is simply wonderful, more than even I could have imagined.*

As a young blonde waitress passed Lucien; her eyes flicked up into his. She smiled. He knew her job required affection for her customers, but as usual, he noticed something deeper in that smile. It was the way of the world for him. He had been blessed all those years ago in so many ways.

He sauntered across to the bar and vied for the attention of the bartender.

"Hello, my good man. I would like to see Mr. McGee," he said.

The bartender couldn't help but notice Lucien's

accent. Internally he wondered how an English ponce like this found his way into McGee's, but outwardly he knew his place with customers.

"You'd be lucky, Sir. If Mr. McGee wants to see you, he'll arrange that himself. Not the other way around."

"So, I just need to be noticed then?" asked Lucien in all innocence.

"I suppose so," said the suddenly confused bartender.

Lucien smiled broadly, "Righty oh, then!"

He turned and moved directly to the nearest waitress. Wrapping one arm around her waist, he crushed her against his chest, causing the tray of drinks she carried to slide from her hand and crash to the ground. In one movement, he brought her face up to his and planted a kiss on her pouting lips. She struggled in vain for a moment, then relaxed into the embrace as Lucien's allure began to work on her.

Within a few seconds, the object of Lucien's intention made himself known. A massive hand clamped down on his shoulder and swung him around. He looked up into a scarred and battered face.

"What the hell do you think you're doing?" the face said, before driving a ham sized fist into Lucien's

stomach and knocking the breath from him.

Another pair of hands grabbed his other shoulder and together they dragged him towards the back of the room. Several patrons dragged their eyes from the semi-naked dancers long enough to see Lucien disappear through the door and after a brief entrance into it, possibly out of their lives forever.

The two heavies lifted Lucien off the ground and dropped him roughly into a straight-backed chair sitting before a large wooden desk. A stocky man in his mid-fifties, with a lit cigar sticking out of the side of his mouth, sat on the other side of the desk. He eyed Lucien, with a level of disgust reserved, by most people, for the appearance of animal faeces on the underside of their shoe.

"Who the fuck do you think you are?" the man said, "I've never seen you before, but you waltz into my joint. No password. No entrance fee. You feel up my girls. Smash my glasses. Upset my customers. For what? You got a death wish or something?"

Lucien smiled.

*This had been quicker than even I thought possible.*

"Mr. McGee, I presume?" he said.

McGee's face screwed up in confusion.

"Give me one good reason why I shouldn't have

Harry and Bob here put you through the mincer and feed you to the pigs?"

"Because I'm going to be your new business partner," Lucien said, studying his nails with an air of one who couldn't care less about the threat of violence hanging over him. "I've come all this way just to meet you."

McGee's reputation had made its way across the Atlantic and into Lucien's ears in London. McGee owned ten speakeasies himself and the supply chain that delivered prohibited alcohol to another twenty around the city as well.

McGee spat, "Partner? I don't need no fucking partner."

Lucien stopped examining his hand and slowly stood up.

"To be honest, I don't think you have a choice," he said as he removed and folded his jacket, placing it neatly on the chair. "I've travelled from London. I want to enter the hospitality business. It seems to be a thriving enterprise," he said, removing his tie, and unbuttoning the cuffs on his shirt.

McGee sat back dumbstruck. He eyed the Londoner as he continued to undress and finally found his voice.

"What the fuck are you doing?"

Lucien stopped, an expression of surprise on his face.

"Oh, sorry, I assumed there would be violence soon," he said, removing his shirt and placing it neatly on the growing pile of clothing. "It's just I only brought a couple of changes of clothes with me and didn't want these getting too messed up or bloody."

Anger bloomed on McGee's face. Veins throbbed in his temple as his rage grew close to erupting.

"Boys! Kill this English ponce," he yelled.

"Oh, damn," Lucien said, looking down at the pants he still wore. Shrugging, he accepted the fact they were black and shouldn't show up too much blood.

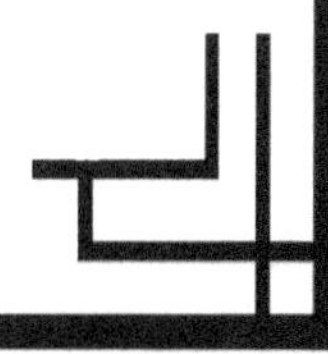

Harry and Bob stepped forward as one. Harry's huge hand caught Lucien by the throat and slammed him against the far wall of McGee's office. Bob stepped around the desk, knocking over Lucien's chair and spilling his neatly folded clothes onto the floor.

"Careful, I just folded those, you great clod," Lucien said, ignoring the crushing pain in his throat. Bob simply looked at the strewn clothing and kicked them away.

Lucien's face sprouted in mock anger.

"Now, you've made me mad," he said.

He reached out his right hand and grabbed Harry by the front of his shirt. He closed his fist, eliciting a howl of pain from the big man, as his fingers dug deep into the folds of skin and muscle beneath, tearing deep rents into the flesh and releasing a torrent of blood. Lucien picked up the bigger man and tossed him across the room. Harry slammed into a wall and crashed to the ground, grabbing at the gaping wounds in his chest.

Bob stared at his fallen comrade, then charged towards Lucien.

The Londoner opened his mouth in a broad sneer. McGee's eyes widened as he saw Lucien's canine teeth slide out of his gums until they were over an inch in length.

Bob hit Lucien like a freight train, both fell backwards and sprawled on the floor. Incredibly, the lighter Englishman lifted Bob's heavier body up like a feather pillow and threw him to the side. Bob crashed onto his stomach; the wind knocked out of him. Lucien jumped back to his feet and lightly stepped across to the guard. He wrenched him off the ground by the shoulders and dragged Bob's neck up to meet his fangs.

The sickly sound of skin and muscle parting from bone followed. A torrent of blood geysered out of McGee's henchman. Bob tried to scream, but only an insipid gurgle emanated from his mouth along with a stream of crimson. Lucien pulled his mouth away and spat a large chunk of red meat onto the floor. Blood poured down his chin in red rivulets. He dropped Bob into a puddle of his own gore with a resounding *splat* and turned his attention to Harry.

The big man stood nearby; his left hand clutched to the ruin of his chest.

McGee noticed and yelled at him, "Harry, get that son of a bitch."

Harry glanced over at Lucien. Pain lanced across his face as he stepped forward.

Lucien held his hands up. "Now, Harry lad, I don't think this is a good idea. You're almost dead on your feet. I don't want to hurt you any further, you could be useful in the future."

Harry tried to articulate a response but could only manage a growl. He took his hand from his chest and held both up ready to grab at Lucien. He rushed towards the Englishman.

"Fine then."

Lucien flicked out his right hand, the fingernails slid out until they were long daggers.

McGee's face dropped in shock. "Oh, crap," he gasped.

As Harry reached Lucien, the Londoner thrust his hand upwards into the larger man's chest, then forced it through and out his back. Blood vomited out from Harry and sprayed the ceiling. The big man's eyes grew wide, then dim as his life left him quicker than his blood.

Lucien held him upright for a moment while he withdrew his hand. He cocked his head and said, "Sorry about that mate, but I did warn you." He let go and Harry's corpse fell to the floor with a dull thud.

Lucien flicked his hand, dislodging the blood in a fine spray across the floor. He surveyed the scene, then turned his attention back to McGee. A wide smile crossed his face as he saw the horror and dismay writ large on the crime boss's face.

"Now, where were we?" Lucien said, pulling the chair back onto its feet and sitting down. He crossed his legs and indicated for McGee to sit down again.

"I believe we were about to speak terms," Lucien said, "I hope this little display is enough to convince you that I'm a man of my word. So, listen carefully."

McGee nodded.

Lucien ran his tongue across his teeth and fangs, licking up the gore that stained them and keeping his eyes on McGee's face. The other man cringed at the sight.

"From now on, you will work for me. You will sign over all your business interests to me. You will not try to have me killed or hurt, even if you could. If you don't follow my orders then what happened to your henchmen will be a circus compared to what I will do to your wife and your children, all while you watch. Do you understand?"

McGee swallowed on a dry throat then nodded.

"Excellent. Now one last thing," Lucien said, looking down at his gore streaked arms, chest and stomach, "Would you have a towel?"

McGee lifted a shaking hand and pointed to a doorway in the corner of the room. It led through to his personal bathroom.

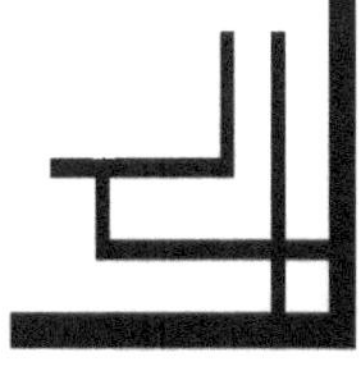

Lucien smiled, "Good, I think this will be the start of a very fruitful partnership."

# Blood Talkies

by Andrea Allison

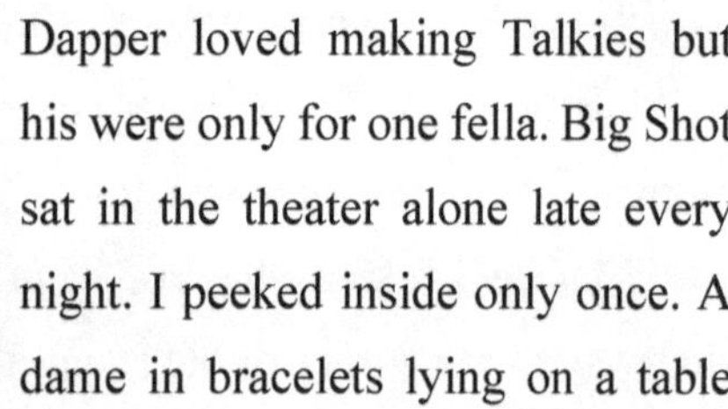

Dapper loved making Talkies but his were only for one fella. Big Shot sat in the theater alone late every night. I peeked inside only once. A dame in bracelets lying on a table being sliced open danced before my eyes. Never seen anything like it before. He laughed as her blood flowed and she went silent. The picture went dark soon after.

He stood and cheered. Dapper bowed and thanked him in kind. Before I let the door close, Big Shot spoke, "The broad's body?"

"Waiting for you at the joint."

I never looked at Dapper the same again.

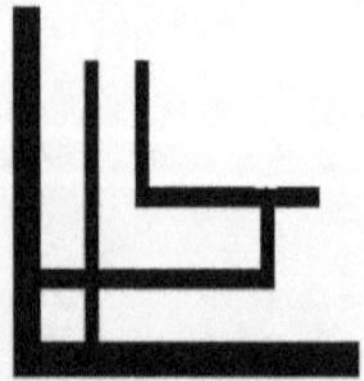

# An Odd Song

by Joshua Gessner

I ask for a drink by the counter, like one does in a place like this. It's the only reason a man might come at all, to a spot so gleefully despicable.

In truly troubled times, when a man can't order a drink, can't unwind, in a place touched by the sun, we've found somewhere else to deliver such pleasures; we call them speakeasies, blind pigs, blind tigers. They are called many things, many places, but in this corner of the world, where even the rats might eat with gold, people like it for another reason other than clandestine drinking. It's got talent. The best talent of all; that's why I'm here. I want to see the dancers dance and hear the singers sing. Ah, yes! The music, the singers! That is the talent I dream so fondly of. I'm not alone in this, of course; the room is packed tonight, as it is every night, and voices of crowds beyond my eye's desire, pile steadily in. Then the music starts to play and I ignore its tune, for I know from the first few notes that Sophie Tucker has taken the stage, singing a song I've heard a thousand times before. Now, I hang my coal coloured fedora, lean over the bar with one hand tucked under my old topcoat, and wait impatiently for my drink, as the bartender floods back into view. I am handed my little pick-me-up, and I know it is a simple one, one I strangely can't recall the name of. I take a nip of the thing and a slight grin begins to wash over me.

With every second I stand now, drinking from my glass, I somehow become more lucid, or rather, more confused. My eyes run across the room looking for an answer to how I arrived here, what drink I actually ordered, and where all these people wandered in from. It all seems a bit odd to me. I glance to my glass, which is empty, and grow curious as to how long I've stood here in this space by the bar. It feels too long, but maybe—maybe like people are sometimes—I'm wrong. I hope to be wrong, so I might stay a second longer in this place, gasping in wonder at all its magnificence, and not force myself out it's door. Finally, I decide to turn my attention away from these thoughts, and suppress them as best I can. My mind, instead, is entirely focused on the audible beauty for which I've come.

Then she appears, the woman of the hour, like a wisp of wind, from behind a curtain. With a black fur scarf, kind green eyes, and curls in her blonde hair brought together in a headpiece that looked like a crown from paradise, the owner of the establishment announces her arrival, but like any fool in love, I lose my will in her presence. Her name has gone somewhere in the audience. She moves with a sway that makes every man in the room wide-eyed, and I see a glimmer of her dress as it flicks its fringe about. It is silver and fine, and suits her well. She eyes the crowd and purses her rose-coloured lips, she's ready and awaiting the music. The audience, in fair wonder, does the same.

A burst of noise comes from the band. They find their footing, and every note begins to fall rightly after the other. I turn my eyes back to the woman and am met with her voice in song, a sound of audible silk that makes me swoon. *Quite a woman*, I think to myself. Then, between a short breath of hers, the music becomes peculiar. It sounds like a record hit a scratch. Then, to my surprise, it picks up and undoes itself. It…the band…is playing backwards, with a rather disturbing tune tagged to its hip, and I think that I am dreaming. Where has my head gone?

Then goes the woman, singing her song—whatever

it might be—in reverse. I feel taken still by her extravagance, but now am taken aback with a fair bit of caution as well. I wish to leave, but am glued to my seat, unmovable entirely. Her voice remains a beautiful one, and I marvel at this tune that makes my stomach sick. Witchcraft, is it? I do not know, but as I look around, I notice no one realising this sudden change; and so, in utter disbelief and with a sense of fear brewing within me, I give her my attention. While I look upon her, I see a thing about her appearance that startles me. I squint my eyes, hoping for some affirmation. Like a spotlight in a dark room, it suddenly becomes apparent. The skin of her face, the flesh of it, is drooping down, like lava running steadily to the base of its volcano, it drips. All the beauty that was resting on her is fleeting quickly, and I am disgusted. My disgust slowly plummets ever downward into repulsion though, as I begin to see flesh sag continuously off her body. A bit of muscle and bone begins to reveal itself on the woman as well, but she does nothing, she gives it no attention, she only sings, and dances, and melts.

I look to all the others in the room for help, because I may be drunk, or dying, or maybe she was. Around me, though, is only an audience who stares at her, ignorant of this monstrosity. They tap their feet, cheer, and smile.

The singer, her voice of beauty and body of beast, keeps singing quaintly, and as her voice presses further, the people themselves begin to melt right along with her; they still cheer, still stomp their feet, and they still drink, until puddles of flesh rest at their feet. Then, as odd as it might seem, I began to laugh hysterically, slamming my fists against the bar's counter.

When they said that a woman's voice can make you melt, I never knew they meant it literally.

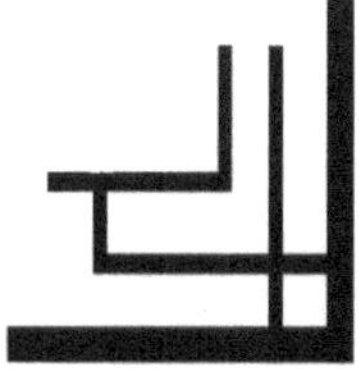

# The Guns Still Sound

by Will Christian

Why do I still hear the guns? Awake, asleep…they will not stop. The war to end all wars, and yet all I see and hear is the *woosh* of the shell and the *thump* of its landing. I still smell the metallic blood and brains spattered on my khaki uniform. Mates who were brutally torn apart, yet we carried on: *next one forward, soldier.*

Five years on, and the only way to stop the noise is to listen to them scream, the poor waifs and orphans that I catch and skin alive.

For a moment's silence in my troubled head.

# MOONSHINE

by Stacey Jaine McIntosh

The barrels full of rum sat three high in the middle of the room. Although cool and damp, the underground chamber smelled slightly of dirt and wasn't the perfect distillery, but it was the humans' only option.

Faeries despite their open dislike of mortals had one advantage when it came to trafficking illegal substances. They were invisible. Humans couldn't see them, not if they didn't want to be seen. A scant few possessed the sight. Which meant they could see the fey as they crossed from one realm into the other. Some said it was fey magick passed down through blood that gave them such an uncanny ability, but nobody really knew for sure how the sight happened, it just did.

Every two weeks, a new shipment of rum was delivered to the Speakeasy down on Lennox Street.

Faerie made oak barrels were just as easily hidden from human sight as the fey themselves, which made them the perfect bootleggers. And once in the Speakeasy, the cloaking magick faded and the liquor continued to flow freely. Almost as freely as the mortals ran their mouths and smoked expensive cigars.

Of course, nobody thought to mention that Faerie made rum also carried a high price.

Faeries were infamous tricksters after all.

So, when some of the more inebriated patrons started sporting donkey ears, the others knew something was wrong.

"Change them back!" Casey shouted over the live jazz music. "Now!"

A Faerie woman sat bound to a chair by iron chains, manacles wrapped around her slender wrists, her black lace fringed dress falling just below her knees. "I cannot undo magick I haven't wrought."

"Then summon the person who did!"

"I can't do that either, for I do not know who wrought it. Each enchantment has its own signature."

"Find out who it is, or so help me, you won't live to see the next shipment come through those doors," Casey growled, one finger aimed at the dimly lit entrance.

"I'm not a genie. I don't just blink twice and things appear instantly," she snapped before softening a little, and with her voice sickeningly sweet, she added, "But…if you release me, you'd find your rum free of all minor enchantments once I track down the culprits responsible, and your fellow patrons will be free of their newly acquired animal parts."

"If we release you, there's no guarantee the rum will keep flowing. And without rum, the patrons will get angry, and then they'll be riots in the streets of New York before too long."

"So, let the people riot," she cried. "Oh, what a sight that would be! I cannot remember the last time I was witness to a riot!"

"Witness, eh?" Casey scoffed. "You probably started it, knowing the likes of you."

"Careful lad, you straddle a fine line, you do. Offend me and you'll have more than a few pixie tricks to deal with."

"A dozen or more patrons with donkey's ears where their own ought to be is hardly a minor enchantment, Trysse!"

Trysse smirked. "Oh, but it is! You've yet to see what the fey are really capable of."

"I've seen plenty," he muttered. "But if the only

way to put a stop to this malarkey is to find whoever it is that's responsible then I suppose the only thing left to do is to have you take me to him."

"You want to go traipsing into Faerie?"

"Do you have a better idea?"

"Hey, Casey?" Jared called. "Have you seen Nick?"

Casey scanned the crowded cigar smoke-filled room. When he'd last set eyes on Nick, he was at the bar. But now there was just an empty stool.

He shook his head and then turned to Trysse. "I want answers. None of this half-truths bullshit. You know something. I'd stake my firstborn's life on it. Tell me what I need to do to turn them back. And tell me where my friend—"

His words were cut short by a fist to the jaw. He saw stars before the world around him went black.

Only when he woke up, he wasn't in the speakeasy surrounded by women in lace dresses, nor was Trysse anywhere to be found. Instead, he found himself in a dark room, chained to a wall.

The captor had become the captive. How utterly ironic.

And he wasn't alone. Two other men, dressed in what had been perfectly tailored suits, were chained

alongside him.

However, something seemed off about the two men. They hadn't met their ends, though it did seem close, judging by the sickly pallor of their skin.

It was then that he registered their missing jackets and the stains of red on their sleeves in the crook of their right arms, along with the thin tubes draping towards the ceiling.

He followed the lines to where they converged at a bag half full of blood hung from a hook on the wall.

But faeries weren't known to drink blood.

Casey shuddered at the notion that vampires were real. All the boogeymen of his childhood came to life in an instant then.

"Oh god!" he murmured, fighting off the urge to vomit. "Trysse!" he screamed.

Even though she need not help him, hers was the only name he knew, and despite her disdain for human life and the fact she was fey, she was the only one who could help him now.

"Hello, Casey," she crooned. "Glad you could join us."

"What is this place?"

"It's a blood bank."

"A blood bank? What do faeries need with a blood

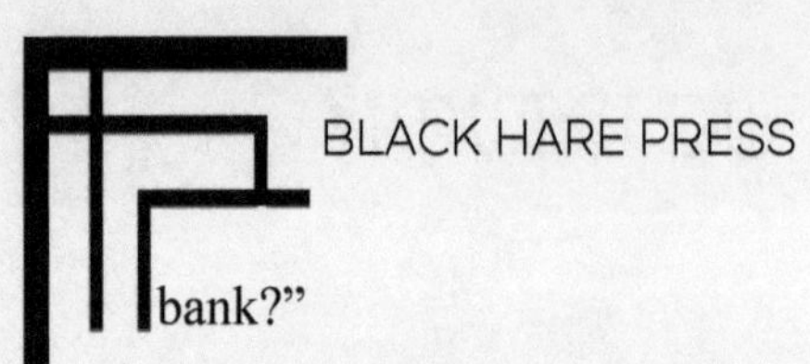

bank?"

"It's not for us," Trysse said haughtily. "Just as the distillery is not for us. But we make a lucrative profit off both. In return for blood, the vampires give us immortality."

"And in return for rum, humans supply the blood for the vampires."

"Precisely."

"So, am I to assume I'm the next sacrifice?"

"You tell me." Trysse rolled up his sleeve and jabbed the needle into his unwilling flesh. "You're the one with a needle in your arm."

Casey groaned. "Fuck!"

# THE PINCH

by M.A. Smith

An old crook once told me, your average man on the street was becoming so suspicious that if you tried to lift his wallet you'd as soon get a mousetrap snap shut around your hand as score a fat wad of cash.

It didn't stop me wanting to try, though, and Charlie The Barley knew all the tricks. He was an old school grifter and took great pride in imparting his trade to a humble apprentice, such as I was then. His area of expertise was agricultural theft, but he'd been a pickpocket since his childhood days and there was, to my knowledge, none better on the Jubilee Line. Seeing him at work among the pigeons as they barged and bolshed on and off the trains was some sort of poetry in motion. I couldn't get enough of it. And I was a fast learner. Time came that I was able to leave The Barley's tutelage and make a path for myself on the London streets.

I had a day job of course. Most of us do. You'd be surprised at how respectable we look. How much like you. But I had plenty of opportunity to ply my trade on busy morning commutes, or after work, as queues gathered outside theatres and galleries, and pigeons of culture were eager to flash around their baubles.

I invested most of my earnings; there was a guy I knew through The Barley called Mickey, who 'converted' jewellery or what-have-you into cash, for a not unsubstantial cut. The deal with this was I had to get to him within two hours of the lift. Now, you could ask, quite reasonably, how this fellow would possibly be any the wiser if I turned up with the goods half an hour late, a week late, five minutes late. You move in my circles, though, you find out sharpish that these sort of folks *do* know. And if you doubt it, get coy about it, try to push your luck the one time, you may find that your life alters from that point on. Maybe you start suspecting that someone's shadowing your steps as you mosey down the Edgware Road. You find your apartment door open one evening when you know you locked it that morning. Perhaps the next day you don't show up for your day job at all. And maybe the next week there's a new grifter

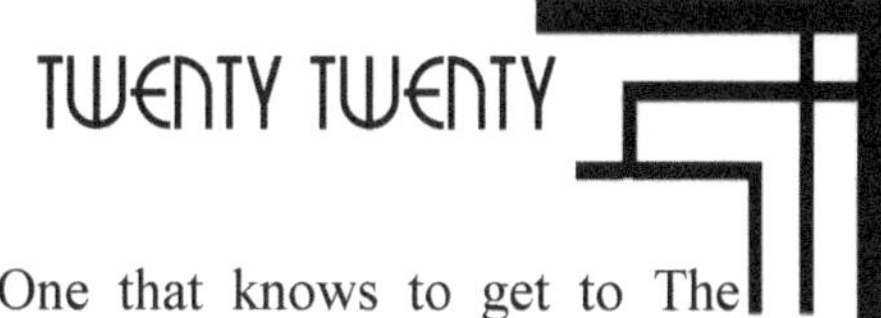

working your patch. One that knows to get to The Barley's man within two hours of a lift.

A summer came when, though, I was considering calling time on the City. I'd put away nearly enough in ready money to begin thinking about taking up the sort of rural life that involves shotguns and trips to muddy floored, over heated pubs serving real ale and pork scratchings that still have bristly little hairs attached to their rinds.

I talked to my broker and calculated that one more season should do it, saving at the rate I had been. I'd maybe have to forego some of my more expensive...'tastes' for a month or so, but I thought I (and a number of Soho's more charming residents) could live with that. You could say I upped production, and as autumn blew in, skittering leaves along Tower Bridge like the dried and brittle bones of dead mice, I found myself staying on the streets later, and covering patches I hadn't worked for years.

A smoky dusk was lingering over the city the evening that I picked the pocket of the woman wearing the red hat, in a side street off Piccadilly Circus. She was looking at the menu stuck to the window of the restaurant she stood outside of. She wore a long black coat, and above its rounded collar slithered a red tattoo that coiled around her neck to disappear beneath her hat. Its inky scales pulsed with her breath, a sinuous and intimate movement that troubled me.

I sensed promise though, so tugged my own hat a little lower, adjusted my scarf, and strolled slowly over to stand a few paces away from her, cupping my hands to the glass as I pretended to look into the restaurant.

After a few seconds I spun away from the window, feigning a sudden remembrance, mocked up a stumble, and collided gently with the woman. She instinctively moved both arms slightly up and out as her centre of gravity shifted, I put a hand on her arm to apologetically steady her, while my other hand slipped unnoticed into her coat pocket and lifted out what felt like a purse and a piece of jewellery. We both muttered quiet exclamations of apology, and parted. Done. Oldest trick in the book. I rounded the corner, without hurrying, and walked to the tube station.

I discreetly looked over what I'd hauled while I sat on the train, waiting for the Hammersmith stop to see Mickey about converting various bits and pieces from the evening's work. The red-hatted woman's purse was a nondescript affair with perhaps a fiver in change inside. I'd maybe read the pigeon wrong: happens sometimes. What I'd taken for jewellery turned out to be a strangely shaped coin. It was like no coin I'd seen before, though: made of steel or iron, it was three-sided, with a pattern of spiralling numbers on one face and a Medusa type figure on the other. The figure's face was worn almost completely away. It weighed much less than it looked like it should.

I tucked the coin away and swung off the train as it slowed to a halt. Tugging on my gloves, I noticed a fine reddish powder on my fingers. I stopped, and the human tide parted messily around me, surging into the street and dispersing into the London suburbs like dust. I pulled the coin back out, and saw what I'd missed before: that same red tinged powder clung to its three sides, impacted deep into the metal's tiny nicks and crevices.

It was full dark by then, and a bitter rain flickered in the cool orange glow of the sodium lights outside. I pushed the coin into my pocket, brushed my hands, hard, on my trousers, and hurried through the emptying streets to this grimy little lane between a newsagent's and an offy: not a place that shouted 'criminal underbelly of London.' Well, one wouldn't want to attract the wrong sort of notice.

I strolled into Mickey's 'office' feeling not quite as chipper as I maybe appeared. We conducted a number of transactions around items I had scored earlier that evening (although, you understand, well within the two hour window), and then I gave him the three-sided coin, fully ready for disparagement and hoping I could at least winkle a few quid out of him to compensate for the tube fare. Instead of doing either or both of these things, though, The Barley's man slipped into a mysterious little back room that I'd never been given the entry of. I could only make out the vaguest of murmurings as he conversed with an unknown associate on the phone. When he came out, he was pale, and I noticed, with a not unsympathetic jolt, how old he'd grown during the years of our business acquaintance. He may have taken me for thousands in cuts, but he wasn't a bad chap. Calling him a lovable rogue would be like calling a medieval castle's dungeon a bijou apartment, but he wasn't the worst. By far.

Mickey lay a brick of notes on the desk between us. I made it disappear.

"May be best to move your business elsewhere, son," he said to me.

"Making you look bad, Mickey?" I returned, a growing unease coiling in my belly and winding a long tail up my gullet.

"That's right, sweetheart. Making me look bad. I

hear Brighton's the place these days."

He produced a card from his sleeve. "Call this guy when you get there. Tell him my name."

With that, the old gudgeon retreated into the back office once more, leaving me bemused, but with the better part of two thousand nicker in my back pocket for that weird little coin with the Medusa on one side.

There being little else to do, I set off home to Northfields, still puzzling, and still with a slightly nauseating sense of disquiet. Opening the door to my apartment, I went straight to the bedroom and lay down fully dressed and shoed, my mind racing and my pulse not entirely steady. I was sure that sleep wouldn't pick the lock of my buzzing brain, but I soon found the light of my consciousness dimming to a fine point, until finally it was extinguished altogether, and I knew no more.

* * *

An old crook once told me, you only leave a job half done when either a copper's breathing down your neck or you get a better offer.

I wasn't getting any heat from the law, and I couldn't see a quicker way to reach my clichéd little cottage in the country but to carry on as was, so I decided to commit the whole incident with the coin to the nether regions of my memory and put Mickey's bizarre behaviour down to some sort of personal crisis. It was hard to do, though. Almost impossible. Especially when every morning I woke to find that same red dust on my fingers, no matter how many times I washed it off. Every single morning it covered my hands like pollen, leaving stains on my sheets and reddish rust around the basin when I sluiced it away…only for it to re-appear again the next day. I wore gloves to bed one night but discovered, on peeling them off at dawn, that same hateful powder on my skin, beneath the fabric. It was easiest to believe that I had developed an unusual skin disorder than consider the alternatives, and so that is what I did, even going so far as to procure a steroidal cream that I applied to my hands each morning, after removing the powder from my fingers. In this way, the top part of my brain, the more gullible part, convinced the wiser part underneath that everything was fine. That underneath part knew better, though. It always does.

The worst was to come. An awful, aching, *pinching*, sensation wracked my hands, so that, sat in the sterile office where I spent my days, I could, at times, barely force my fingers to curl around a ringing telephone. I began to suspect arthritis, as I watched the joints stiffen and solidify, like little fossilising corpses. Barely a week after the first presentation of these symptoms, I was working the pigeons pushing off the tube at Green Park, always a rich fishing ground as excited pigeons of the tourist variety were all glazed over with the thought of Buckingham Palace and all that old tosh. In hindsight, it was foolish, attempting a lift in the state I was, but there had taken root in my mind a kind of desperation, a weird feeling that perhaps if only I acted as though nothing had changed, miraculously, nothing would have.

It was a clumsy job, even without my mangled hands. The mark felt the jolt before my fingers even came into it and turned, all suspicion and hostility, looking at me with eyes that clocked my every feature. I only caught the clichéd, "What the—" as I melted back into and through the crowd. I sprinted on foot to the next tube station and caught the first train that came down the line. And what do you know, ended up back at Piccadilly Circus where this whole sorry palaver began. That my mind was far from clear is the only excuse I have for my footsteps taking me, as if following an unseen track from which there was no detaching, to the dark little side-street where I'd first encountered the woman in the red hat maybe a fortnight past. If I told you that she stood there still, right outside that closed up restaurant, as if she'd not moved since, you would quite rightly think that my mind had come loose under the pressure of my double existence, and maybe doubt the credibility of the whole of this tale. And maybe you'd be right; maybe I'm right now spinning my wheels in an institution somewhere, rattling on to an orderly about nicking wallets, women with weird tattoos, and an infinite red powder that covered the skin of my hands like an obscene dust.

Whatever the truth of it, I saw that woman standing there in the grey light, that fleshy snake tight to her neck and flashing now dull ochre, now silver to the beat of her pulse.

I came nearer.

My hands shook inside my pockets, and I felt the familiar ache intensify, so that it was like a foot stood on each, grinding the small bones beneath the skin and pulling, nauseatingly, at the tendons.

She turned her head to look at me, and I saw how the tattooed snake crossed her temple before sliding beneath the fabric of her hat. I can't explain this next part very clearly; the best I can do is to tell you that she began to talk to me, but her speech was in no language I have heard the like of before or since; guttural, and somehow meaty: animalistic. And that I was able to, in some horrific fashion, understand the sense of it. I realised, too, that, up close, I couldn't see her face clearly. It seemed to shift and swim and never come completely in focus, as if I were looking at her through spectacles with strong prescription lenses.

The essence of what she said was that old chestnut: "You have something of mine."

I held my hands out in a gesture I hoped would indicate that the coin was no longer in my possession. I also bought from my pocket, with withered fingers, a little pile of notes, and proffered it. "Please."

She touched my hands with hers, and the feeling of her skin on mine was so grotesque that I barely suppressed a scream.

Before turning away, she gave my fingers a last caress.

"Keep the change," she said.

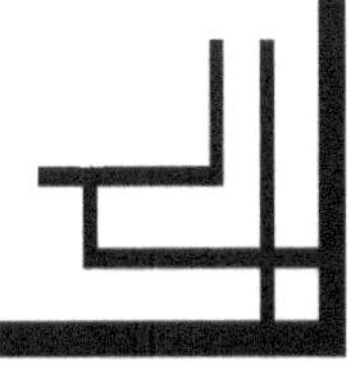

# ΠIGHT FLAPPER

## by Eddie D. Moore

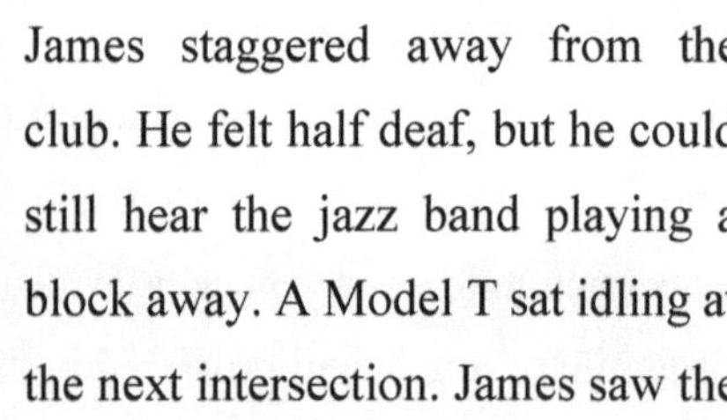

James staggered away from the club. He felt half deaf, but he could still hear the jazz band playing a block away. A Model T sat idling at the next intersection. James saw the driver studying a map as he approached the passenger side. He grinned when he noticed the driver was a gorgeous flapper.

"Hey, doll. That's a nice Tin Lizzy you're driving. Can I catch a ride?" He winked. "To your place?" Her smile made his heart race as he closed the passenger door. The fangs that sank into his neck a moment later was a complete surprise.

# DEATH WAS HER VOICE

by Chris Bannor

The joint was hopping as Mia made her way across the room. Prohibition made the speakeasy possible, but it was blood money that made her family thrive. Gin flowed like water into crystal cups and into parched clientele. They could drink all night, but it wouldn't stem the tide of what they really longed for though.

On the other side of the bar, guns and backroom alliances shifted power. The old money that had once run the city found itself on the edge of extinction with an insurgence of new money and new power. They were just a bunch of grifters and goons in her eyes, but she knew to keep her trap shut.

Except in song.

Her stepbrother ran the place. The liquor flowed, and the dance floor was full of footers showing off the latest dances. The city was on the verge of history, and it learned the new right and wrong inside these doors.

She slid past the dance floor and up to the bar where the bartender sent a hanky panky her way before she had to ask. She smiled at the man, dressed in his best digs and hair slicked in a respectable manner. He was still new, but he'd learned fast. He was just another up-and-comer in her brother's army of thugs, but more cultured on the outside. He treated her all right, so she wasn't going to dissuade her brother. She had her uses for thugs, the same as he did.

She sipped her cocktail and watched the regulars mingle and the newcomers fling themselves from one drink to the next. They were self-made men and women of the newest fashions. Not a drop of the old Blood in them. Not a drop of the Ancient.

Everything was changing, spinning out of control with this new age. Old money meant less, as gun and whiskey runners bought their way into society. She sneered at the notion, but her brother didn't agree. A man with no Blood, but he thought they needed young blood.

She ignored the press of bodies and the stench of mortality around her. It was inevitable, especially on nights she was going to sing. Tonight, she wanted the ignoble masses.

Her brother waved at her from the other side of the room and the band played the introduction that the regulars would easily recognise her by. The noise died down to a pleasant hum as she walked across the floor.

"Nice to see you out, Commissioner," she offered to a man at a table close to the stage. The mayor, as well as the police chief, were there, staunch supporters of prohibition during the day, but real boozehounds under the dim lights of the club.

"You're looking mighty fine, Ms Mia. I hope you'll save a dance for me?"

"What would your girlfriend think?"

"Shouldn't you be worried about my wife?"

She laughed. "Your wife is on a toot in the back room, but your girlfriend is sittin' two tables over, staring daggers at me."

"A man has his needs, Ms Mia." The table roared with laughter, and as she walked past, she looked over her shoulder.

"And boys will have their toys."

She didn't speak to anyone else as she approached

the stage, but she waved to a few regulars and people of notoriety. When she took her place on the raised dais, she watched as the bartender put wax in his ears. So did two of the doormen.

Her brother didn't notice, and she smiled at him as the music swelled around her. She crooned the introduction, the initial notes delicately coaxing each listener to lean slightly closer, to pay a little more attention.

By the time she sang the first chorus, she had enraptured the audience.

By the time she sang it a second time, they were ripe. As the band broke into a musical interlude, she smiled off to one side of the stage. "Who can butt me?"

A young man stood to bring her a cigarette, but another threw a punch to his jaw to gain himself the honour. The brawl spread quickly, men and women all throwing themselves at the stage to get closer to her, to perform the one task she asked of them. Her faithful three came forward and blocked the path so no one could get within reach, but she didn't fear the mortals.

She sang again, the band as unaffected as any real Blood would be. The riot became a massacre as her brother's guns tore through the crowd and gore splashed against the walls in vivid colours. Death was visceral;

on her tongue and in her voice and over her lips.

When the music stopped, her faithful three went among the fallen and finished anyone that still tried to catch a breath. The piano player held out a gun for her as her stepbrother tried to pull himself to the stage. She smiled as she pulled the trigger on the mortal who dared to make a Siren nothing more than a speakeasy songbird. She handed the gun away as the bass player offered her a hand to help her across the slippery floor. She carefully made her way behind the bar and pulled out a bottle of her private stock.

Red filled her cup as she poured for the band and the few thugs she'd kept with her tonight. She raised her glass, and they toasted together.

"To a great show, and new beginnings," she offered.

They laughed with her, drank their fill, and by sunrise her legend was established.

The mortals would never know the truth, but the Blood did. The Sirens ruled this town now. Death was her promise to those that didn't follow. Death was her promise to those that rose against her.

Death was her voice. She need only say the word and they would all fall.

# Prohibition Brings Everyone Together

## by Nikki DeKeuster

"A toast! To my good fortune and all you fine people!" Sam raised his shot glass along with the other scalawags. Cops and crooks alike took a table at the Blind Pig.

They didn't know him or why he was celebrating, but they were part of it now; everyone choking and clawing at their throats, unable to scream as his concoction sealed their fate.

It tasted like peppermint.

Sam poured his shot back into the bottle. "Waste not, want not." Smiling at the bartender's corpse, he

# TWENTY TWENTY

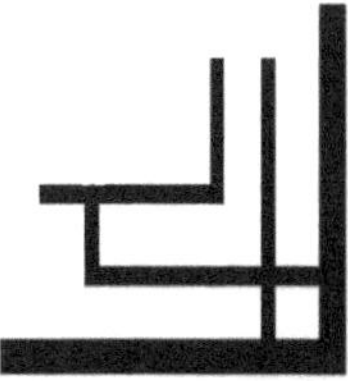

picked up his twice-illegal brew, tipped his hat, and strode away.

Next stop, Milwaukee.

# COWARD NO MORE

by J.M. Ames

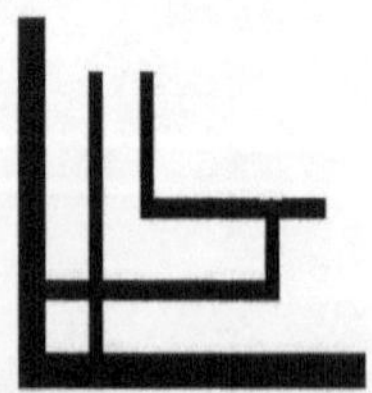

Zeke roared so forcefully, his mane shook and spittle flew from his fangs. Don backed away, feet unsteady from his dance with the green fairy at the speakeasy the evening prior. He barely registered the rage in Zeke's eyes before a tan paw shot out and flayed open his face, spraying crimson on the dancing Vaudeville Vixens. They, and the audience in the stands, shrieked in terror and scattered. Zeke paid no mind. He bit down on Don's neck and shook—hard. The snap of Don's bones let Zeke know the whippings he had endured for years were finally over.

# THE COST OF DIAMONDS

by Catherine Kenwell

"Oh, it's the *bee's knees*!" she gushed as she pulled the needle-beaded dress from its paper wrapping. "Thank you thank you thank you!"

Agnes ran to her fella and threw her arms around his neck. "Oh baby, I can't wait to wear it!"

Big Joe smiled and hugged her, carefully balancing his cigar between his left fingers and his old-fashioned glass in his right hand. "You're welcome, baby, you're gonna look swell in it. Big Joe has to treat his best dame with only the best, and lemme tell you, the thing has real diamonds sewn into it. Anything for you, doll."

Agnes hurried back to the box and picked up the

dress, scouring it for the decadent gems. "Diamonds!" she gushed, holding the ornate frock up to the light. "Real diamonds! What a lucky gal I am!"

"Listen, babe, I gotta go finish some business," Big Joe said, bringing Agnes back to earth. "Why don't you get dolled up, get your glad rags on, and we'll head to the casino when I get back. I wanna introduce you to some of my colleagues."

"Gee, Joey, that sounds fine," Agnes replied. "I'm always ready to hit the town with you, Big Boy."

Big Joe slapped down his empty glass, bit his cigar, and slipped on his overcoat. The garment concealed the gun holstered at his waist. Without a kiss, he let the door close behind him.

Agnes grasped the heavily adorned dress in her hands. It was weightier than most gowns, although it was the new sleeveless flapper style—straight and above the knee. It *was* gorgeous, she thought.

But her mind wandered to Big Joe. She knew Big Joe was second only to the mob kingpin, and 'finishing some business' often meant making a deadly deal or 'finishing off' a rival or a rube who was causing trouble. She gazed at her shimmering gift and wondered where the money for it came from. She sometimes had a difficult time reconciling the big bear she adored with

the crime boss she knew he was.

Big Joe kept Agnes in silk dresses and t-strap shoes, and was generous with jewellery and meals out on the town; at first, she didn't question his gifts, and she believed him when he told her he was a regular successful businessman. But she was puzzled as to why he always carried a gun, and why sometimes he'd come home with what appeared to be blood spatter on his suit jackets.

He'd eventually confided in her that he ran a bootlegging ring, and that the ring was part of a bigger 'corporation'. When she'd dined with some of his business partners and their gals, she was struck by the attention and bend-over-backwards service they always received. They were big shots, like movie stars—and Agnes was awestruck by the excitement.

Her parents would be so disappointed to discover she was a gangster's moll; when Agnes took the 'El' from Chicago to visit them in their stately Oak Park home, she was careful to wear the plainest of her frocks, and downplay her vamp-like makeup. She was a wealthy girl by birth, but her new riches gave her a thrill she couldn't get from her family. Her mother and daddy, meanwhile, believed Agnes was working as an assistant editor for *The Chicago Daily News*. She wasn't about to tell them anything different.

Agnes tore herself from her reverie and set out her adornments for the evening; slinky silk stockings, silver t-straps, and sparkling crystal chandelier earrings…and of course, her diamond slip-over dress.

As she slipped her gossamer stockings up to her garter, Agnes anticipated the evening's events. They'd head to the casino where the cocktails would be free-flowing. Prohibition didn't mean a thing in mob circles, except for the fact that they were getting rich from it.

She slid her feet into her delicate t-straps, crafted from the finest Italian leather. They were like butter on her soles. Agnes hoped there wouldn't be talk of take-downs or rub-outs tonight. She felt more than a little guilty knowing that her Joe-bear mighta offed someone to pay for the evening's revelry.

Finally, Agnes lifted her needle-beaded shift over her head and let it slide down her lithe body. It fit perfectly and fell to an inch above her knee. Wow, she thought as she gazed in the full-length mirror, she looked like the cat's meow. Each bead shimmered and reflected a tiny version of her image. The only problem was, it was a little itchy, as if the beads were slightly poking her in places. Never mind, she thought, she'd get used to the heaviness and any discomfort would glide away once she'd downed a couple of gin-laden South Side Fizzes. More often these days, Agnes found she needed to down a few drinks before she was comfortable with the dubious celebrations the gang gathered for.

As she clipped on her gem-flickering earring drops, Big Joe burst in.

"Ready, baby? We're celebrating the ultimate deal tonight!" he exclaimed. "We're in the money now, doll, no looking back!"

Big Joe stopped in his tracks and dealt a loud wolf-whistle in Agnes's direction. "Look at you, Miss Cat's Pajamas! Wowee zowee, you're somethin' else!"

Agnes knew how glamorous she looked, and she felt proud to be heading out on Big Joe's arm. But she avoided asking what the ultimate deal entailed; her stomach felt a little nauseated and when she bent down to grab her fox stole, the diamond dress prickled uncomfortably.

The casino was in full swing when they arrived. The big jazz band was already playing, and white-gloved black waiters were bowing before taking orders.

"A round of Fizzes," Big Joe bellowed. "Hell, make it two rounds—we're more than flush tonight!"

Agnes slipped into the leather banquette and placed her hands on the lacquered table in front of her. As she bent to sit, her dress poked her skin at the waist. The beads felt like real needles, digging into the backs of her thighs.

Thankfully, the waiter arrived with their cocktails and set two at each place. Agnes picked up her first Fizz and downed it. She needed the numbness the alcohol would give her.

The boisterous conversation around her was of no consequence; all she could think about was the beads jabbing her thighs, her belly, her chest. She couldn't cry with complaint, after all, she was wearing the most expensive, most luxurious dress in the place.

Big Joe hugged her from the side. "That's my gal, enjoy yourself! You deserve everything I can give you, Dollface!"

The hug drove the needles further into Agnes's skin. The pain was excruciating. Her head spun. *I...deserve everything...she heard. Ill-gotten gains...proceeds of crime...who died for this....* The guilty words danced around her brain. "Blood money," she murmured, words delivered unintelligible. *I shoulda never...I...deserve...* her mind continued.

Big Joe stared at her, noticing her bewildered expression.

Agnes looked down at her diamond-needled dress.

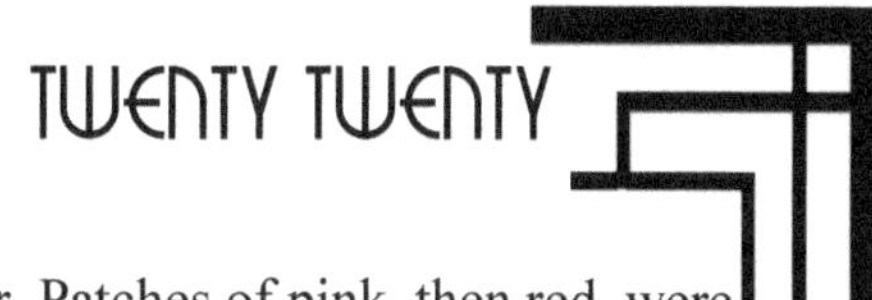

Her eyes popped in fear. Patches of pink, then red, were blossoming through the beaded fabric. The dress was stabbing her with every slight move.

The woman sitting across from her shrieked in horror as the dress transformed to poppy coloured. Agnes pulled at the neckline, desperately trying to tear off her dress. Her tears loosened the kohl from her vamp-lined eyes, and coal-coloured streaks ran down her pale face. Her crimson lips were open in silent scream.

Big Joe grabbed her in his arms, not realising his actions drove the needles deeper into her. The longest of the diamond beads scratched her ribs and poked through to her lungs. He tenderly wiped the blood running from her nose.

Big Joe held her limp body against his, unconcerned that his fancy suit was becoming drenched in her blood.

"I'm sorry I lied, Mother and Daddy," Agnes whispered. She looked into Big Joe's frightened eyes. "Joey, please don't tell my folks I was a gangster's moll."

# St. Valentine's Day Massacre

by Dawn DeBraal

The Twenties were roaring. The States weren't at war.
Booze was illegal contraband liquor worth more.
The gangs took to Chicago, to sell their bootleg,
Many a man shot and killed for a keg.

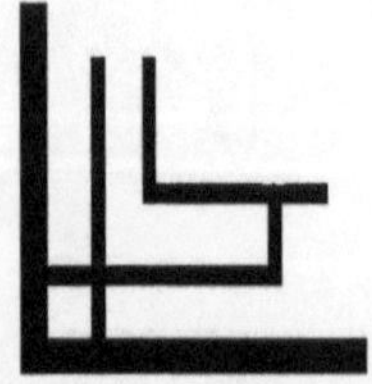

#  TWENTY TWENTY

Flappers, they danced in feathers and beads,
while selling their bodies to fulfil the men's needs.
Machine guns and autos, gangs prowled the street.
When violence erupted, they died on their feet.

Lining them all up against the back wall
In a hail of bullets, each man did fall.
Seven men dropped to the floor where they lay,
Shot in the massacre of Saint Valentine's Day.

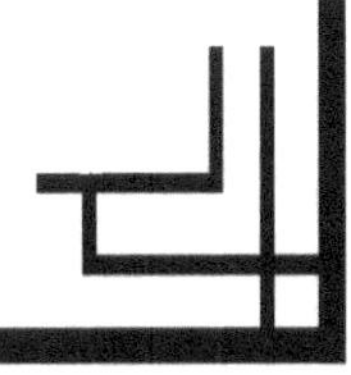

# BODY PARTS

## by Andrew Kurtz

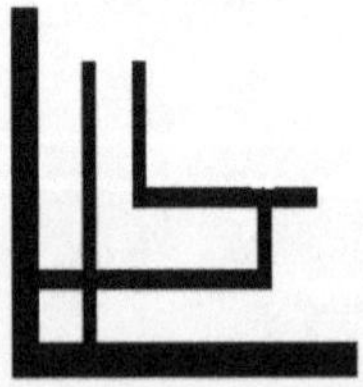

The seven bodies were brought to the laboratory of Doctor Kilmo. Five were members of Bugs Moran's gang, and two were not.

"Remove all the heads, arms, and legs. Bring me the jar of their dried blood from the warehouse where they were unjustly murdered," Kilmo ordered his assistant.

Five hours later, a monstrosity composed solely of seven heads, fourteen arms, and fourteen legs stood in front of the doctor.

"First, seek out the two police imposters who murdered you. Bring the dead bodies back to me. More monsters will soon be born." Kilmo laughed.

# STRAIGHT TO THE BONE

## by Gabriel Hart

It was 9:30pm when Jacob Schick jumped, startled by a fierce knuckle-rap at the door of his office in the building of Magazine Repeating Razor Company in Stanford, Connecticut. Working overtime after his employees left for the day, he was over-caffeinated and thin-nerved as he put the finishing touches to his big deal with American Chain and Cable Company—it would be the most lucrative contract he would sign in his life. Whoever it was at the door, he was already sure it was the last thing he needed.

Before he could react, they knocked again.

Harder. Louder.

His chest tightened as he stood, shaking his head.

He opened the door to three men that looked more upset than he was. The one in the middle wore a strapped-tight German leather trench coat under his black Fedora, which he lifted up to reveal his piercing gaze. The two flanking him wore black slacks, white button-ups, their ties at half-mast.

"Can I help you?"

"We shall see how this goes," said the German. "My name is Johan Henckels, heir to the Zwilling J.A. Henckels company. As you know, we are the makers of the world's finest straight-razor."

"Ah ha, that's great!" said Schick, his mood lightening. He assumed this was no more than a poorly-timed international elbow rub to talk shop, so he perked up professional. *Germans and their wacky time-zones,* he thought.

"Would you like to—"

Before he could invite them inside, the three pushed past him.

"Mr Schick, these are my American colleagues from Proctor and Gamble who make many fine products. Specific to this visit, I will note they provide the best quality shaving creams, soaps, and badger-hair shaving brushes."

Schick reached out his hand to shake. The two men nodded, hands remaining in their pockets as they rocked back and forth on their loafers, impatient.

"All right, gentlemen. Great to have you here. What is it I can do for you?"

"Mr Schick, first of all, we are concerned," said Johan. "Concerned that you are making men...soft."

"Soft?"

"Yes, your magazine razor patent. It was unfortunate enough for our company when the safety razor was introduced, but at least men were still at one with the blade when changing them out. While I admire the fact that you were once a colonel and your magazine strip blade replacements resemble a clip for a classic repeater rifle, the problem is that men don't get to handle the blades anymore. Not only has it hurt my company, but you have helped erase a vital part of masculinity in our morning ritual."

"Sure, well... it's a lot safer. No more getting cut, that's why it became so popular."

"Yes, but you are making them scared of their own grooming tool. In addition, you've grown so arrogant by the success of your product that you are going a step further. We understand that you are about to forge a substantial deal with American Chain and Cable?"

"Correct, to patent the world's first electric razor!" He beamed. "I can show you the prototype right over at my desk..."

"That will be unnecessary, Mr Schick. Now, we also understand that while it's electric, it is also being called a 'dry razor.'"

"That's right," said Jacob. "No more soap or brushes to get in the way." Realising his faux par, he looked up at Misters Proctor and Gamble and his sales pitch nose-dived.

"Aha, you're starting to understand why we are here," said Johan. "Mr Schick, while I commend you on your invention, I'd like you to think very hard about what that means for the future of our companies."

Jacob could feel his pores giving hard birth to cold sweat.

"I...I'm not really sure what to say."

"Have any contracts been signed yet?"

"No, that's all happening tomorrow."

"Oh, good. So, we still have a chance," said Johan, finally cracking a smile.

"A chance for what?"

He hadn't noticed the Proctor and Gamble guys at his sides until they grabbed both his wrists, holding them behind him like a downhill skier.

"What the—"

"Mr Schick, when was the last time you had a real blade against your skin?"

"I...I...I don't know. I..."

"I'll take that as so long you can't recall."

Johan pulled out his own personal Henckels Solingen blade from the inner pocket of his jacket. He slowly put it to Jacob's straining neck.

"You see, the thing with an electric razor, is that they serve only one purpose—shaving. And not very well. Is it true that the electric razors will actually *stimulate* hair growth, as it cuts just above the surface of the skin? Like right about here, like this?"

Johan hovered the blade, barely touching Jacob's flesh, so it just skimmed the flecks of his incoming growth. Jacob's whole body shivered as he tried to scream through the hands over his mouth.

"Well, sometimes the old ways are the best ways, Mr Schiff. The way the straight razor gets the closest shave..."

He pressed the blade into Jacob's bulging jugular, flesh pillowing around the metal.

"... getting right in there, deep...to the real root of the problem!"

He swiped diagonally, unzipping skin to a crimson-flood. Then, the same slash of pre-emptive vengeance on his left, the rip briefly interrupted by Schick's collarbone before he gouged it back in for a third. Jacob's life ran down his neck from both sides in a heavy, pulsing deluge. Hands remained over his screaming mouth to muffle his protests, following him all the way down to the floor. His eyes grew wider until the pleading ceased.

"I think there is a bathroom down the hall we can use," said Johan, pointing the way out of the office to his two accomplices.

They closed the office door behind them and walked down the hall, entering the bathroom. They turned on the hot water. One of them pulled out a bar of Proctor and Gamble Ivory Soap, and the other presented a shaving brush which would be perfect for getting deep under their fingernails.

# THE LIQUID LUCIFER

by Galina Trefil

Nearly forty years ago, after her husband's complete collapse into the world of the bottle, Carrie's grandmother, Maggie, had joined the so-called "Women's Crusade." While she'd roared and protested, sung hymns and held public prayer events against the "devil's poison," Maggie's husband continued to do as he pleased up until his liver could take no more. Forevermore, Maggie had brought his unpleasant demise up as a lesson to all who would listen.

Raised on this story and the many other unpleasant ones bandied about by the Women's Christian Temperance Union, even as a child, Carrie's future husband's sobriety had been of the utmost concern and importance. Ernest had been quiet, religious, and serious. He hadn't seemed at all the type to drink. Oh, the many secrets that one discovers only after getting married…

It wasn't long after they tied the knot that Ernest began taking his fists to his young wife. Afterwards, as she lay sobbing on the floor, Carrie couldn't help but think to herself that the incident had been exactly like all the tales that other women had related. As he beat her, Ernest had reeked, positively stank, of liquor. His face, a massive, twisted, flame of red flesh, hadn't even looked like the man she knew and loved. This hair-trigger temper wasn't him. It was that stuff, that vile stuff, which he'd swallowed! And when she told him so later, he quickly agreed, yes, of course it was the drink. Of course, *he* would never hurt her. It was the booze; just the booze. And he promised that he'd never ever touch it again.

But he did. Touched it again and again and again, in fact. Eventually, he stopped even bothering to go through the standard lies, apologies, and pleas that she forgive him.

"You must find some way to get through to him, Carrie," Maggie insisted over tea one afternoon. "The bruises may be on your face, but Ernest is also suffering. He is intoxication's prisoner; indeed, its slave! Only when you free him will you free yourself."

Maggie pointed out a few Biblical passages which Carrie might instruct Ernest to read with her later. Carrie looked at the Good Book which lay between the two of them with miserable skepticism. Perhaps this method would have worked on other men, but all of these passages were already familiar to Ernest. None of them had penetrated his psyche enough to make him stop.

"Be strong," Maggie instructed. "It takes tremendous strength to triumph over the Liquid Lucifer. Don't forget, your namesake Mrs Carrie Nation, was not afraid to enter a saloon with a hatchet in order to destroy its bar and all the contents too. I sincerely hope that you find the courage to follow in her footsteps."

Carrie winced. Her grandmother did not appear as sympathetic about her physical condition as she had hoped she would be. Carrie had heard, from time to time, of women leaving their husbands on account of this very problem. But it wasn't legal. Though more women sought to divorce in Carrie's day than they had in the 1870s, when Maggie had been young, there were still only three reasons which would result in a judge dissolving the union: adultery, bigamy, and impotence.

Maggie tilted her head to the side, her wrinkles creasing as she frowned suspiciously. "I think I know what is going through that head of yours… I always can tell, my darling. You see all these irresponsible hussies abandoning their vows and you think that you might want to do the same." Carrie swallowed, lowering her eyes. "Ah, yes, that's it. For shame! There never has been a divorce in the history of this family and there never will be, at least, not while I'm breathing! The day that I hear of such a thing happening is the day that I fall down dead."

"Grandma, times have changed. Many women today are much happier for having divorced. They remarry easily enough and—"

"Yes, I know the awful state of things!" Maggie snapped. "These modern times breed Godlessness like mutts breed fleas. But not in our family. Not you, Carrie. You can't have a divorce! A little beating now and then isn't worth throwing away your dignity like that. You think that women whined like this; aired their dirty laundry like this, in my day? No! They bore their suffering with poise, morality, and, above all, respectability.

"You girls these days, with your short, revealing dresses... Putting rouge on your kneecaps so men will look more at your legs. Wearing swimsuits not big enough to swaddle a baby in. I've seen you do it, Carrie, so don't even deny it. You may have met Ernest in church, but you certainly have never presented the proper, nice image for him. So, if he's drinking, what do you expect to happen? Husbands can only take their nose being tweaked so much before they become jealous."

"You're saying this is my fault? I thought that it was his fault because he keeps coming home from the speakeasies."

"It is not necessarily your fault, no. Nonetheless, I am sure that there are many things which you could do which you have not yet done. Dressing more modestly, for example, could certainly do you no harm."

"What would Carrie Nation have said regarding that?"

"Carrie Nation was called to Jesus in 1911," Maggie huffed. "She never lived to see our country's young ladies display themselves so vulgarly. Had she endured the changes of the past decade, such as I have, I assure you that she would have had indeed voiced a great deal of condemnation on the subject."

"So, she would have blamed my beating on my dress, rather than Ernest's drink?"

"She would have told you not to divorce. Divorce has only ever been a means through which men may exercise undue control and abuse of women. They use it as a threat, knowing the financial and familial ruin which ensues for divorcees. Such beasts treat their wives no differently to how they would a painted lady. A terrible trick has been played upon the girls of your generation, propaganda really, which has convinced them to believe otherwise. Only after the sorry legal mess has concluded do those female unfortunates begin to realise the depth of their own ruination. At that point, poor things, there is nothing to be done for them. They have dug their own graves…and enthusiastically too!"

"Ernest hits me so hard, Grandma. I don't know how I can stand it."

Maggie sipped her tea, giving it thought for a few moments. "After leaving the saloons, these 'speakeasies,' as you call them, does he walk home or does he stagger?"

"He walks, I suppose."

"Well, dear girl, be grateful for that much at least. Not only may he yet be saved, his and your reputation may be protected as well. Many an unhappy wife that I've known would have given anything if only her husband could present as sober when he was not... In the meantime, on the days when Ernest's resolve has slipped, do not go on any errands. While there are certainly many women in this town in the same circumstances as yourself, they see no need to advertise their domestic difficulties and nor should you—"

"But I haven't," Carrie protested.

"A revival is coming to town two months from now. Make sure that Ernest attends. Perhaps it will help break him of these chains which bind him."

"Surely, Grandma," Carrie finally snapped, "prohibition did not become drafted into law through prayer alone. There must have been stronger methods used!"

"Oh, most certainly," Maggie nodded. "As I said, our great leader herself employed very harsh measures. But what good would such brutal soldiering do you? If it were illegal for Ernest to drink, I might advise the planning of his arrest. Unfortunately, the law does not bar the actual act of drinking. Tell me who sells Ernest his liquor and I promise you, Carrie: your grandma will see that both the manufacturer and seller are sent straight to the jailhouse for their part in this."

"I don't know who they are. He won't tell me."

Grandma Maggie nodded. "Well, take heart. Sooner or later, they will be caught. And all the nefarious things which they did, all the sleazy profits which they made, yes, everything that led to those black and blue marks on you, that will cost them, Carrie; cost them dearly. A fine which might take their life savings and more, plus five years in prison. They'll walk out a starved shadow of who they were, with not a nickel to their names. And, for the Hellfire which the two of you were made to walk through together, you and Ernest will only be stronger."

That night, as Ernest repeatedly kicked Carrie in the stomach, she found herself thinking afterwards that her grandmother and the other ladies of the temperance meetings were wrong; maybe had been entirely wrong from the beginning on this issue. So many wives were positive that, if only not for the alcohol, this would stop happening. But was Ernest's smirk above her truly a result of the little fermented monster? Was it that monster taking the sick and sadistic pleasure at the sight of her pain?

Perhaps Ernest was just a bastard. Perhaps all these husbands beating their wives were just bastards, and together they had conspired to avoid consequences for it by inventing the monster. After all, any woman that even minimally loved her husband would be so keen to believe that something else, something truly beyond the men's control, was making them act so hatefully.

Carrie felt stupid; brainwashed by the movement. "Take away the drink and end the beatings," had always been said, in a thousand difference ways. But even in the beginning, there had been WCTU members that had said that, even when the alcohol was gone, their husbands still acted every bit the part of drunks. They still had the rage. They still had the irresponsibility, both professionally and to their families. Sometimes, the husbands pulled themselves out of it, but many women had reported this act of drunkenness would go on for many years.

Bleeding and broken, Carrie knew that, even if Ernest stopped drinking this very night, she didn't have those necessary years left. At the rate that he was going, he'd wind up killing her before then.

There was no preacher's sermon, no weekend revival, no Gospel passage, which was going to make this situation change. Only Carrie could change it. But the law was not on her side. If she tried to leave, she knew that none of her friends or family would be either.

Divorce had only ever been a dream; something done by the women in other states and other counties. This was a small, rural town. It wasn't just Carrie's family that had never had a divorce here. Among the locals, none were divorcees. And Carrie knew that, if she went the uncomfortable road of being the first, the fallout would quite likely lead to her having to leave the area. Could she move far away to the big city? Embrace a culture, another side of America, so different from her own? Perhaps other girls would have, but Carrie wasn't that kind of brave.

Wiping at the blood dripping down her chin, she stiffened though. She wasn't *that* kind, maybe, but she was *some* kind. Tonight, by God, she vowed, was the night that she took matters into her own hands. After all, women in these parts had always, when pushed to the limit, taken it upon themselves to handle such business privately.

Dr Adams had never been the most scrupulous individual in the first place. He cared little, one way or another, about prohibition in the second. As a child, he'd briefly treated Carrie for asthma—a condition which she had outgrown, but also one for which medicinal whiskey was known to be prescribed. Carrie insisted that her asthma had returned. Did he believe her? Did it matter? It wasn't the first liquor prescription that he had found himself filling out. He appreciated the added income, as so many doctors did, that such prescriptions brought him. As for Carrie, she now had the means to purchase a pint of alcohol every ten days.

She had it waiting on the table for Ernest when he came home from work. "Please," she begged. "Just don't let my grandmother find out. She'd be so angry."

"How did you get it?" He marvelled, reverently caressing the bottle as though it were a lover.

Carrie explained. "Marriage is difficult, Ernest. You and I both need to try to make the best of things. You haven't been very happy, I know. I'm going to try harder to make sure you're happy."

Well, now, that certainly sounded good to him. She watched as he drank. And drank. Carrie's regular contribution wasn't enough for him, so he still travelled to the speakeasies. Nonetheless, the apparent peace offering smoothed down some of his ruffled feathers. The beatings still came, but Ernest became more aware that Carrie's appearance was important. If she looked battered, picking up her pint from the pharmacy might be more troublesome. He began to try to at least avoid her face when the violence came.

Maggie did find out, eventually, what Carrie was doing, and when she did, she delivered the slap to Carrie's countenance that Ernest was no longer delivering. "How could you?" she shrieked. "How could you betray our values like this?"

"There's plenty of women whose problems weren't fixed by prohibition!" Carrie yelled back at her. "I'm going to survive this marriage, by any means possible. And I won't be ashamed for it either!"

Afterwards, the two women, for a great while, stopped their visitations with each other.

Everyone knew that too much alcohol could destroy a person. A few were even dissuaded from their bad habit by this, but not the truly determined drunks like Ernest. Oh no. Those fellows were always so sure that a severe decline in their health would never happen to them.

Well, it was going to happen to Ernest. Tonight.

Drop. Drop. Drop. *Drop!* Four drops of methanol in the medicinal whiskey, placed neatly in the centre of the table. Oh, but how Ernest looked forward to the days when he could just come home and have his hooch without having to risk anything by going out. Immediately on walking through the front door, he kissed Carrie's cheek and then, like an elated and ravenous wolf, he set upon the bottle. Four drops, Carrie observed, soon became four generous swigs down his gullet. He smiled at her and she smiled right back. After all, she wanted him to remember later that she was smiling right now.

Would he be blinded by her first attempt to take his eyes? She didn't know, but she was willing to do this again, as many times as it took. True enough, Ernest could die in the process, but she hoped that he didn't. A lifetime of disability and the suffering that it entailed seemed incredibly fairer to her at this point, however his demise *was* a risk worth taking.

No one, including Grandma Maggie, ever even considered Carrie was directly responsible for Ernest's ultimate, pitiful misfortunate. After all, to further enforce the rapidly failing state of prohibition, the United States government had announced that they were increasing the concentration of methanol and benzine in the products which moonshiners used. All across the country, thousands of drinkers were going blind and, in the worst of cases, even losing their lives.

Big Sam was to blame for Ernest's terrible agony; not the battered wife…or so it was believed.

*How strange was life?* Carrie noted. The law body that had granted her no protection and ultimately no rights, through its own mass maiming and murdering of its own citizens, had provided her with the very means of escape which she had needed. How many wives, she questioned, in similarly horrid and helpless circumstances, had used the same route with which she had freed herself from violence? Impossible to say, but one couldn't help but wonder.

The only thing either way which Carrie was sure of

was that perhaps the fanatical Miss Nation had been, at least occasionally, correct. Some women used prayer. And others used hatchets.

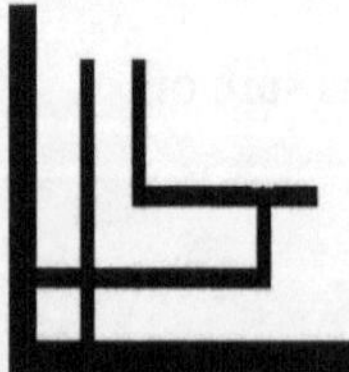

# LEAHY CASTLE

## by D.J. Tyrer

"This one was not like the others," Liam said, spitting blood as O'Rourke drew back his foot to deliver another kick to the prone man while the others watched, impassive.

"Now, don't you be lying to me, son. You're one of the gang who've been burning 'big houses' in this district."

"I don't deny it. I don't deny it."

O'Rourke held his foot ready as the young man cringed on the floor of the empty stone room.

"But, this one isn't like the others."

The CID man relaxed. "What are you blathering about, boyo?"

There were plenty of different reasons offered for the destruction of the 'big houses', Ireland's mansions and castles; that they belonged to the Anglo-Irish landowners; the Imperialists hated by the Republicans; some were home to the Free State senators de Valera's mob were trying to overthrow; that their owners were accused of being spies and informers. But the truth was always the same; a desire to sweep away the old order in favour of the new. O'Rourke saw no reason to expect anything different from his lips.

"It's about the evil," Liam sobbed.

"What the hell are you talking about?"

"It's a local superstition," said Father Mulhoney, cigarette quivering on his lip as he spoke. "A silly peasant superstition."

It had been the old priest who'd tipped them off that a gang intended to torch Leahy Castle. Empty since the death of the old Baron a few years before, the castle had been earmarked as a potential barracks for National Army troops in their battle with the Republicans—one the Irregulars would love to deny them.

O'Rourke sniffed. "What do you mean?"

"They say the Baron and his ancestors invoked the Devil here. He used to hold séances and dabble in the occult. The peasants believe an evil remains trapped within these walls."

"We have to destroy it."

The rest of Liam's gang had either died or run away, but they'd caught him setting dynamite in the cellars beneath the castle. The old tapestries and paintings stank of the petrol with which they'd been doused. The gang had been determined the place be destroyed.

"Night is falling." Liam groaned. "We must be gone soon."

"I don't share his superstitions," said O'Leary, O'Rourke's number two, "but, we should leave soon if we want to get back to town."

The civil war, as a straight conflict, hadn't lasted long, but whilst the army controlled the towns and cities, the Irregulars moved at will through the countryside, ambushing forces loyal to the government.

"Very well. We can take the lad, here, back to Dublin tomorrow for some further interrogation. Go get the van started."

O' Leary nodded and stepped out of the room.

"Smith, McGuinness, bring the prisoner."

The two plain-clothes CID officers grabbed hold of the prone man's shoulders and dragged him to his feet and out after their boss.

O'Leary met them at the entrance to the courtyard, expression grim.

"The van won't start. I keep turning the damn crank handle, but it just won't start."

"McGuinness, you know about these things."

"Sir." He nodded.

"Go take a look at it with O'Leary, see what you can do."

"Sir."

Liam gave a liquid laugh, blood dribbling down his chin.

"It won't let you go."

O'Rourke cursed at him. "I don't want any of your nonsense." He tapped the bulge in his pocket that was his revolver and nodded towards the door behind which were piled the bodies of three of Liam's cohorts.

Liam spat a curse back.

"Boys, boys," said Father Mulhoney, hands up as if trying to placate a pair of squabbling choirboys.

"We have to leave," said Liam. "Forget your van. If we walk it, we might make the village by nightfall."

"And, say 'hello' to a merry band of your pals? I don't think so, boyo."

O'Leary returned and his boss looked at him expectantly.

"No luck. Van still won't start, no matter how hard we crank it. McGuinness took a look at the engine—the

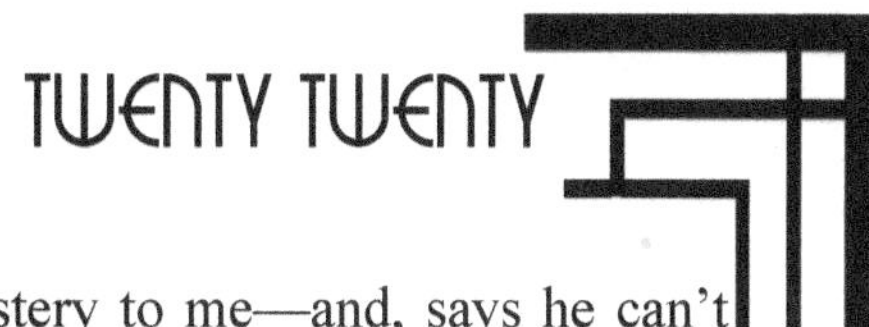

thing's a complete mystery to me—and, says he can't find anything wrong with it."

"We have to leave—now!"

O'Rourke laughed. "Oh, yes, you'd just love that, wouldn't you, son?"

"Yes, I would. I'd love to be gone from here before it's too bleeding late."

"Well, it ain't going to happen. O'Leary?"

"Sir?"

"Go barricade the gates, make it difficult for anyone to get in. Use the van, if you can shift it."

"Sir."

"Then, we do the same with these doors, before finding somewhere to lock up this little traitor and a place for us to kip down."

"Is that wise?" Father Mulhoney asked. "I mean, this place *has* been soaked in petrol. If they come and try to burn us out..."

The old man shuddered in his cassock.

"I'd rather take my chances behind stout stone walls than try wandering about country lanes in the dark, surrounded by assassins, Father."

"Fair point."

Liam shook his head. "Well, if we're staying, is there any chance of the good Father taking my

confession? I don't value our chances of surviving the night."

"Sure, damn you. Back in there –"

He had Smith drag Liam back to the room with the blood-splashed floor where he'd been interrogated.

"We'll be just outside…"

O'Leary and McGuinness returned after a few minutes, carrying their rifles.

"The gates aren't much, sir, but we managed to push the van in front of them. We can drag some furniture over to block the door and, if we smash that window there, we'll have a fine view of the courtyard and gate, in case anyone manages to break through."

"Get to it."

"Sir."

Father Mulhoney stepped out from his makeshift confessional.

"All yours."

O'Rourke nodded. "Are there any other ways in or out of the building?"

"There's a small door from the kitchen, I believe. Let me show you."

"Smith, stand guard over the prisoner."

The burly CID man nodded.

The kitchen door was easily blocked with a

cupboard and the heavy kitchen table and O'Rourke felt pretty confident nobody would get in that way.

What he took to be the drawing room seemed the most-practical place to settle down in. He lit some candles and tossed some blankets, from the van, over the chairs so the petrol splashed on them wasn't soaking directly into their clothes. Although a little musty, the room was comfortable enough and close to the entrance, where O'Leary was taking first watch through the shattered window.

McGuinness had settled down for a snooze on a chaise longue.

An old oak wardrobe, dragged in from another room, was serving as a simple cell for Liam, its doors tied shut with twine. O'Rourke sat opposite with his revolver ready in his lap. Smith sat nearby

"We have biscuits, Father," O'Rourke said, "but our only drink is whiskey. Will that be acceptable?"

"The Water of Life, it is—there's nothing finer."

"You can do the honours, Father."

"Of course." He poured them each a generous helping into bone-china teacups from the kitchen. "*Sláinte!*"

"*Sláinte!*"

A sudden gunshot made O'Rourke spill his drink.

McGuinness sat up in shock.

"What the hell? Smith, go take a look."

The CID man nodded and exited the room.

"Sir!" More gunshots. Sounds of a struggle.

O'Rourke jumped to his feet. "Father, McGuinness, stay here."

Father Mulhoney crossed himself as he stood.

"Hey, what's happening?" Liam's muffled voice called.

O'Rourke reached the door to find Smith retreating across the entrance hall, his semi-automatic pistol in his hand. O'Rourke looked past him and swore.

Moonlight flooded in through the shattered window to reveal O'Leary laying on his back, his rifle just beyond the fingers of his outstretched hand, a figure atop him.

For a moment, O'Rourke thought an Irregular had broken in through the barricaded door and was choking the life out of his colleague. Then, as he realised the barricade was still in place, the figure looked up from O'Leary's twitching form and O'Rourke cried out in horror.

It was one of Liam's gang that they'd shot; O'Rourke could see the bloody hole in the man's chest, and his lips were covered in the CID man's blood and

bits of flesh dangled from his teeth.

The other two would-be arsonists, O'Rourke realised, were alternatively crawling and flopping their way towards him and Smith on bent and broken limbs, snarling like rabid dogs.

He stared as Smith fired at them and they jerked without being further impaired than they already had been by their death wounds.

It was impossible. It was impossible, yet he was seeing it…

"Sir!"

Smith's shout tore him out of his shock and he fired, blowing away half of one's head. It made no difference.

O'Leary had ceased to twitch and the one atop him began to crawl towards them, too.

Then, O'Leary twitched and spasmed and rolled over and began to crawl after it, growling horribly through his torn throat.

"Back inside the room," O'Rourke told Smith, who'd emptied his magazine. From somewhere within the castle, O'Rourke was certain he could hear more sounds of movement, more snarling…

"What is it?" Father Mulhoney asked as they slammed the drawing room door shut behind them.

"Seems those peasant superstitions were true, after all, Father."

"You're not making any sense, son."

"You remember those Republican lads we shot?" The priest nodded. "Well, it seems they decided death wasn't to their liking, so they got back up and tore out my man, O'Leary's throat. Oh, and he got back up, too!"

O'Rourke, McGuinness and Smith dragged a table and a couple of chairs in front of the door, which shuddered as the dead men flung themselves against it.

O'Rourke pointed to the other door. "That, too…"

"I told you," Liam shouted through the wardrobe door. "There's an evil here. Evil spirits. Devils."

The priest crossed himself. "Nonsense."

O'Rourke jabbed the barrel of his revolver towards the shuddering door. "That nonsense is busy flinging itself against that door, intent on killing us, Father." He turned to the wardrobe. "Hey, lad, you willing to stand with the living against the dead?"

Liam shouted back that he was, and O'Rourke let him out.

"There's a couple of good, sturdy candlesticks there, boyo. You and the good Father, here, should arm yourselves. Bring one of them down on a skull and it should crack."

He glanced at the shuddering door and wondered how long till they'd have need of them. Did dead men need rest, or would they go on flinging themselves at it all night until the door finally gave way? Would there be respite with the dawn?

He wished he knew the answers.

"I'm not usually a praying man, Father," he said, "but, if God's listening, now's the time to ask Him for His help, wouldn't you say, eh?"

"Aye." Father Mulhoney got down on his knees and Liam joined him, head down as he prayed.

"So, my boyo," O'Rourke addressed the local youth as he stood, "you seem to know something about this place and its evil. So, what should we do?"

"What we should've done is blow the place to Hell, but you put a halt to that. Now, all we can do is pray we last till morning…"

The door shuddered heavily.

"They'll be gone at dawn?"

Liam shrugged. "Hopefully."

McGuinness swore.

"Evil shuns the light of God's grace," the priest opined.

"Thank you, Father, for the fine words of wisdom." O'Rourke shook his head.

There was a loud crack and they all turned to see that the upper hinge had partly broken away from the door.

"I don't think we've got till morning," said Smith, holding his pistol to his chest as if it were a talisman.

"Maybe you Republican bastards had the right idea, after all," O'Rourke said.

Liam shrugged. "It was never about the Republic. As I said, this one was different."

"How long would it take for you to finish setting the dynamite?"

"Depends… did you pull out all the fuses?"

"That we did. If we'd had more time, we would've packed it all up."

"Well, thank God, you didn't. Give me five minutes and I reckon I can have the fuses back in place and we can blow it."

"Well, my boy, let's see if we can get you down into the cellar. Smith, McGuinness, help me clear that other door. We'll go out ready to fire, cover the lad and the priest as they head for the stairs."

Father Mulhoney crossed himself. "Pray God is with us this night." He sighed. "Sometimes, as brother fights brother, I think He may have forsaken our country."

O'Rourke patted his revolver. "Better hope this is reliable, then, Father."

He and the others began to drag the barricade away from the second door. The main door was beginning to hang inwards; fingers reached through the gap…

"Better hurry," Liam said as he swatted at a hand.

Smith opened the door, O'Rourke covering him, McGuinness just behind.

They stepped out into the passage and looked down to where it met the entrance hall: There were more than four figures throwing themselves against the door, several of which were no more than skeletons.

"Run!" O'Rouke shouted as he, Smith and McGuinness opened fire.

Liam and the priest ran for the cellar stairs.

The dead turned and began a spasmodic charge towards them, those that were skeletal practically seeming to fall apart and, then, reform in a rolling tide.

They began to fall back, after the others, still firing.

McGuinness shrieked as something seized him and dragged him off into the shadows, screamed, then fell silent.

O'Rourke winced.

"Our guns are having no effect." Smith cursed.

"Then," O'Rourke said, "you'd better put your faith

in that lad's dynamite."

The priest shouted in alarm and O'Rourke turned and ran for the stairs, calling for Smith to follow him.

"More of them!"

Father Mulhoney was beating a skeletal thing back with a candlestick near the bottom of the stairs. Fingers like claws had already gouged bloody tracks down the priest's cheeks.

O'Rourke stepped down and fired, blowing the thing's skull into pieces. The remaining bones fell back and apart, scattering down the stairs, and the CID officer whooped in success.

Only, there were more, and the ones from the hallway above were stumbling down the stairs after them.

They fought their way past those below them, sustaining several cuts along the way, and reached the first cellar.

"I don't think you've got time to do all the dynamite, boyo. Would just these work?"

He and Smith shut the cellar door and braced themselves against the battering of the dead against it.

"It'll probably topple the castle. And," Liam gestured to a couple of barrels of oil that sat amongst the bundles of dynamite, "it should send up a fireball."

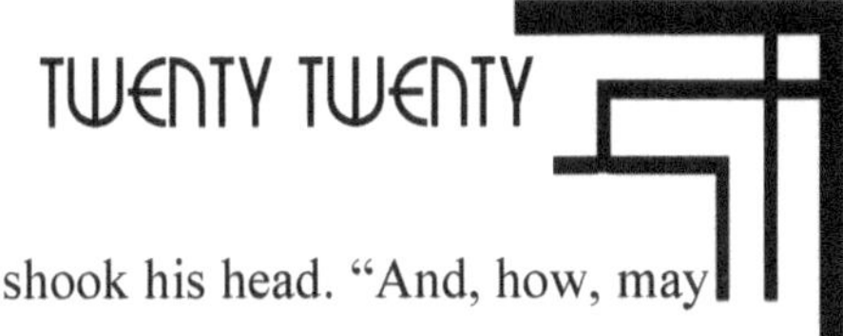

Father Mulhoney shook his head. "And, how, may I ask, do you propose we get out of here?"

"I don't think we're getting out, Father," said Liam from where he was crouched with the fuses.

"You fools! You've doomed us all!"

"We were hardly in a position to fight our way out through the front door, Father," O'Rourke said, "and, we sure as hell weren't going to last the night."

"We ought to have headed for the kitchens, gone out that way."

O'Rouke shrugged. "Yeah, maybe. Too late, now."

He almost fell over as the door shuddered against him and Smith.

"How does God feel about self-sacrifice, eh, Father?" He looked at the youth. "How's it going?"

"Nearly there," Liam said with a nod.

The door nearly burst open and O'Rourke cursed.

"Whenever you're ready, son. Whenever you're ready."

He shook his head, suddenly regretting all the waste of the civil war, now they were all trapped facing death together.

"Whenever you're ready."

The door shuddered, and he began to pray.

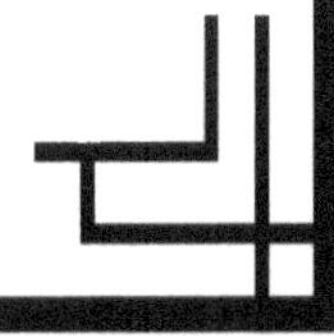

# Three Colours

by J.A. Hammer

Katsuko's world narrows itself from Nikolaevsk-on-Amur to white, red, and black.

Snow drifts down, flakes kissing frozen tears on her cheeks.

Blood flows, pours onto the ground after bayonets thrust forward.

Light fades as her shaking body is stuffed into a hole chipped out of the iced-over river.

Katsuko's world opens itself from death to black, red, and white.

Hair grows longer, strands writhing, twisting in the water.

A crimson haze stains everything a midnight sun's beautiful wrath.

She flees her body, calling forth ice and death as

Nikolaevsk-on-Amur burns, reeking of betrayal.

Following Tryapitsyn's army would be Katsuko's revenge.

# PIGS FOR PIGS

by Lynne Phillips

The policemen pushed the terrified girl through the barn door.

"Thanks, guys. I'll take it from here," Johnny Torrio said.

Realising she had been betrayed, Louisa struggled, but the policemen held her firm.

The knife slashed across her throat. She slumped to the ground.

"Good job, guys. Diamond Jim is grateful," Johnny said as he passed them brown paper packages. They shuffled their feet, mumbled their thanks, and turned.

Johnny shot them in the head.

"Sorry, guys. Can't take any chances."

Johnny the Fox fed the bodies through the woodchipper, straight into the sow's pen.

"Pigs for pigs," he chuckled.

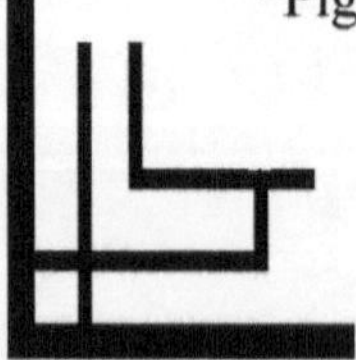

# The Surrealist Painting

by Michael Kellichner

Raymond Bisset had come back from Paris a few months before, ecstatic about some new art scene going on over there. Thought he could make a name for himself, finally, bringing some ideas back and really turning some heads. He went around to the important people in the city, asking them to sit portraits. Naturally, he came to me, and though I don't understand art beyond mortals' desire to try to achieve immortality, I do understand the power that can come with being seen among the publicly acknowledged elite. Often, if you're known to be important, people will do as you want without needing to resort to any unpleasantness.

Sometimes, though, unpleasantness is the only choice.

He'd been correct in assuming his new paintings would get the attention of a rich collector in the city. One of my frequent clients, a banker named Harry Bradford, bought up all the paintings Raymond made and threw a lavish party to show them off. All the big names were there, and of course he asked me to supply a little jag juice for his guests. My presence was welcome as well because he understood the importance of having powerful people close by.

And there it was, displayed in the main room, so that when I walked in, it was like looking into a giant mirror.

The table and chair were the same bland wooden affairs that I had sat in while Raymond had worked secretly on the other side of the canvas. The pose was the same: a cigarette exhaling smoke between my fingers arched over a whiskey glass. Charcoal suit, pristine chalk stripes. My homburg resting on my knee. He'd said the pose summarised me well, and I figured there was nothing more to worry about. Raymond had always been a decent sort, if a little eccentric and bad with money.

But in the painting he'd pulled off my face and left it hovering over the table. Inside my head, there was nothing but viscous drippings streaked with ochre and

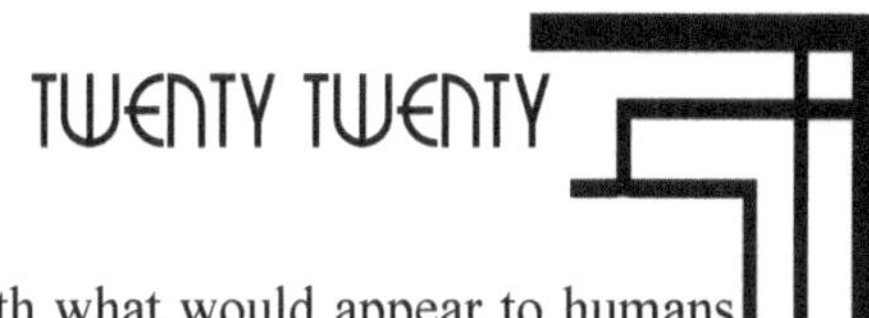

vermilion, mixed in with what would appear to humans as clumps of struggling bees.

In the forty-five years since I crawled into this meatsuit, no one had been able to see my real face.

But even if he'd somehow stumbled upon my face in ignorance, the background assured me Raymond Bisset knew too much. He'd set the table and chair in a stretch of swirling, burning reds and browns beneath swashes of umber and black streaked across the sky. Nothing special, but the mountain that rose up out of the desert, far off in the distance, was too perfect to be anything other than the mountain I'd grown up seeing every morning of my youth. The rocks twisted and swirled in on themselves, like vortexes that could open up and suck in everything in existence.

Anger is very much a human emotion, and one that I've had to learn to mimic to avoid suspicion. But it would be dishonest to say that I was angry at Raymond. Surprised, perhaps. Self preservation, however, is consistent across all sentient creatures, and even some non-sentient ones. And humans are also quite consistent about destroying things they didn't understand. Thus, I was certain that anyone who realised Raymond's painting wasn't just some new style of art and actually true to life would not try to practice their empathy, an emotion they all had but rarely bothered with. Whether Raymond had somehow figured out what he shouldn't have, or maybe he wasn't human himself, was of little consequence to me. He'd exposed my true face, to too many people and needed to be dealt with, regardless of whether the social elite wandering about the mansion sipping champagne and smoking and mingling realised what they saw or not.

A little asking around to learn Raymond had already drifted out of the party earlier in the night, headed for his favourite speakeasy. Celebrating selling so many paintings. He'd probably already be smoked, but if he was, that would only make my job easier.

* * *

The house band at *The Crimson Crescendo* had some swing, and the horn player was red faced and sweating through a solo when I walked in the door. The bar was crowded and most of the tables were filled. The dance floor writhed with bodies. The lights were drawn dim. A good place to meet people where no one would be paying attention.

It would take too long to find Raymond on my own, so I took off my hat and shouldered my way to the end of the bar. The bartender was a young man named Tom

Hawley, and when he saw me, he rushed toward me, drying his hands on his slacks.

"Hey there, Mister Collins," he shouted with a smile too full of teeth. The boy had a kind face, the kind of face that meant bad things were going to happen in his future. Too soft. But he was smart, and knew who to listen to in this town, so he was okay by me.

"Hey there, Tommy," I said, setting my hat on the bar. I stretched the skin of my mouth into a wide grin. Tommy seemed pleased. Approachable expressions were always the hardest, but honest people always had an easier time trusting them. It was part of the reason I liked the kid.

"The normal Mister Collins?"

"You bet, old sport."

The boy mixed up a nice old fashioned and poured it across some fresh ice cubes. I gave it a sip, nodded, and said, "Hey, Tommy, you seen Raymond Bisset in here tonight? I heard he was here celebrating selling a bunch of paintings."

Tom nodded. "Yessir." He pointed over his shoulder with his thumb. "He's at the table in the corner with a couple of skirts. Really putting on a show for them."

"Thanks, Tommy," I said. I picked up my hat and pointed at him with it and said, "You keep out of trouble now. You need anything, you know I'd like to help you out."

"That's very kind of you, Mr Collins. Thank you."

I took my drink and made my way between the tables. I kept my face fixed into the relaxed smile that made people want to talk, the one I used when trying to do things the easy way. Never know who is watching, and with at least Raymond somehow seeing my true face, there was good reason to be extra guarded. A lot of people meant either that no one was paying attention to what you were doing, or someone who wanted to pay attention was using the crowd to hide themselves. Even if most everyone in the joint knew who I was and knew better than to cross me, I didn't get to be where I was by being careless.

Raymond was sitting at a table with three dames all fawning over him and a bucket of ice with a champagne bottle shoved in it. He saw me coming, clapped his hands, and shouted, gesturing at me with such wild movements he looked like he would upend the table. His face was already flushed and his forehead gleamed with sweat.

"Robert!" he shouted when I arrived at his table. "Please, please, sit." He gestured to the dames. "Robert, this is Ruth. This is Dolores. And Lillian. Ladies, this is the esteemed Robert Collins. I'm sure you've heard of

him. A very close personal friend of mine."

"Now that can't be true," Lillian said.

I took the time to light a cigarette before I said, "Oh, it's true." I took a sip of my whiskey and smiled.

"See?" Raymond yelled. "Sit down, Robert. Sit down! We can have more drinks."

I sat and said, "I like Raymond here so much that I sat for one of his new portraits. Did any of you happen to see it?"

"You saw it?" Raymond said. "Wonderful! Isn't it fantastic?" He drank and pointed at me emphatically. "It's because of Robert here that I could sell the whole bunch. His was the best one. The one that had everyone talking."

I watched him over the rim of my glass, trying to figure out what he saw that others didn't. His eyes were shining bright, surrounded by sweaty, flushed flesh.

"Actually, Raymond, that's what I'm here about."

His face fell a little and his lip twitched. "You didn't like it?"

I threw back my head and gave a hearty laugh. Loud enough that even the bartender could have easily heard. "No, no, no, that's not it, Raymond," I said. "You're absolutely right. It was definitely the standout of all of them.

"I actually needed your help, though. You see, I managed to acquire a few dozen paintings from overseas and they've just arrived today. I didn't want to bother you, especially since you're so busy at the moment. But I didn't know who else I could ask to come and take a look at them. Make sure that I actually got what I was promised. Some of them seem a little hinky." Flattery is an excellent cover when you need someone to let their guard down.

"Paintings you say. I'd be happy to take a look at them," Raymond said. "After all, I owe you, don't I? Ladies, did you know that old man Bradford couldn't pay me fast enough when he saw Robert's portrait? Called me a genius, he did."

"Well, that's nice of you to say," I said. "I'd actually hoped to go down and take a look at them right now. But I can see you're busy. We can go some other time."

Insistence on not inconveniencing is the fastest way to inconvenience.

"No, no, Robert. A few dozen, you said? Sounds like a perfect evening. Ladies, you'll have to excuse me. You can't leave someone like Robert here just waiting. We'll pick this party up again some other time."

"I mighty appreciate that, Raymond," I said. I reached into my jacket and pulled out my wallet. "Ladies,

let me pay for your drinks while I borrow your company. It's the least I can do."

*  *  *

The drive down to the docks was slow. The streets were crowded, and if Raymond figured out why I was really taking him to a more secluded location, he'd have a chance to bail and escape. No need to take the risk, so I eased through the city that didn't seem to possess fatigue. People were coming and going from all the establishments that had made me a man of import within the city limits.

Raymond seemed none the wiser and chatted along merrily the entire time, telling me about the artists and bars and dancers in Paris. I wasn't listening, but Raymond was ossified enough that my few nods and open questions kept him prattling on the entire time. I focused on ensuring that the drive felt like a leisurely, friendly excursion.

When we left downtown behind, I could drive a little faster, and just as Raymond was finishing a story about a dancer he'd been following around the city without any luck, I pulled up beside one of the warehouses near the water's edge. We got out, and

Raymond continued going on about how the dancer rebuffed him at every turn. We went between the silent buildings sitting in the darkness, the silence shattered by Raymond's boisterous story.

At the water, boats creaked in their rhythmic rocking. I took him all the way down to the end of one pier, where I knew one of the mafia's empty boats was waiting. It was a small one used by a colleague who was in the cooler and wouldn't be around for a while. I took Raymond up onto the boat, opened the door, and let him stumble down the stairs into the cabin. I followed closely and shut the door behind us.

At the bottom of the stairs, Raymond patted along his pockets. "Sure is dark down here, Robert. You got a light? Can't see a thing."

I reached up to where a lantern hung next to the door. I struck a match and lit it, turning up the wick to illuminate the empty hull. Raymond swayed for a moment, turning to each corner, as if he had simply missed all the paintings at first glance.

He laughed. "Very funny, Robert. Where are they?"

He turned and took a step back. I didn't bother to twist my face into one of the approachable facades or a genial, trustworthy expression. I let it settle into the blank, slack appearance that came most naturally, one

that always set people on edge.

"How did you know, Raymond?" I asked.

The intoxication seemed to drain out of Raymond's face and was replaced with one of great consternation. He tried to smile, but the corners of his mouth just twitched. "Know what, Robert?"

I took a step toward him, and he took one back. "My face, Raymond. How did you know?"

Raymond looked all around. "What? Are you talking about the painting?" He laughed, but it was higher than usual, more panicked. "Didn't you like it? Robert, it's just the style that's keen right now. It's nothing personal." He forced out another laugh. "You should see some of the weird stuff they're selling over there. Really weird stuff. It doesn't mean anything, Robert."

I slowly reached up and pulled off my face. The skin peeled away easily, and Raymond stared into the ochre and vermilion clumps. I asked him again how he knew, but without a human mouth the sound emerged as a sticky, coughing buzz.

His scream told me that he didn't understand my native language.

I had more questions, but the important thing was that Raymond not paint any more pictures and certainly that he not talk anymore. He struggled as I grabbed him, but when I oozed out of my borrowed skin, his screaming stopped quickly. It took a few hours to consume him completely, leaving nothing behind. By the time I crawled back into my meatsuit and exited the boat, the sun was already colouring the horizon a beautiful mixture of orange and red.

I took a moment to watch the sun coming up, smoking a cigarette to get the taste of Raymond out of my mouth. When I finished, I flicked the butt into the water, adjusted my tie, and headed back to my car.

Later, everyone wondered where Raymond had gone. When I told them he had gone back to Paris to chase some dancer, no one ever wondered about him again.

The painting still hangs in Harry Bradford's parlour, something people glance at when they enter, comment upon. "Yes, it came by way of a young artist from Paris," Harry tells them.

"Charming," they reply, and carry on as they had been.

# GIN AND JINKS

by Nicola Currie

Bernie Blue was the smoothest grifter I ever saw. He could charm the ice from around the necks of broads who gave every other guy the cold shoulder. There was just something about him. He was a good-looking fella, sure, real put together, but he had something else, something I could never figure.

There was one time, no word of a lie, I watched from the sidewalk as he talked his way out of a pair of bracelets for bumping off some poor Joe he'd conned, the guy too stupid to realise how things would end for him if he peached. I watched as Bernie made the officer dance along to his own special kind of jazz while he sang of his innocence with blood still on his hands. The copper released Bernie from his cuffs as resigned medics loaded the dead chump into a meat wagon,

413

already a ghost beneath a white sheet.

I asked him one night, a little while after that, "What kinda name is Blue, anyhow? I'll bet you a nickel that ain't the name your daddy gave ya."

Bernie grinned a smile, twisted in a way everything about Bernie was twisted, a little off-center, a little out of sight. I always let people be, no matter what kind of goon they was, minded my own business, so Bernie liked me. Even a con man needs a buddy to shoot the breeze with.

"Could have won yourself a dime because Bernie ain't neither," the man I knew as Bernie said. "But I bet a wise guy like you had that square. Bartender, a gin for myself and the genius here." Bernie fixed me with a still hard stare.

Was he on to me? Bernie was a flitter, always ready to jink out of a place in a swift second. It gave him a breezy quality, like you could turn back a second after looking away to find he was no longer there. You might even convince yourself, once he was gone, that he had never been real in the first place.

"But why Blue?" I asked, taking my gin and raising it in thanks, trying to act casual. The thing was, I was running my own con. It wasn't a coincidence that I was on the street outside the bar the night Bernie sang himself out of a date with the electric chair, just like it wasn't a coincidence I'd been there every night since. I was no hotshot like Bernie, but I was known to get things done for people, on the sly, in the shadows. I had something of a reputation with the higher-ups as a man who could be trusted to get his hands dirty on behalf of richer, gentler folk who had need of some muscle. Mostly it was scaring off business competitors or pistol-whipping some cake-eater who had got too friendly with another guy's lady. But Bernie was worth more than any job I had ever pulled.

"It's the name the devil gave me, when I sold my soul for a last glass of gin. Everyone underestimates the coolness of blue, the devil told me. If you're smooth as blue sky and quick as water, nobody can catch you. You just flow in and out, like a river."

That's exactly what Bernie did to upset the state governor. He flowed into his daughter's life and, when he had taken her money, flowed away again. The governor was rich enough to take the hit, but Bernie had promised to marry her and the dumb Dora believed him, got herself in the family way. The governor was left with a hole in his pocket and a floozie for a daughter. He couldn't move on the guy in the open, not without his daughter's secret getting out, so he came to me. I'd never sent anybody to the Big Sleep before, but the money was too good to pass on.

"You sold your soul to the devil?" I said all casual, sipping my drink, knowing that tonight was finally the night I could complete the deal and collect my fee, after weeks of learning how much Bernie drank, where he lived, how dark the alleys were as he walked home. "A guy as slick as you?"

Bernie smiled that twisted smile again, and the shadows in his eyes almost sent me running.

"That's him. I was a poor sap, a regular dope fiend, completely on the nut and on the lam from the button man. It was the end. All I wanted was one last gin. But I guess the master scammer saw something in me. He's had me playing the confidence game ever since, jinking from east coast to west coast ten times over."

We talked a little longer, a little lighter, of baseball and starlets from the pictures. I took one more drink, for courage, but no more. I needed a clear head. As Bernie bid me good night with a wave of his hat, I stood, ready to follow. Only my head was woozier than a dame in love all of a sudden, the lamplight seeming to flicker black and bright, black and bright.

"Careful there, pal," Bernie said, catching me, looking at me with that twisted grin. "Let me help you

out." The shadows in his eyes flickered too, jinking black and bright, black and bright.

I don't know when my mind went down, but it didn't come up again until hours later. I didn't understand it at first, the red everywhere, the sirens in the distance, no Bernie in sight. I couldn't put two and two together as I heard the police say the governor's body was stone cold, his daughter's too, and as they asked me about the letter I had written saying why I did it, the pills I took that didn't take.

A few months into my stay in the Big House, the electric chair almost juiced for me, my bunkmate showed me a picture in the paper of Belle Gracy. She was the prettiest dish America had ever seen, the darling of the silver screen. I barely gave her a glance. I stared in horrified defeat at the man she held onto.

Like I said, once he was gone, you half convinced yourself he was never real in the first place, but I knew I would die knowing the truth.

Knowing I was a prime chump forever thinking I could take him.

Knowing he was still out there, on the breeze.

# AUGUST 18TH

by Neen Cohen

Mother's tears soak into my dress as she holds me tight. Over her shoulder my father smiles, a look more confused than pleased. She puts me back down amongst my blocks and smiles although tears still slide over her cheeks.

"Remember this day."

She laughs, racing back out the door.

My father continues to smile as he shrugs and closes the door behind him, following my mother. I never tell the policemen about the butcher's knife in father's hands.

It was years before I understood mother's joy and father's confusion. But I never did forget August 18th, 1920.

# Under the Weeping Willow

## by Robin Braid

My little bird. I fell for you before I even saw you. That night you got up to sing at the Cameron place, and I, perched low by the fireplace, cup at my lips, vowed I would sip from it no more until I found the one capable of such enchantment. As I looked around the room, my soul took flight, following the dips and swoops of your melody, and I knew then that you would be mine, and I would be yours, forever. You were always my little bird after that.

Through spring and summer, we walked the fields and hills around the village. Everything looked bright and new with you, and I felt like we were waltzing through a world all of our own, destined to go anywhere, do anything. You lifted me to a place I'd never known, and when we were apart, my mind was consumed by thoughts and wishes for our future. We may not have had much, but we would build something to which wealth and possessions could not compare. I can still feel your hand in mine, so light, but always so cold. All I wanted was to keep you safe and warm. If only you had let me.

I pulled up the collar on my overcoat and headed down the wooded lane. The earth felt hard beneath my feet now the land was on the cusp of autumn. The air was crisp, and the leaves were beginning to lose their lustre. Without you, everything was fading. I walked flanked by row upon row of trees, and with every rustle of fallen leaves, I almost caught sight of you, long red hair, the hem of your skirt, dancing in the light between the silver birches.

On the far side of the woods was the arched stone bridge. This was our place where we could throw our worries to the wind and just be together. We would spend hours there waiting for the southbound train to pass. Your arms tightened around me as a pillar of smoke appeared on the horizon, and when the carriages flew under the bridge, we were there arm in arm with our luggage overhead, on our way to London and

watching our old life disappear into the past. That was our plan. If you'd only believed, little bird.

I crossed the bridge with my head bowed. It was nothing but an ashen memorial now and I dare not look down the tracks lest I fall victim to thoughts of what might have been. The pitted path ahead wound up and over the grassy hill, our final walk.

Out in the open, the wind was at my back, pushing me on. From the top of the hill I could see the still, dark pond below, the golden weeping willow by its edge, branches swaying gently in the cold morning light, beckoning me down.

It was there, beneath the willow tree that everything ended. We were lying in each other's arms, I remember you had felt distant that day, and your eyes looked down, avoiding mine as you told me you were leaving for Canada. How you had to keep the family together, a new start for you all. How your mother had never gotten over her beloved son going off to France a proud local hero and never returning. Fallen and lost on a grim and lonely battlefield.

Fallen and lost.

I knelt and touched the dirt at the foot of the willow tree. It was undisturbed, the white flower still pinned to the ground beneath the rock I had placed there. My last act. I never dreamed our story would end this way, but the devil was in me that night. Your throat so smooth, so fragile, and my hands not my own. You never even screamed. I don't think either of us really knew what was happening. Until the light went out.

I turned and stood by the pond's edge. Looking down, I saw my silhouette in the murky water, framed by the shadow of the weeping willow hanging low across my shoulders. Somewhere in the branches, a soft sound broke the silence, and a lone bird began its song. The sound glided in and around me, and on the water, another glimpse, your eyes closing for the final time.

From a distance, the rattling of the train came on the breeze and a thick plume of smoke rose to kiss the darkening clouds. I stepped and placed a boot into the pond. The mud below the surface gripped my heel, and I cried out, "My soul is lost," and walked forward, the cold, black water taking me in.

"We'll fly little bird. We'll fly together."

The train passed beneath the bridge and disappeared beyond the horizon. The smoke drifted and faded against the grey sky, and in a moment, the water was still once more.

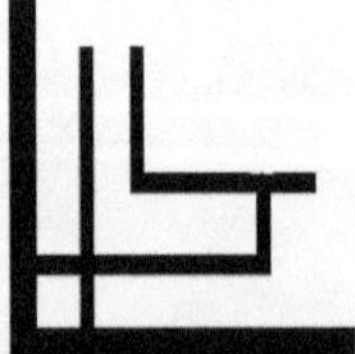

# The Making Of A Star

by Ximena Escobar

Red lacquer on her toenail, in the exact colour of the *Duesy* parked outside. One good thing about putting up with Fritz was the cabbage.

"Money, money," she mouthed mutely as she placed the cupid-bow stencil on her lips, painting them to match the car and the nails.

Another good thing was that a man was never going to replace her in this business. No matter how wonderful the Maybelline, no one will ever want to see scantily clad men in the movies.

She thought about this as she slipped into her shoes, carefully doing the straps to protect the perfection of her fingernails. And if he ever fancied himself a woman's experience, knowing Fritz, he'd have to have *real* blood. All for the *authenticity*…

Blood's what the lip-paint was really all about… The blood-filled flesh of a man's desire. Under the lipstick. Like the nipple tassels only draw attention to that which they are covering.

She marvelled at the strength of the adhesive, gently pulling the long shiny threads.

It had its advantages, putting up with Fritz.

"Alright, damn it!" Fritz's voice exploded from below the planks, muffled somewhat like when a man's palm smothers a woman.

He knocked. And paused. And knocked again. But Brigitte twisted shut the metal lipstick-lid, savouring the satisfying *click*.

"Is it time, baby?" She asked.

(Sometimes, the paint was all about losing one's humanity… Quite literally, 'dolling up.')

"Brigitte!"

There was a delicious sensation associated to the idea of standing on Fritz, even if a plank of wood would separate them. She imagined digging her heel into his cheek, and a red mark lingering—like a man's handprint often does on a woman's face. But remembering the way

his eye had last looked through the square hole, she thought of him as a dog; vulnerable, innocent.

"C'mon! Brigitte!"

And she'd always give a dog his water. Nevertheless, she took her time rubbing her small lips together; careful not to smudge the lipliner perfection.

"Ready for some bread then, baby?" She asked him, eyes fixed on the mirror.

She looked like a real movie star. She *was* a real movie star. Well on the way to becoming one.

Wooden legs screeching on the floorboards, she pushed herself on the stool. Maybe... She was a different kind of star.

"Cigs! I'm ready for cigs!"

Brigitte turned and looked at the large cushion bobbing awkwardly and heavily on the floor, on the planks, as Fritz poked it from inside the vault, with the three fingers he could fit through the hole. Fritz had cut it, but she'd nailed the planks to the floor herself, where a trapdoor had once been, following the instructions he shouted at her from his would-be prison. (Before she'd done her nails.) Like she needed direction to use a hammer.

She stood up, slightly repulsed by the idea of his fingers wriggling through the hole, looking at the fine lines of light, like threads of gold, between the old floorboards. She kicked the cushion out of the way; strings of tiny gold beads dangling on her thighs.

"Didn't you say, 'a minimum of food and water *only*'? It's not even been two days, baby. And you're not supposed to turn the light on until bread time."

Towering above him, she watched his mouth appear in the square. It reminded her of the lip-stencil.

"I know what I said," he said. "I don't give a damn."

"*The Fated* wouldn't get any cigarettes, would they?"

"Butt me quick, Brigitte. I mean it. I feel enough of their despair alright. I can have a damn cig."

He'd nearly set her on fire, all for the 'authenticity' of the film. Of course, he'd never take it too far on himself. He'd never deem it "necessary" for the director to understand a character's ordeal, if it didn't suit him. He didn't give a damn what suited his actors. Broke Bill's teeth so his speakeasy scene would look authentic.

She stepped away for the cigarettes.

"How's the costume?" His eye replaced the mouth, but she wasn't there to see it. Nor to be seen.

"Oh, you're going to love it," she answered from the vanity.

"Rudy seen it on you yet?"

"It's just you and me here, baby. No one else is crazy enough to come to work before production officially resumes. Not even Rudy. Just that runaway gal… Bonnie."

"Let me see you."

"That Bonnie gal with the southern accent… She came looking for you."

"Don't know who the hell you're talking about..."

"And *I* don't know what 'an extra' thought she was doing here, in between production runs. But there you have it."

(She knew. It had all come together by now.)

"C'mon. Let me see you. Our first film, Bearcat."

"There's not much of it to see. Besides, isn't that bending the rules? Again?"

"They're my rules, don't you forget. Hurry up with that cig."

Brigitte lit the cigarette, taking a deep slow puff. The smoke bounced on the mirror as she exhaled—a foggy highway stretching before her; nothing else before her in the dead of night. Fritz always kept plenty of gasoline cans; that was another good thing about him.

"Brigitte!"

Brigitte's heels clicked on the floorboards as she

went. She stood on the plank, covering the hole completely with her sole.

"Just pass the damn cig."

She removed her foot, watching his fingers pop out again.

"Let me see your mouth, baby," she said.

The fingers disappeared; his eye glared at her.

"Pass the damn cig, Brigitte."

She crouched down, hovering upon him. Her face darkened by the ceiling lamp.

"I said 'your mouth', baby. You have no rights, remember? Remember what you wrote? You're not Fritz Weber anymore. You're nothing but a cog in a great big machine. Worthless on your own. Replaceable. Scum of society; put to the good use of the *Luminous*. So, when I tell you I want your mouth, I want your mouth…"

The eye widened. The lips took its place.

"Atta boy. You know I only wanna kiss it."

Brigitte lowered her face and blew a full breath of smoke in through his lips.

Fritz held it. Fritz exhaled. Smoke like a steam-train blowing out of the square as she stood up and disappeared out of view.

* * *

Fritz never suspected that was the last he'd ever see of her. Brigitte herself didn't know what had come over her when she saw Bonnie, but she soon came to think of her as an angel. It was all part of a larger plan. A *higher* plan.

She hadn't been jealous, just humiliated, once again; not that she wasn't used to that. She didn't even think about it at the time... She only saw the road, and the fog, and then the Bonnie head like a broken mask under a brick—hair like muddy grass because of the blood; and she knew that was the future... Mostly, she believed in her own strength right then. And that had to mean something. She visualised the adhesive on the dresser, because of the hair all stuck together maybe, and that was that; ended up gluing Bonnie's lips shut until she gathered the courage to give it to her with the hammer. Duck soup. People will do anything for a movie star.

She dragged her slight corpse easily into the dressing room, despite being just as small; pretty much her exact same build. All that dancing, before Fritz discovered her and brought her to the studios, had sure paid off. She was strong; but mentally strong too. The incessant knocking, Fritz's incessant screaming she dreaded; she didn't even hear it... Screaming and screaming her name, but that wasn't her name anymore. She only listened to the soothing sound of Bonnie's body sweeping the floor.

Sweeping is always so satisfying because you see the results immediately; kind of like painting your nails. Other things take time, patience. Resilience. Not this. This was immediate. Retribution. The gurgling of the gasoline, the flame flaring on the match, the highly flammable celluloid…by far the most penetrating sound. The erasure of Brigitte's character, Molly; the erasure of *the Luminous* and of all *the Fated*; the erasure of Brigitte; piercingly satisfying; the moment when breath becomes exhalation. The moment when Brigitte puts on Fritz's raincoat, but it's Bonnie who climbs into the *Duesy*. Poor doll even had her papers with her—angel fallen from heaven probably wasn't there to have an affair with him after all but, if she did, least they're 'dead happily ever after.' His cabbage in the pockets, the knowledge that the nail lacquer matched the car. The knowledge that no one would recognise Bonnie's charred remains as Bonnie's.

* * *

Headlines told of a cursed film, feeding the prudes. Always starved for arguments to suppress the making of motion pictures.

Others put it on the mob.

And Bonnie… She eventually ran out of gasoline. Met a nice fellow with puppy dog eyes. A nice fellow called Clyde, in the gas station.

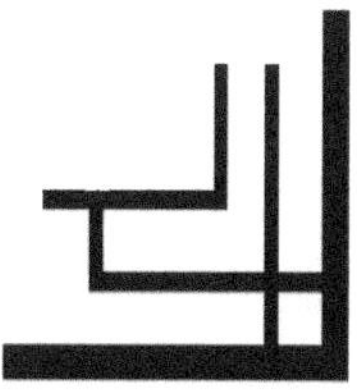

# The Weighing of the Heart

by Matthew M. Montelione

*The Valley of the Kings, Egypt. 1923*

King Tutankhamen's gold mask gleamed in the torchlight; his tragic eyes transporting me from the present into the mute past. I felt deep solemnity in the presence of the mummy of the teenaged king, until he stirred!

Tutankhamen stepped forward, his frayed linen bandages dangling from his over three-thousand-year-old corpse.

My heart raced.

Suddenly, a massive jackal-headed shadow lunged towards me. Anubis had come! He tossed me atop a

large scale. On the opposite pan was a feather, symbol of Truth. Anubis cackled as my scale plummeted into the jaws of the Gobbler.

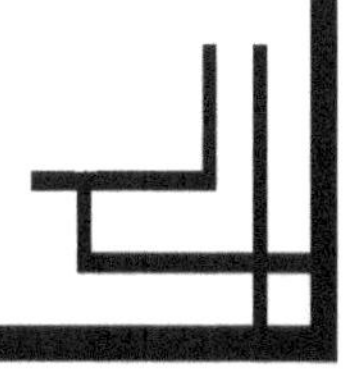

# NOSFERATU

## by D.M. Burdett

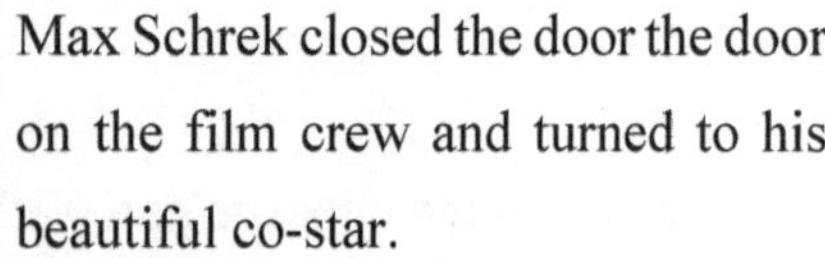

Max Schrek closed the door the door on the film crew and turned to his beautiful co-star.

"My darling," he said darkly. "At last, we are alone."

"Oh Max," Greta breathed, "The filming has exhausted me. I should go home."

"Please! Just one drink?"

Greta Schroder blushed. "Maybe, just one."

Max led her to the drawing room, ushering her into a seat as he poured a single brandy.

"Are you having one?" Greta asked, brow furrowed, as she took the glass.

Max took a seat opposite. "Yes, my dear," he said, watching the curve of her neck and the way the vein pulsed a beat just beneath the surface of her skin, "I do believe I will."

# A Song for the Prince

by Donna Cuttress

Hangers bent under the weight of expensive furs and tailored overcoats. Patsy leaned against the counter of the coat check room, examined her off white gloves, and sniffed at a stain she found on the right hand one. She stifled a yawn. *The Stormers Jazz Band* screamed into life every time the double doors to the ballroom swung open. She watched as two young ladies, who had arrived prim and polite but were now more than tipsy, stumbled into the restroom across the corridor.

*At least they're having fun,* she thought. The homemade liquor that was served as 'lemonade' had seen to that.

Patsy would always keep a watchful eye on the younger girls. She'd hold their purses as they vomited, then wash their faces and get them a cab. "We gotta look out for each other," she would tell them.

The music slipped into chaotic raucousness as the night passed. Usually she would have been dancing herself, going crazy in the cloakroom, but not tonight. Patsy felt irritable and restless. She felt like there was not enough air and what there was, was thin and stale. She wanted to sit by an open window and let the fresh sea air fill her lungs. The twisted knot in her stomach cramped.

*Something's going to happen tonight. I can feel it,* she thought.

Her tip jar had a few dollar bills inside, as well as some change, but that still didn't lift her mood. Taking coats and hats in a seaside hotel was not how she envisioned her life panning out. Patsy ran her hands down the white silk lining of one of the coats. The contrast made her gloves look even greyer. The man's dress coat smelled of perfume, probably French and expensive cigars and cologne. This coat had graced the hangers of the Neptune hotel many times before. It was a return visitor. Sometimes it was draped over the back of a young lady, to keep her warm. Another pretty face that the coat's owner would call his 'latest girl' or 'the one'. He would always wink whenever he said that, a joke at their expense. He would arrive with an entourage, ready to take the best table in the ballroom, and cause mayhem all evening. The staff called him, The Prince on account of him being the owner's son. He would press folded up twenty-dollar tips into grabby palms and shout loudly about how his father would know about the excellent service he had benefited from. There was a rumour that one lucky bell boy got a hundred-dollar tip, just for bringing him the baseball scores. He was destined to inherit the Neptune Hotel, when his daddy died, despite not taking an interest in the place other than how much of the profits he could waste. Patsy called him 'Mr Sleazy'. *Must be great to be the boss's son!* she thought as she fiddled with her kiss curls on her cheeks.

Patsy tried to see the raw skin at the back of her neck with the small cracked mirror that hung from a nail in the cloakroom. She had dyed her hair red, just like Clara Bows, but she had that itchy, irritated feeling that she'd left the smelly dye on for too long. She returned to the counter and glanced at her wristwatch. She straightened her cap, slid her movie magazine onto the counter and flicked through some of the pages.

"One day I'll get to Hollywood Land," she whispered, "And some director will see me and say, *that's her*. That's the girl I need!"

A freezing wind blew down the corridor. It was straight from the sea; Patsy could smell it. *An ill wind...* she thought as she threw her magazine back under the counter. The doors from reception swung violently on creaking hinges, almost hitting the wall either side of them. The clicking of heels echoed on the marble floor. Patsy smoothed her skirt, flattened her apron then stood up straight, ready to meet the clientele. The footsteps grew nearer, measured and hurried. The overhead lighting flickered throughout the hotel.

"Must be a storm coming in."

Patsy began to rip a ticket from the coat check booklet and stifled another yawn. She stopped when she saw the woman who had suddenly appeared at the coat check counter. Patsy almost dropped the tickets.

"Jeez! You frightened me!"

The lady wore a long black shimmering coat, with the lapels pulled high around her neck. A black velvet cloche hat sat low over her forehead with an intricately patterned veil attached that covered her face. Patsy could only see the glisten of her dark eyes and the yellowy whiteness of her teeth against plum coloured lips. For a

few brief seconds they stared at each other.

"I'm so sorry… Good evening, Madam."

The woman pulled the coat collar around her face as though protecting it. Her hands looked cold, the skin red and mottled. Her nails were long and black, but not painted.

"Would you like me to take that, Madam?"

Patsy pointed to her coat.

"No, thank you."

The woman looked beyond her into open the cloakroom. Her lips moved, but there was no voice, yet Patsy could hear her.

"Can I ask you a question? You don't have to answer if you don't want to."

Patsy noticed she was staring at the white coat. It seemed luminescent.

"Of course, Madam. Ask me anything."

Patsy had never met anyone like her. Was this the '*it*' that the movie magazines wrote about? Did this woman have 'it'? She tried to fix her face, or what she could see through the veil, to one of the movies she had seen lately.

The woman let go of her lapels exposing a long white neck. The muscles constricted as blue veins pulsed. There was that cold wind again along the corridor, and thunder began to roll above the hotel, drowning out the jazz music. The woman pointed to the white coat.

"Is he here?"

Patsy nodded.

"Yes. He went into the ballroom about an hour ago. He's sat at his usual table."

"By the dancefloor, I presume? I was told he likes to watch the ladies' legs as they *'shimmy'*."

Patsy nodded. She felt shy of the lady, but fascinated.

"Would you like me to get a bellboy to take a message to him for you, Madam?"

"No, thank you. There is one thing I would like you to do though. I'm going to go on stage in a few moments…"

*Ah, she's a singer!* Patsy thought. *Of course she is! The glamour and the mystery! She has to be a performer.*

The woman smiled at her. Patsy froze. Could she read her thoughts? Hear them as clear as if they were chatting in a cafe?

"Patsy, when you hear the music stop, I want you to go into the cloakroom and close the door tightly."

"What?" Patsy said.

"Cover your ears. Block out the sound. Don't listen.

Understand? This might seem strange, but it's for your own safety. Do you understand?"

She nodded, even though she felt bemused, but she would do it anyway, she would do anything for her. The woman gently rolled the veil up from her face. Sharp wolf-like teeth formed into a hideous smile, wet eyes rolled in the flashing overhead lights. She dropped a folded bill into the tip jar and winked at Patsy. Despite her terror, Patsy winked back. The woman slipped the veil back over her face, turned away and walked along the corridor toward the ballroom. The doors slowly opened, it seemed by themselves, letting the raw jazz music escape and dance around the hotel. Then they closed behind her, dulling the party. The storm exploded above the hotel. The thunder boomed as rain hit the windows. The sea smashed into the exposed side of the hotel. Everything suddenly seemed too loud. The lights flickered again above her. The change in the tip jar began to tremor.

Patsy hesitated, her breathing had become heavy. The anticipation of something horrific made her shake. *Is this some kind of joke?* she thought. *Should I really do what she said?* She could hear the band slowing down, then stopping. Someone booed, another yelled

"Get off the stage!"

The M.C. said into the microphone,

"I guess the lady wants to sing... What was that, Madam?"

Someone blew a raspberry sound. A slow hand clap began.

"And she wants to sing it for the man at the front down here, our *very own prince.*"

A slow round of applause began. No one wanted to anger The Prince.

Patsy felt overwhelmed, but she did not know what by. Her mouth became cold, her teeth chattered. She wanted to scream.

"Can't you see what's happening? The storm is *inside* the hotel! It's *in front* of you!" she shouted. Nobody took any notice of her. She ran into the cloakroom, slamming the door behind her. Her hands fumbled with the key, as she swallowed down bile in her throat. She then cowed into the furthest corner, pulling the white silk coat over her and covered her ears with her hands. Her breath became staggered, as her heart seemed to pump in her brain.

The lady's voice was high pitched and operatic. She sang a melodious song that danced around the surprised crowd. They nodded at her talent, smiled when she looked at them and sipped their hooch in appreciation of the refrain. They stared, beguiled by her, eager to hear more from those dark sensuous lips. The lady directed her song at the man sitting at the table next to the dancefloor, the owner's son, The Prince. He sucked and puffed on his cigar as he watched her, smoke drifting around him like sea fog.

The song slowly changed. It became unrecognisable, then unlistenable, as it mutated into a howling scream. It echoed, and with each rebound it became stronger and ferocious. Each note seemed to shatter like splinters of glass, burying themselves into the audience's soft flesh.

It made Patsy think only of death. She felt like she wanted to tear at her eyes and yank out her tongue from the root. Her brain swelled inside her skull. *What is this? What's happening to me?* An icy wind blew through the hotel, making the walls shift against the foundations. She screamed louder and louder, her throat becoming raw and just as she was about to collapse, it stopped. There was silence.

Patsy fell back against the wall and pulled the coat from her face. She paused to breathe, inhaling long gulps of air as though she had been held underwater. Her gloves felt wet against her hands. They were soaked with blood that had run from her ears. She could still feel it trickling down her neck. She struggled to stand and trampled bloodied footsteps on the white coat as she did. After she unlocked the door, she paused. The quiet terrified her. Patsy opened the door slightly, then peeked out. She could see no one and hear nothing. The band had stopped playing, the party had stopped, and the storm seemed to have passed over the hotel and back out to sea.

The double doors of the ballroom opened slowly. The lady walked into the corridor, heading for reception. She pulled at the lapels of her coat, covering her neck, then nodded at Patsy and blew a quick kiss. The lady disappeared as she walked toward reception, disappeared with the popping of the chandelier bulbs.

Patsy stumbled toward the ballroom doors and pushed them open. A man in a tuxedo stood before her, his eyes were bleeding from the sockets, his lips were bitten to pulp. His hands shook as he tried to cover his face.

"We need help Miss,'' he said, slowly trying not to swallow too much of his own blood. Patsy could not help him; she could barely take in what she saw. A woman stood in the centre of the dancefloor, just screaming, long terrified roars of fear. She scratched at her own face, leaving long thick welts as she stared at

the bodies that were scattered around her. The party goers were in various states of injury. Eyes were gouged, necks broken, and arms twisted. Everyone had blood from their ears, running down their necks staining shirt collars crimson. Everything that could break, glass, wood or bone had broken into pieces. Patsy held hands to her mouth, trying to cover her nose from the stench of piss and hooch.

"It's like a battlefield!" someone shouted, "Has a bomb exploded? Have we been attacked?"

The Prince, or what was left of him, was by his favourite table. His face had melted like hot wax. His body was contorted into a horrific shape, his bones had snapped like canes. Patsy watched as his cigar still burned, clenched between his shattered fingers.

She closed her eyes.

The hotel seemed to shudder, like it could collapse at any minute. The cracks in the walls seemed to be widening, spreading like veins across the ceiling. The Neptune Hotel was going to collapse into the sea, taking everyone within, alive or dead. A man grabbed her arm, his face scalded and blistered, he could hardly see through his swollen eyes. He leaned on her, muttering into her ear.

"She said she wanted to sing! She said it was for

*him!"* He pointed to The Prince, "A message from his family, an old, old song from the old country... All of this *horror* happened when she sang. *She was a banshee. I swear she was a banshee!"*

Patsy forced the man's hand from her arm and began running toward the doors, kicking shoes and smashed champagne bottles as she did.

"I have to get out of here!"

She met the manager running toward her. He had blood running from his ears too.

"What happened here?"

The manager blocked Patsy's way. His face was sweaty and red. He grabbed her arm and pulled her toward him.

"I asked you, *girl,* what the hell happened?"

"It was the song ..."

He stared at her, then pushed her aside, almost throwing her through the ballroom doors. Patsy straightened up. Her mind was suddenly clear.

Patsy ran into the cloakroom and stared at her own reflection in the cracked mirror. Her pale face looked grotesque. She ripped off her cap, tidied her hair and wiped the dried trickles of blood around her ears.

"It's time to leave, Patsy," she said to herself. Then she selected one of the glamorous dress coats from the hangars and slipped it on. In one of the pockets was a pair of scarlet gloves, and she put them on too. She grabbed a dark silk cloche from the hat shelf, brushed the nap of any dust and discarded the ticket pinned to the inner rim. She checked her reflection. She was a different woman now, a lady, *Patricia*. Ignoring the pandemonium and death around her, she retrieved the cash from the tip jar. The neatly folded one from the *banshee,* had the face of Benjamin Franklin on it. It was a hundred-dollar bill. More than she had ever seen, and enough to buy her escape to Hollywood Land. "We girls gotta look after each other," she whispered as she ran, toward reception.

# THE FINAL COFFIN

by K.B. Elijah

It's hot in the burial chamber. I push my glasses more firmly onto my nose, barely daring to breathe in any of the musty dry air as sweat pools on my forehead and down my back. The long cotton shirt feels constrictive, and I wonder whether I should start donning the linen clothing of the Egyptian workers, who seem significantly less bothered by the heat. And then I chastise myself, because it doesn't matter, not here, not now.

Six long years of fruitless searching, three more of careful excavation, brick by brick and statue by statue. I thought it couldn't get any better when I peered through into the antechamber for the first time, my eyes adjusting to the candlelight I held out through the gap as I spied furniture and figurines in remarkably well-preserved conditions.

And then even that paled in comparison to when we broke through into the funerary chamber, and that to when we discovered the shrine...Tutankhamun's tomb is one huge, wondrous construction of Russian dolls, each layer more special and wondrous than the last.

It feels like a dream sometimes, being this close to history. I often wonder what would have happened if Lord Carnarvon had been a little more stubborn, or myself a little less so, and I was not given that final season to dig in the Valley of Kings, desperation making us often work through the night. Would the world be dimmer? Has our triumph inspired courage back in London for people to fight for what they want, live for the now, and celebrate how far humanity has come?

Or am I so arrogant as to believe I could make a difference to our world?

I take a deep breath, feeling dizzy in the dry heat, and glance up at Lord Carnarvon. His eyes are alight with fervour, perhaps even more than mine, and he's clutching his hands so tightly that some of his fingers are turning white.

"Ready?" I whisper.

"Ready," Lord Carnarvon confirms, his gaze flicking to mine briefly, before returning to the resting place of the boy pharaoh.

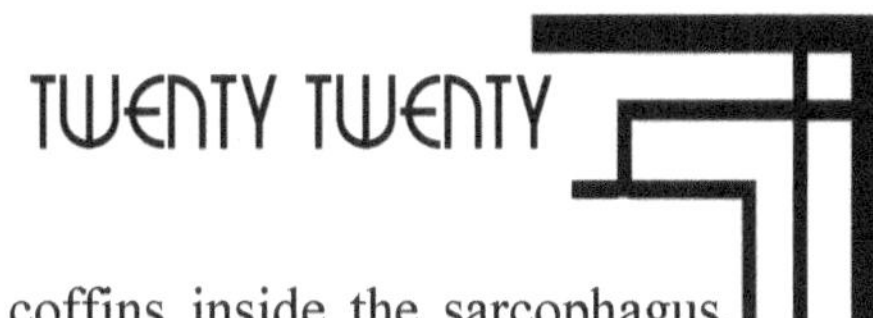

There were three coffins inside the sarcophagus, and today is the day we open the final one.

I nod at Harry and Alfred, and the three of us carefully lift the lid and place it on a blanket stretched across the floor, a puff of stale air erupting from the seal as we break it.

I can't believe my eyes. The mummified pharaoh is unbelievably intact, impossibly untouched by time itself. The quality of the wrappings, the shape of the limbs, the delicate etchings on the inside of the coffin...

Delighted murmurs hit my ears and I catch the eyes of my colleagues, all of us wearing the same stupefied look of wonder.

The treasures in the outer chamber pale in comparison to this. It is an unprecedented find, the discovery of the decade...no, forget the 1920s. The discovery of the century! It is-

"Yes, yes," Lord Carnarvon mutters impatiently. "Toss him over there and let's get a look at what's underneath."

"Toss him? Toss the mummified pharaoh?" I repeat disbelievingly, and he has the good grace to wince.

"You're right, Carter. I apologise. Handle him very carefully so we don't have to explain to the media what happened. But do it quickly: I've waited too many years

for this already."

Confused, I start to protest, but Lord Carnarvon shuts me down in less than three words, reminding me of his power over our excavation. One command from him, and this whole project comes down around my ears. Fuming, I gingerly heave Tutankhamun's fragile body out of the coffin, and Alfred and I lay it down next to the lid of the coffin. His corpse is both heavier and lighter than I expected, and I can't help but gasp when I see how short it really is. I knew the pharaoh died in his teenage years, but it's one thing to read the hieroglyphics about him and another to have a child's body in your arms.

I swallow hard as I turn back to Lord Carnarvon, who is running an ungloved hand around the inside of the golden coffin. My hands curl into indignant fists, but I'm powerless to stop him. "Let me see," he mutters, clearly not speaking to any of us. "Further up, I'd say, what about...there!"

With a triumphant cry, he heaves up the base of the coffin, a loose plank of wood that he carelessly casts over his shoulder. I grit my teeth as it shatters against the wall, another piece of history lost to the barbarism of uncaring men.

"It's beautiful," Lord Carnarvon breathes, and despite my anger, I'm curious what he has found.

Leaning forward, I catch sight of a small gelatinous blob curled up on the true base of the coffin, rounded unlidded eyes blinking up at us. Its colouring is a pale purple, but I can see the grain of the wood through its translucent body.

"What is that?" Harry scrambles backwards, his limbs splayed, and I catch his arm before he falls onto the pharaoh. He gives me a brief nod of thanks, but his eyes are wide and scared.

"It's what the Egyptians truly intended this tomb for," Lord Carnarvon says, reaching in a hand to scoop the creature out. It was about the size of his palm, and he was able to ease it between his fingers without too much difficulty. "King Tut's body was just another protection, the same as the statue guards, the blocked wall, the curses. A distraction from the real royalty that lay within. But," he adds, frowning at the thing as he raises it to his face for closer inspection, and it waves two tiny tentacles feebly at him. "All the hieroglyphics speak of it as an egg."

"Three thousand years might have had something to say about it," I mutter under my breath, annoyed. For all of his pretending to share my interests, it is clear that this was what Lord Carnarvon has been searching for all along, using my archaeological knowledge for his own purposes.

It's a find, to be sure: either some type of ancient mutant creature, or a being from beyond the stars, but that wasn't my area of expertise. I was about mummies, the dead King behind me and the markings on the walls that surrounded us which told of generations of pharaohs and their complex politics.

The creature abruptly leaps from Lord Carnarvon's hand to his face, and the man lets out a wet scream.

It is piercing but muffled, as if a mermaid were screeching from the depths of the ocean, and I can only stare in horror. His face is completely enveloped by the translucent glob of the creature, his arms clawing at the substance to no avail. And then...he falls still. Not as if he's steadily grown weaker as the thing cut off his air, flailing around in his death throes, but a sudden and unnatural stillness as if he were an automobile that has been turned off. He's still standing upright, his hands frozen in the air, and he reminds me far too unpleasantly of one of the wax figurines at Madame Tussauds.

"Sir?" Alfred takes a tentative step towards Lord Carnarvon.

"Don't touch him!" I shout, but my voice took too long to come back to me, and it's too late: the thing slithers down Lord Carnarvon's neck with impossible

speed, clamping onto Alfred's outstretched hand.

He screams and tries to shake it off, one hand shielding his face, but whatever the creature did to Lord Carnarvon is far different to how it's choosing to kill Alfred. And killing him it is: everywhere it touches, be it skin or clothing, boils and bubbles with a stench of charred meat, and within seconds it has glided over Alfred's arms and his torso, leaving nothing but blistered skin with a sticky, melted texture.

I can't breathe again, and this time it's for completely different reasons. This thing, this creature, is far worse than anything the Egyptians had done to each other, more disturbing than any of the curses or ancient punishments I'd read about, or maybe it was because this was real, and right here, and burning a man to death in front of my eyes...

"Harry, we need to get out of here!" I croak hoarsely, letting my eyes rest for the barest of seconds on King Tutankhamun, and knowing if I leave, I'll never see him again. But even history, as precious as it is, is not worth dying for.

Harry is already ahead of me, his feet dislodging rock as he climbs through the opening into the antechamber, not even offering me a second glance as he flees. I take a step, intending to follow, but a streak of purple flashes past me, shooting across the floor and wrapping around Harry's ankles.

The man falls head first onto the loose rock, a sickening crunch accompanied by what could only be described as a slurping sound as the creature makes its way up the body, boiling it as it goes. But there are no screams this time: mercifully, Harry knocked himself out with his fall.

I don't think I'll be so lucky. With the only exit blocked, I back away, my eyes darting around for a weapon. But everything in here is too fragile and would crumble to dust in my hands. And besides, what can possibly stop a monster like that?

So I let myself fall to my knees instead, reciting the Lord's Prayer under my breath. Science has driven God from my thoughts over the years, preferring logic and reason to the immeasurable and indeterminate fantasy of religion. But there is no logic to this creature, no reason. It's not of this earth, and science has failed me, so where does man go when the darkness falls?

Back to his Maker.

My eyes are closed, so I can't see the thing coming. I don't want to face my death.

But nothing ever touches me, no fiery pain meets my skin.

And so, reluctantly, I open them again.

For a moment I can't see it, and a flutter of hope builds inside me that it followed Harry's intended route out to the excavation site outside, sparing me in its excitement for freedom.

And then Lord Carnarvon speaks.

"Car...ter."

It's his mouth moving, his voice coming out, but it's not him. There's something eerie about the sound, unearthly and strange.

"Car...ter. His mind tells me this is...you..."

Lord Carnarvon's eyes stare glassily at me.

"George?" I ask, my mouth dry. "George, are you in there?"

"He is gone," the creature hisses, using Lord Carnarvon's mouth. "I sucked out everything that made him...him. He was tast...ty. It is only...me...now."

"What are you?"

"It...does not matter...even if I told you, your...brain would not con...ceive it..."

"Are you going to kill me?" I ask, in a very small voice.

"No, Car...ter. Not if you do what I...say."

I stay silent for a moment, processing my options. Not that I have many.

"What do you want of me?"

"This body...he is power...ful, is he not?"

I nod my head. "Yes." It only strikes me afterwards that the creature may not have been talking about influence, but rather physical strength, but it seems to find my answer acceptable at the time.

"You will remove them," the creature says, lifting one of Lord Carnarvon's fingers to point at the corpses of my colleagues. "And you...will not speak of this day to anyone. I require privacy for my work: do you understand?"

I want to ask what its 'work' is, spoken in such a creepy and determined way, but I hold my tongue out of a sense of self-preservation. "There's no way you - or I," I correct, "can cover this up. The whole world is waiting for us to tell it what we found in here!"

"Then bring a...camera," the creature says, forcing Lord Carnarvon's tongue around the words. "Open the king's sarcophagus and show them there's nothing inside."

"I don't understand."

"So simple," it hisses. "So weak."

My face flushes.

"Reset this coffin, and ensure the world sees it open," the creature explains. "No one will ever know that the king did not lie here alone. I have other business to attend to."

"Wait, wearing...him?" I blurt out, gesturing at Lord Carnarvon's body, being directed around like a puppet with invisible strings. "You'll never get away with that!" But even as I speak, I realise that its speech has become less disjointed in the last few minute, its movements smoother. It's passing for human already.

"Don't fail me, Carter," Lord Carnarvon says, adjusting his shirt collar. "Or I'll be back to finish you off as well. Your life is as long as your usefulness."

The creature, hidden inside the man's body, saunters out of the tomb, treading on the two corpses as he leaves.

I sit there for a while, staring at the pharaoh as if he can give me answers to what I should do. But the dead— the true dead—are silent.

* * *

It's fifteen years later that the iron grip on my tongue fails, the complete absence of the creature from the last decade and a half of my life convincing me that it holds no sway over me. I write down all that happened that day in careful script, triplicating it across three letters that I intend to distribute: one to the London Museum, the second to the Egyptian Antiquities Service, and the third to Yale University.

Bile rises in my throat as I tuck the certificate conferring my honorary degree into the final letter. I don't deserve it.

I'm scrawling the addresses on the envelopes with a determined hand when I hear a voice behind me. A woman.

A woman with the voice of darkness and death.

"Cart...er..."

# THE SCREAMS OF THE ELEPHANTS

by Thomas Vaughn

"Them's good. Ain't they?" The man smiled with tobacco-stained teeth, a meaty hand stirring the large kettle of pork scratchings that boiled in hot oil.

His customers, a man and woman, watched as their little boy took his first, hesitant bite. The three of them were arrayed in their finest clothes. She wore a white, satin dress with a blue cameo, and he a tweed suit. The little boy was adorned in formal breeches and a sailor hat. He chewed apprehensively, then his face lit with joy.

"Mama, these are swell!"

The woman laughed and the man patted his son on

the head. "It looks like you've won another convert," he said, winking to the cook who was carving more pig fat and tossing it into the cauldron where it sizzled in protest.

"Yes, Sir! Ain't nobody makes scratchings like I can. Learned it from my pa in Louisiana. You tell folks you see. You tell em' about Old Moses."

The little boy dug into the bag and stuffed another piece of blistered flesh in his mouth.

"You'll get no argument from us," said the woman, her teeth shining beneath the June sun. It was a perfect day and the crowd gathered on the hillside pulsed with anticipation. There was a slight breeze coming through the pines from the west and few among those assembled failed to take note of just how beautiful the world seemed at that moment. It was one of those incandescent afternoons, the type that beguiled one into believing they might live forever.

The train wreck was scheduled for two o'clock in the afternoon. An entrepreneur named Spratt had built three miles of track outside of Lexington Kentucky just for the occasion. He could be seen strolling through the crowd in a tuxedo and bowler, bowing to the ladies and tweaking his large moustache as he surveyed the scene. Each person had paid the considerable sum of five dollars a ticket for the privilege of witnessing the catastrophe. The locomotives, both purchased from the Frisco Line, puffed patiently just beyond the eyesight of the crowd. After shouldering so many burdens for a young nation emerging from its first world war, the machines had one last task to perform before they were scrapped for good. The iron horses would be stoked to maximum capacity and driven straight at one another. At the first mile marker the lone engineers on each train would jump from their respective cabs into specially arranged beds of hay bales arranged alongside the track.

All around merchants were selling food and souvenirs. There were peanuts and candied apples. One man was selling hand-carved toy trains. Embossed brochures with pictures of the locomotives could be had for twenty-five cents. To one side, a motion picture crew was perching a cumbersome camera atop a massive tripod. A lone clown in a tattered coat rode a unicycle alongside the tracks, navigating expertly across the newly upturned earth. The air was redolent with the smell of food and the hillside rang with laughter.

"Are they really gonna wreck those trains?" asked the little boy.

The man beamed at him. "That's right, Tiger. They're gonna hit each other at sixty miles an hour. Can

you imagine that?"

The little boy looked down at the tracks. "Is it gonna make a loud noise?"

"It's going to be a noise like you've never heard before."

"And a noise like you'll never hear again," echoed his mother.

The young couple stood arm in arm, soaking up the sunshine. They were part of that great mass of humanity, yet marked by their singularity. Each of them vibrated with expectation. This was a day of celebration, though no one could articulate the occasion. They were the first generation to grow up in a world of machines. The power of automation encompassed them on all sides. Perhaps the display was an exercise of autonomy. The act of driving the iron behemoths headlong into one another was a means for reasserting control over an increasingly uncertain technological future. After the machine guns, rifled artillery, and cumbersome tanks of Europe's killing fields had claimed so many, it was a moment where their collective anxiety might be transmuted into joy. The machines would be set against one another for entertainment, producing an amnesia about the piles of rotting corpses now mouldering beneath the distant battlefields, victims of an age of steel

and gasoline.

"Mama, why doesn't that clown smile?"

The man and woman were surprised to find that the clown was suddenly next to them, still balanced on his unicycle. Only a moment before he had been some distance away. It was almost like he had simply materialised. The clown looked weak and thin.

"Well, how did you get up here?" asked the man good-naturedly. He looked down at the milkweed and marvelled at the strength and skill it had taken for the clown to reach them. His coat was worn, and dirty toes poked through tattered shoes. The clown saluted with one gloved hand, then answered the man's inquiry by dodging back and forth among the clumps of weeds.

"That's something," crooned the boy, delighted. "Can I get one of those?"

"A unicycle?" asked his mother with a mixture of amusement and concern. "Only when you are a good bit older."

"And when you have your own insurance policy," teased his father.

The woman struck him on the chest playfully.

"Stop that, Art."

"But how come he doesn't smile?"

The clown's face was covered in what appeared to

be black axle grease. In fact, his clothes stank of petroleum. His lips were highlighted in grey ash, accenting the down-turned features.

"Well, let's ask him," said his father, turning to the clown. "Say, Fella, why don't you smile?"

The clown balanced for a moment, then suddenly lost traction in the grass and began to tumble down the hill. The woman put a hand to her mouth, but just as she was about to speak the clown emerged from the tumble still seated on the unicycle.

The boy squealed with delight. "Mama, I want a unicycle!"

The woman laughed with relief. "You're definitely not getting one now."

The boy's face screwed up in consternation, and it appeared that he was getting ready to protest, but his father redirected his attention to the tracks and the coming train wreck. They lost interest in the clown who continued to bob and weave up and down the hillside. It was true that he didn't smile. In fact, he hadn't smiled in ten years. It's hard to smile when all you can hear are the screams. The whole circus had been headed to Chicago by train. Somewhere around Hammond Indiana the engineer fell asleep and didn't perceive the second locomotive parked on the tracks ahead. It was the dead of night and most of the performers and roustabouts were sleeping in the cars along with the animals. Dozens died in the initial collision. Yet the worst was still to come. Crates of lamp oil ignited and set the railcars ablaze. With only one stagnant pond nearby, there was no way to quell the flames.

As the clown dodged amid the crowd, he could still hear Sheeba's screams. She was an ancient elephant housed in one of the cars. Her screams echoed throughout the night, almost drowning out the humans. But most of all, he remembered the woman and child trapped in the wreckage as the fire crept closer. He grasped bloodied hands, nearly pulling arms from their sockets in a desperate attempt to free them.

But still the fire crept closer.

And still Sheeba screamed.

Finally, some bystanders restrained him lest he be consumed by the fire. He sat by and wept as the flames took them all, their screams reaching up to heaven like so many unanswered prayers. Sheeba bellowed even as she was roasted alive, the smell of her cooking flesh mixing with the pall of toxic smoke. After that the clown never smiled. He no longer careened around the big top as the spotlight followed him, trying to flee from his own shadow while the crowds howled with delight. Now, he simply rode the unicycle, his face contorted in a permanent rictus.

"Ladies and gentlemen, may I have your attention!"

When Spratt mounted the specially made platform, all thoughts of the clown were lost.

"For the past century we have conquered this land from coast to coast. This sacred conquest was ordained by our creator. No single tool has been more useful in fulfilling this task than the locomotive. The iron horse has linked all forty-eight states of this great country, making us a strong people. With their help, we are now the greatest nation on earth."

Here the people took a moment to cheer themselves and their great nation while Spratt beamed benevolently, his moustache strangely resistant to the light breeze.

"Today these engines serve a different design. Today we will pit Titan against Titan. Coming from the south you will observe the Shamrock and from the north the Monon Bell. These trusty steeds, recently retired from the Frisco Line, will clash in this very valley on this very day in a celebration of our greatness as a people and as a civilization."

The crowd cheered again, this time with greater zeal, the tension rising in their gullets.

"But it's not me you've come to see."

Brandishing a great pistol, he pointed it upward.

"May the best engine win!"

With this he pulled the trigger and a ball of fire arced into the sky.

"What's that, Daddy?"

"That's a flare gun, Tiger. He's signalling to the engineers.

The crowd surged toward the tracks to get a better view. Now the family found themselves buffeted uncomfortably and the man picked up his son to keep him from falling underfoot.

"Here now!" he admonished those around him. "It will take the trains some minutes before they can get up to speed. Be patient!"

The crowd pressed together, and necks strained toward the distant horizons. For a long time, there was nothing but silence. No one noticed that the clown had come to a complete stop. He balanced in the open like a scarecrow on its stake. He didn't face the tracks, but toward the Northwest. It was as if he was straining to pierce the distant haze, to perceive that cemetery plot called Showman's Rest. There lay so many of his friends, some with grave markers reading *Rags* or *Baldy,* because no living person could remember their Christian names. There also lay the ashes of a woman and a child, the ones cremated the night the elephant screamed.

But no one thought to look at him just then, with his head bowed and shoulders slumped. Instead, their heartbeats quickened when they heard the braying of a whistle to their right. They cheered. As if on cue came the answer from the other side.

The woman took her husband's arm. "My God, the anticipation is simply killing me."

He smiled reassuringly. "Mark my words, Lela. We'll never forget this day as long as we live. Isn't that right, Tiger?"

"Right, Daddy!" said the boy, transfixed.

Soon they could hear the sounds of the engines as they laboured toward one another, the rhythmic chop of the pistons growing more frantic as the great beasts increased speed. Sweat beaded on foreheads and guts jangled with the mounting tension. Before long the two machines came into view, each pulling a lone coal car. Both smokestacks were belching smoke, as if warning the other of its infinite lethality. In the end, the crowd didn't have time to cheer. There was only a collective intake of breath as the two machines charged at one another, cold and implacable in their mission. The impact was so sudden those standing near the tracks didn't have time to react when shrapnel shot forth from the crash zone. The steam casings buckled like accordions before the echoing tremor could be absorbed by the surrounding hills. Bits of rivets and gears riddled those on the front row, many collapsing with bloody wounds. Only the motion picture man remained where he stood, his hand slowly cranking. His own peril didn't figure into any calculation since he was nothing more than an extension of the camera.

"Good gracious!" exclaimed the woman, as she surveyed the damage. With nowhere else to go, the Shamrock and Monon Bell had each lifted off the tracks in a tortured archway, then fallen back to earth with the sound of thunder. They lay smouldering in a twisted heap.

"Are you hurt?" asked her husband, raising his voice over the rain of metal and screams of the wounded. Mr Spratt was striding here and there, calling for calm, but no one was paying any attention to him. The people genuflected to the death throes of the metal monsters that burst into flames before their eyes, scorching those who had ventured too close.

"This is madness!" cried the man, clutching his weeping son close to his chest. But even as he did this, he felt a countervailing force trying to extricate the boy from his arms. He looked up to see the darkened face of the clown. The strange creature was still perched on the unicycle. He had wrapped his gloved hands around the boy and was trying to pull him from his father's arms.

"What the hell is wrong with you?" he yelled, clutching his son tighter.

But the clown continued to pull, his downturned lips never wavering. The woman soon joined in the struggle and it seemed to them that the clown was weeping. It was as if a lifetime of sadness had concentrated itself in a single moment of pain. They didn't look the clown in the face, for his continence was too sickening to behold. His eyes spoke of a quiet desperation. One would be tempted to dismiss him as mad, but he also seemed to see through the world around him—the only one who could perceive the terrible reality that lurked beneath the simulacra.

At last the man pulled his son free. Tossing him to one side, he dealt the clown a savage blow to the face. Again, the clown rolled back down the hill, popping upright as he had before, like some automated gear. All around him people were pushing and shouting.

"Get the hell away from us or I'll kill you," growled the man.

The clown's dark eyes peered first at the boy, and then at the woman. The desperation was replaced by sad

resignation. Without a word he began to pedal back up the hill. The man watched the clown until he no longer posed a threat, then turned to his son.

"Are you all right, Tiger?"

"What's that sound, Daddy? What's that terrible sound?"

Man and woman reached down together, forming a protective shield around the boy. All over the hillside the shouts of surprise had given way to the moaning of the wounded and cries for help.

"What's happened?" asked the woman.

"A damned, stinking mess!" the man replied.

"What's that sound?!" shrieked the boy, placing small hands to either ear.

But they couldn't answer him. The only one who knew was still pedalling. He rocked precariously from side to side, smoke beginning to waft from his clothes. The grease on his skin bubbled, causing the flesh to sizzle and curl. Though he faltered, he never lost his balance, even as the flames licked up from beneath his collar. The smell of pork cracklings mixed with that of petrol and scorched metal. He was the clown that never smiled. He was the clown that listened to the screams of the elephants. Once he circled the big top, trying to escape his own shadow while the audiences roared with

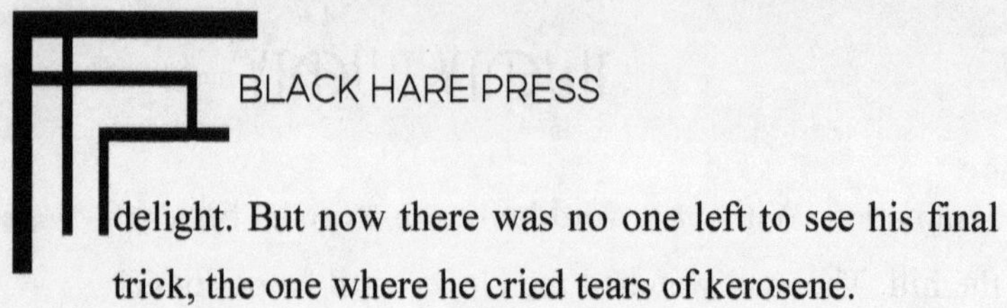


delight. But now there was no one left to see his final trick, the one where he cried tears of kerosene.

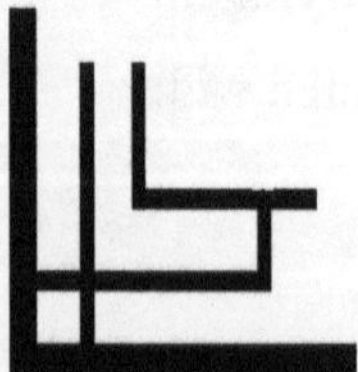

# Sebastian and the Speakeasy Adventure

by Scott Harper

Sebastian relished the decadent splendour of his first night on the town in Atlantic City. He'd rarely gone out socialising in the old country. The towns there didn't offer much in the way of entertainment…inhabited by peasants with clinging body odour and garlic breath and stagnant blood. But the cities of the new world…they offered him something very different. Something vibrant and alive. Something potent enough to pique his curiosity and lead him to load up his old dirt coffins and leave his homeland behind.

*The name itself quickens the senses...Atlantic City!* Sebastian marvelled.

He walked the streets amongst them, a cross section of the city, the poor and misbegotten, the rich and profane. Darkness made animate, he slipped from one shadow to the next, moving about unnoticed. He passed a garishly lit speakeasy named Babette's. The flow of foot traffic in and out enticed him. The American government had decreed alcohol to be illegal, inadvertently spawning a thriving black market that filled the void. Noting the "All Welcome" sign above the front door, Sebastian entered and took a seat.

It wasn't long before a woman joined him at his table. She reminded him of a tryst he'd had many years ago with a young flower in Bucharest. This one was pleasing enough in appearance, alabaster skin with soft brown eyes and a winsome smile. Her name was Ruby, and she was a frequenter of Babette's. She offered Sebastian some "giggle water," stating that it was "the berries," though he saw no evidence of fruit. He would have to get used to colloquial phrases that weren't listed in his books on the English language.

Sebastian sipped the grainy, bootlegged whiskey out of courtesy, but his attention was drawn to the steady pulse of the arteries on Ruby's neck. The trip across the

Atlantic had been long and exhausting. He'd fed only sparingly from the crew, reluctant to create a scare and wind up being tossed overboard in his coffin in the middle of the day. He caught Ruby's eyes and held her gaze, sifting through her thoughts, savouring them as he regaled her with tales of distant, exotic places she'd only read about. She stared at him with rapt attention, fascinated by the dark, handsome stranger who exuded such poise and confidence.

They were interrupted when two large thugs in grey suits and noisy boots thundered up to their table. Sebastian noted the bulge of pistols under their jackets.

"The boss wants to speak to you and the swell, Ruby. Now," the larger thug ordered, his beady eyes looking out from under a black fedora.

Sebastian was not intimidated by the men, but he was curious. What would the owner of such an establishment be like? Based on the thoughts he had sampled earlier, he knew that Ruby feared the man. Sebastian decided that he wanted to meet this "boss," but first he would engage in a little mild banter to further fine-tune his English.

"Sir, were you by chance addressing me? I believe you are mistaken. My name is not 'Swell,' it's Sebastian. Count Sebastian Alonso Alvarez."

Both thugs squinted and grimaced. Sebastian hoped he had succeeded in agitating them but wasn't sure. He hadn't spoken English with any regularity for many years and knew his speech bore a distinct accent. He continued needling them, nevertheless.

"Now if you'll excuse us, the young lady and I are otherwise involved at the moment." Sebastian looked back to Ruby.

The smaller thug placed his hand over the gun in his waistband.

"Maybe Marco didn't make himself clear, Mr Swell Fancy-pants Alonso Alvarez. Get your ass up and get moving!"

Sebastian smiled and nodded his head, not wanting to push the matter in front of so many people. He stood and complied. They were led upstairs and to the back of the building, passing a large mirror panel. Fortunately, no one noticed Sebastian's lack of reflection.

The boss's room was expansive and windowless, old world paintings decorating the walls. The man himself sat behind a large wooden desk, flanked by another jacketed underling, a scar-faced man with cold blue eyes. Sebastian recognised an assassin when he saw one, sensing a fellow predator.

The boss was dressed immaculately in a pinstripe

suit and tie. Light reflected off his bald head as he scowled.

"Now, just who da fuck do you think you are, mister, coming into my drum in your glad rags and getting half-seas over with my choice bit of calico? Do you know who I am? I'm Alonzo Diavolo, the devil. I run this town, *capisce*? And nobody messes with my moll!"

"I saw no signs with your name on them, Mr…Diavolo, is it? And I do believe the young lady's name is Ruby, not 'Moll,'" Sebastian replied.

The lights flickered, the laws of physics going askew in the presence of a vampire.

Diavolo became incensed. "Alright Mac, you think you're funny, eh? You think you're tough? Let me show you tough. Giuseppe!"

Upon command, the smaller goon withdrew a pocketknife and sliced Ruby's neck with expert precision. Blood sprayed as she gurgled and collapsed to the ground.

Sebastian was not surprised. He'd "lived" for many centuries and was familiar with the psychology of brutes. A show of force meant to intimidate a rival.

*How trite,* he mused. He regretted the shameful waste of precious blood.

Giuseppe levelled the blade in front of Sebastian's face as Diavolo continued.

"Now you seen how I handle my business. If you're smart, you'll take your cake-eatin' ass out of this town and back across the pond where your kind belongs. Ya follow? But first Giuseppe is gonna take one of those pointy ears of yours for my collection."

Diavolo's pomposity made Sebastian smirk. *The unbridled arrogance!*

Sebastian drew upon the tenebrous depths of the room's shadows and called them to him, his form swelling with dark power that reflected the blackness of his soul. The sclera of his eyes bled red as his fingers lengthened and nails grew into claws. He smiled, showing fangs, then gestured with his hands, exposing the fur on the palms. The faces of Diavolo and his goons blanched.

Sebastian savoured the look of absolute, wide-eyed terror frozen on their faces. "You have no idea what 'my kind' is, do you Mr Diavolo? You're a petty boor who fancies himself a purveyor of evil, but you merely leach off other's misery. Running liquor and gambling rings and selling females. You're more of a parasite than I am. Your methods are droll and hackneyed. You've not lived even a single mortal lifetime. I was butchering men far

more significant than you centuries before your great-grandfathers drew breath. Now, let me show you true evil!"

Giuseppe overcame his shock and stabbed Sebastian in the torso and neck. His steel blade found no purchase and drew no blood. Marco pulled his pistol from his waistband and emptied rounds into Sebastian, the gunshots deafening. The bullets caused no more damage than would a passing breeze.

Sebastian chuckled at the feebleness of their attacks. As a vampire, he existed on both the positive and shadow material planes, and was more spectral than corporeal in nature. Conventional weapons posed little threat to the eldritch durability of the cursed undead.

He shot out his hands, seizing the two men about the neck. Their eyes bugged and their tongues lolled out their mouths as their windpipes were sealed shut. Sebastian lifted them off their feet and smashed their heads together with a nauseating crack, pulping their skulls. The corpses slumped to the floor.

Diavolo jumped to his feet, upending his chair. He motioned to the assassin.

"Cipriano, do your job. Kill this egg!" he screamed.

Sebastian had noted that the blue-eyed assassin remained impassive during the entire incident, his hands at his sides. Diavolo began to panic, cold sweat breaking out on his forehead.

"What the fuck is your problem, Cip? Don't just stand there like a dew-dropper! Bump this spiffy off!"

"He knows his station, Mr Diavolo. He recognizes an apex predator," Sebastian remarked, looming between the two corpses. Blood pooled around his feet as he licked a stray drop from his finger, savouring the adrenalised fear within. He caught Diavolo's gaze.

"Look at me, cur! Look deep into my eyes and know yourself for what you truly are!"

Diavolo fell to his knees and began to bark like a dog, his tongue out. He sniffed the ground, raised a leg and pissed himself.

Sebastian spoke to the assassin.

"What say you, assassin? Shall I feed on this wretch, add his strength to my own?"

The assassin paused for a moment, then spoke.

"The wine has gone bad, sir. The vintage has turned to vinegar."

The vampire smiled. "Then, would you do me the honours, Cipriano? I grow tired of our friend's theatrics."

Cipriano stepped forward from behind the desk, drawing a pistol from his coat. He put one round into the

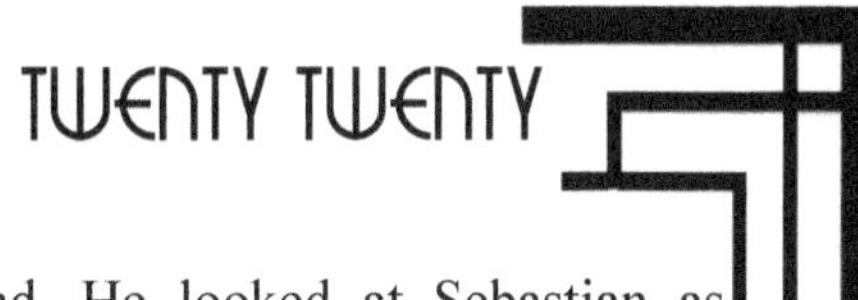

back of Diavolo's head. He looked at Sebastian as Diavolo fell like a stone to the floor.

Sebastian approached.

"I like your style, Cip. I've got big plans, you see. This town is just begging for someone with a bit of panache to come in and paint it red. And I'm a paint-it-red kind of guy, as you can see. So, let's just cut to the chase, shall we?"

Sebastian extended his fur-palmed claw to the assassin.

"Would you like a job?" the vampire asked.

Cipriano smiled.

"The world is our oyster," Sebastian said as they shook.

BLACK HARE PRESS

# THE BOX

by Owen Morgan

Billy Parker, Ned Armitage, and Peter Watkins, veterans all of the Great War, having observed the first Armistice Day ceremony, had ventured into the comfort of the local pub to escape the bitter north British weather, and huddled next to the snapping and popping flames, which outlined the trio in its orange glow. Billy reached for his pint and gulped down the last mouth full, then ran the back of his hand over his stubble rimmed mouth.

Ned held up his still full cup. "I know we're all unemployed soldiers who fought for King and Country with little to cheer about, but I propose a toast."

Peter rolled his bloodshot eyes. "I propose you down that drink so we can go home."

Ned banged his fist on the tabletop, sending plates and cutlery dancing. "Oh, have a bit of respect, this is my fourth pint, I thought it proper to make a toast after all this time."

Billy smiled, revealing a mouthful of teeth only a tart would call attractive. "Hold on there, by my count, that's your fifth. But I digress, who do you want to toast?"

"Michael Stratford."

His drinking compatriots remained silent, Peter glanced at Ned, who nodded and both raised their mugs.

An hour later, they departed the Pig and Whistle Tavern, propping each other up in the misty rain, singing a song from the Great War. An old man approached with a black umbrella held aloft, who listened to their slurred words then joined them in song.

"Oi, hold on," Ned pointed to the man who sheltered beneath the umbrella. "Were." He wobbled for a moment, then continued. "Were you in the war?"

"Why, yes, don't let the touch of frost in my hair make you think I was too old to have served. I was at the Somme with the East Lancashire Regiment."

Billy, Ned, and Peter linked their arms. "Three cheers for the regiment."

The man smiled. "I know you lads have already had a grand evening but would you honour a fellow Tommie and join me for a drink, on my bill, of course."

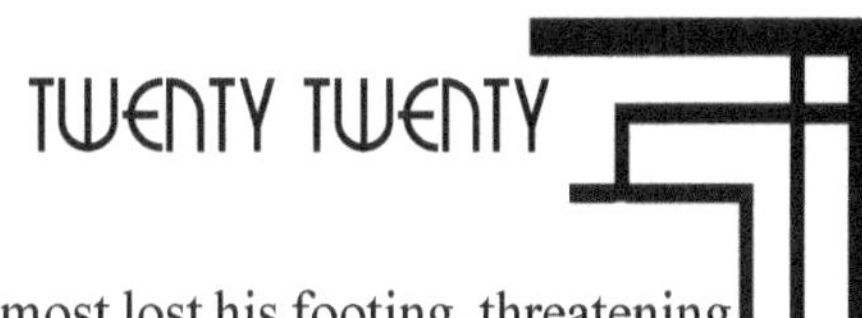

Ned swayed and almost lost his footing, threatening to take down his linked mates. "I say, that's a fine idea. Let's go inside and partake in a drink with Mr…"

"Henry Horrocks, Lieutenant."

Peter opened the door. The common room was devoid of patrons. Only Derrick, the tavernkeeper, nodded from behind the bar. Someone had pushed all the round tables into a corner, and only a square table occupied the middle of the room. In the centre of the table was a plain, sandalwood box devoid of any markings, resting on a slip of red silk. Billy and Ned shared sidelong glances. Peter shoved his hands into the pockets of his trench coat.

Ned turned to Horrocks. "What's all this then? Where the rest of the gents?"

"I apologise for the subterfuge. For you see, I was tasked with meeting you, gentlemen. As to the other patrons, they were each given a pound note and sent on their way home. For we require some privacy."

Billy pushed up the peak of his hat, revealing a jagged scar from a piece of shrapnel. "All right, mate, I'll play along, as long as I get that drink you told me about."

Horrocks sat and gestured to the remaining chairs. "Please, gentlemen, I promise not to keep you long."

All three took their seats. Ned jabbed his thumb at the box. "What's in there?"

A voice issued from the box. "Don't you lot stand to attention when an officer is in the room?"

"God in heaven," Ned almost shrieked. He tumbled from his chair and fell backward, disgorging a flask, lighter, and a package of cigarettes from his pockets.

Billy laughed and shook his head. "Now, that's one hell of a trick. I admit that does sound like Captain Stratford. What do ya have in there a recording of his voice?"

Peter stiffened, eyes darting around the table, his gaze settling on Horrocks. "What..what's this all about?"

Horrock's leaned his elbows on the table and rested his chin atop his interlaced fingers. "Open the box and find out."

Billy leaned forward and flipped open the lid. Inside, resting atop a cloud of purple linen was the head of Captain Stratford. His eyes remained shut, but his mouth opened. "Normally, you men would be on report for not standing to attention, let alone not saluting a superior officer, but under the circumstances, I shall overlook this violation of the King's Regulations."

All stared, unblinking, Ned tried to speak but could

form no words while Peter shook in his chair. Billy recovered first, and flung off his cap, producing a folding razor and opened the blade. "Hold on, what kinda trickery is this? I mean, bravo for having some puppeteer make the mouth move and all, but this ain't funny."

"Don't interrupt when an officer is speaking. As I said, I can overlook the breach in military protocol, but what I cannot turn a blind eye to is the killing of an officer. I suppose you lot had shot your bolt before we went over the top back on July 1st. You obviously thought entering my dugout the night before our big push and taking an axe to my head would solve your problems. And then to unceremoniously leave my body in no-man's-land, obviously hoping some stray jerry shell would dispose of the evidence."

Billy, Peter, and Ned alternated between curses and threats and utterances of disbelief. A door opened in the back of the tavern and Stradford's headless body entered the room, pointing a Webley revolver at the men, and motioning with the weapon toward the front door.

"Horrocks," Stradford continued. "Be a good gentleman and lift me."

Horrocks lifted the head to turn in the direction of the men. Stradford's eyes opened, steely and blue.

"Thank you. As for the rest of you, I trust you can show more backbone before a firing squad than you did in the trenches."

# THE STORY OF ROSCOE OWEN CLYDE

by Michael D. Davis

My father told me this story when I was, but a child. I believed it back then, just as I believe it now. Whether you will believe it or not, I don't know.

It all starts with my great uncle Roscoe Owen Clyde. He was just over twenty-years-old in the year 1926, and he knew the dirt roads of Hinchley County like the inside of his eyelid. His black demon of a car zipped through the back roads, just a shadow in the wind. Every night of the week he was out, driving under the moon carrying the moonshine.

He made deliveries all over the county, gallons of the stuff being moved from place to place. There would be a chase every now and again, but no one ever caught Roscoe Owen Clyde's car.

One particular night when he was out on a delivery, Roscoe pulled off and parked on the side of the road. There was nothing wrong, he just had to take a piss. Stepping into the grass, Roscoe Owen Clyde dropped his pants and proceeded with relieving himself and watering a small patch of weeds. As he did so, he looked up at the night sky, at the moon that seemed to float amongst the stars. That's when he heard it first; a rustling, a movement. Shrugging it off, he figured it to be a rabbit or a squirrel chasing its tail. But just as he did so, a little green man, no bigger than a boot, and what seemed to be a hound dog, came out from behind a bush.

"Excuse me, can I talk to ya a moment?" said the little green man, looking at Roscoe Owen Clyde still with his pants down.

"Didja hear me alright, fellar?" said the little green man again.

Roscoe Owen Clyde slowly pulled up his pants saying, "Yes, I heard."

"Good. My name is Floyd and I'm not from around here, as you can probably tell." The little green man

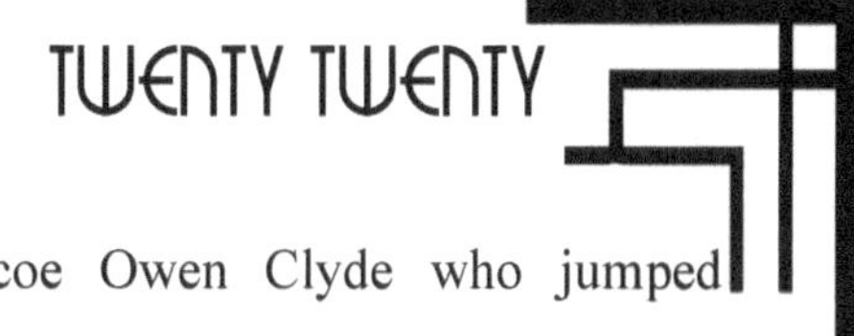

started towards Roscoe Owen Clyde who jumped backward towards his car.

"In all honesty, Floyd ain't even my real name, just somethin' I'd call myself while I was here. I'm from a planet a ways away, and I'm here offerin' Earth bein's a trip. The only catch bein', we gotta learn a bit from ya. We'd do us some blood tests, x-rays, and you can tell us all about Earth. Simple as that."

Leaning safely against his car, Roscoe Owen Clyde said, "I tell you 'bout Earth and you take me away to a distant planet?"

"That's the deal. Tests won't hurt, and you can tell us the goin's on. This one here already agreed." Floyd pointed towards the hound dog.

"What can a hound tell ya?"

"You'd be surprised there… So, you agreein'?"

"I…I think I am. It will be astoundin' to go 'bout the stars."

"Certainly will. Now, there ain't enough room in my vehicle for you and him, so I'll tell ya what I'll do. I'll pop over, drop him off, then come back and get you. How 'bout that?"

"How do I know you're comin' back?"

"Glad you asked," said Floyd.

Roscoe Owen Clyde finished his deliveries that

night, then went home and retold the story. No one believed him. He told his mother, his father, his brother, and his sister, all of them thought it was crap. That was until he showed them. Roscoe Owen Clyde took his shoe and sock off his right foot and extended his leg forward in front of his family. They stared in disbelief at his missing big toe. It wasn't cut off or chopped, but simply gone; like he was born without it. The other four toes sat untouched.

It was his ticket, Roscoe Owen Clyde had explained. The proof that showed Floyd was coming back. But he didn't come. Roscoe Owen Clyde sat and waited, living his life, delivering the moonshine, with an unrelenting belief in Floyd's return.

That was until three years later when Roscoe Owen Clyde walked out of the house in the middle of the night, never to be seen again. The morning after Roscoe Owen Clyde disappeared, his mother found, on the front porch, lying at the front door, a big toe. It didn't look cut off or chopped, not even wilted.

That big toe is now buried in the dirt under an old stone that says: *Roscoe Owen Clyde gone but never forgotten*. I've seen that grave with my own eyes. I've dug that dirt myself. I've held that toe in my own hand. If you don't believe the story, come around the farm one

day, Hinchley County, Iowa. I'll show you the gravestone. I'll dig the dirt. I'll show you the toe. Not cut or chopped or even wilted, is the toe of Roscoe Owen Clyde.

BLACK HARE PRESS

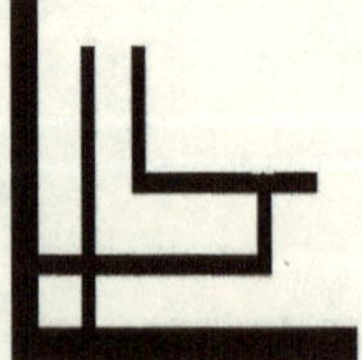

# TWENTY TWENTY

BLACK HARE PRESS

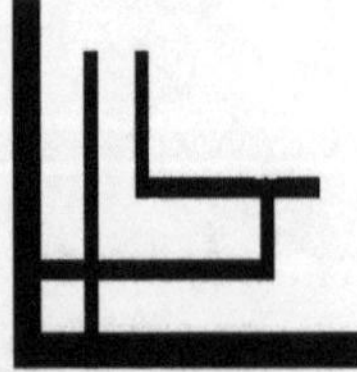

# AUTHOR BIOGRAPHIES

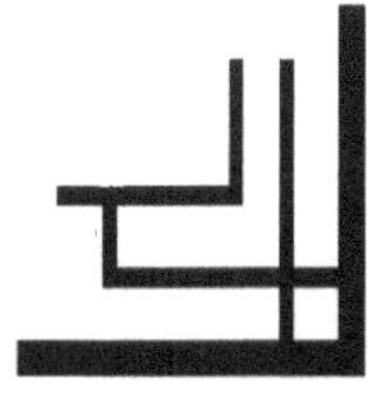

BLACK HARE PRESS

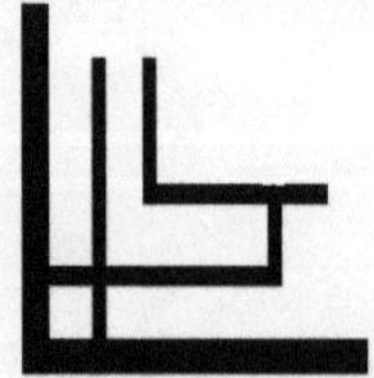

## A.R DEAN

*A.R. Dean is a dark and twisted soul. Dean has spent their whole life spreading fear with the tales from their head. Best known for stories that terrify and show the evilest side of human nature. So, look for Dean haunting your local cemetery or under your bed, because they're here to spread the fear. Turn off your lights and enjoy a scare. Dean is being published in Black Hare Press's Beyond and Unravel Anthologies. Keep a lookout for more stories.*

*Facebook: A.R. Dean Author & Ghoul*

* * *

## AMBER M. SIMPSON

*Amber M. Simpson is a dark fiction writer from Northern Kentucky with a penchant for horror and fantasy. Her work has been published in multiple anthologies, as well as online. She assists with editing for Fantasia Divinity Magazine, where she's gotten to work with many talented authors from all over the world. While she loves to create dark worlds and diverse characters, her greatest creations of all are her sons, Max and Liam, who keep her feet on the ground even while her head is in the clouds.*

*Website: ambermsimpson.com*
*Facebook: authorambermsimpson*

* * *

## ANDREA ALLISON

*Andrea Allison writes and resides in a small Oklahoman town. Her work has appeared in Trembling With Fear, NoSleep Podcast, Speculative 66, Sirens Call Ezine and various anthologies.*

*Website: www.andreallison.com*

## ANDREW KURTZ

*Andrew Kurtz is an emerging writer of horror, influenced by Stephen King, H.P. Lovecraft and Wells. He has stories published by Black Hare Press, Eleanor Merry, Renaimted Writers' and R.J. Roles.*

* * *

## CATHERINE KENWELL

*Catherine Kenwell is a Barrie, Ontario, mediator and author. After 30 successful years in corporate communications, she sustained a brain injury, lost her job, and joined the circus. She writes both horror/dark fiction and inspirational non-fiction. Her works have been published in Chicken Soup for the Soul, Trembling with Fear, Siren's Call, and HellBound Books.*

*Website: www.catherinekenwell.com*

* * *

## CHRIS BANNOR

*Chris Bannor is a science fiction and fantasy writer who lives in Southern California. Chris learned her love of genre stories from her mother at an early age and has never veered far from that path. She also enjoys musical theater and road trips with her family but is a general homebody otherwise.*

*Facebook: chrisbannorauthor*
*Website: ChrisBannor.com*

# TWENTY TWENTY

## D.J. ELTON

*D.J. Elton is a writer living in Melbourne's west. As a child she came from England to Australia, on the last boat down the Suez Canal, where she underwent a sacrificial dunking ritual in the court of King Neptune, and has never looked back. She likes creating speculative micro fiction and short stories, as well as random essays. Her work has been published in several anthologies, and she has written a historical fantasy novella, 'The Merlin Girl.' When not playing with a pen, she likes most of all to go to the green country.*

* * *

## D.J. TYRER

*D.J. Tyrer is the person behind Atlantean Publishing and has been widely published in anthologies and magazines around the world, such as Chilling Horror Short Stories (Flame Tree), Steampunk Cthulhu (Chaosium), What Dwells Below (Sirens Call), and EOM:Equal Opportunity Madness (Otter Libris), and issues of Sirens Call, Hinnom Magazine, ParABnormal, Kzine, and Weirdbook, and in addition, has a novella available in paperback and on the Kindle, The Yellow House (Dunhams Manor) and a comic horror e-novelette, A Trip to the Middle of the World, available from Alban Lake through Infinite Realms Bookstore.*

*Website: djtyrer.blogspot.co.uk*

* * *

## D.M. BURDETT

*D.M. Burdett initially roamed as an army brat, but now lives in Australia where she spends her days avoiding drop bears and killer spiders. She has published a Sci-Fi series, has short stories in various anthologies, and has published two children's series. She is currently working on the first book in a dystopian series.*

*Website: www.dmburdett.com*
*Facebook: DMBurdett*

 BLACK HARE PRESS

## DAVID BOWMORE

*David Bowmore has lived here, there and everywhere, but now lives in Yorkshire with his wonderful wife and a small white poodle. He has worn many hats in his time; head chef, teacher and landscape gardener. His first collection of short stories 'The Magic of Deben Market' is available from Clarendon House.*

*Website: davidbowmore.co.uk*
*Facebook: davidbowmoreauthor*

* * *

## DAVID M. HOENIG

*David is a multiclass surgeon/writer with the "time management" feat. He's had stories published with Grim Dark Magazine, Flame Tree Publishing, Cast of Wonders, and others. He has published a novel-told-through-surreal-verse-and-art with Oscillate Wildly Press, called "Queen To His King". He is editing his first novel (sci fi), at somewhat slower than the speed of light. He's also a soul-gem carrying member of the HWA.*

*Website: davidmhoenig.wordpress.com*
*Twitter: authordmhoenig*

* * *

## DAWN DEBRAAL

*Dawn DeBraal lives in rural Wisconsin with her husband Red, two rat terriers, and a cat. She has discovered that her love of telling a good story can be written. Published stories with Palm-sized press, Spillwords, Mercurial Stories, Potato Soup Journal, Edify Fiction, Zimbell House Publishing, Clarendon House Publishing, Blood Song Books, Black Hare Press, Fantasia Divinity, Cafelit, Reanimated Writers, Guilty Pleasures, Unholy Trinity, The World of Myth, Dastaan World, Vamp Cat, Runcible Spoon, Dark Christmas, Siren's Call, Iron Horse Publishing, Falling Star Magazine 2019 Pushcart Nominee.*

*Amazon: amazon.com/Dawn-DeBraal/e/B07STL8DLX*

## DEREK DUNN

*Derek Dunn is a film enthusiast and musician who writes primarily horror and mystery stories. After obtaining a degree in Media Arts Studies and dabbling in film production, he's turned his efforts to writing fiction. Several of his works have appeared in recent anthologies. He lives in the American northwest with his family, dog, and fish.*

*Twitter: DerekTDunn*

* * *

## DESTINY EVE PIFER

*Destiny Eve Pifer is a published author whose work has appeared in numerous anthologies and magazines. Her stories have been featured in FATE Magazine, True Confessions, Spotlight on Recovery and Country Magazine. A lover of all things supernatural and spooky she resides in Punxsutawney, Pennsylvania with her son Dartanyan.*

* * *

## DONNA CUTTRESS

*Donna Cuttress is a short story writer from Liverpool, U.K. Her work has been published by Crooked Cat, Suicide House, FoF Publishing and Black Hare Press. She has had work published by Sirens Call as part of Women in Horror Month and been included in Flame Tree Publishing's, Chilling Ghost Short Stories. Her work for 'The Patchwork Raven's' 'Twelve Days is also available as an art book. She is currently completing her first novel, and has been a speaker at the London Book Fair.*

***Twitter:*** *Hederah*

# BLACK HARE PRESS

## DREW STARLING

*Drew Starling is an author of horror and dark fiction. His short stories have been published in over a dozen anthologies and his collaborative novel "Storming Area 51: Horror at the Gate" spent time ranked as Amazon's #1 Sci-Fi Anthology. His only rule of writing is the dog never dies.*

*Website: www.drewstarling.com*
*Twitter: @ScaryStarling*

* * *

## EDDIE D. MOORE

*Eddie D. Moore travels hundreds of hours a year, and he fills that time by listening to audiobooks. When he isn't playing with his grandchildren, he writes his own stories. You can find a list of his publications on his blog or by visiting his Amazon Author Page. While you're there, be sure to pick up a copy of his mini-anthology Misfits & Oddities.*

*Website: eddiedmoore.wordpress.com*
*Amazon: amazon.com/author/eddiedmoore*

* * *

## EMMA K. LEADLEY

*Emma K. Leadley is a UK-based writer, creative geek, and devourer of words, images and ideas. She began writing both fiction and creative non-fiction as an outlet for her busy brain, and quickly realised scrawling words on a page is wired into her DNA.*

*Website: emmaleadley.co.uk*
*Twitter: @autoerraticism*

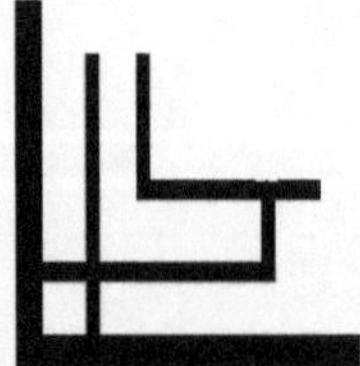

## ERICA SCHAEF

*Erica Schaef worked as a Registered Nurse for many years before becoming a stay-at-home parent. Her short stories have been featured most recently by: Visual Verse (Vol. 06- Chapter 09), Blood Moon Rising Magazine (Issue 77), and HellBound Books ("The Toilet Zone"). More of her short stories will be in featured in upcoming anthologies by Fantasia Divinity ("Isolation"), and Jitter Press (Issue 8), as well as in the forthcoming issue of Still Point Arts Quarterly. She lives in rural Tennessee with her husband and two children.*

* * *

## EVAN BAUGHFMAN

*Evan Baughfman works in a very scary place: a middle school! He writes all genres, but horror is where he's most comfortable. Much of his writing success has been as a playwright. He's had many different plays produced across the globe. Heuer Publishing has published his Poe adaptation, "A Taste of Amontillado". Additionally, Evan has adapted a number of his short stories into screenplays, of which "The Emaciated Man" and "The Creaky Door" have won awards in various film festival competitions. Evan's "Just Plants" was recently published in Soteira Press's horror anthology, The Monsters We Forgot - Volume 1.*

## GABRIEL HART

*From Morongo Valley in California's High Desert, Hart's debut twin novel Virgins In Reverse / The Intrusion (Traveling Shoes Press) was released January 2019, with foreword by avant-rockabilly provocateur Tav Falco. His chapbook Cinema of Life (2016) and novelette Nothing To See Here (2017) will be incorporated into his upcoming desert speculative fiction novel Lies of Heaven, to be released unabridged by Space Cowboy in 2020. His short-fiction and poetry have recently been published in Cholla Needles, the Howl 2018 and 2019 Anthology, and the Desert Writers Guild Anthology, and the new issue of Luna Arcana. Hart is a regular contributor to Space Cowboy's Simultaneous Times podcast, as well as L.A. Record, a Los Angeles underground music publication. Currently, Hart is teaching the writing workshop for Mil-Tree, a non-profit reach out program for Vets and Active Duty Military to heal the wounds of war.*

* * *

## GALINA TREFIL

*Galina Trefil is a novelist specializing in women's, minority, and disabled rights. Her favorite genres are horror, thriller, and historical fiction. Her short stories and articles have appeared in Neurology Now, UnBound Emagazine, The Guardian, Tikkun, Romea.CZ, Jewcy, Jewrotica, Telegram Magazine, Ink Drift Magazine, The Dissident Voice, Open Road Review, and the anthologies "Flock: The Journey," "First Love," "Sea of Secrets," "Coffins and Dragons," "Organic Ink volume One," "Winds of Despair," "Waters of Destruction," "Curses & Cauldrons," "Unravel," "Hate," "Love," "Oceans," "Forgotten Ones," "Dark Valentine Holiday Horror Collection," and "Suspense Unimagined."*

*Website: galinatrefil.wordpress.com*
*Facebook: Rabbi-Galina-Trefil-535886443115467*

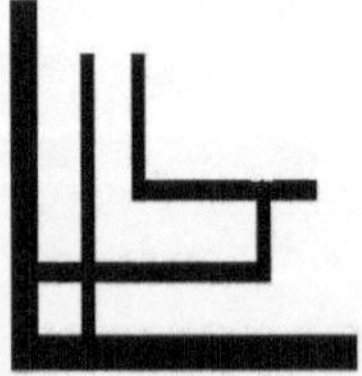

## HANNAH RETALLICK

*Hannah Retallick is a twenty-six-year-old from Anglesey, North Wales. She was home educated and then studied with the Open University, graduating with a First-class honours degree, BA in Humanities with Creative Writing and Music, and is studying for an MA in Creative Writing. She is working on her second novel and writes short stories and a blog. She was shortlisted in the Writing Awards at the Scottish Mental Health Arts Festival 2019, the Cambridge Short Story Prize, and the Henshaw Short Story Competition June 2019.*

*Website: ihaveanideablog.wordpress.com*

* * *

## HENRY SNIDER

*For over two decades, Henry Snider has dedicated his time to helping others tighten their writing through critique groups, classes, lectures, prison prose programs, and high school fiction contests. He co-founded Fiction Foundry (fictionfoundry.org est. 2012) and the award-winning Colorado Springs Fiction Writers Group (1996-2013). While still reserving enough time to pursue his own fiction aspirations, he continues to be active in the writing community through classes, media work, editing services, and advice. Henry lives in Colorado with his wife, fellow author and editor Hollie Snider, and numerous neurotic animals, including, of course, Fizzgig, the token black cat.*

*Website: fictionfoundry.org/members/henry-snider*

## J.A. HAMMER

*J.A. Hammer is a coffeeholic in the wild concrete city of Tokyo. Known online as CoffeeQuills, they are a multi-genre writer who enjoys a wide range of speculative fiction. Previous publications include Apocalypse and Unravel by Black Hare Press and Trembling with Fear Year 2 by the Horror Tree. To catch up on future 2020 projects (a LitRPG serial and a superhero romance), feel free to find them on Twitter and at their website.*

*Website: www.coffeequills.com*
*Twitter: @coffeequills*

* * *

## J.B. WOCOSKI

*J.B. Wocoski is the author and narrator of the shortstorypodcast.com with three flash fiction short story books published in the last three years. He is currently working on book 4 "Short Story Podcast 2019." He writes mostly science fiction, fantasy, and horror stories. He won the 2016 Little Tokyo Short Story Writing Contest with his short story "The Last Master of Go"*

*Website: shortstorypodcast.com*

* * *

## J.M. AMES

*J.M. Ames is an award-winning multi-genre speculative fiction author native to Southern California. He has multiple short story publications dating back to 2016. One thing holds true throughout all of his stories - you can Expect the Unexpected.*
*When not working his day job or enjoying his fatherly adventures, he writes short stories and novels, including an upcoming series. You can follow him on a variety of platforms, details on his website.*

*Website: jm-ames.com/contact-jm/*

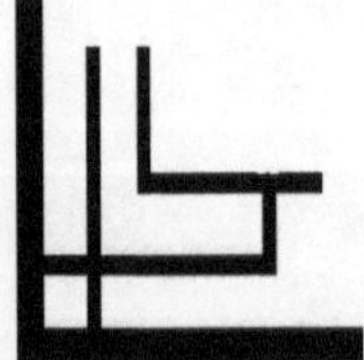

# TWENTY TWENTY

## J.W. GARRETT

*J.W. Garrett has been writing in one form or another since she was a teenager. She currently lives in Florida with her family but loves the mountains of Virginia where she was born. Her writings include YA fantasy as well as short stories. Since completing Remeon's Quest-Earth Year 1930, the prequel in her YA fantasy series, Realms of Chaos, she has been hard at work on the next in the series, scheduled to release August 2020. When she's not hanging out with her characters, her favourite activities are reading, running and spending time with family.*

*Website: www.jwgarrett.com*
*BHC Press: www.bhcpress.com/Author_JW_Garrett.html*

* * *

## JACK LOTHIAN

*Jack Lothian is a screenwriter for film and television and currently works as the showrunner on the HBO / Cinemax series 'Strike Back'. His short fiction has appeared in a number of publications, including Weirdbook, Hinnom Magazine, the Necronomicon Memorial Book, and 'The New Flesh: A Literary Tribute to David Cronenberg'. His graphic novel 'Tomorrow,' illustrated by Garry Mac, was nominated for a 2018 British Fantasy Award.*

* * *

## JACQUELINE MORAN MEYER

*Jacqueline Moran Meyer is a writer, artist and small business owner living in New York. Jacqueline loves to read and write stories in the horror, mystery and paranormal genres. She also enjoys hiking with her dog, Molly, and doing everything, or nothing at all, with her husband Bruce, and their three children, Julia, Emma and Lauren.*

*Website: jmoranmeyer.com*
*Amazon: www.amazon.com/jacquelinemoranmeyer*

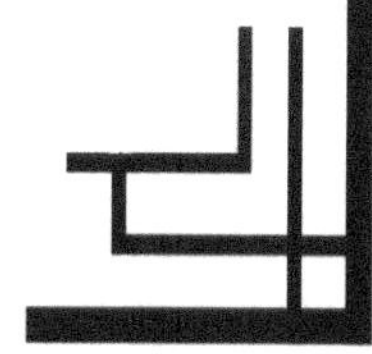

## JIM BATES

*Jim lives in a small town twenty miles west of Minneapolis, Minnesota. His stories have appeared online in CafeLit, The Writers' Cafe Magazine, Cabinet of Heed, Paragraph Planet, Nailpolish Stories, Ariel Chart, Potato Soup Journal, Literary Yard, Spillwords (Dec, 2019, Author of the Month), The Drabble, The Academy of the Heart and Mind and World of Myth Magazine. In print publications: A Million Ways, Mused Literary Journal, Gleam Flash Fiction Anthology #2, the Portal Anthology and the Glamour Anthology by Clarendon House Publishing, The Best of CafeLit 8 by Chapeltown Publishing, the Nativity Anthology by Bridge House Publishing and Gold Dust Magazine.*

*Website: www.theviewfromlonglake.wordpress.com*

* * *

## JOHN H. DROMEY

*John H. Dromey was born in northeast Missouri, USA. He enjoys reading—mysteries in particular—and writing in a variety of genres. In addition to contributing to the Black Hare Press series of Dark Drabbles anthologies, he's had short fiction published in Alfred Hitchcock's Mystery Magazine, Martian Magazine, Mystery Weekly, Stupefying Stories Showcase, Thriller Magazine, Unfit Magazine, and elsewhere, as well as in numerous anthologies, including Chilling Horror Short Stories (Flame Tree Publishing, 2015).*

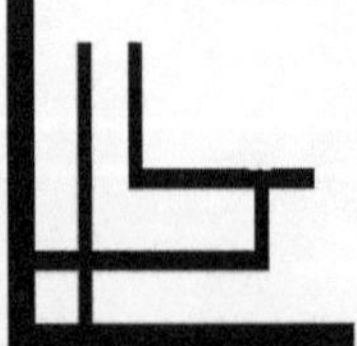

## JOSHUA GESSNER

*Joshua Gessner is a full-time college student, enrolled under the English major at his local community college. He is nineteen years old, and lives with his family in Manchester. Joshua Gessner has been published for the first time ever in January of 2020, and was published again one month later in February of 2020! He now continues working diligently on his craft, hoping to enter literary contests. In the near future he also hopes to publish: novels, novellas, short stories, and poetry!*

*Facebook: joshua.gessner.98*
*Twitter: @joshuagessner41*

* * *

## K.B. ELIJAH

*K.B. Elijah is a fantasy author living in Brisbane, Australia with her husband and three cockatiels. A lawyer by day, and a writer by...also, day, because she needs her solid nine hours of sleep per night (not that the cockatiels let her sleep past 6am). K.B. writes for various international anthologies, and her work features in dozens of collections about the mysterious, the magical and the macabre. Her own books of short fantasy novellas with twists, The Empty Sky and Out of the Nowhere, are available on paperback and Kindle now.*

*Website: www.kbelijah.com*
*Instagram: k.b.elijah*

## KEVIN J. KENNEDY

*Kevin J. Kennedy is a horror author & editor from Scotland. He is the co-author of You Only Get One Shot & Screechers, and the publisher of several best selling anthology series; Collected Horror Shorts, 100 Word Horrors & The Horror Collection, as well as the stand alone anthology Carnival of Horror. His stories have been featured in many other notable books in the horror genre. He is an active member of the Horror Writers Association. He lives in a small town in Scotland, with his wife and his two little cats, Carlito and Ariel.*

*Website: www.kevinjkennedy.co.uk*
*Amazon: : amazon.com/Kevin-J.-Kennedy/e/B016V0NA7M*

* * *

## LYNDSEY ELLIS-HOLLOWAY

*Lyndsey Ellis-Holloway is a writer from Knaresborough, UK. She writes fantasy, sci-fi, horror and dystopian stories, focussing on compelling characters and layering in myth and legend at every opportunity. Her mind is somewhat dark and twisted, and she lives in perpetual hope of owning her own Dragon someday, but for now she writes about them to fill the void... and to stop her from murdering people who annoy her. When she's not writing she spends time with her husband, her dogs and her friends enjoying activities such as walking, movies, conventions and of course writing for fun as well!*

*Website: theprose.com/LyndseyEH*

* * *

## LYNNE PHILLIPS

*Lynne Phillips, a retired teacher, lives in the beautiful Northern Rivers Region of New South Wales Australia. Her stories, across all genres, have been published in anthologies and various online magazines. Her priority is spending time with her family. Her passions are reading, writing and keeping fit.*

## M.A. SMITH

*M.A. Smith writes from Gloucestershire, UK, where she lives with her family. Her short fiction has appeared in magazines including Mythic, Dark Moon Digest, Gallery of Curiosities and Outposts of Beyond, and her novella, 'Severance,' was published by Fantasia Divinity in 2018.*

*Website: www.masmithwriting.com*
*Facebook: masmithwriting*

* * *

## MATTHEW A. CLARKE

*Matthew A. Clarke is a new face in the world of horror. He has been writing short fiction as a hobby for two years and has decided to share his passion with likeminded people. Matthew loves all things that go bump in the night, having been introduced to slasher movies at a young age. He lives on the South Coast of England with his fiancé, Isabelle, and a little dachshund called Frank.*

*Facebook: matthewaclarkeauthor*

* * *

## MATTHEW M. MONTELIONE

*Matthew M. Montelione is a horror writer and American Revolution historian born and raised on Long Island in New York. His work has been published in many titles, including MONSTERS: A Horror Microfiction Anthology, Quoth the Raven: A Contemporary Reimagining of the Works of Edgar Allan Poe, Thuggish Itch: Devilish, WHAT IF?: History Rewritten, Long Island History Journal, and Journal of the American Revolution. Matthew lives with his wife in New York.*

*Website: maybeevils.com*
*Facebook: maybeevils*

# BLACK HARE PRESS

## MICHAEL D. DAVIS

*Michael D. Davis was born and raised in a small town in the heart of Iowa. Having written over thirty short stories, ranging in genre from comedy to horror from flash fiction to novella he continues in his accursed pursuit of a career in the written word.*

* * *

## MICHAEL KELLICHNER

*Michael Kellichner is a writer and poet from Pennsylvania currently living in South Korea. Other short fiction of his has been published in Black Denim Lit, Trigger Warnings: Short Fiction with Pictures, and Three Crows Magazine. Flash fiction has appeared in a previous Black Hare Press anthology, Angels: A Divine Microfiction Anthology, and Horror Tree's Trembling with Fear.*

*Twitter: @mithalanis*

* * *

## N.M. BROWN

*Since N.M. Brown made her first post to a popular Internet forum, she's taken the horror community by storm. Her ability to create, terrify, and drive home her stories is insurmountable. N.M. Brown's published works can be found in multiple anthologies for all to read, but be forewarned, if you do... you may want to call your therapist after, her stories are terrifying, disturbing and devilishly unsettling. She is not only a fright visually, but also has a creepy tentacle in horror podcasting as well. Sinister Sweetheart writes, voice acts and is the media director of the Scarecrow Tales podcast.*

*Website: Sinistersweetheart.wixsite.com/sinistersweetheart*
*Facebook: NMBrownStories*

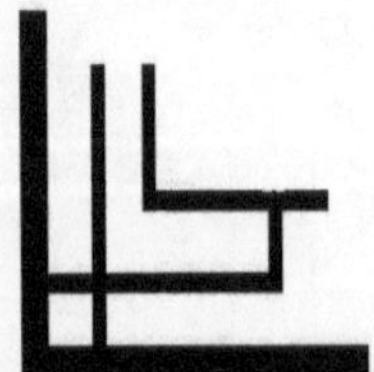

# TWENTY TWENTY

## NEEN COHEN

*Neen Cohen lives in Brisbane with her partner, son and fur babies. She is a writer of LGBTQI, dark fantasy and horror short stories and has a Bachelor of Creative Industries from QUT. She can often be found writing while sitting against a tombstone or tree in any number of graveyards.*

*Website: wordbubblessite.wordpress.com/*
*Facebook: neen.cohen.82*

* * *

## NICOLA CURRIE

*Nicola Currie is from Cambridge, UK where she works in educational publishing. She has published poetry in literary magazines, including Mslexia and Sarasvati, and short stories in various anthologies. She has also completed her first novel, which was longlisted for the Bath Children's Novel Award.*

*Website: writeitandweep.home.blog*

* * *

## NIKKI DEKEUSTER

*Nikki DeKeuster devours souls. She spits them onto her glowing screen and toys with their lives for your amusement. Reading this story makes you an accomplice to their suffering. You're welcome. A storyteller with decades of experience crafting tales with her friends, she's bound some of them to bring into the wider world. The stories, not her friends. She enjoys throwing stones into Lake Michigan with her daughter and keeping her husband up past his bedtime with her ramblings. The first novel in her horror series will claw its way out of the earth in 2020.*

*Website: NJDeKeuster.com*

## OWEN MORGAN

*Owen Morgan writes science fiction, fantasy, and alternate history, and lives in the fishing port of Steveston, British Columbia.*

*Website: httpwwwkingauthor.wordpress.com*
*Twitter: @owen_morgan1066*

* * *

## PAUL BENKENDORFER

*Paul Benkendorfer is an English and history teacher from Scottsdale Arizona who mainly writes historical fiction, poetry, non-fiction. He is currently working on his novel A Bridge Outside of Limerick based on the events of his great-grandfather who fought in the Irish Revolution of 1916. Paul has nearly 15 years experience working with at-risk youth and children with special needs and continues to primarily work with them to this day. In 2014 Paul received a Bachelors in Creative Writing from the University of Arizona and is currently process of obtaining his Masters in Teaching Writing from Johns Hopkins University. Paul's work has been published in The Write Launch, Allegory Ridge, Eerie River Publishing's anthologies, and many other journals. Paul prefers to spend his time at the dog park with his two rescues, Rudel and Daisy.*

*Twitter: @PBenkendorfer*

* * *

## PEDRO INIGUEZ

*Pedro Iniguez lives in Eagle Rock, California, a quiet community in Northeast Los Angeles. Since childhood he has been fascinated with Science-Fiction, Horror, and comic books. His work can be found in various magazines and anthologies such as: Space and Time Magazine, Crossed Genres, Dig Two Graves, Writers of Mystery and Imagination, Deserts of Fire, and Altered States II.*

*Website: pedroiniguezauthor.com*

## PETER J. FOOTE

*Peter J. Foote is a bestselling speculative fiction writer from Nova Scotia. Outside of writing, he runs a used bookstore specialising in fantasy & sci-fi, cosplays, and alternates between red wine and coffee as the mood demands. His short stories can be found in both print and in ebook form, with his story "Sea Monkeys" winning the inaugural "Engen Books/Kit Sora, Flash Fiction/Flash Photography" contest in March of 2018. As the founder of the group "Genre Writers of Atlantic Canada", Peter believes that the writing community is stronger when it works together.*

*Twitter: @PeterJFoote1*
*Website: peterjfooteauthor.wordpress.com*

* * *

## RAVEN CORINN CARLUK

*Raven Corinn Carluk writes dark fantasy, paranormal romance, and anything else that catches her interest. She's authored five novels, where she explores themes of love and acceptance. Her shorter pieces, usually from her darker side, can be found in Black Hare Press anthologies, at Detritus Online, and through Alban Lake Publishers.*

*Twitter: @ravencorinn*
*Website: www.ravencorinncarluk.com*

* * *

## ROBIN BRAID

*Robin Braid writes stories of the mysterious and macabre. A resident of Fife, Scotland, he graduated from Dundee University with a degree in English Literature. When not working in his regular job he can often be found rambling over hills and glens in search of inspiration for further tales.*

*Twitter: @robinbraid*

## SAM M. PHILLIPS

*Sam M. Phillips is the co-founder of Zombie Pirate Publishing, producing short story anthologies and helping emerging writers. His own work has appeared in dozens of anthologies and magazines such as Full Metal Horror, Flash Fiction Addiction, World War Four, and Dastaan World Magazine. He is also a prolific poet and his poetry can be read on his blog. His debut short novel is available in SCIENCE FICTION DOUBLE FEATURE: Phosphorus and Into The Eye.*

*Website: www.zombiepiratepublishing.com*
*Blog: www.bigconfusingwords.wordpress.com*

* * *

## SCOTT HARPER

*Scott Harper is an avid follower and consumer of speculative fiction, particularly the vampire genre. Inspired by the works of Bram Stoker, Marv Wolfman and John Steakley, his writing combines aspects of horror, dark fantasy and superhero fiction. He lives with his wife, son and two dogs in California.*

*Amazon: amazon.com/Scott-Harper/e/B07F5DKMK4*

* * *

## STACEY JAINE MCINTOSH

*Stacey Jaine McIntosh was born in Perth, Western Australia where she still resides with her husband and their four children.*
*Although her first love has always been writing, she once toyed with being a Cartographer and subsequently holds a Diploma in Spatial Information Services. Since 2011, she has had a vast number of stories and a few poems published online as well as in various anthologies. Stacey is also the author of Solstice, Morrighan, Lost and Le Fay and she is currently working on several other projects simultaneously. When not with her family or writing she enjoys reading, photography, genealogy, history, Arthurian myths and witchcraft.*

*Website: www.staceyjainemcintosh.com*

## STEPHEN HERCZEG

*Stephen Herczeg is an IT Geek based in Canberra Australia. He has been writing for over twenty years and has completed a couple of dodgy novels, sixteen feature length screenplays and numerous short stories and scripts. His horror work has featured in Sproutlings, Hells Bells, Below the Stairs, Trickster's Treats #1 and #2, Shades of Santa, Behind the Mask, Beyond the Infinite; The Body Horror Book, Anemone Enemy, Petrified Punks and Beginnings. He has also had numerous Sherlock Holmes stories published through the Belanger Books - Sherlock Holmes anthologies.*

*Amazon: amazon.com/-/e/B07916SQQS*
*Facebook: stephenherczegauthor*

* * *

## THOMAS VAUGHN

*Thomas Vaughn has had stories published in over twenty-five different magazines and anthologies over the past two years. This includes publishers such as Deciduous Tales, Sanitarium, Allegory and Riddled with Arrows. He was also honored to finish second in the 2019 Dark Regions writing contest. When not writing, he poses as a college professor whose research focuses on apocalyptic rhetoric and doomsday cults.*

*Website: brokentransmitter.com*

## TIM MENDEES

*Tim Mendees was born in Macclesfield in the North-West of England. He has recently been published in Death and Butterflies (suicide House Publishing,) Solitude (DBND Publishing,) and has had several short stories accepted for publication in forthcoming anthologies and magazines. His debut novella 'Miracle Growth' is coming soon from Black Hare Press. Tim is an active and recognisable figure in the UK Goth scene in his role as DJ, promoter and podcaster. He currently lives in Brighton & Hove with his pet crab, Gerald, and an army of stuffed cephalopods.*

*Facebook: tim.mendees*

* * *

## TRACY DAVIDSON

*Tracy Davidson lives in Warwickshire, England, and writes poetry and flash fiction. Her work has appeared in various publications and anthologies, including: Poet's Market, Mslexia, Atlas Poetica, Writing Magazine, Modern Haiku, The Binnacle, A Hundred Gourds, Shooter, Journey to Crone, The Great Gatsby Anthology, WAR and In Protest: 150 Poems for Human Rights.*

* * *

## TRISTAN DRUE ROGERS

*Tristan Drue Rogers has had his writing and poetry featured in literary magazines (such as Vamp Cat, Genre: Urban Arts, Weird Mask, and more), and horror anthologies (such as 100 Word Horrors Book 3 & 4 and Twenty Twenty). Tristan lives with his lovely wife Sarah and their son Rhett in Texas.*

*Website: www.tristandrue.wordpress.com*
*Twitter: @RogersDrue*

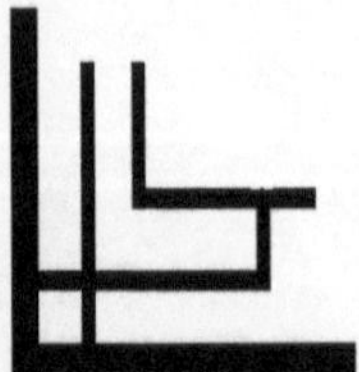

## WILL CHRISTIAN

*Will Christian is a father of two writers and a husband to his beautiful wife (who paid him to write that). With a sense of humour that his eldest daughter calls "adorable and groan-worthy dad jokes with surprising creativity", Will can usually be found wandering the local beaches, writing poetry and drabbles, and wistfully daydreaming about the boat that his girls haven't yet agreed to buy him.*

* * *

## XIMENA ESCOBAR

*Ximena is writing stories and poetry. Originally from Chile, she is the author of a translation into Spanish of the Broadway Musical "The Wizard of Oz", and of an original adaptation of the same, "Navidad en Oz", both produced in her home country. Since 2018 she has published several short stories in various anthologies and online platforms, and is now slowly working on her own collection. Ximena has a degree in Arts & Communication Science and lives in Nottingham with her family.*

*Facebook: Ximenautora*
*Twitter: @laximenin*

* * *

## ZOEY XOLTON

*Zoey Xolton is an Australian Speculative Fiction writer, primarily of Dark Fantasy, Paranormal Romance, and Horror. She is also a proud mother of two, and is married to her soul mate. Outside of her family, writing is her greatest passion. She has featured in dozens of anthologies to date, and has recently celebrated the release of her debut short story collection 'Darkly Ever After'. You can find further details regarding her various publications, including her eBook series the 'Fast Fiction Collection', on her website!*

*Website: www.zoeyxolton.com*

BLACK HARE PRESS

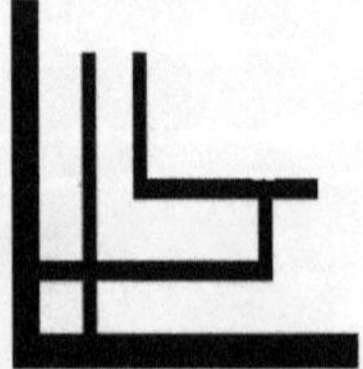

# ACKNOWLEDGEMENTS

When we embarked on our Black Hare Press journey back in late 2018, we never envisioned the huge support we'd get from the writing community. We have been truly humbled by the number of submissions we've received (around 3,000 over our first eight publications!) and have loved reading every single one.

So, thank you to everyone who crafted tales just for us—from the tiny tales in our Dark Drabbles series to these Jazz era twisted tales in Twenty Twenty—we thank you from the bottom of our hearts.

To our families and friends, collaborators, random strangers who took pity on us, and everyone who has helped us on the way: we couldn't have done it without you.

And to you, our discerning reader, we and these talented writers did it all for you. We hope you enjoyed these tales, and if you did, don't forget to leave a review.

Thank you all—see you next time.

*Love & kisses*
*Ben & Dean*

www.blackharepress.com

# Publications